COUNTRY
OF THE
HEART

A N O V E L

COUNTRY OF THE HEART

KAY NOLTE SMITH

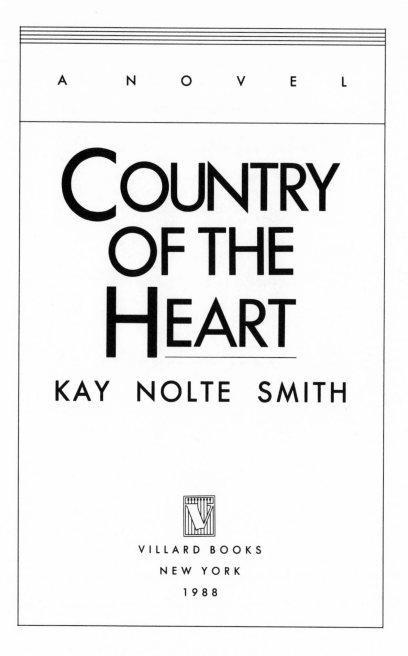

VILLARD BOOKS
NEW YORK
1988

All rights reserved under International and Pan-American Copyright
Conventions. Published in the United States by Villard Books, a division
of Random House, Inc., New York, and simultaneously in Canada by
Random House of Canada Limited, Toronto.

Library of Congress Cataloging-in-Publication Data

Smith, Kay Nolte.
Country of the heart.

I. Title.
PS3569.M537554C6 1988   813'.54   87-40190
ISBN 0-394-54655-5

Manufactured in the United States of America

9 8 7 6 5 4 3 2

First edition

BOOK DESIGN BY JO ANNE METSCH

To all who stand against the censors

Like a white stone deep in a draw-well lying,
As hard and clear, a memory lies in me.
I cannot strive nor have I heart for striving:
It is such pain and yet such ecstasy.

It seems to me that someone looking closely
Into my eyes would see it, patent, pale;
And seeing, would grow sadder and more thoughtful
Than one who listens to a bitter tale.

The ancient gods changed men to things, but left them
A consciousness that smoldered endlessly.
That marvelous sorrows might endure forever,
You have been changed into a memory.

> Anna Akhmatova
> "Like a White Stone," 1916
> (translated by Babette Deutsch)

CONTENTS

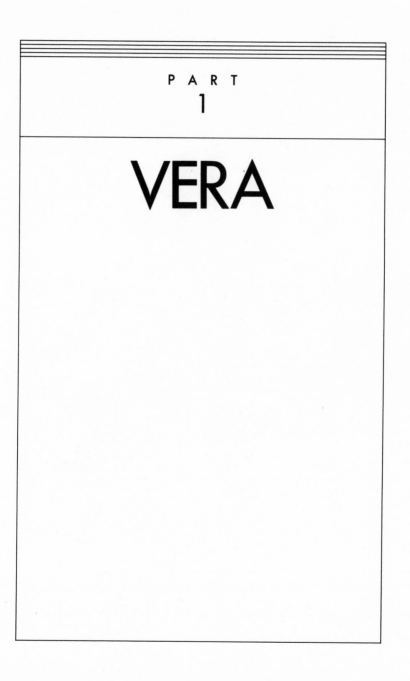

**PART
1**

VERA

CHAPTER ONE

She stepped into the store and gazed around with a smile of content. Books. By the yard, the acre, the mile. Stacked in piles and packed in bursting rows, spilling out as if propelled by the energy of their words. And everywhere the smell: must and wood and aging paper and, somehow, a hint of spice. It exhilarated her to plunge into the past, as long as it wasn't her own.

She moved past the tables of shiny new review copies, toward the remainders and secondhand books. The shelves were separated by such narrow aisles that she had to walk between them crablike and angle her head to read the spines, so that the long braid of her hair slid to one side. The color of ground cloves, it was coiled around her head during the week, framing her oval face and dark brown eyes, but on weekends she freed it to swing with her motion.

She edged her way into the poetry section and blew dust from the top of a row. It went up her nose like pepper, and she sneezed. "God bless you," said a disembodied voice from the row behind her.

"Thank you," she said. And after a moment, "Excuse my dust."

"Dorothy Parker, I presume?" said the voice, and she smiled. She could have answered again, and then he might, and they might peer around the shelves and begin a conversation; but she had never been able to believe in the kindness of strangers.

She bent to hunt for some Swinburne. It was with his work that she had felt completely at home with English verse for the first time, the images blooming in her mind without hesitation, their meaning emerging and deepening like a photograph that developed while one watched. *If you were queen of pleasure, and I were king of pain. . . .* The lines had sung into her mind and stayed, the first of the permanent residents in English. But there was no Swinburne on the shelf. Too out of style even to be secondhand.

She straightened and moved along, thinking that *secondhand* was a poor word. It suggested that a book's life stopped with the second pair of hands to find it, the pages kept forever white and stiff and crisp, like crinolines that had barely danced. *Crisp,* on the other hand, was a splendid word, which, for absolutely no reason, advertisers had ruined, turning its military snap into a simpering *crispy*. People could treat their language shamefully; she knew it for a fact but didn't understand it.

She wandered down another maze of shelves and aisles, happily spending a Saturday as she most liked to do: an invigorating run, a few hours at the Metropolitan Museum, lunch alone in its cafeteria, then off to a matinee or down to one of the bookstores on lower Broadway. It had been a while since she had a Saturday to herself. Jess was in

Washington working on some legislation. Her mother was entertaining a former student, her fine little face no doubt inclined to a steam of tea and, when she talked, a thin hand playing the lace tablecloth with violin fingering.

She could never resist the biography section, which had a copy of her first book, *Souls in Hiding: The Lives of the Brontës* by Hedy Lucas. It had taken a year and a half to research and plan, including a lovely summer in Yorkshire and at the British Museum, which she had squeezed out of her teaching salary, then two years to write. The thoughts had come easily enough but had resisted being caged in proper words. They still did. In her view, her prose was workmanlike, with the merit of clarity and an occasional touch of grace. It would never come without struggle—even though the modest success of *Souls in Hiding* had enabled her to work at it almost full time ever since—and it would never be Art. Art, with its dangers and ecstasies, was for others to achieve.

She took down the copy of her book and was pleased, for it had been well used, with passages marked in yellow ink. Once, when she was quite young, she had marked something in a fairy-tale book because she thought it so beautiful; her teacher had reprimanded her for calling attention to herself and for failing to show respect for the book. She hadn't agreed, about that or many other things. Writing in books, she had felt—not defacing them, of course—was a compliment. Proof that one had read them carefully and found their choicest parts.

She checked her watch. If Jess were there, he would already have checked his watch several times, with the tight little smile that masked impatience. He had come with her only once. Crouching before a bottom shelf, she had twisted to look up at him and said, "I guess you're not one of life's browsers."

"Only along the primrose path," he had said. "But I wanted to come. I want to know the things that please you." Much of the time, he did.

The next time she looked at her watch, it said five-thirty, and there were six books she couldn't leave behind. A work on singing that she had never seen, some Hawthorne she hadn't read, and books on Wagner and Freud, for in the back of her mind, in spite of what she had promised her mother to do, lay a wish to write a biography of Lou Salome, using that intriguing turn-of-the-century woman to explore the intellectual world in which she lived. "More books?" her mother would ask when she walked in with them. Then, as she had lately taken to doing, her mother would smile and add, "Ah, you were always reading. Every time we called, you were reading."

Hedy paid and walked out into the late April afternoon. The day had been clear and bright. Remnants of sun lit sparks on the grit of the sidewalk. She decided to take the subway instead of a cab. Everybody told her she was crazy to submit to life underground, but cabs could eat away an author's precarious income in voracious bites.

She went down the broad steps at the Union Square station, a tall woman so thin that people felt the hint of bones beneath her olive skin, just as her soft, measured speech hinted at the deliberation that lay behind it. There was something intense in her manner, but also an air of reserve. The two should have contradicted each other but instead coexisted, so that she had a solidity of presence but lacked the hard edge of so many of her peers. Where some women were honed to metal against the pace and crush of Manhattan, Hedy Lucas offered a more subtle resistance, absorbing and muting rather than confronting.

People waited in the subway caverns with sullen edginess. When the train came, its inside walls were caked with graffiti. Hedy had long since acquired a New Yorker's obliviousness to the ugly. Twenty years earlier, when she had arrived in the city, she had been amazed that underneath the towers which lifted her head lay a world so grimy and loud, so unlike the vast, clean, opulent Metro on which she had grown up. Then she had laughed to hear herself complain about dirt and noise in the new world she had miraculously reached. Where could it take her, anyway, that Metro with chandeliers and stained glass and statuary?

She made a tiny grimace of impatience, realizing she had been looking backward again. Though she tried not to do so, and had been quite successful for many years, her mother was now spending more and more time in the past. "You must write about it so it won't be lost," her mother had said, and what could she do but agree?

She transferred and got out at Fifty-seventh Street. Her mother's apartment was not far from Carnegie Hall, on the fifth floor of a building that had housed musicians and teachers for decades. Baritone vocalizing floated down the hall. Behind a more distant door someone attacked a Bach cello sonata. Hedy let herself into the apartment, inhaling the familiar scent of old woods and velvets. Everything was quiet; the former student must have left. "Mama?" she called.

"In here," came the voice, still strong.

She went through the living room, crowded with dark furniture and glass cases of china and spoons, down the hall papered with photographs, and into the little bedroom, once hers, that had been converted into a study when she left. Vera Lucas sat by the window, in the blue silk she wore for visitors because it disguised how thin she had become. She had been a small woman even at her best, and she was not yet at her worst. Thank God.

She took Hedy's hands and leaned up for a kiss. Her face was doll-shaped, with dark eyes that could shine like glass when she was excited, which was often, and skin like fine, rose-scented paper.

"Did you have a good time with your student?" Hedy asked.

"Yes, yes. He is playing now with the Cleveland, for two years. And he has three little girls, all studying piano." Vera opened Hedy's bookstore bag, studied each title, then put the books down on top of one another, their edges aligned. "We sent you to evening music school when you were eight," she said, "but it was useless. You never wanted to practice. You were always reading."

The knowledge that one day she would never hear that sentence again came at Hedy like a knitting needle. She managed to smile anyway, took off her coat, and sat in the chair opposite. In silence, the two of them looked down at the street in the thinning light.

"Sometimes, in the old days," Vera said, "it used to be so quiet, with your father composing in his head and yours stuck inside a book. I would look at the two of you and think, My silent ones."

"Mmmm," Hedy said.

Vera spoke fluent, idiomatic English but had never lost her accent. The consonants wore heavy boots, the r's rolled like waves, and "th" was a mountain rarely climbed. She had tried hard to conquer the practice sentences—"Mr. Smith says thank you for the red radishes"—but finally had laughed and given up: "Hedy, my darrrlink, I leave Mr. Smiss and his rrredishes to you."

She leaned forward and pointed across the street. "That man, the heavy one there, has stood on that corner for at least an hour, watching something over here. Or someone." She shook her head. "Like the old days."

"He looks innocent to me," Hedy said. "Probably waiting for a friend who's late, and they're going to the movie up the street." After a moment she added, "I'll fix dinner, shall I?"

"Yes. Is there some nice fruit? I can't seem to get enough fruit." Vera laughed. "That's like the old days too."

"Plenty of fruit," Hedy said. "Come sit in the living room and watch the last of the news while I work."

Vera nodded and stood.

"Shall I help you?" Hedy asked.

Vera's eyes flashed. "I go by myself as long as I can." But her gait was becoming a bit unsteady. She settled at the big table that had been the scene of dinners lasting for hours, with the apartment full of friends and laughter.

Hedy switched on the TV. The anchorwoman was saying, ". . . left the auditorium, he was asked about the recent banning of four books from a Long Island library." A minister who had been more and more in the news of late appeared in a film clip, saying smoothly, "We believe in free speech. That's the American way. But the family, too, is part of the American way. Christian parents have the right to protect their children against the kind of smut that is peddled these days between book covers." As he talked, he smiled and nodded, features and hands busy around the cold, immobile rectitude of his eyes.

"Ah, I don't understand such people," Vera said.

Hedy's teeth locked on her lower lip. She and her mother had talked often of the mysteries they found in America, but for some there was no explanation.

"I'll start dinner," she said and went into the kitchen. The old cabinets, Vera's favorite blue, had begun to lose chips of their color and reveal glimpses of a former, yellow life. On the wall, Vera's pride of copper pots and bowls hung like huge buttons, beginning to show streaks. She must try to do them after dinner, Hedy thought. She tied on an apron and started cutting the chicken, telling herself not to think of the way Vera was walking, to think of something else. Of Jess.

Probably he was still in his office in the House building. Sometimes he worked until ten or eleven, he said. She was ambitious too, but Jess was in a different league, propelled by some energy she could not imagine and some greed she did not share. Once his name had been in the papers as possible presidential timber several elections down the road. He had laughed. But he hadn't called it ridiculous.

"Hedy!" The call was so high and sharp that she threw down the knife and a piece of chicken and went in at a run. Eyes huge, Vera was pointing at the TV screen, and the photograph that, with piercing familiarity, filled it.

"—widely regarded," the anchorwoman was saying, "as one of the great composers of our time. Boris Nikolayev has not left Russia for almost twenty years, not since a trip to Paris to conduct one of his works, during which his wife and daughter defected to the West. The festival in Finland, to take place early in July, will present a number of his works. Observers say the Soviet government's decision to allow him to attend reflects the current climate of cultural thaw. Whatever the reason, Boris Nikolayev's appearance will be a major event in the musical world. Turning now to other cultural news . . ."

The woman must have continued talking, for her mouth kept moving, but the only sound Hedy could hear was the pump of her own blood. She went to the set, switched it off, and turned to her mother. When the glitter in Vera's eyes welled into tears, Hedy went to kneel by her chair.

"He's coming out." Vera spoke in Russian. "Haven't I always said that he would try to join us one day?"

When Hedy took her mother's hands, they fluttered

within her own like small birds. Gently she said, "Mama, you know he's going at the Kremlin's pleasure."

"Yes, but perhaps he . . . He might try . . ."

"And he's only going to Finland."

"Oh, Anna," Vera said, using the old name. "Why didn't he come with us? What happened to him? What did they do to him? If only we could know, Anna." The words had been worn thin by twenty years of saying them.

There was only one response. "Yes, *Mamochka*, if only we could."

"Don't you think it means anything, then? That they are letting your father come across the border?"

"I don't know what it means," Hedy said finally.

Her mother pulled her hands away. In English she said, "I must go to him. I must go to Finland."

"Mama!" Hedy cried.

"How can I not go? How can I not be there if they are going to let Boris come out? Call and make me a reservation immediately."

"Mama, I know how you feel, but that is absolutely out of the question. The doctor would never allow it, and if he did, which he won't, I would lie down on the tarmac in front of the plane before I'd let you get on it."

"You want me to sit here in my chair in New York while your father comes out? I can't. I am not a woman who sits in her chair and does nothing!"

"You are now," Hedy said, keeping her voice even.

It was the first time either of them had made such an admission. They looked at each other, fighting it, accepting it.

At length Vera sat back in her chair. "Please take the receiver from the telephone," she said. "Tonight I don't want to talk to anyone but you."

"The press won't call, Mama. They don't know where to

look for Nikolayev's wife and daughter. Certainly not after all this time."

"I wasn't thinking of them. I don't want to talk to my friends. Not yet. Not even to Zoya. So please, darling, fix the telephone."

Hedy rose and went across the room. She did as her mother asked and then stood staring at the receiver but looking across the miles and the years until the phone began making the high-pitched whinny that warned it was off the hook. She picked it up and took it into the hall.

She couldn't just go in and make dinner, she thought. Nor could she talk to her mother, at least not for a minute, because she didn't know what else to say, or whether there was anything else to say. Or do. She went to the bathroom, drank some water, and laid her forehead against the cool of the mirror.

When she got back to the living room, Vera was composed. "Make the dinner, please, will you?" she said. "I want just to sit here for a while and . . ."

"Are you all right?"

"Yes. Yes."

Hedy pushed back her braid, which had slid over one shoulder. Vera said, "Tonight I want to help you with the book. Very much I want to do that."

"Of course, Mama." What else could she say? She had promised to write a biography of her father—"So it's not lost," Vera had pleaded, "so the world will know about his life"—even though they knew so little of his past twenty years. And when her mother was gone—long before the book could be finished—she would have to keep on, would actually have to write it. Wouldn't she?

In the kitchen, she put the chicken pieces in a pan, added some wine and herbs, and laid out the mushrooms for slicing. In the woods near Moscow there were dozens of varieties of mushrooms—some in spongy ground, some near

birches, some in the gloom underneath low-lying pine
branches. You had to learn which kinds lived where, and
try to keep the good hunting grounds secret. In the fall she
and Vera, like practically everyone else in the city, it
seemed, used to put on waterproof boots and old clothes,
take baskets and good, sharp knives, and head out to go
mushroom-picking. Sometimes they would be at it for ten
hours at a time. Sometimes, but not often enough, Papa
would go with them, lumbering ahead in his most ancient
pants and jacket. When he gave the signal, they could stop
and unpack the picnic. . . .

She lifted a mushroom from the cutting board and
rubbed its cap, smooth as suede. She turned it over to reveal
the brown velvet filaments underneath, brought it to her
nose, and smelled the earth, and life, of the old days. How
could she fight the undertow of the past? Now more than
ever Vera wanted to take her there, to make her its hagiog-
rapher, because Vera's future had shrunk to months, they
guessed, but the past stretched out forever, endless.

After dinner Vera said, "Now get your things, won't
you? I'd like to tell you how I met your father. I haven't told
you, have I?"

Many times. "I want to hear it." Hedy went to get her
notes and tape recorder.

Up along Herzen Street and through the doors of the
Moscow Conservatory, carrying her violin. At the age of
eight Vera had begun studying it; by ten it was a friend, by
twelve an extension of her body, lodged between shoulder
and chin. *Veruschka the little fiddler,* her mother had called
her, and had been awed when she was accepted for the
Central Music School and then the conservatory. Despite
the hardships of the war—the food rations that sometimes
seemed little better than starving, the failures of heat and

light and spirit—music went on. It had to; it was as essential as bread.

There were *Americantzis* in the city, for America was an ally, and people sang American songs, like one they called "Coming In on a Wing and a Machine." But for Vera, the voice of the war was Boris Semyonovich Nikolayev, whose *War Choruses* even Stalin liked. They were like nothing she had heard before: dark and rich as earth, with unique combinations of brasses and reeds and flinty syncopations. Every great composer had his own sound, which one could recognize at once and take for no other, and Boris Nikolayev had such a sound. It had pinned Vera to her chair the first time she heard it, and she had known she would have to meet the man who created it.

He taught in the Composition Department. She would sometimes see him in the halls: an oak of a man, with a heavy branch of brown hair casting a shadow over his deep-set dark eyes, and an air of unapproachability. He was unmarried, they said, and had never been seen with a woman. He was only thirty-seven, they said, although his face seemed granitic and timeless.

In the spring, after the American forces and the Red Army met in Berlin from their separate directions and split Germany in half, V-E Day finally arrived. All night people had gathered, quietly waiting, and when the news came, they went wild, shedding the reserve normally shown in public. Waves of humanity flooded the sidewalks and streets. Vera and two friends joined the sea that poured into Red Square, hugging and laughing, dancing and screaming. A man trying to play an accordion was as squeezed as his instrument. In the time-honored way of showing admiration, people tossed every uniformed man they could find into the air and, for once, lowered all bars between themselves and foreigners. They sent roars of joy up at the twined Soviet and American flags and kissed every American they encountered. Vera embraced left and right. Suddenly her arms were around an oak and her eyes looking up at Boris Semyonovich. For a moment she didn't grasp who it was; would the great, silent Nikolayev be part of such emotional abandon? She pulled back. "Victory!" she cried, and then, losing herself completely in the glory of the day, and of meeting him, she reached up and kissed him on the lips.

She didn't know which of them was more startled. He frowned down at her. "Conservatory!" she said. "Violin! A student of Lermontov!" He pushed the hair back from his forehead. She heard herself continue, but he shook his head, unable to hear, so she leaned up to his ear and shouted, "Thank you for your music. You are Russia's greatest composer." His heavy eyebrows lifted, then he patted her on the shoulder and pushed on into the crowd, his head riding above most others'. Once he turned to look back at her.

It had to be an omen that they had met on such a day.

From then on, she watched for him in the halls and went up to speak to him, nervously at first, but soon quite boldly, always armed with something to say about his music or to ask him. Once she even asked if he would someday compose for the violin. Gradually his responses grew less gruff and peremptory. One day, when she approached him, he made a polite little bow with his head and said, "Vera Andreyevna, I invite you to come with me and have a glass of tea."

"Oh, yes," she said. "Oh, yes."

CHAPTER TWO

"What does *bodacious* mean?" Hedy asked. "It's not in any of my dictionaries."

Jess looked over the top of The Week in Review section of Sunday's *Times*. "Beats me. How's it used?"

She read out the sentence from the book review. " 'The leader of this motley and bodacious crew . . .' "

"Audacious? Rhymes with," Jess said.

"Maybe." She sipped at her coffee. "I have to get one of those unabridged dictionaries."

He grinned. "You'll have to hang it from the ceiling."

They were having breakfast in her apartment. "Good Lord," Jess had said the first time he'd seen it. She tried to explain: It made her feel secure to line her life with books, at the expense of furniture. Books were a kind of padding against . . . she didn't know exactly against what. She had always lived that way, and now, when you could buy any book you wanted, with no restrictions but money. . . . Jess had given her a strange look, which she hadn't understood until he told her something about his ex-wife. A willowy blonde improbably named Alice, she preferred book reviews to books, he said, because they were "more condensed," and saved her concentration for the fashion magazines whose pages she might well have graced.

On the grounds that she would have to deal with the answer, Hedy had decided not to ask Jess why he'd married Alice. But he volunteered it one night. "She was beautiful and fun, and that's what I wanted when I was twenty-five." Then he had added, with the candor she loved and regarded as archetypically American, "The perfect wife for a politician, I thought. Until I became one." And a moment later, "She had money, of course. Lots."

He had retreated to his paper. In a minute his voice came from behind it. "A buck says I know what you're doing over there."

"What?"

"Figuring out how many other rhymes there are for bodacious."

"Gracious," she said. "You're perspicacious."

"And tenacious. Give me my dollar."

"And rapacious." She got up, went to the Toby jug that held loose change, fished out four quarters, and took them to him.

"And salacious," he said and tugged on her braid to bring her down and kiss her. His lips were soft and wanted to pull her in, but she stood up. They had been out of bed only half an hour. Too soon to go back.

He settled back to the paper amiably. *Sagacious,* she thought. *To be more efficacious, I need more spacious.* She made herself stop.

Jess had come from Washington late the night before, his first time in two weeks. They would spend the afternoon

with his twin daughters, who were thirteen, halfway between giggles and sophistication, and very pretty. The
more they grew to look like their mother, the more Jess
treated them like little girls, so that they were always utter-
ing unison cries of "Oh, Daddy, *really.*" They seemed both
embarrassed and fascinated by the fact that their father had
a *girl friend,* for heaven's sake. When Jess held her hand or
kissed her, the twins shot each other furtive glances and got
elaborately busy doing something. They liked Hedy but
seemed to want her to be an androgynous pal whose apartment their father just happened to visit when he came to
town.

Jess put down the paper with a snap and leaned over it.
"Why didn't you tell me about it?"

"About what?"

"That your father is going to be at some festival in Finland." She said nothing. "Why do I have to read it in the
paper?" he asked.

"I'm sorry. I just wanted to live with it by myself for a
while."

He sighed. She knew the words that lay behind the sigh:
Didn't she know he would understand, didn't she feel close
enough to share things? It was an old conversation. Sometimes they had it silently, sometimes in words, though on
that subject she wasn't good with words. She would try to
joke, and it would come out flat-footed: "I know Russians
are supposed to be emotional, gypsy songs and weeping in
the vodka and all that, but I never like to do what I'm
supposed to." Then he would say things like "You don't
keep anything away from me in bed, so why out of it?" And
then she wouldn't know what to say.

"I want to help," he said. "Wouldn't you like to talk
about it?"

She thought of the piece she'd read recently, a woman's
complaint made only half in jest: Is there such a thing as

too much understanding from a man? Is it too late to bring back the good old days, before males acquired sensitivity? She'd been hesitating to show Jess the piece because she wasn't sure he'd find it amusing; then, one weekend, grinning, he'd brought it to her.

"OK," she told him. "I'll talk about it."

"So how does it sit with you?"

On my chest, she thought. *Heavily.* "I'm not sure yet."

"And Vera?"

"I think Mama feels she's going to be vindicated. You know what she's believed all along—that he wants to get out, that they've been preventing him."

"But he's not getting out. He's only being allowed to go to Finland."

"I know that. So does she. But she's . . . alive with hope."

"How about you?"

Hedy looked away. "In almost twenty years they haven't allowed him to emigrate—if that's what he wants to do. In almost twenty years they haven't allowed him out of the country—if in fact he's wanted to go."

Jess reached over and put a hand on hers.

"Mama wants to go to Finland. It's impossible and crazy, but if she could, she'd get on a plane and go." Hedy pulled the last piece of her English muffin in half; butter had cooled in its holes. "And since *she* can't go . . ."

Jess gave her the steady gaze that meant he was trying to see past her own. "Do you want to see your father?"

"If I went, if I could see him and somehow talk to him alone, I might be able to find out the truth of what happened to him. And bring it home to Mama."

"What if the truth was something she wouldn't want to hear?"

Hedy put the muffin pieces on the plate and fitted them back together. "Yes. What if?"

Quietly he said, "Surely it wouldn't be wise to go."

"I could just be an American writer preparing a biography of him. Which I am. I specialize in biographies of artists—that's a matter of record. My name is different now. I look different now. They wouldn't know I'm his daughter."

"There'll be KGB all around him. Doesn't that scare you?"

Terrifies me, she thought. "I'm an American citizen now."

"If they could get you alone, it might not make that much difference."

She nodded. Another wonderful thing about Jess was that he understood the realities.

He folded his arms and tilted back in his chair, moving closer to the window behind him, where sun poured in. It drew an aureole around his curly dark hair and square face. His chin had a cleft, and an old football scar cut a tiny white line through the tip of his right eyebrow. "I can't believe you're actually thinking you might go," he said. "But if you are, by some gypsy quirk in your soul, I'd sure as hell be opposed."

She wanted him to say that, of course—and also to say he wouldn't get involved in her decision. What's the best way to have things? Why, both ways.

"Jess, I really don't know what I'm going to do." She had shared as much as she could; the decision had to be made in that inner space where no one else went, and from which she had learned the dangers of sharing. "I need to think about it. OK?" She hated tacking "OK?" onto the ends of things, like a little flag sent up to test the wind, but sometimes it flew of its own accord.

He waited so long to say "Fine" that she knew it wasn't.

After a moment he got up and stretched. The yellow terry robe pulled open across his chest, where the hair lay in black whorls. "Going for a shower," he said. "Care to join me?"

"Rain check?"

She watched him go down the hall. Shoulders that made jackets hang right, broad back, good legs. A good man, who had been hard to find. Not that she been looking for A Man at the time—just wishing for someone in politics who saw things as she and her émigré friends did, and would say so. She was not an activist—her work claimed too much of her energies and emotions—but there was one issue to which she couldn't be indifferent even if she had wanted.

For some time after arriving, after she and Vera had managed to hide from the bewilderingly aggressive press, she had been able to deal only on a personal level with the new world. Physically, it was a sensory assault: the vivid clothes, the open faces, the constant presence of bright signs and advertisements. Practically, it was a series of challenges: learning a new way of paying, in which you wrote the sum on a paper called a "check" and people trusted they would get their money; working to lose the accent that branded you as alien. Psychologically, it was a struggle with the nakedness of freedom: what to buy when nothing was scarce and everything came in a dozen colors and kinds; what to study at a university that would let you study anything; what career to plan when the planning was up to you; how to live in a world full of choices.

Only gradually had she become aware of larger issues, which were infinitely more puzzling than idioms and charge accounts. She had heard Americans denouncing their government for being in Vietnam, denouncing it as loudly and viciously as *Pravda* had ever done. She had learned there were people in the government who were more critical of Washington than of Hanoi or of the Kremlin itself, who were not able, or willing, to remember that Red Square was the same color as blood and who talked smoothly of the "idealism" of communism, as if the nightmare she had left had no reality. Almost as hard to credit were those whose perception of communism should have made them friends but couldn't, because not only did they believe in forcing young men into the army to fight for freedom, they seemed to oppose tyranny only when it was red. They knew of the jails of Chile and Haiti and the Philippines and Iran but called the rulers "friends" and filled their coffee with "aid"—sanctioning one kind of oppression because it opposed another. Oh, this wonderful, naïve, bewildering America, which often contradicted its magnificent mandate; which gave its money all over the globe and got hostility in return.

She and Vera had stopped trying to understand and turned fully to their private worlds. So she knew nothing of a congressman from New York named Jesse Newman until one night, flipping the TV dial, she heard a deep voice on a talk show arguing that it was wrong to distinguish between "left" and "right" dictatorships, for oppression was like slavery: unacceptable in any degree. Five minutes later he was saying that no, he didn't believe in cultural exchanges with Russia—though he would change his mind if the Soviets stopped dictating which artists could go abroad and which couldn't. She began to follow his career. Perhaps his manner held a touch of slickness, but perhaps that was a cavil.

One day, leaving her publisher, she had gotten on an elevator, given its sole other occupant the customary visual frisking (possible mugger?), and then, realizing who it was, reacted with a double take that must have been comic, for he laughed and said, "What's the matter? Sorry you voted for me?" "No," she said. "Sorry I didn't." It was the end of the day; he invited her for a drink. She learned that he had read not only her book on Garcia Lorca but most of Lorca; that he was still trying to reconcile the pragmatism of politics with the idealism that had first sent him to law school and then made him abandon a career as a prosecutor because the only way to change the law was to be a legislator; that there were compellingly rough edges in his deep voice. Within a week he called to say he had read her other books; how interesting that her subjects were always artists suffering under one kind of oppression or another—a common thread she actually hadn't realized herself. Within two months he was staying at her apartment on every trip to the city, although, for separate reasons, they decided to keep a low public profile.

He came back down the hall, hair still damp from the shower, and went into the tiny kitchen behind her to pour himself more coffee.

"Jess," she said, "when are you going to make some kind of public statement about those self-appointed censors who are cropping up everywhere? Banning books, bombing abortion clinics, doing their-God-only-knows-what next?"

"I don't know."

"You are going to do it, aren't you?"

He came around and took the chair across the table. "You know I share your opinion of those people."

"So when will you share it with the public?"

He drank coffee slowly, stared into the big mug, and set it down as gently as if it were eggshell china. "How about if I let you decide what to do about your father, and you let me decide when to make public statements."

If you truly loved a man, Hedy thought, wouldn't your instincts warn you? Would things happen so fast that your face couldn't catch up with them and you were left with a smile while the hairs on your arm were bristling?

"That sounds like a good arrangement," she said carefully.

"I think so."

The silence lasted, became a tightrope.

"It's too bloody silly," he said, "to sit and fight on Sunday morning."

"That's true."

"So . . ."

"So we won't do it." If you truly loved a man, wouldn't you sometimes *want* to fight with him, just for the pleasure of feeling your passion in a different form?

"We're meeting the girls at one o'clock, so if you want to get in a run . . ."

"Right," she said. "I'll get going."

They all went to a movie starring two boys with smooth faces who looked to Hedy like babies but who transfixed the twins. Afterward they walked over to the Children's Zoo, which had reopened. Jess said they had to go because he had always taken the girls there as the first rite of spring. They said, "Oh, Dad, *really*," and tried to rise above the fact that they were having a good time.

The air was warm and smelled of salt. Balloons sailed high, trying to escape their strings, and young children gathered in front of the cages in brightly colored knots. As the four of them strolled along, Laura, the more inquisitive twin, said, "Hedy, I guess you didn't have a zoo when you were young."

"Of course. Right in Moscow. I used to go often." In fact it hadn't been much of a zoo at all, but she felt a surprising, perverse desire to defend it—to challenge the unspoken assumption that life in Russia was unrelievedly cheerless and drab. "Moscow has a wonderful open-air market," she said, "where you can buy any kind of pet and everything you need to take care of it. We used to go there on Sundays."

The twins gave her the slow, grave look that seemed to acknowledge her as an exotic—or was it an eccentric?—and Jess raised an eyebrow at her because she rarely volunteered information about her past. She smiled at all of them.

They wandered over to the polar bears and leaned on the railing to watch one of the animals lumbering over a rock.

"Gross," Laura said. "If I had to walk like that, I'd never get up."

"He's just old," said her sister Lindsey matter-of-factly.

"Remember the brown bears they used to have?" Jess asked. The twins nodded.

Hedy leaned her head back to catch the sun, and, without warning, the music was in her mind . . .

Hey, old bear, can you still dance at the end of your chain?—the voice grating, the words bitter, the melody riding an insistent beat. Alik singing and playing, his body angled on a stool but one leg planted on the floor, the guitar across his broad chest like a shield that made him vulnerable even as it protected him. . . .

"What's the matter?" Jess asked.

She blinked, came back to reality. "Nothing. I stared at the sun too hard. That's all."

"Sure?"

"Of course."

"OK." Jess clapped his hands. "Hey, everybody, a ride on the carrousel!"

Lindsey and Laura looked at each other and gave up all pretense of adult superiority. "Come on!" they shouted and raced ahead.

"OK!" Hedy yelled and went after them.

"Hey!" Jess cried and ran to catch up.

They waited until four horses were free, two abreast, and clambered on, the twins in front. The music started, like a dozen wheezing flutes, and the horses began their wooden prance, soaring and swooping with light-headed ease, painted nostrils flaring. Young children squealed on all sides, the twins' blond hair sailed up and down, and Jess looked over at her and mouthed, "I love you." She was going to yell back, had her mouth open for the words, but the wind of her motion blew them back into her throat, and all she could do was smile at him hugely. For the first time she felt that maybe she really could join them, could make a unit of four with this hard-driving yet easy man and his daughters. But the flute music slowed, the horses glided into stillness, and the feeling turned back into a question.

Afterward they all went for ice cream at Rumpelmayer's, which the twins swore not to confess to their mother, and then Hedy and Jess walked them up Fifth Avenue and across town to their building. Once Alice Newman had been waiting for them in the lobby, so blond and perfect that Hedy felt quite foreign beside her, but she was no-where in sight. The girls hugged Jess and gave Hedy little kisses on the side of her cheek.

As the two of them walked away, Jess said, "They like you."

"I know. And I like them."

They had had the exchange before: three little incanta-tory sentences that both hinted at things and forestalled discussion of them. Could the divorced politician remarry with political impunity? Did the quiet dark woman want to be part of his official life? Would his daughters be able and willing to sit for a new family photograph?

They stopped to pick up Chinese food and ate it sitting on the floor in front of her coffee table. He talked about the immigration bill he was fighting for and the reelection campaign he'd have to begin soon. Could he ring still an-other change on the slogan that had elected him the first time: "You Need a NewMan in Washington"? In the mid-dle of the discussion, apropos of nothing, he looked at her and said, "When you decide what you're going to do about your father, you'll tell me, won't you?"

"Of course I will."

"Don't look as if it were self-evident. You're full of sur-
prises."

She said nothing. Surely he was the one whose reactions
were unpredictable. Surprise was supposed to stimulate a
relationship; that was the conventional wisdom. But where
was the dividing line between surprise and alienation?
How many facets of two people had to match for the center to hold? *If you were queen of pleasure, and I were king of
pain. . . .*

"What are you thinking?" Jess asked.

"Nothing." He started to frown, so she said, "I was wondering why some people seek out their opposites but others
seem to want a mirror for a partner."

"What's the answer?"

"I don't know."

"Which kind are you?"

"The kind that likes you," she said, and he grinned.

Later, they made love. It was good, had always been
good: two facets that locked securely. He fell asleep soon,
for he had to catch an early shuttle to Washington, but she
was restless and went to the window. Arms leaning on the
center sash, she stared at all the lighted squares of other
people's windows, rising in stacks halfway up the sky.

When she turned back to the room, in the moment before
her eyes adjusted, the man in the bed looked like someone
else, not Jess. In that fleeting, alien glimpse she knew, for
the first time in words, that she had been drawn to him
because in his body and voice she found echoes of Alik.

She slid back into bed. He stirred but didn't reach for
her, and she lay on her side, apart, watching the shadows
move with the moon.

There was a gathering at Lidiya's. What was the occa-
sion? No one knew. No one cared. Just so there was tea and
more tea and vodka, and something for *zakuski*—sliced fish

and cheese, perhaps, and some meat pies and salads—and around the table, the circle of friends that knew and trusted one another and could behave freely.

She had been brought into the circle recently by Volodya, who was in one of her classes at the university. Nervous and pale, lank hair hanging over sad eyes, he looked nothing like the keen-minded student and lover of poetry that he was. Appearances were not reliable; she had learned that as one of her first lessons. She had gotten to know Volodya during the obligatory month that all students spent at a *kolkhoz* digging potatoes. Stooping in a field, dirt caking their hands, they had talked of books and traded the latest cynical jokes about the compulsory political courses that would be with them throughout their university years. Soon she had known, with the extra sense one had to develop, that Volodya had the heart of a rebel, if not necessarily the courage. And his sister Lidiya had splendid gatherings.

Many of the guests wore Western jeans and jackets and smoked American cigarettes. The air was turning into a fog, through which everyone talked excitedly, dropping English words into sentences like raisins into a cake. Beside her, two fellow students argued as they ate, stabbing the air with pickled gherkins: "Art has the right to remain free of politics!" "No, art must be the instrument of social change!" Versions of the argument were in progress all around the table. At its far end, Lidiya held court, smoking black cigarettes and gesticulating, miraculously not dropping ashes on a pile of cakes someone had just brought in.

She stood holding her tea, looking around the room, drinking in the warmth and animation. A strange image came into her mind: What if they all went out the door, and into the world, just the way they looked and sounded now, none of them slipping the public masks of caution and passivity over their faces? What if there was no need to be two people, the real one and the official one. . . .

Volodya loped over, grinning. "Guess who will be here later? Aleksandr Romanovich Markov!"

"And who is he?"

Volodya batted hair away from his eyes. "Our Alik? Haven't I talked about him? Right here in this room he used to play and sing for hours. He was the best."

Many circles had a balladeer, someone who composed irreverent songs and sang them with his guitar. Some of them were becoming widely popular, but she had not heard of this one. "Has he been away?"

"In the camps," Volodya said. "Three years. After that he was out in the country for a while, but now he is back in Moscow, and Lidiya says he will come tonight."

She was curious. It was a fact of life that people disappeared; one of her earliest school memories was the sudden absence of the girl she had liked best of all, whose father, they said, had been exposed as an enemy of the State. Her own father, she knew, had never lost the fear of being arrested, even though he had been in favor in recent years. Twice the door opened and her gaze went to it, but no one was greeted with more than the usual cries of welcome.

The smoke and noise increased; the food shrank to odd scraps. Someone put records on the phonograph, and couples danced, bumping into each other and the furniture. She was revolving in a tiny space with Volodya when he let go of her abruptly and begin to grin. "Alik!" The dancing stopped, and people surged to the door and the man who had just come in.

He smiled and nodded, and was hugged and kissed and pounded on the back, but she felt at once that it was not his usual way, that he kept people at arm's length even while embracing them. They led him to a seat of honor, pressed

vodka on him, piled all the food that was left onto one plate
and set it in front of him. She got close enough to hear him
laugh and say, in a deep, rough voice, "Where I've been,
friends, this is a month's ration." Lidiya sat close to him,
one hand frequently resting on his arm, but he seemed not
to notice.

She could not stop watching him. Very tall, shoulders
bulking under a heavy sweater, hair a thick crop of black
wire. He seemed to be drawn in brighter, harsher colors
than anyone else in the room, except for his eyes, which
were a pale, hard blue-green. Like aquamarines. He talked
of life in the camps, the wretched food, the isolation, but
also the camaraderie. Then he picked up the guitar he had
brought with him.

" 'The Ballad of Ivan and Dmitri'!" someone called.

He nodded and bent his head over the instrument.

The song told of two seventeenth-century peasants who
played a balalaika outside the main gates of Moscow and
were ridiculed, beaten, and exiled for disturbing the peace.
Ostensibly it was about nothing more than the peasants'
"three-cornered friend," which became a victim of oppression under the czar. No censor could have objected. But the
mocking delivery left no doubt of the double meaning; each
chorus ended with "Exiled for talking to Mother Moscow
in the free, bright voice of the strings." The song might
have been plucked on barbed wire.

When he finished, to shouts of approval, he looked all
around the room and then fixed his gaze on her. "Here is
someone I don't know," he said.

Volodya said, "This is Anya Nikolayeva."

Alik's left eyebrow rose. Did he recognize the name and
know whose daughter she was? "Hello, Anya."

"Hello, Alik."

"You can trust her," Volodya added firmly. "She is a
good friend."

"Ah," Alik said. "Good friends are life." His fingers did a drumroll on the guitar. He smiled at her, then announced, "I wrote this one in the camps."

"Wait, Alik," Lidiya said. She got up, went across the room, and took a small tape recorder from a drawer. Everyone murmured in agreement.

When the tape was running, he sang:

Hey, it's nice here, in my cell.
Not too cold, because seven of us
Keep each other warm;
Seven in a space built for two,
Just like home.
No meat, no eggs, no fruit, no unemployment . . .
Just like home.
No, better!
Here we can say whatever we damn well like.
What are they going to do? Send us to prison?

The cords in his throat swelled into branches when he sang, and his voice was like no other she had heard: a rich bass raspy with cigarettes and bitterness. It made her think of razors with velvet laid over their edges.

He sang again, and again, stopping occasionally to drink vodka and to smoke. Sometimes, through the smoke, he looked at her and smiled.

Once, when he stopped, she asked, "Why were you in the camps?"

"Poetry." He played a soft river of notes. "Not even my own—other people's, though some of it was worth being arrested for." He said that he had helped with many of the public readings of protest poetry that took place during the brief relaxation of official attitudes—helped not by reading his own poems, which he did not consider good enough, but by tending to practical matters. The KGB had detained him several times, once for a month, and when official attitudes hardened once more, they had manufactured a reason to expel him from the university. One night he had been picked up again for questioning; someone, he never learned who, had reported the lyrics of some of his songs, and he had been sent away, for anti-Soviet agitation and propaganda. "I started as a good Communist and a bad poet. Now I am neither."

He laughed, struck off a chord, and sang again.

Brothers, remember how we love the winter?
Ice grows thick on the river,
Walk on it, dance on it, stamp on it,
But take one step wrong and it gives beneath your
    boot like an egg.
Down you go, up to the chest.
Cold crushes your heart, ice fills your veins.
Don't let it seal your lips.

She watched his blunt fingers work the guitar with delicacy and thought that if he put his arms around her, she would feel both safe and in danger.

She came out of her class on dialectical materialism, huddling her books against her because the wind was cold, and so was her mind, still frozen with the heavy, meaningless lecture and the struggle not to know how bitterly she resented the waste of so many precious hours of her life. Face sunk in her coat collar, she didn't see him until suddenly he was in front of her on the walk.

"Anna Borisovna," he said with mock formality.

She was too surprised to say anything but "What are you doing here?"

"Looking for you." A fur hat hid his hair and made his face seem broader, but his aquamarine eyes were just as she had been thinking of them in the weeks since Lidiya's party. "Volodya told me you would be here, coming out of class."

"Yes?" she said uncertainly.

"Apparently Volodya is reliable, because here you are." His voice seemed even deeper and more rasping than before. "Are you on your way somewhere?"

"To the Metro. Home."

"I'll walk with you," he said, not a question. He put her books under one arm. The last time she had seen him, she thought, Lidiya had been hanging on to that arm. They started off, boots making little squeals on the frozen snow.

He glanced back at the university and said, "I was there for a year. What are you studying?"

"History and literature."

"Are you a writer, then?"

"No. Only someone who admires them."

"Your father's music is magnificent," he said.

So that was it; he had learned who she was and hoped for an introduction.

"I heard his violin concerto at the conservatory five years ago. A friend got me a ticket."

"I was there," she said wonderingly.

"Is your father like his music?"

She was silent for a dozen steps. She had never quite put them together: the music that sometimes touched her as directly as an embrace and the distant, difficult father whose sporadic eruptions into warmth only made his retreats harder to accept. In her mind's eye he was a still figure, frozen in the posture of her earliest memories: bent over a pile of score paper, eyes fixed on visions she couldn't see, fingers locked against his temples. She had used to think that some spirit—half benign, half terrifying—had taken him away and left only his body behind; Papa was with Demon Music. "I don't think I can answer your question," she told Alik. "Why do you care what my father is like? I suppose you want to meet him."

"The more I admire someone's artistry, the less I want to meet him."

"Why?"

"Because art is the only safe thing to believe in. But what if the artist doesn't live up to his creations?"

It was a new thought. Was her father the equal of his music? No, he was its master. Or was he its slave?

"Meeting your father isn't the reason I came to find you," Alik said. "I could have met him years ago if I'd wanted. One of my mother's cousins, in the Ministry of Culture, knows him. Rodion Sergeivich Orlov."

She turned to Alik in surprise. Rodion Sergeivich, that small, meticulous man who came to dinner occasionally, in neat suits and a perpetual smile, his graceful hands moving as if yearning for reins—he could have no relation, familial or otherwise, to the big, rough man beside her. "I've never heard Rodion Sergeivich mention you," she said.

"Possibly he doesn't appreciate my contributions to the glory of the Communist Party," Alik said gravely. "Or the fact that, for my mother's sake, he has to try to keep me out of trouble." His eyes went even more brilliant, and he laughed. She couldn't help laughing with him. In the icy air their breath made two ragged clouds.

When they reached the Metro, Alik said, "If you come to my place, we can be alone for an hour or so."

She nodded as if it were the most natural thing in the world.

The place was near Gorky Street, a two-room apartment shared with his brother, his brother's ex-wife, and their young son. The couple had divorced a year earlier, Alik said, but neither had been able to find another place. So they stayed, giving the apartment still another tenant: their hostility. It was a drearily common story.

Alik slept in the "parlor," in the curtained-off end. One wall held books; the other was a montage of sketches, photos from foreign magazines, and scraps of paper with music notations and lines of verse. "We can talk here," he said. "They haven't bugged it yet. And by a miracle, no one will be home until six." His guitar lay on the narrow bed, in the center. He picked it up and sat in the one chair, cradling the instrument as they talked, fingers holding a faint, often silent dialogue with it. She sat on the bed, in the guitar's place.

He had read everything, including most of the English and American authors she knew. They agreed about Chekhov, not Turgenev; Twain, not Hemingway. "I want to write poems and songs and play the guitar," he said. "I don't want to be political! But they force politics into our lives. And it will never end, not when things like the invasion of Czechoslovakia can happen. But why do I tell this to the daughter of Boris Nikolayev?"

" 'We have art in order not to die of the truth,' " she said softly.

"Ah!" His eyes glittered. "Who said that?"

"Nietzsche."

"Are you studying to be an artist, then, like your father and mother?"

"I could never be like them. But I want to understand art, perhaps to write about it someday."

He bent over the guitar, fingers busy but silent. There were fine black hairs on the backs of his hands. The top of his head was a mat of curls the color of coal.

"Aren't you afraid," she said, "that if you keep singing, someone may report you? The way they did before?"

"What else can I do? When art is a crime, artists have to

become criminals. I didn't want to write political songs, but they've made me into someone who has to. If I stop altogether, then they've turned me into a permanent prisoner, someone who's locked up even when he's out."

"I suppose my father feels that," she said slowly. "He's afraid of being arrested, though he never has been."

The front door sounded; someone had come into the apartment. "My ex-sister-in-law," Alik said. He rose, put down the guitar, and pulled her to her feet. "Natasha?" he called loudly, but while he said it, and while a voice called back, he ran his thumb slowly all the way around her mouth.

The next time she was at Lidiya's with Volodya, Alik came in. He waved at her but paid her little attention; Lidiya was at his side, and he made no attempt to dislodge her. When people asked him to sing, he angled himself on a high stool and sang something he called "Birches," different from the others she had heard. Over an intricate, delicate guitar accompaniment his voice was more gentle than she had thought it could be, singing of birches that stood at the edge of a smooth, dark sea, shaking their leaf-hair into the wind, watching for a ship that never came.

When the song was finished, she told Volodya she felt ill and had to leave.

Three days later Alik was waiting for her again when she came out of one of her classes. Without a word, he reached for her books, but she stepped back and said, "What do you want?"

"To see you," he said.

"Why?"

"I like you. I want to talk to you again, the way we did before."

She was going to say she had to get home. Instead she heard, "Why don't you talk with Lidiya?"

"I do." He looked at her expressionlessly. "Lidiya is a good friend."

Something—the wind?—was stinging her cheeks. "I have to get home."

"Fine," he said. "Let's head for the Metro." He walked on the balls of his feet, springily, as if part of his energy came up from the ground, even through the snow. "I talk to Lidiya," he said, "I dance with Lidiya, I sleep with Lidiya, if you're wondering, because Lidiya is safe. I'm afraid you are dangerous."

She stopped. "If you think I'm a *stukach,* why talk to me?"

He took her arm, and even through her coat and his gloves, she felt the life in his fingers. "The university may be full of KGB stool pigeons, but I don't think you're one of them."

"Then?"

"You're dangerous because I want to be with you too much."

They walked on in silence. At the Metro entrance, she said, "I don't have to go home yet." He nodded.

His nephew was in the apartment, reading at the table. Alik tousled the boy's hair and said, "Go read in the bedroom, Mitya, will you?" The child looked at her with no curiosity and left.

"Your nephew seems used to having you bring women here in the afternoon."

"No. He's used to doing as he's told and asking no questions. He'll be a good citizen."

Inside the alcove, the guitar was propped on the chair. She sat on the bed. "What did you want to talk to me about?"

"Oh," he said, "the glory of socialist realism. No, even better—the number of housing units required to fulfill the next five-year plan."

"Why are you angry?" she asked.

"I'm not."

She ran her hands along her arms, feeling the rough wool of her sweater. "Socialist realism," she said, "is the only art worthy of the Soviet people. The number of housing units required to fill the next five-year plan will be larger than for the last five-year plan. What else shall we talk about?"

He made a fist of one hand and slammed it into the other. "I wanted to stay away from you. You're only eighteen. Volodya told me. I'm twenty-five."

"So?"

"Why are you here? Why are you willing to come into my life?"

"Why did you ask me to?"

"Don't you know it's dangerous to care about people?"

"Is that what you're going to teach me?"

"Oh, oh, oh," he said, the anger leaving his voice in steps, "the things I'd like to teach you."

They looked at each other in silence. She felt the steadiness of her gaze, and the pulse that contradicted it. He reached down and put his hands around her neck. "I can't do this," she said, "if you're not going to care."

"I know."

"If you're not going to care, stay with Lidiya." He was pulling her to her feet, against the length of his body, when she felt a last spurt of panic. "Maybe we should be friends, Alik, just friends."

Into her neck he whispered, "Too late."

CHAPTER THREE

"What wonderful smells," Vera said. "No one can make your mouth water like the French."

They were five at the table, in a quiet corner of a small, elegant restaurant. It was Vera's birthday, her sixty-third. At Jess's insistence and expense, Hedy was taking her and her three oldest friends out to celebrate. Jess had planned to be there but had been detained in Washington by a crucial vote; the reservation was made, he said, so they must go without him. In the afternoon he had sent dark red roses to Vera, who pursed her lips over the extravagance but buried her face in the flowers as if their scent were oxygen.

"Tonight," Vera said, "I shall eat like a pig." She broke a chunk of the hard-crusted country bread into pieces, crumbs flaking from her fingers. "Well, perhaps a piglet. But you'll see. The appetite is still good."

Lately, Hedy noted, her mother had begun referring to her body and its condition in the third person: "The appetite is good." "The legs are better today." The same way singers spoke of "the voice," and probably for the same reason; when the physical self, or a part of it, acquired such importance, one thought of it as something separate, outside one's control.

Tonight Vera was happy, or behaving as if she was: face animated above the blue silk, eyes glittering in competition with her favorite crystal beads. She lifted her wineglass. "We must toast our absent host."

Still engrossed at his post, Hedy thought before she could stop herself. Maybe it was just as well Jess wasn't there, for in his presence Vera's three friends would have been more formal and more inquisitive, glances flying among them like darts as they tried to assess the situation between Hedy and "her special friend." They were single women—one widowed, one divorced, one unmarried. The *babushki,* Hedy called them fondly, although only one was Russian and none—that was the joke—were like those grandmotherly figures in drab dresses and thick stockings who could seem omnipresent in the Soviet Union, offering advice, encouragement, and reprimands to everyone, including total strangers.

Zoya, the widow of an émigré professor, lifted her glass. "Now we toast our dear Verushka!" Always inclined to flamboyance, she tossed back her scarf, then her head, and then the wine, in one gulp, the way vodka went down a Russian throat. The others followed suit, but Dorothy didn't get it right; she spouted wine on herself and laughed merrily. Dorothy, a high school music teacher, was always in good humor despite a chronic struggle for health and money. "I was a happy baby," she would say, apparently believing it to be an explanation. Perhaps it was; had psychology offered a better one?

Lucille rolled her eyes and handed Dorothy a napkin. Lucille's efforts had kept her husband's business afloat for twenty-five years. When he decided efficiency wasn't feminine and left her for a clinging vine, she had built a successful business of her own, in discount art supplies.

Dorothy sponged her dress and said, "Let's try that again."

Zoya laughed. "You are impossible!"

"In Russia," Vera said, "no one would drink with you!"

"Enough of this," Lucille said. "It's time to order. If I don't have an appetizer pretty soon, I'll get silly."

That was quite untrue; no glass or two of wine would dare affect Lucille, who could down three Scotches without her eyes, or even her nose, turning shiny. She was simply masking her solicitude for Vera. Hedy felt a rush of warmth for her, for all the *babushki*—for the trust that tied them to one another, and to Vera, as solidly as a chain. Trust was the bedrock of relationships, she thought. The thought was like a burr.

She picked up the menu and tried to concentrate: parchmentlike paper, copperplate writing, *Les Potages, Les Poissons.* . . . That first time in Paris, it had been strange to experience French as a language of real life, not just of the schoolroom and books. . . . She shook her head; she had eaten in dozens, perhaps hundreds of French restaurants without recalling that twenty-year-old visit to Paris, so why now? Especially since, during that visit, they had avoided restaurants, had come with their luggage full of tea and sugar and potatoes. . . .

The waiter appeared, in response to Lucille's raised finger, and recited a long list of specials. "Too many choices," Zoya said when he finished. "That was splendid, young man," Vera said, "but you don't expect *us* to remember such a list?" The waiter laughed as genuinely as if she were the first customer ever to make the comment, and said,

"May I recommend for madame?" Strangers had reacted that way to her mother, Hedy thought, as soon as they arrived in America. At first Hedy took it to be American friendliness, and though that was part of it, the greater part was something in Vera herself, a combination of eyes, voice, and smile, perhaps of her small size and the tilt of her head, that made people feel she saw them as individuals. In Russia Vera's public behavior had been as guarded as everyone else's, but in America she became, except in degree, the same person out in the world that she had always been at home. Had she known such a thing would happen? Hedy had wondered. Was it one of the reasons she had wanted to leave Russia? When asked, Vera had cocked her head, thought, then said, "I dreamed always of the things we could do if we left. I never thought how it would *feel* to do them. I don't think you can know what you will feel when you leave your life. You just have to . . . leave it, and find out."

Vera touched Hedy's hand. "Darling girl, this nice man is waiting to take your order."

"Of course. Sorry." Hedy obliged. The waiter bowed, smiled at Vera, and said, "Madame and her friends have made excellent choices."

As soon as he was safely away, Dorothy said, "Why didn't I tell him to forget the sauce? Or at least put it on the side. I could hardly get into this skirt. Tonight, in your honor, Vera, I have thrown caution to the wind."

"I've got a better idea," Lucille said. "In her honor, why don't you spare us all and not mention your damn diet for the next three hours?"

Dorothy rolled her eyes. "The supreme sacrifice? All right." The others began to joke about her eternal plumpness. The friends liked to dwell on one another's peccadilloes, in affectionate celebration of the fact that none of their psyches held more important problems.

Hedy leaned back and watched her mother. Flushed in the glow of friendship and wine, she didn't seem ill. No one who didn't know would suspect. If she didn't know her, Hedy thought, if Vera were not her mother but just a woman having dinner with other women, she would see . . . what? A small, dark lady—perhaps too frail?—but still strong enough to be intense and charming. . . . It couldn't be done, she thought. You couldn't strip motherhood from your mother, who was forever locked inside (or freed by?) your childhood perspective on her.

As a father was too?

> *Annushka, darling, come listen. Papa has written the most glorious song for tenor and French horn. Play it for her, Boris, let her hear what you have done while she was at school.* And somehow, when he sang it in a deep, cracked voice, there was the soaring of a bird in the sadness of his song. . . .

The thought, which had been invading Hedy's mind all week, pushed its way in again: If she saw her father, if she went to Finland and talked to him, that would make Vera all right. The cancer would go into remission, and her mother would live.

They were of equal power: her acceptance of the thought, and her knowledge that it was irrational.

She heard silence around the table, felt them looking at her. "I'm sorry. Did you say something, Zoya?"

Zoya leaned back theatrically. "I asked what you were thinking. You were many miles away."

Dorothy laughed. "In Washington, I'll bet. With her nice friend."

"That's right," Hedy answered, because it was simpler.

"Aha!" Zoya said, as if she had caught a spy, and they all laughed.

A waiter materialized, lifted the wine from the ice

bucket, and refilled their glasses. When he left, Vera said, "Now, listen to me, my dear daughter and friends"—and as she spoke, the sound of laughter ran from her voice like water rushing down a drain—"now I would like a toast, please, to Boris and to the book his daughter will write about him."

The four women looked at Hedy. Pinned in the circle of their eyes and lifted glasses, she could only join it. They all drank.

Softly, Vera said, "But how will she finish the book? How can she know how it should end?"

The *babushki* looked at Hedy, throwing smiles over the silence.

Finally Zoya fluttered her hands and said, "Hedy, tell us, your nice friend with all his connections in Washington, have you asked him to find out what he can about your father?"

She hadn't asked, but Jess had done it anyway. "He did talk to the State Department," she said, "but there wasn't much the press hadn't covered. Apparently the request for my father originated with the Finnish festival, with no prompting from Washington. The Soviets agreed pretty quickly and they've played up the story in *Pravda* and on TV. There hasn't been any official U.S.-Soviet discussion about the fact that he's going. The government sources don't know anything new about him." As Jess had put it: "There's been no change in his circumstances, whatever the hell they really are."

"So," Zoya said, "if the State Department has nothing to add . . ."

There had been one item, over which Hedy had hesitated before passing it on to her mother: Boris Nikolayev had last been seen publicly thirteen months before, at a Kremlin reception for some Eastern bloc dignitaries. Vera's face had clouded; she hated to think of him in the Kremlin. But she had to be told such things. If things were true, and knowable, people had to know them. Didn't they?

Lucille leaned forward. "Exactly what do you know, then, about your father's situation? What can you be sure of?"

Vera answered, firmly. "Boris is alive. Finland wishes to honor him, and he will be there. And if he could, he would try to come to us."

Lucille lifted her wineglass and replanted it. "What's the last information you had that you could trust? The letter four years ago?"

"Who could trust that?" Vera said. The letter, posted in Zürich, had been addressed to "Family of Boris Nikolayev," in care of the conductor of the New York Philharmonic, who had given it to the third-chair violin, who knew Vera's name and address and had sent it on. No trace remained of the chain of hands that must have gotten the letter to Switzerland. It was in English, unsigned, the writing physically bold but the words crabbed, as if anticipating a censor's slash: "There have been reports in the bourgeois press that Boris Semyonovich was ill but has now recovered. Boris Semyonovich wishes personally to assure you that these reports are true. He is at work on his music, in the peace of his home, happy and secure in the watchful care of his friends."

Hedy and Vera had spent hours trying to decide the actual meaning and provenance of the letter, which was written in a hand they didn't recognize. Had a friend sent it at Boris's behest? If so, why no personal comment, however superficial? Had someone sent it in Boris's behalf but without his knowledge? What was its real message—that Boris was under constant surveillance? Or was the letter a plant for some purpose only the KGB knew?

Zoya put her hand on Vera's. "How many letters, over the years?"

"Five. And the one note in Boris's own hand."

That had been written six months after their last sight of him and sent on by the State Department, which would not divulge how it had been received. The note had said only: "This way is best, for all three of us. Be well and safe in the new life. I will keep you always in my music. Boris. Papa."

Had he written the note freely? Had he failed to write again because he couldn't, or was it because he didn't want to? There never were any definitive answers to those questions, or to the larger one: Why had he failed to follow his part of the plan—to meet them at the American embassy in Paris, where they would all defect to the West?

When Vera first learned the official Soviet position about that day—that Nikolayev's wife and daughter were traitors but he himself would never think of leaving his country—rage had twisted her face and voice into a stranger's for half an hour. Then she had collapsed in tears and locked herself in her room. After two days she had emerged, pale and calm, and refused ever again to consider any possibility except that Boris had been prevented from leaving by force—that was it. That was all.

There was another possibility, but she didn't know it because Hedy had never told her. Some weights had to be borne alone.

"How long has it been since you tried to call him?" Dorothy asked.

"I don't remember," Hedy said. "Some time now." Her mother had agonized before each of the few times she tried, knowing that her efforts to contact him could harm him, might even get him arrested. Once, in the beginning, she actually had reached him, but before she could say more than two sentences, she had been cut off. After that, either the operator would not put the call through, or else a strange voice would answer and say that Boris Nikolayev was out. Then there had been a period when no one answered at all. Even if they had reached him, or thought it safe to try one of their former friends, what could they have said on phones they knew to be tapped?

The waiter brought their hors d'oeuvres and set Vera's in front of her with a flourish. They ate in silence for a while.

"There must be a lot of Western musicians going to this festival in Finland," Lucille said. "Won't some of them be able to bring you news? Or even deliver a message for you?"

"Maybe," Hedy said. "Mama just learned that Kim Wan Lee will be there."

"Kim Wan Lee!" Dorothy cried. "Vera, didn't you teach his older brother?"

"Yes, and Kim himself, for a short while. The brother was a nice boy with a good bow arm, but everyone knew Kim would be the exceptional one."

"I'm sure he'll help you," Dorothy said.

"Yes," Vera said. "Musicians make good friends."

Good friends are life. The words pushed into Hedy's mind in a rasping voice. Only when the others looked at her did she realize she had repeated them aloud. "I mean," she said quickly, "that much of what we know about Papa has come from musicians." Occasionally someone who had played in the Soviet Union would report seeing Boris at a concert or a reception, but no one had managed a conversation with him about anything other than music; there was always a functionary at his side, and he never tried (was never allowed?) to ask or talk about his family. Once in a while an émigré would bring news: Someone had a brother who knew someone who had seen Boris and said he looked well. Then relief would flood Vera's face—until someone else

knew someone who had heard he was in a hospital, and
Vera would pray it wasn't for "psychiatric treatment."
From year to year the stories might conflict: Boris Nikolayev had been honored for his music—or his music wasn't
being played anywhere, officially. Boris Nikolayev had in-
curred the anger of the Composers Union—or, worst of all,
he had joined the Party and delivered a speech to the union
on the glory of the Party and Soviet music.

Vera put down her fork. "You ask exactly what we know
about Boris?" She lifted her bread plate, turned it over, and
let the pieces of crust fall on the cloth. "Crumbs, that is all
we know. Crumbs." She covered them with the plate and,
without warning or sound, began to cry.

"*Mamochka,*" Hedy whispered, and put an arm around
her shoulders. Beneath the blue silk, her mother's bones
felt as small and sharp as a cat's. The *babushki* were looking
at them, frozen in a self-conscious tableau: Zoya wanting
to touch, Dorothy indecisive, Lucille holding back.

As suddenly as she had begun crying, Vera stopped. "A
tissue?" she said. Three were proffered so quickly that she
had to smile. She made a ceremony of taking all of them,
rolling them into one ball, and dabbing her eyes. "I am
sorry. Weeping into wine! And there is not even truth in
this wine—I am not sad, I am happy to be here with all
of—"

"Mama," Hedy interrupted. For one last moment she
wondered if she really were going to say it, but there was
no choice. There never had been. "Mama, I have a present
for you."

"Already you gave me my present, the beautiful blue
sweater that I will—"

"I've decided to go to Finland."

Vera went quite still. "What are you saying?"

"I'm going. So I can try to talk to Papa."

Vera made fists of both hands and put them to her heart. "Do you mean it?"

"Yes. I know I can count on Lucille and Dorothy and Zoya to look after you while I'm gone. Can't I?"

The *babushki* murmured, Yes, of course.

"No, my darling girl," Vera said, "you cannot go. It could be dangerous."

Hedy smiled. "When you talked about going yourself, I didn't hear a word about danger."

"What difference could danger possibly make to me?"

They all looked away, unwilling either to challenge the question or to answer it.

"I'm going," Hedy said firmly. "And that's all there is to it."

Vera rolled her eyes and said to the *babushki*, "Now you see why she had to leave the Soviet Union—someone who always wants her own way."

"I take after my mother," Hedy said, and they all laughed.

The *babushki* patted Hedy's hand and called for more wine, for toasts.

In spite of herself, Vera began to relax into happiness, her eyes turning darker and shiny, her smile sometimes stretching as wide as her face. "What a wonderful evening," she said. She clutched Hedy's wrist. "Tell Jesse his French restaurant was a good omen, because now Paris will not be the end of the story. *Vive* the book! *Vive* Jesse! *Vive* Paris!"

Paris! she thought as soon as Boris came in.

"You've had news?" she said, and he nodded. Their months of waiting were over, Vera could tell. But she knew he would say nothing more until he had taken off his jacket and hat and put on his slippers. He was methodical in all unimportant, daily matters, as a relief, she thought, from the savage concentration he gave his music. So she made herself stand by the table quietly, answering that no, Anna was not home yet nor was his mother, who had gone out to hunt for meat. Finally he came over to her, took her hands, and looked down into her eyes. The room trembled around her. "They have given the permission," he said. "We are going to Paris."

"Anna too?" she whispered.

"Yes. Thanks to Rodion, Anna may go also."

Vera felt as if she might start rising toward the ceiling. Boris's hands, and his eyes, were all that anchored her. A miracle had taken place: Months before, the French had issued an invitation, and at last the Ministry of Culture had approved it. They were actually going to go, all three of them: Boris to conduct the Moscow Symphony in the Western premiere of his Third Symphony, she to take her usual place in that orchestra, and Anna to accompany them. Anna not made to stay behind as security for them! They must have accepted that Boris's mother was security enough.

She could not stay still. Crying *"Vive* Paris!," she pulled Boris with her and began to whirl around the room—or as much of it as could be whirled around without hitting the divan or the table or the buffet. *"Vive* Paris! *Vive* Nikolayev! *Vive* the Third Symphony!"

But he slowed her to a stop, not so much by pressure as by frowning and casting his eyes to the ceiling and the walls. He was afraid someone might hear or see, or pound at the door. Or arrest him. That fear had crawled into his eyes two years after they married, when his music, which Stalin had praised, was denounced as "anti-Soviet"—at Stalin's wish, of course—and their lives had gone silent, except for the sound of minds and opportunities slamming shut against him. They had gone hungry, and been scared, and expected Boris to be arrested. But he hadn't been. After Stalin's death he had come back into favor for a while, and no other seesaw of official opinion had been as bad as that first one. But the fear had never crawled back out of Boris's eyes; it burrowed deeper and grew fatter. He had to get to a world where the fear would die because it had nothing to feed on. That was why she had prayed for Paris, and worked so hard to make him think beyond Paris.

She gripped his hands. "Borya, is it really going to happen? Are you sure?"

"Of course. Rodion told me this morning." Rather stiffly, he added, "Rodion Sergeivich will also be going to Paris."

Vera nodded. They had expected him to go—had made it part of their plan, in fact.

"I asked him to dinner on Sunday," Boris said. Vera nodded again; miracles had to be paid for. Boris added, "He is lonely now that his wife is gone."

Who could live with such a man? Vera wanted to say but didn't. She rarely said anything negative about Rodion Sergeivich Orlov, not because he used his growingly influential position in the Party and at the Ministry of Culture to help and shield Boris, but because Boris wouldn't listen. He would murmur, "Yes, yes," but his eyes would get that look of wearing glasses even though he didn't, and her words would slide past his gaze like drops of rain. Boris and Rodion's father had known each other since they were boys in Young Pioneers, and somehow that bond had been passed on to Rodion. Whatever was its nature, Boris would not, or could not, explain it beyond saying the obvious: that Rodion tried to help when he could, and that he not only admired Boris's music but understood it. She had silenced herself completely, of course, when it turned out that Anna's new boyfriend was actually some kind of cousin to Rodion.

Boris pushed hair back from his eyes. "We have a lot to thank Rodion Sergeivich for."

"Let's not talk of him just now," Vera said. "I want to talk of Paris. Do you think the full orchestra will go? How many performances? When do we leave? How long do we stay?"

Boris put his arm around her. "Give me a kiss and some tea, and I'll tell you all I know."

They were still at the table talking, Boris on his third glass of sugared tea, when Anna came in. She had been with Alik; Vera knew that in an instant, the way all the states of Anna's being registered in her own. Didn't Boris see it—the soft look of satiety and the impatience of hunger, both at once? "Annushka," she said, "there is such wonderful news. Boris, tell her."

She folded her arms on the table and sat between her husband and her daughter, content to hear Boris say the words and watch their meaning reflect on Anna's face—at least as much as Anna would allow to be seen. "Paris? I can go with you?" she said, her dark eyes sunstruck with wonder. "I am truly going to Paris?" She struggled to believe it, and succeeded. She opened her mouth as if to shout her joy, but closed it instead. Because, Vera guessed, she had thought of going without Alik.

"We leave in two months," Boris said.

Anna got up and, almost religiously, embraced him.

"We have much to plan," Vera said. And added the logical next thought, "Tomorrow let's have a day in the woods."

Perhaps it wasn't really necessary to be there—in one of the parks outside the city, walking among the birches, with the huge curve of the river appearing now and again through the trees—but Boris, very nervous, wouldn't have the discussion anywhere else, not even at the dacha. Perhaps he was right; they could be sure the trees held no listening devices, and could take protective coloration from the other strollers and mushroom-pickers. The air was still warm, and a breeze ran pizzicato through the tops of the birches.

Boris led the way, branches parting before his tall, broad frame, twigs occasionally snagging on his shirt or in his heavy hair. At length he found a spot with no one else in sight or hearing. The three of them stood facing one another. Vera took their hands to close the triangle. Anna's were very cold; she smiled and said, "Like the witches in *Macbeth*." Anna had been in love with Shakespeare, perhaps with all of English and American literature, for years.

Boris's expression did not change—couldn't he have smiled back at his daughter's little joke?

"Listen, Anechka," Vera said. "Your father and I have decided . . ." She stopped.

"Yes?" Anna's lovely face was eager but tense.

"Your papa . . ." She had not thought it would be so difficult to say. "Boris and I, when we first learned of the invitation, we agreed that if we could get to Paris, we would try . . . not to come back."

Anna's hand leaped within hers.

"Yes," Vera said, answering her look. "We will try to get to the West."

In the distance a child called, "Papa, come see this toadstool!" Above their heads a bird shrilled and then went silent again.

"Papa?" Anna said wonderingly. "You, to the West?"

Why wouldn't Anna be amazed? Vera thought. For years she had heard her father speak contemptuously of "Western humanists" and angrily of his one trip to New York

and London many years earlier, when the bourgeois press
had pursued him relentlessly. Vera had worked just as
relentlessly to offset those perceptions: coaxing, cajol-
ing, whispering when she curled beside Boris in their
bed. . . .

He bowed his head, almost formally. "Your mother has
convinced me that we must go."

Anna released their hands and stepped back, as if she
needed distance to accept what he had said.

"Your papa must go where his works are understood
and loved and he will be free to write what he wishes,
where they will not admire his music one year and keep
it from being played the next. Your papa cannot live and
work where they give him prizes but refuse to give him
work unless he tips his cap to them like a serf, where the
son of some school friend has more power over his life
than—"

"Verochka!" Boris chided.

He was right, she was rattling on, but the thoughts were
in her mind so strongly, dammed up, that they rushed out
like water when the tap was finally opened, the way water
should rush out if the plumbing worked right, but it never
did, nothing ever worked as it should. . . . She took a deep
breath. "We will stay in the West, Papa and I, if we can.
If you will go with us."

Something scuttled in a bush near them. Boris's head
jerked at the sound.

Anna stood very straight. The decision was hers to make.
How could it be otherwise when Vera had from babyhood
encouraged her to see things for herself; had worked to
undermine the schools' constant lesson of conformity; had
let her play freely in the park, splashing into ponds while
other children stood passively at their edges and other parents and *babushki* muttered disapprovals. . . . A leaf drifted

behind Anna's head. Not a blue one, Vera thought, and smiled. Once in kindergarten Anna had come home puzzled and unhappy because in art class she had drawn a tree with blue leaves and a yellow trunk and the teacher, upset, had told her to draw green leaves and a brown trunk, like everybody else. "I thought it would be pretty to make it different," Anna had said, and Vera had had to explain that in school you must try to seem like the others, to keep your blue leaves to yourself. . . . How Anna had grown, how adult was the slant of her cheek! Gravely she said, "I have been thinking of staying in the West ever since I knew there was even the smallest chance of going to Paris with you."

"Ah," Vera said. She had been sure of it, but Boris had refused to discuss anything with their daughter until and unless the permissions came through.

"I was wondering whether I would have the courage to do it," Anna said. "Whether I would be able to leave you. And now you tell me you are going . . ." A smile began to curve her lips.

Then she shivered almost imperceptibly, and Vera knew she was thinking of leaving Alik. Vera would never tell her so, but that separation would be a relief. If they stayed in Moscow, Alik could only mean trouble. For Anna, for all of them. A talented young man, even brilliant, with his poetry and songs, but he could not, or would not, keep more than a step ahead of trouble. They had already had enough trouble for six lives. Now that the permissions had come, Anna really shouldn't see him again, even if he was a cousin to Rodion Sergeivich. Perhaps *because* he was.

"To the West," Vera said. "The three of us!" She embraced Anna, holding the warm, sweet body that had grown so tall and solid. For nineteen years she had felt its growth in its changing positions against her own.

"To the West," Boris said hoarsely.

Vera pulled him into the embrace, and the three of them stood, clutching one another beneath the birches. Now their joining would be forever, Vera thought, and a wordless ecstasy filled her, until she realized Boris and Anna were holding her so tightly she could barely breathe. She pulled away, laughing and gasping. "To Paris and the West!"

"Yes," Anna said. "The three of us. To Paris and the West."

CHAPTER FOUR

"Hedy," a voice said, or maybe it was saying "Hey," and a hand was gently shaking her shoulder and pulling her up out of a black hole of sleep, though she struggled to hold her eyelids over it as long as she could.

She gave up, and blinked. "Jess?" In the sliver of time before she fully knew it was he, before her thoughts and feelings and confusions about him could swoop into their accustomed places, she saw his face without them, and knew exactly how she felt about him. "Jess, hi," she said softly, but the saying of it dispelled the wonderfully clear perspective, which slid away like the content of a dream. She blinked again, realized she was lying on her couch, remembered she had been reading something about Freud. "What time is it?"

"Two-ten," Jess said. "I just got in."

Other things slotted into place: He had had to go to a

reception at an African embassy and had hoped to get a late plane out of Washington. "How was the party?" she asked.

"The ambassador wore the most beautiful gold robe I've ever seen and talked about Beethoven. Great food, but I think I ate some chocolate-covered ants."

She sat up. The books she had been reading had been put back on one of the piles on the coffee table. Jess's coat and weekend case were on a chair.

He sat beside her and put his arm around her. "Wearing anything under that robe?"

"No."

"Then it's better than the ambassador's." He pulled a pencil from the coil of her braid. "When I came in, you had Freud on your chest and letters from Verdi across your thighs. How can you read two books at once?"

"I don't. I read one for a while, then the other."

"Why?"

"I don't know. Why not?"

He looked nonplussed. "It's not the way I do it."

"You're linear," she said. "A straight arrow."

"That sounds dull."

"No. It means you're one of the good guys."

"That sounds dull."

"No, no. You're so—how can I explain it?—so . . . American. No accent. No import tax."

"Now it sounds like a compliment. But what the hell does it mean?"

"Oh, dear." It had started as a joke, but suddenly she wanted him to understand. "You're so straightforward and generous, and you believe in things, and you get things done, and even though you're sophisticated, you're still innocent, and—"

"I hate me. Whatever happened to good-looking and great in bed?"

"That too," she said.

He kissed her ear. "Let's go check it out."

"Soon." She leaned against him and thought about telling him her decision and wondered how he would react. All that came out was "I need some tea."

"I'll fix it."

"No, I'll do it, Jess, I—"

"Sit!" he said and made a face at her before he went into the kitchen.

The stupid thing was that she felt odd when he waited on her. A carryover, perhaps, from her other life, where they could say all they liked about equality and on International Women's Day could broadcast sugary songs ("Bouquets to you, Soviet Woman, how you inspire us") and stage huge celebrations, but the reality was that women did not only their work in the world but everything at home as well. Her mother had accepted without question that Papa would offer no help, not even during the times when they had no maid or before his mother came to live with them. In the afternoon Mama had to rush from rehearsal to stand in queues for hours, string bag in one hand, violin case in the other; in the morning one of them had to stand by the washing machine for hours, constantly pushing its buttons to coax it to do one small laundry; but Papa was always at his piano or bent over his desk, deep in his own world. . . . Decades later, when Jess was in the kitchen making her some tea, she liked it, but it felt odd. Could you ever erase the emotional imprinting of your youth?

Jess looked too big for the kitchen, but he moved easily in the cramped space, taking out cups and filling the kettle. She thought of the first time he had shown up with a bag of groceries and announced he was making dinner for them. She had hung about the kitchen offering to do this or that until he laughed and told her to go write deathless prose. When he called her to the table, the steak had been perfect, ditto the rice and the asparagus and the wine. He had been so easy about it all.

His life might not have been easy, she thought, but it seemed so: the athletic prowess, the law degree, the gradual easing—there was the word again—into politics, the wealthy, gorgeous wife, the daughters who were blond mirror images of health and smiles. She looked around the clutter of her apartment, at the books leaning in crooked stacks like *baba yagas*.

He brought out two cups and raised his eyebrows until she cleared a space on the coffee table. "Did you used to wait on Alice?" she asked.

"Sure," Jess said. "Until she got to like it."

She laughed and tried to drink her tea, but it was too hot.

He sat beside her again, stretched his legs, and kicked off his shoes. "This weekend I'm not going to see the girls."

"Why not?"

"Alice wants to take them somewhere, and I want her to. It's been too long since I had a weekend with just you. Without seeing the twins, or your mother, for that matter. What say we both put our families on hold till Monday?"

"That might be difficult."

"Why?"

"I was getting ready to tell you what I've decided to do about my father."

"Oh." She watched the small lift of his shoulder and jaw.

She tried some tea: drinkable, but still so hot that after she swallowed, muscles from her ears to her breasts tightened in revolt. She put the cup down and said, "I looked up *bodacious*. You were right—audacious, bold. I guess I'm going to do something bodacious."

She had hoped he might smile, but his expression didn't alter by a millimeter. "I knew you'd decide to go," he said.

"I'm sorry you don't like the idea, Jess, but I—"

"What I said was I'd hate it."

"All right, I'm sorry you hate it, but I have to go."

"When did you make this decision?"

"Last week. At Mother's birthday dinner, to be precise, when we were all celebrating. On you." She smiled, but he looked as if he didn't believe her. "I have to try to get the truth about my father."

"For your mother or for yourself?"

She hesitated. "I don't think I can separate the two."

"So you're not going just for her sake?"

"I . . . No. And it's also for the book. If I'm going to write about my father, I have to see him."

"So it's definite you're going to do the book?"

Until that moment it hadn't been. "Yes," she said, and added, almost defiantly, "It's in my category—artists who work under oppression."

He pushed his hands into his hair. "I've got to say this; there's no way I could keep from saying it. It's possible there won't be any problems and you'll be safe. Maybe the KGB won't find out who you are. Maybe they'll decide they don't care who you are. But you'd sure as hell be foolish to count on it. And don't tell me you're counting on the Finns to keep you safe, because you know the Finns have to be very careful about not cooperating with the Russian bear. Besides, you can't know what the Russians are going to do until you get over there, which could be too late. Do you really think your mother wants you to take such a risk? Hedy?"

"Mama is aware of the risk, but I'm keeping her from focusing on it. What's important is that she wants to know certain things before she dies."

"OK. But what the hell are you doing to her if you go over there and get drugged and put on a plane back to

Moscow so they can announce Nikolayev's daughter has returned to the motherland?"

She said nothing. He took a swig of his tea and yelped. "Jesus, how can you drink it like that?"

"I don't know. I always have. My father liked it that way, with four sugar cubes."

"And you decided last Saturday night that you had to go see him?"

"Yes," she said, puzzled.

He rose abruptly and went back into the kitchen. She thought he was walking away from the discussion, but he opened the refrigerator, popped an ice cube out of the tray as if he were mad at it, dropped it in his tea, and came back. "Here's what I don't get," he said. "I've known you almost a year. You hardly ever talked about your father until now, and I sure never heard you say you'd like to see him."

"I didn't expect I'd ever have the chance."

"In fact I got the strong impression you don't care much about him."

She tried to protest, but the sentence had harpooned her. It wasn't fair that someone could throw a shaft of words at you and leave it there, quivering, so you had to ask whether it was true or not.

"Am I right?" Jess said.

He couldn't be. Whatever that dense cat's cradle of her feelings for Boris Nikolayev summed up to, surely it wasn't indifference.

"Not that I blame you," Jess said. "If your father had wanted to, he could have managed some kind of contact with you and Vera. I know the difficulties involved, but he could have done better than one letter in twenty years. I understand how you feel."

If so, she thought, he was smarter than she. She cleared her throat and said, "Of course I care what happened to my father."

"I'll tell you what else I think. Sure, you want to do this for your mother and maybe even for a book, but something else is involved."

Her mind still pinned by his comment about her father, she took a moment to follow his switch. "What else could be involved?"

"Your past. Your life in Russia." He was standing over her. "You won't let go of it."

"What are you talking about?" He was looking at her as if she should know. "I can't expect you to approve of this trip," she said, "but why can't you at least sympathize with my need to make it?"

"Because I want us to have a life together. You'll put your future at risk over this trip to Finland, which says you care more about the past than about the future with me. I'm willing to commit myself, but not you. You can't accept a future with me—or maybe with any man—because you're still tangled up in the past. Hung up on it."

She gaped at him. "I have no idea what you're getting at."

"No?" He began to pace, but the smallness and clutter of the room hedged him into a small, tight oval. "How about that poet and balladeer you left behind?"

"Who?" she said, not meaning it to come out so faintly.

"Alik Markov. Isn't that his name? One night you sat right on that couch and told me about him."

"Because you asked me," she said. He had had so many questions about that other life—the university, the city, the weather, the apartment, the news on TV—and finally, when she volunteered nothing personal, "Did you leave a lover behind?" She could have said no. Should have. But she wouldn't lie to him.

"I saw the look on your face while you talked about him," Jess said. "And dammit, I see the look on your face right now."

She lifted her cup in both hands; it was warm and steadying. "This is very crazy," she said. "You think my going to Finland has something to do with some . . . with a man I used to know? But he's not going to Finland, and I'm not going to Russia, God knows, so what can he have to do with anything?"

He shook his head.

"What? Jess, what is it?" She took a deep breath. "All right, I'll tell you the true reason I'm going. The others are true, but there's something deeper. I wasn't going to tell anyone, but I'll tell you." He nodded, satisfied but defiant. Like a boy whose dog had been run over, waiting to hear it was all right, knowing it wasn't. But it *was* all right. So when she told him, his face would change. "I can't defend it," she said, "but I have this deep feeling that if I go, if I can talk to my father, it will . . . cure my mother."

His face did change, but not as she expected. "And you want me to believe that," he said, not a question.

"Jess, I know it's not rational. But it's no worse than your idea about some . . . man I used to know. Let's just say we both had crazy notions, and talk about something else."

He gave a cynical little grunt.

"Anyway," she said lightly, "I thought we had a deal. You don't interfere with my decision about my father, and I don't ask you when you're going to attack those people who want to censor books."

His teeth sank into his lip, then released it. "A man named Aleksandr Markov," he said, his gaze fixed on her like a microscope, "is going to be at the festival in Finland."

"Oh, no," she said, almost smiling at the impossibility of it.

"Oh, yes."

"It must be someone else with the same name."

"Aleksandr Romanovich Markov. Popular Soviet singer and guitarist. Going to the festival to perform the Niko-layev Concerto for Guitar."

There were two possibilities, calm or panic. She willed herself into the former by concentrating on Jess: on the two lines made by the cleft in his chin and the scar in his right eyebrow. "How do you know?" she asked.

"The State Department is keeping me posted. I got this early last week. Days before your mother's birthday dinner. At which you made your decision."

"You think I knew. You think that's why I decided to go."

"If I could get it from State, it had to be known in the musical world your mother belongs to. Or on the émigré network."

"If it was," she said, still calm, "no one told me." *But how could Alik be there? Why would they allow him to go?*

Jess pulled off his tie and threw it on his coat like a whip.

"I didn't know," she said. "I can only tell you the truth. Either you believe it, or you don't."

She watched him struggle. Finally he said, "If I say I believe it, will you believe me?"

"I'll try. Will you?"

"Deal," he said. The struggle wasn't over, though. "But now that you do know . . ."

"It doesn't change my mind."

He sighed and sank into the opposite chair, both actions heavy.

They drank tea in silence. Hers was cool and tasteless. *Would they really allow Alik to go? Why would he be playing a piece of her father's music when he wasn't a classical musician?*

"I suppose you're thinking I should be feeling foolish," Jess said.

She wouldn't lie, and she couldn't tell him she wasn't thinking of him at all. She said nothing.

"I don't feel foolish because what I said was true. Even if you didn't know that man would be there—"

"If?"

"OK. You didn't know. I accept that, Hedy. I do. But you haven't let go of him. Or, Jesus, am I such an egotistic fool that I can't accept it if a woman isn't interested in me?"

"Are you crazy? We're always together when you're in New York. I don't see any man but you, I don't *want* to see any man but you, and you think I'm not *interested* in you?"

He pushed aside some papers on the lamp table and set his cup down. "I think you're not in love with me."

"I never said that."

"That's the problem, isn't it?—the things you never say."

She said nothing.

"You had affairs before you met me," he said. "In this country, I mean. Did you tell those men you loved them?"

She stood up. "All of them. At once. I lined them up every morning before breakfast—'I love you, I love you, I love you.' "

"Goddamnit, Hedy!"

"Goddamnit yourself! I'm not someone who says personal things easily. I'm sorry, I know you don't like it, but that's the way I am, the way I've always been." She stopped, aware that finally she had lied to him.

"OK. Go to Finland. Never mind the danger, never mind our future. Go over there and root up your past. I can't prevent you."

"Right. You can't."

She folded her pillow into a new shape that, like the others, felt right at first but soon hardened into a bag of sand. *Fight,* she thought. *Uptight. Contrite. Who's right?* No answer.

She tried something else. Build up a word in steps, adding letters front or back only, never in the middle, no proper names, and each addition had to form a word on its own:

a
at
rat
ratio
ration
rational
irrational
irrationally

Eight steps. Eight was good; nothing below five was worth doing. She had begun the word games soon after coming to America, to help make herself think in English, and they had become a habit, a kind of rosary of language to relax or distract her. To keep her from thinking about—She punched her pillow and refolded it. How many words could be made from Jess's name? Newman: New, man, anew, mane, wane, wean, wan. . . .

The bed that never seemed empty when Jess was in Washington felt acres wide now that he was out on the couch. He had refused to let her sleep out there—"If I don't get the couch, I go to a hotel"—and she had agreed because she didn't want him to leave but she didn't want to be close to him either. At least not for what was left of the night. In the morning they would have cooler heads. He would realize he was being unfair, and she would realize, well, something, and then maybe he would calmly tell her exactly what he had heard about Alik. . . .

A-L-I-K. Could any English word be made from all four letters?

. . .

She went through her life like a sleepwalker, her whole inner being focused on him. Crash-studying for oral examinations, she couldn't keep the pages from blurring into the sight of his curtained-off corner; listening to a song Papa had just written, she couldn't stop wondering how it might sound played on a guitar; helping Grandmama with a meal, she would tell herself with each potato that if she could peel it in one long strip, she would see Alik the next day.

Often she didn't. He refused to make formal plans; he would simply appear somewhere he knew she would be. She didn't complain because she understood. It was his way of not surrendering totally to the relationship, of keeping part of himself outside it. She would have done the same if she could, but she had no choice. Sometimes she was frightened by the depth of her involvement in him; it made her think of her father's surrender to his music.

Sometimes Alik would show up for days in a row, or it could be longer than a week. Sometimes he would laugh at everything; other times she couldn't coax out even a smile. They would visit friends of his, to argue about books and listen to Western jazz records, or attend poetry readings, or sit and talk in Pushkin Square like so many other lovers. Whenever they could, they would go to Alik's. If there were others in the apartment, which happened most of the time, they would try not to touch each other, but usually they would fail, and would make love behind the curtain with a caution and a silence that were exciting in themselves. The words and sounds she had to suppress seemed to grow and slide back down her throat to become a pressure in her stomach and legs. Afterward she would tell herself it was only the enforced silence that kept him from saying he loved her.

She hadn't been able to keep what was happening hidden from Mama. One night, when her eyes were blank over a paper on the foundations of Marxist-Leninist aesthetics because she had been with Alik all afternoon, her mother had sat beside her and put a hand over hers. "My darling child, I watch you, and I think your heart has found someone. Am I right? Are you in love?"

So she had had to make Alik come to meet them.

The visit had not been a great success. The apartment, with its grand piano covered by an embroidered cloth and its bookcases full of dusty editions of the classics, suddenly had seemed huge compared to Alik's place. Alik had been stiff with reverence for Papa, and strangely cautious. Papa had responded in his most withdrawn and gruff manner, Grandmama had been as silent as if she weren't there, and Mama had chattered too brightly, her voice a needle trying to stitch the ragged edges of conversation together. They had talked of Rodion Sergeivich in awkward platitudes— "A very able man"; "He has been a good cousin to my mother"—and of music in words not much more meaningful.

"Boris Semyonovich, allow me to tell you that your cello concerto has been a source of great inspiration to me."

"Thank you. Anna tells us you are a composer of songs. Political songs."

"I couldn't presume to discuss my efforts in the presence of musicians like you and your wife."

During it all she had sat there, mostly mute, knowing she could not expect her parents to love and trust Alik as she did. Not on first meeting. Not in a world where you had to assume everyone was a spy until proven otherwise, where that proof could take years. *To know someone*, went the old proverb that Papa often quoted, *you have to eat a pood of salt together*. And there were many kilograms in a pood, many years. Why had she loved and trusted Alik so quickly?

Perhaps because he was fearless. Or perhaps because of the way he confessed he was not.

"I wish my father weren't afraid," she told him one day. "I wish he were like you."

"Don't put me in the same breath with Boris Semyonovich. Besides, I am afraid too."

"I don't believe that," she said indignantly. "Of what?"

For once he spoke hesitantly. "Of what prison made me feel."

"What was that?"

"I felt . . . like everybody else. All with the same clothes, the same food, the same hunger, the same stink. The glorious goal of equality, that's where you reach it. The camps are the true *kollektiv*. I felt as if the thing that was me was being peeled off in layers, like cabbage leaves, and they would take those leaves from all of us and make soup. And the only way to stay out of the soup pot was to keep writing and singing."

"I've felt things like that," she said. "I don't mean that anything could compare with being in prison, but . . ."

"Tell me."

Dimly aware that she had never confessed it to anyone but Mama, she said, "I remember feeling it the day some of us were taken into Young Pioneers. After we swore the oath, after we promised to live, study, and fight as the great Lenin bequeathed us, as the Communist Party teaches . . ." She stopped, recalling it, then went on. "When they were tying the red scarfs around our necks, I suddenly seemed to be able to see us all in a big mirror. I saw how alike we all looked—blue shorts, white shirts, and now the red kerchiefs. I thought, 'They want us to be the same, all tied together by the same scarf.' I started to imagine the scarf growing into my neck, and suddenly I didn't want to wear it, I wanted to pull it off, but of course I couldn't. I couldn't think of making trouble for Mama and Papa. But through the rest of the ceremony, I kept saying in my mind, 'I am Anna Borisovna, Anna Borisovna Nikolayeva' . . ."

"Yes, you are," he said softly, and laid his hand on her cheek. A delirious sense of freedom filled her. With him, the part of herself that was real—the self that had to be hidden so often in the gray Soviet world, and was choking—came effortlessly to the surface. With him, she was not two persons, private and public, but only one.

She cherished the ways in which they were alike and, equally, the ways in which they weren't: their common, early disillusionment with the smothering presence of slogans and Lenin-worship and the *kollektiv*—which in him had turned to moodiness and anger but in her had become a quiet, rocklike refusal to accept; and their shared passion for America, acquired through daily, unremitting streams of anti-Americanism, by means of the survival skill they had had to develop: reading between the lines of "official truth" to learn what was true.

One day he took something from under his mattress, wrapped in protective paper: a copy in Russian of the Declaration of Independence. "How did you get it?" she asked. All he would say was "Somehow." They read it many times, admiring its simplicity and wisdom. Sometimes he would speak angrily of the Soviet constitution: "That also guarantees rights, but who would know it? Every day they are violated as a way of life." Sometimes they would try to imagine living in a place where people had rights in reality, not just on paper, where there was nothing one couldn't read or write or sing or learn about. It was a distant, unattainable ideal, which gave her the comfort of inspiration, even hope, but for him was a torture.

On the wall with his photos and sketches was a postcard from New York showing the skyline, the harbor, and the

Statue of Liberty, which had been sent to him by a retired
couple who lived next door. They had gone to America to
visit the woman's wealthy brother, who had wanted to
finance their permanent stay; it was understood that the
Soviet Union would not object, for they were old and
unimportant. One day Alik came to get her at the university, drunk. The couple, he told her, had just returned from
America—by choice. "Do you know what Olga Ivanovna
said? She said the shops were nice, but what would she do
all day long? She said, 'Why do I need political freedom?
I'm not an activist.' " Eyes glittering with vodka and fury,
almost lurching on the sidewalks, Alik could not let go of
the story: "So many people in this city are like her. But
why, Anya? Why? If I could just understand it! What do
they want? What matters to them?"

She had no answer. She could only make sure that he got
safely home to sleep it off. Riding the Metro back to her
place, staring at all the stolid, staring faces, she thought
how different Alik was: not only from the couple who had
no need for political freedom but from many of their
friends, whose fascination with America seemed no deeper
than the slang they affected and the jeans and posters and
records they endlessly schemed to find on the black market.
Alik was different, and so was she. But what was it that
made them different?

She didn't see him for five days; then he was restless and
distant. "I have to get to the West," he kept saying. "But
they'll never let me emigrate. Bastards!" He had a plan,
which he half believed and half considered hopeless: "If I
can become popular enough with my songs so they can't
send me back to prison, and at the same time troublesome
enough so they'll exile me to the West . . ."

She hadn't told him about Paris when it was only a
chance; it had seemed so unlikely that she hardly dared
think of it herself. She knew the envy and pain he would

feel at even so remote a possibility, and the effort he would make to hide them. But when the miracle happened and the trip was definite, she had to tell him. Not about trying to stay in the West—that couldn't be told—but about going to Paris.

He gripped her hands so tightly she feared the bones would break, yet the look in his eyes made her feel far away. She didn't move, only waited. At last he said, "Paris," like a word he'd never spoken before, and then, quite calmly, "We can't let anything stop the trip. We'll be even more careful. You mustn't be seen going anywhere or doing anything that could be reported to my dear cousin Rodion Sergeivich."

It seemed a great irony when, the very next day, Papa said to her, nodding his head in slow emphasis, "I remind you to be particularly careful where you go now, whom you speak with. The Ministry must not have the smallest reason to change its mind."

"What do you mean?" she said defensively. "Do you think Alik is a reason? But Alik is Rodion Sergeivich's second cousin. Are you asking me to stop seeing him?"

Mama sighed and took her hands. In her eyes was Yes, but she said, "No. We ask you only to remember that there is a family relationship. That we should not be making any . . . difficulties for Rodion Sergeivich. That's all."

"But Alik is careful!" she cried. "He is as worried as you are!"

He stopped taking her to any place where he, or anyone else, might perform political songs or poetry. Perhaps he stopped going to those places himself; she couldn't ask, and didn't. She even brought herself to suggest that perhaps he should be seen with Lidiya sometimes. She didn't ask whether he did that, either.

It was summer, so they could leave the stuffy confines of buildings and go out into the parks and woods—even more aware, as they headed for those temporary escapes from it, how tight a grip the city and everything it represented had on their lives. They took books and picnic food and lay beneath the trees and read, sometimes to each other, or talked about Paris—how it might sound and look and smell, what books and records might be in the stores—though it was always Alik who raised the subject, in a careful, controlled voice that touched her deeply; and, defying convention and respectability, often hearing families and groups chattering only yards away, they made love as slowly and as long as they liked because the leaves couldn't hear and the birds wouldn't gossip.

One beautiful day at the end of September they wandered along, looking for a spot, through birdsong and faint calls from other lives, passing overlooks that showed them the broad curve of the river and its freight of barges and, beyond that, the solid spread of the city she would be leaving soon. "Let's stop here," Alik said. She realized the place was only a few dozen yards from where Papa had led her and Mama, that first day they had talked about defecting in Paris. She felt it must be some kind of omen.

It was *babye lyeto,* the last bloom of summer, and the pure yellow leaves fell around the two of them like a slow golden rain while they made love with a sweetness that made her cry because, when her body left his, she thought of leaving it forever. "What's wrong?" he said, more tenderly than he had ever spoken. She choked out the word: "Paris." "I know," he whispered, "I wish we could be there together. But you'll be back, and you'll tell me everything, and bring me things . . ." He put his fingers on her eyes to wipe the tears and said, for the first time, that he loved her.

In that moment, because of what he had said and the place he had said it, she knew how she would prove her love; she would repudiate a world in which fear was chronic and spying was the norm. She raised herself up to

lean on his shoulder; she kissed the skin of his neck, which
was faintly salty. "I love you too, Alik. I love you, and I
trust you, more than I know how to tell you, so I want to
show you. I am going to tell you the truth about Paris, not
just that Mama and Papa and I have permission to go but
what we are going to do in Paris. We are going to defect,"
she whispered, and saw the words lodge deep in his eyes,
like arrows of light. Arrows that hurt the archer as much
as the victim. Yet with the pain, she felt a queer exultation;
she felt defiantly non-Soviet—as if in sharing the secret
with him, she was leaving Russia in spirit and taking him
with her, taking him even as she told him she was going to
leave him. "Mama has worked out a plan, and we are going
to do it. Yes, it's true." She saw the arrows go deeper, and
twist. They twisted in her, too, and she put up her hand to
touch his face, to comfort both of them—

She sat up violently, disoriented, staring into the dark,
reaching out one hand as if to blot out a sight. Or to call
back the words she should not have said, which had pulled
her from sleep, their edges still too sharp even though they
had lain in her memory for nearly twenty years.

Her eyes cleared. She shivered. Her hand fell back;
awareness of her bedroom, and her life, settled around her.

She lay down again, turned the sheet over the spread,
smoothed it, and put both hands carefully at her sides.

CHAPTER FIVE

Jess opened his eyes. Beneath him was the hard, unfamiliar texture of the couch. Something in the dark room had waked him, he thought. He sat up, groped for the lamp on the end table, found the switch.

Hedy stood in the doorway from the bedroom, looking at him.

He sat up, ran his hands through his hair, and remembered why he was on the couch. "What is it?" he said. "Something wrong?"

"It was . . . I couldn't sleep."

"I didn't do very well either. I kept thinking about the fight we had."

She came a few steps into the room. Her hair was loose and long, and against the white nightgown her olive skin seemed even darker. Often he thought there was something of the gypsy in her, and never more than now. "I hate fighting," she said.

"Me too."

"I did sleep a little, but I started dreaming about things that happened in Russia, and then . . ."

He wouldn't ask if she'd like to tell him about it; he asked her that too often.

She gave him a fractional smile. "There's room in the bed. Three feet of choice New York real estate."

"Is that a firm offer?"

She nodded.

He got up, went to her, put his hands on her thin, bare arms. "I'm sorry I said the things I did."

"Didn't you mean them?"

"Well . . . yes. Some of them. It's risky for you to go over there. The place will be crawling with KGB, you know that. I'm going to worry like hell about you. I can't help it. But I was wrong to dump on you that way. You're under a lot of strain over Finland. I didn't mean to add to it."

"Which things didn't you mean?"

He had to smile even though she was putting the screws to him; that quiet focus on precision was so typical of her. "OK, I'm not actually jealous of a man you knew almost twenty years ago." He meant it, he thought; he wasn't just saying it for her. "That'd be childish and stupid, which I try to avoid on weekends. But I am jealous of something with a powerful hold on you, which I think your past has, because I don't know how powerful *my* hold is on you."

She put her hands on his arms and said, "It's powerful."

He thought of three different replies, but none were completely safe, so he put his face into her hair, which was thick and dark and always seemed full of life, even restrained in a braid. Finally he said, "I'll try to keep my feelings about the two of us out of any discussions we have about Finland."

She sighed: no sound, but he felt it in her body. "OK," she said.

"I want to help you, not complicate things for you."

"I know. And I know I complicate things for you. I'm sorry."

They held each other. "Let's go back where we belong," he said.

Once in bed, she settled deeply against him. He was aware of the firmness of bone beneath her warm, soft skin. He sensed her eyes closing, heard her breaths grow long and even, felt her body become as relaxed as a cat's.

Holding her that way, which he loved to do, brought a dark flood of pleasure he could never fully explain, except to know it wasn't sexual. He told himself that maybe one's deepest feelings were always beyond language, like the primal connection he felt to his daughters. Still, because he was an articulate man who deplored the platitudes of public life and enjoyed the challenge of finding words to express his meaning, he wished that when he lay in the dark holding Hedy like a shield that he in turn shielded with his arms, and felt a pleasure that seemed to lie at the heart of loving her, he could name it, to himself and then to her. He knew only and dimly that it was something like what he had felt as a child for his family.

They were immigrants from Eastern Europe who, as World War Two was breaking out, had managed to get to America—to Queens, where other members of their clan had settled earlier. One Sunday every month and on all holidays, an extended family of aunts, uncles, and cousins had gathered at one of their houses, at a long dinner table where, in homemade wine that Jess discovered was lethal, there were toasts to those who had fought against the Germans and then the Russians. Those Sundays were no more. Jess's parents were gone, and most of the uncles and aunts. But sometimes he would imagine taking Hedy to one of the dinners and introducing her to his father. The man whose first act in America had been to change his family name, unpronounceable by American tongues, to Newman—"because that is what I will be now, in freedom, a new man"— he would have liked the Russian woman who had come with her mother to America and, needing to change their name to feel safe, had chosen Lucas "because it means 'light' and that is what we thought our life here would be. Light, after dark."

She stirred against him. Jess put his hand on the flat of her stomach. Of course, he thought, the old man wouldn't have liked her not being religious. The old man had believed that communism's evil was caused by atheism—no use reminding him how many of the world's despots had been religious—and had credited God with all the family's good fortune (but none of the bad). When Jess learned he would graduate from law school third in his class, the first thing the old man had said was "God has been good to you, son." His eyes still burning from a late study session, his mind stuffed till it hurt with cases and statutes, Jess had retorted, "Dammit, Pop, four years of night school with a full-time job during the day, making Law Review—God didn't do any of that, *I* did it!" The old man had slapped him, the only time in his adult life, and they had fought.

When Jess told Hedy the story, she had said, "I bet it was partly your fault, though. You make things look easy, even if they aren't."

Maybe she was right, he thought. He liked to be in control of whatever he set out to do, and by definition, control meant you weren't also heaving and gasping with effort. But easy? Nothing had been easy, except perhaps the sports

in high school and college, for which his body had had a
natural affinity—and getting married to Alice. About
which he might say the same thing.

He thought for a moment of Alice: of loving her, being
intimate with her. Although he could remember clearly,
the memory had no power. A film with no emotion track.
If only Hedy could see her past that way.

If only she wouldn't try to pretend she was going to
Finland in order to cure her mother of cancer.

He pulled her even closer against him. Once more the
special pleasure stirred: dark and proud and protective,
holding echoes of his family but unique to Hedy and the
contradictions she embodied for him: delicate but tough,
passionate but private. The scholar with a streak of gypsy
wildness that kept their relationship off-balance.

No, he thought, be precise: kept it out of his control. And
he was a man who liked to be in control.

Across the room the clock glowed 4:38. A breeze belled
the curtain like a dancer's skirt, revealing that pale streaks
were marbling the sky. The two of them would have a good
weekend, he thought. He would keep himself from saying
a word about Finland. He would grit his teeth and make
it look easy.

The pale blond wig sat above the faceless face of the wig
block, speared by a long pin. Nothing could look less like
her and still be credible, Hedy thought, which was why she
had chosen it after hunting all over the city. She had had
to settle on something because she needed a new passport,
with a new photo, which she couldn't get until she decided
how she was going to look.

She felt almost embarrassed, as if she should be preparing her disguise behind locked doors; yet it had to be done,
if only she could figure out what to do. Presumably an
actress would know, or a makeup consultant, but she didn't

want anyone to know what she was planning. Not her mother, and certainly not Jess.

She looked into her dressing table mirror, then back at the wig, wondering how to marry her face to that hair. Something about Hedy Lucas, she thought, was fundamentally non-blond. Was in fact opposed to blond, and not just because of the stereotype that clung to it. She felt incompatible with blond, which suited a woman like Alice Newman but did not accord with a certain darkness in her own soul. The moment she had the thought, she knew it was true. A moment later she knew she was in fact attached to that darkness—as Alice Newman no doubt was to her spiritual blondness. As everyone, perhaps, was attached to whatever inner colors he or she had, and had probably started developing in the cradle. Did you then fall in love with someone of your own color, or did you want the contrast? *If you were queen of pleasure* . . . she thought, knowing she had never truly been a creature of pleasure; the line had resonated within her because of the *king of pain*. Whom she would not think of today.

She made a grotesque face in the mirror, then frowned at the stupidity of trying to joke away her tension.

She had thought about announcing publicly that she was Nikolayev's daughter before going to Finland. The press would love such news, and publicity might help protect her. She had even considered trying to get word to her father that she would be there. But if the KGB didn't want him to see her, or if he himself didn't want to, a possibility not to discount just because it was unpleasant, she might ruin everything by revealing in advance who she was.

The best and safest way to go, she had decided, was as the impersonal biographer, with no advance notice to anyone, and with a look different enough from the old days to make her feel safe and allow her to conceal her Russian identity as long as she saw fit.

But how had she looked in the old days? She opened the envelope she had pulled from a box at the back of the hall closet: photos, but only four because she had never liked being photographed and had hardly ever thought to do so in the first years in America. She laid out the pictures: on the Staten Island Ferry with the Statue of Liberty behind her, an emotion clogging her throat that the picture couldn't show; on the steps of the New York Public Library beside one of the lions; outside one of the buildings at the university; and at the table with her mother during their first Thanksgiving dinner.

She had been heavier then by at least twenty pounds, weight she had later lost without trying, as if it had been the bloat of fear and secrecy and had simply drained away. But there was more in the photos than a difference of pounds and years: There was an overall look of not-quite-fitting, like a peasant in a city suit, except the not-fitting had more to do with her spirit than her clothes. As if she hadn't yet reclaimed her mind from the omnipresence of caution. Or her self from self-consciousness. She tried to recall how that had felt from the inside, but the state of mind of being in America though not yet part of it was gone. She did remember how Americans had seemed to her at the time: confident, trusting, untroubled. Was it possible that over the years she herself had acquired that manner?

Perhaps no disguise was necessary after all. The added years, the subtracted weight, and the "Americanization" might be enough to deflect any KGB suspicions. She had never allowed a picture on the jackets of her books. Besides, authors were invisible in America—not revered as they were in Russia, where people turned out by the thousands to hear poets read their works. With the KGB watching both poets and listeners . . . as they would watch her father in Finland, and anyone who spoke to him. . . . She shivered. She could not guess what the KGB might do, specifically, but she could be certain that her desires, and life, would mean nothing to them.

She poured a glass of water, drank half of it at once. Maybe Jess was right. Maybe it was crazy for her to go. She thought of him—the shape of his face, the concern in his eyes, the tenderness with which he held her. He hadn't mentioned the trip since the night they fought about it. If she didn't know both of them better—if she hadn't several times caught him looking at her with his mouth held in control too tightly—she might even think the trip was a dead issue between them. Wasn't it a major insanity not to say "I love you" to Jess and then find someone else, with nothing at risk, to take the trip and if possible make contact with Boris Nikolayev?

"Yes," she said aloud. And added, "Don't make a mess, Of life with Jess."

She drank the rest of the water, picked up a soft, dark brown pencil, and began drawing her right eyebrow higher. Whatever she did, if it was going to work, it had to be good enough to keep even her father from recognizing her. A wave of bitterness rolled against her hand and made it slip; her father would be easy to deceive. Even when she lived with him, he hadn't known who she was half the time. All the more reason to go, she thought, and drew the eyebrow line a little higher. The person who would be hard to deceive— She stopped, before his name could slide into her mind. Bad enough that he had been haunting her dreams; the waking hours had to be in her control. She bent closer to study the brow she had drawn, which made her eye look more deeply set, and shifted to the other one to try for a match. The pencil moved steadily for half a dozen strokes, but then her fingers let it slide through, to the table, and she was inches from the mirror, staring at questions in her eyes that she had lived with for half her life.

The flight to Paris was coming nearer on the calendar, and it was harder to arrange meetings with Alik. She had to undergo with her parents the political indoctrination for a trip to the West—there were special lectures to attend, lists of "no's" to learn, political topics to study to make sure they would answer foreigners' questions according to party line: Be familiar with the five-year plan; remember that we have no homeless persons abandoned on the streets; do not forget that all Soviet citizens are guaranteed the right to work. . . . There were maps of Paris to study, French to practice, and extra time to spend with Grandmama in hopes she would look back on it after they were gone and understand why. Blessedly, Grandmama had good friends to help and comfort her. Like Alik. . . .

Each meeting they did manage was measured by its closeness to the flight date and colored by their knowledge that the store of such hours was finite. Time became a tyrant, rapidly making the days too cool for trysts in the woods, where rowanberries soon grew in red clusters among the bare birches, and shrinking the number of white-smocked women selling produce in the farmers' market, where one day there were no more parsley and dill and another, no mushrooms. The first snow fell a month earlier than it had the previous year. As she always did, Grandmama said that summer and winter followed no rules but came as God wished. As he always did, Papa came in brushing that first snow from his coat and recalling some of the country wisdom he had heard as a boy: "If wolves howl near the village, it means either a harsh winter or a war." He had used to quote the sayings with relish. Now it was with a heavy sigh.

Time brought two things closer and closer, each pulling

her in its own direction: the hope of America rising in her throat, the thought of leaving Alik sinking in her stomach.

Two weeks before the date of the Paris flight, she said to him, "I'm not going to do it. I can't leave you. I won't leave you."

She had expected his eyes to widen with love and relief; instead they hardened into metal. He stood up and said, like a slap, "You can't. I won't allow you to give up such a chance for me."

"You can't prevent me."

"I can. If you have the chance in Paris and refuse to take it, I will have nothing to do with you when you come back."

"Really?" She kissed him thoroughly, to prove both her power over him and her confidence in it.

He pulled away, put his hands on her arms, and said, with the quiet force of a man who had survived years in prison with his spirit intact, "I mean it, Anya. I will go back with Lidiya, or someone else. Anyone else."

She couldn't let him see that she believed him. She kept her expression defiant while he said the things she knew he would say: She couldn't sentence herself to the rest of her life in Russia; she had to get to America and live for both of them; if she didn't try, she would begin hating him for holding her back; if she didn't try, her father might not try either, and how could she ruin her father's chance to live and create in freedom? How could she ruin her own, when she had begun rebelling against communism in her heart as early as he had, and for the same reasons?

They argued, walking and whispering tensely, finally stopping in a warm, steamy blintz house where they stared at each other in silence. She knew he was right. The next time, when they had two hours alone at one of her friend's, she said, "But you'll get there too someday, Alik. And I'll be waiting."

On that, too, he was adamant. She must go and forget about him. "Make a new life without looking back. You must, Anya! It will be a miracle if I ever find a chance to get out, and we can't live waiting for miracles. Don't leave me with such a burden—that you're waiting for me and I can't get there, so I've made your whole life unhappy." The more she protested, the colder his eyes got, and the harsher his voice, until finally he held her hands as if his own were manacles and made her swear that, if she did reach the West, she would forget him and never make any attempt to contact him.

What made her agree was not the pain in her hands but the one that bloomed in her mind: He wanted her to go because he needed to be free of the relationship, which he had fought from the beginning because caring was "dangerous."

The day before the flight she saw him for the last time, briefly, in Pushkin Square. They sat on one of the benches that ringed the poet's statue, saying very little, so she carried the scene away with her in scents and images: The tiny, hard granules of snow that kept landing on Alik's hat and melting into the fur. The smells of the city, intensified by the cold air: strong tobacco, gasoline, wood fires. The people scurrying past on their way to the shops, like ants streaming to some common goal she had never understood. The hard, tight look on Alik's face, like a mask over what she herself was feeling. And finally his voice, very hoarse: "Be happy. Be free. For both of us. I will always write songs for you, even if you never hear them."

"I will always love you," she said. Her eyes ached with the effort of memorizing his face.

She turned and left the square, biting one hand through the wool of her glove, trying to make it hurt enough to blot out everything else.

From then until she and her parents landed in Paris, her

mind was cleverly merciful; it let her think of Alik and see him clearly but wouldn't let her feel. It held him behind a glass wall, a figure who sang without sound.

Mama's plan for the defection had been discussed that day they had all gone to the woods. In Paris, she and Mama would go out for some kind of errand at a place from which they could walk or take the Métro to the American embassy. Perhaps the famous Galeries Lafayette, or the food-store Fauchon. The best time to do it would probably be late morning. At that time Papa, who they assumed would be constantly accompanied by Rodion Sergeivich, would insist on lunching somewhere near the embassy, in a restaurant or bistro from which he could slip out a back door or a washroom window, to join them at the embassy.

Their behavior, and their luggage, must look as if they were simply going on a tour. They could take nothing except clothes for Paris and must pack as everyone else did, cramming their cases with food, saucepans, and hot plates, because touring Soviet artists never wasted their daily government stipends on food when there were so many wonderful things to buy and take home.

She had been over the plan so often in her mind that it seemed as if she had already lived it: the store that would glitter with clothes or food, perhaps both, the Métro that would carry them on pneumatic tires, the language that would be light, precise, and dry until it changed to English inside the doors of the embassy. . . .

When it actually began to happen, there was a sense of déjà vu. Their hotel was close to the Opéra, as expected. The three of them went out for several walks—to see the sights, they told the KGB "companion" who went with them everywhere, but in reality to locate a bistro suitable for Papa's lunch with Rodion and to become familiar with streets and stores they knew only as lines and dots on the maps they had memorized.

At eleven-thirty on the fourth day of the visit, they
were ready. She and Mama kissed Papa good-bye in the
hotel room, all trying to seem casual but passing tension
among one another like electricity, and stepped out into a
hall already filled with the odor of cabbage soup that the
Soviet musicians were cooking on their hot plates. Feeling the "companion" at their heels, forcing innocuous
comments about shopwindows through their dry lips,
they walked to the Galeries Lafayette and into the center
building. There were so many kinds and colors of soap in
one display that, involuntarily, they stopped to gape, their
purpose almost forgotten for a moment. They went up
the escalator, Mama's heart thudding as badly as her own,
for she could see it beating above Mama's collar. Near a
large, very crowded counter, Mama gave the signal by
squeezing her arm. They went opposite ways around the
counter, and suddenly she was alone in the crowd, watching the companion hesitate over which of them to follow.
She made her way back to the street by the most circui-
tous way she could find and ran to the corner they had
decided upon. For a blinding moment she didn't see
Mama; then Mama was there and they took each other's
hands and walked as fast as they could without calling
attention to themselves, blood beating in their fingers as if
it came from one heart.

Then came the part that wasn't déjà vu because it hadn't
been planned at all: the unexpected desire not to do it, the
backward pull so strong that she felt she was walking into
a headwind, the sound of Alik's voice drowning out the
chatter of French around her; how beautiful was Russian,
was Alik, how wonderful life with him would be, even a
terrible life, why was she heading for the unknown. . . .
Then they were at Avenue Gabriel and the embassy.

They made their prepared speech, clutching each other's
hands.

And waited. Waited while the light and hope drained from the day, and people were kind but could get no answer in Papa's room when they rang the hotel, and her eyes, hot and dry, saw their questions reflected and twisting in Mama's: Where was he? Should they keep waiting, or go back? Which would be worse for him?

Around four Mama began to cry softly, ashamed of the tears.

Around five they accepted that he wasn't coming, that he had been stopped.

Around six the question came to her for the first time, fleetingly, like something at the edge of a desert, a speck that could be on the horizon but perhaps was only in one's eyes: Had Alik told Rodion of their plan?

She tried to dismiss it, but as the hours passed, the question grew, first into a plume of dust, then into a figure riding hard and bearing down on her: Was Alik the reason Papa hadn't come? Had Alik betrayed her father? Had she betrayed him by telling Alik what they would do?

She saw that her eyes were staring into the dressing-room mirror, under one brow that looked too high. She pushed herself back, away from the reality of Paris, and reached for the glass of water. It was empty, so she got up, refilled it, and drank, looking back at the blond hair on the wig block.

In the first weeks and months in America, while she and her mother grappled with its splendors and puzzles, while she tried to help Vera accept life without Boris, the questions had ruled her days.

Over and over, she built the case: Alik was the only one besides the three of them who knew they planned to defect. He might have revealed it inadvertently to Rodion Sergeivich—not deliberately, she couldn't bear to think that. Or he might have been forced to it, to save himself from being sent back to the camps because someone had reported his songs. Yes; and Rodion could have decided to allow Boris Nikolayev's wife and daughter to defect—he thought them a troublesome, distracting influence, she knew he did, no matter how he had smiled over the dinner table. He would let them go but would save the great Nikolayev for the glory of Soviet music.

Over and over, she destroyed the case: Alik was too smart, too prison-wily, to give away such a secret without realizing. And he loved her too much—he had said it not only in words but with his whole being—to betray her trust. He wouldn't destroy the future of the man who was not only her father but an artist he profoundly admired. It was crazy to imagine otherwise. Only her years under communism, with their harvest of mistrust, could have made her consider such a thing. She would honor her new, chosen country by not soiling Alik's name and memory with suspicion.

She would say it firmly, and believe it, and get on with her amazing new life. Stores not only had every kind of fruit and vegetable but put them out in boxes on the sidewalks, and no one stole them! People had apartments of two and three rooms, sometimes even more, and did not have to share them with any other families! She would be going headlong through her days, and suddenly she would hear the question that was always in her mother's eyes and sometimes on her lips: Why didn't your papa come with us? And her own question would return: Had Alik betrayed him?

No. Not possible. But then why had Alik insisted so violently that she forget him and never think of contacting him if she got to the West? Didn't that sound as if he knew what he was going to do to her and her father? No. Not possible.

The questions ran in an airless inner circle. To discuss

them with someone might have helped, but there was only her mother, who had enough to struggle with, especially the guilt that sometimes came over having "abandoned" her husband. How cruel to burden Mama with a mere possibility about her daughter, to put emotional distance between the two of them when they needed each other in the new life. If she *knew* Alik had betrayed them, she would have to tell her mother no matter what the consequences. But she would have to be certain.

Or was that concern for her mother just a rationalization, to protect herself from the anger Vera would surely feel against her?

The questions, which had begun in Russian, changed to English and finally receded, not because she answered them but because she had to send them into internal exile in order to live her life. They stirred only when she heard something about Alik, as she occasionally did from émigrés. When she heard that his songs were becoming known throughout the country—the blander ones allowed to be recorded officially and the barbed, political ones circulating by the thousands in the private recording and distribution networks known as *magnitizdat*—the questions had new forms: Was he being permitted to have a career as a reward for preventing Nikolayev's defection to the West? Or was he still following the plan he had first announced to her in that tiny, curtained corner of his brother's parlor: become popular enough to stay out of prison and troublesome enough so they might exile him to the West?

It was the latter, she decided—until years later, when she heard that he had married a Party official's daughter. The Alik she knew couldn't have done such a thing; either he had changed drastically, or she hadn't known him at all. What could you know about a man's character when you weren't even twenty?

How about when you were almost forty and had the chance to find out?

I have to try to get the truth about my father. That's what she had told Jess. She hadn't told him she was terrified of learning that the truth might mean she had betrayed her own father by trusting her lover.

Was that what going to Finland was really all about? she thought. Perhaps, in a way, Jess had been right: The crazy notion that getting the truth could cure her mother wasn't what was driving her. It was the guilt whose possibility had hung over her since Paris.

She shook her head. She couldn't give in to cowardice. She must go to Finland. Besides, the truth could be something quite different from what she feared. Or her father might not know the truth. Or if he did, she might not find a way to get it from him.

The truth couldn't involve a betrayal on Alik's part, she thought, not if he was going to Finland to play a concerto by her father. Then the thought slithered inside out: Maybe Alik had joined the Party, like his father-in-law and no doubt his wife, and was going to Finland as a reward.

After a long time she put the glass down and went to the bedroom, to a box so far back in the closet that her clothes seemed to have grown roots over it. After a struggle, she finally pulled out a record she hadn't looked at or played in eight years. Not since she had found it in a Russian-language bookstore.

It was officially recorded and released: "Made in USSR," it said, but everything else was in Cyrillic, including his name. All the songs were bland, apolitical. The only one from the days when she had known him was "Birches." In the cover photo he looked just as she remembered him, yet like a different man. Maybe it was the smile, which seemed posed, or the fact that the angle of his head kept his eyes largely in shadow. Or maybe he was a different man.

She took the record into the living room, put it on, and stood waiting for the first sound of his voice, her shoulders lifting in tension and hope.

Vera Lucas sat by her open window. Down on Fifty-seventh Street, people bustled in the bright sun. Sometimes she watched them; sometimes her eyes closed. The tenor who lived two floors directly above was working on *Di quella pira;* the high notes rang in and out of her reverie.

She thought of the opera and how the character was singing about avenging his mother . . . as Anna was going to Finland for her. . . . Often in her mind now, her daughter was "Anna." Often now, the Hedy she thought of was her own mother, whose name Anna had taken in America; Anna had wanted a name that was all new, for the new life, but at the last minute, as if unable to jettison everything, she had chosen to honor and remember her Romanian grandmother. . . .

Di quella pira. Thrilling, if well sung. Verdi was a splendid composer, and Wagner . . . but there was nothing like *Boris Godunov,* which, praise God, had been written before Stalin came along and laid down his three rules for opera. How Boris, her Boris, had sneered at those rules: a Socialist theme, folk song as the basis of the music (no dissonance!), and a happy ending glorifying the State . . . sneered only to her, of course . . . and had never written an opera, at least not that she knew of. . . . Ah, *Boris* in the glorious Bolshoi production . . . the half-mad emperor, and the crowd: the huge, cruel mass of the Russian people. . . . Lenin had said, "Art belongs to the people." And Boris Nikolayev had said, only to her, of course, that the people had nothing under the czars, and nothing under communism either, except slogans telling them they had everything. . . . In the Revolution they had nationalized all violins, in the name of the people, but from her first lessons she had felt, This violin belongs to me, it's *mine*, it's part of me. The teacher said she must not have such imperialistic, capitalistic thoughts and must work on her bow arm. Arm. Someone was touching her arm. . . .

"Mama?"

"Anna . . ." She opened her eyes. "Ah, Hedy. I didn't hear you come in."

"Good. Have you had lunch?"

She sat straighter and tried to recall. "Yes. Zoya was here and made the two of us a four-person fruit salad. She put things in the refrigerator, too."

Hedy kissed her. "Shall I make some tea?"

"Not yet. Just sit here with me."

She took the other chair. Vera looked at her, at the hair coiled around the oval face, the waist set off by a wide belt, the slim legs below a full print skirt. "You're so very pretty, my darling."

"Thank you, Mama. But we both know I'm not."

"Ah, how stubborn you are. The first time I saw you, in the hospital, when they brought you to me all wrapped up so I could see only your face, I saw that you had a stubborn chin."

Hedy smiled.

"They wouldn't let me see you until you were twenty-four hours old. No hospital would. And how bundled up you were, like all Russian babies, swaddled in a *pelyonka* like a little mummy. They thought it was bad if babies were left free to move." Wryly she added, "To be born in Russia is not to be born free."

"I got my ticket today," Hedy said. "I leave for Finland two weeks from tomorrow."

Vera blinked and turned to her. That was the bond between the two of them, she thought, always had been: ready to fight, to do something, not to sit passively waiting. "I want to go with you," she said.

"Mama, no more of that."

"If something happens to you . . ."

"I'll be fine."

"I know the dangers, maybe better than you."

"Then you know I can't have the distraction of a sick woman with me."

Vera sighed. "You and that stubborn chin."

Hedy smiled but said no more, content to sit quietly while life went on inside her head. In that respect, so like Boris. Perhaps because she had been conceived for his sake. Vera had never told that to either of them. She had planned the "accident" of her pregnancy in the hope that a child might help Boris live with the denunciation. With the resolution the Central Committee had put out one day, accusing all the giants of Soviet music, and even some of the dwarfs, of "formalism" in their music. The very men who had been praised until then as the glory of Soviet music!

What did the charge mean? It had no musical meaning. To be "formalist" was to be anti-Soviet; nothing more was needed to prove evil. Just in case, they also said his music was "antipeople" and "individualistic." But what else could art be but individualistic? Surely they knew that, no matter what their rhetoric. . . . Many meetings took place; speakers rose to podiums like scum to the surface of a pond and, in the name of the people, denounced the artistic crimes of Shostakovich, Prokofiev, Khachaturian, Nikolayev. . . . She and Boris had sat in an auditorium, surrounded by his students and colleagues but apart from them; she put her leg as close to his as she could so he could feel her warmth, while he bowed his great, beautiful head to the scum. In that moment all the dissatisfactions with her country that she had felt all her life gathered into a new awareness: that it was not enough to be dissatisfied and hope for change, that they would have to leave. . . .

As the others also had to do, Boris Nikolayev—People's

Artist of the USSR, laureate of the Stalin Prize—went up to the platform to thank the Central Committee for the resolution and to apologize for his artistic crimes. *Music must be understandable to the Soviet people, who have pointed out my creative errors. I shall work to make my music reflect in a realistic manner the image of the heroic Soviet people, as expressed in their folk songs.* . . . Later he had joined the other denounced composers in writing to Comrade Stalin to thank him personally for the criticism. Giving thanks for their own destruction! And then he sank into silence. He would sit for hours, staring into space as if it were hell, chewing on his lip as if to punish it for shaping the words of his confession. He wouldn't talk about how he felt, only about their practical difficulties. He said no one would perform his music now, and he was right. He said the State would not buy any new works from him, but they couldn't tell if he was right because he didn't compose anything new. There was nothing she could do; that was the worst part. No one to appeal to; all around her—at the conservatory, in the orchestra, on the street—eyes were coated with fear. She could only talk and talk to Boris, trying to lift him up with a net of words, but failing. She had to do something to shake him alive again, but what? Could a child do it? All Russians revered babies, who had melted stonier hearts than Boris's. . . . Desperate, needing vodka to help him, she coaxed him into bed and was able to conceive. At first he was angry—how could he support a child when he had no work and their money would run out even faster if she had to take a leave from her orchestra work? Gradually, as she had hoped, he began to talk about the child that was coming and, if they were alone, to place his hand on her abdomen and smile.

And somehow they survived.

CHAPTER SIX

Deputy Minister Rodion Sergeivich Orlov finished studying a report on the proposed tour of a provincial drama group and tapped the papers into a neat pile, which he laid in the exact center of his desk. Two thoughts occurred to him: First, it was important to bring to Moscow representative theatrical activity from all the republics; second, if the activity was in fact representative, no one in Moscow with any taste or *klass* would want to see it. He wrote a quick, neat approval on the appropriate form and clipped it to the report.

He was a slight man with reddish hair that had barely grizzled and a round face that had refused all lines except for crosshatching below the eyes. His dark suit was well cut and his leather shoes nicely made; imported from West Germany, they were available in the category of special shops that he and others of his position were entitled to patronize. Shoes were a particular passion with him. When a new shipment arrived, he would have himself driven to inspect it at once. It disappointed him that the festival would be held in a small, fairly rustic Finnish town where he might have trouble finding good shoes, especially ones from England. However, some very fine musicians would be there, like Kim Wan Lee, the young Asian whose recording of the Brahms had been amazing.

One of the phones on the desk rang. He waited a moment before lifting the receiver. "Orlov," he said, in a light voice.

It was one of his subordinates. "Rodion Sergeivich, arrangements have been made for the commission to attend a rehearsal of the Kirtsov play next Tuesday night."

"Kirtsov will be there himself?"

"Of course."

"Very well."

Rodion hung up and made a note. The commission was one of the bodies responsible for approving plays for ideological content. The playwright Kirtsov was famous for pushing hard at the edges of the permissible, and the director of the theater always fought to defend his productions. The two men had already been through eight levels of approval, starting with permission to begin rehearsals. Both of them knew that Rodion Sergeivich Orlov was the only commission member who understood anything about art, and always appealed to him to save the lines and business they cherished most. No criticism of the Party itself, its top leaders, or the goals of communism had been, or ever could be, allowed, although at present the orders were to allow, even to encourage, criticism of corruption and reference to certain problems. Some relaxation was now regarded as necessary, to make international and domestic goals easier to achieve. Only so much relaxation, however. Things must not go too far.

It was good to have such a theater in Moscow. For one thing, correspondents from the bourgeois press went to the productions and wrote about the liberalization for their papers. For another, the productions were damn good.

Rodion replaced his pen, his glance flicking with customary pleasure over his row of telephones. Besides one for regular office use, there was one for the minister and another for his family and friends. The family was not immediate, for his wife had remarried many years before and never been replaced, and he had no children. He did have a network of nieces and nephews and their offspring, to whom he felt umbilical ties of loyalty that transcended political differences, and friends chosen from the elite of the artistic world that, to an extent he never ceased working to enlarge, was under his care.

He had several phone lines that did not pass through his secretary's office, to prevent listening in. If he became minister, he would also have his *vertushka*, a special phone on which he could call the private numbers of many of the top members of the Party hierarchy. The nickname amused him: Russia's most powerful men reached by means of an "empty-headed woman." Ten years before, he had been passed over for minister because of a power play at the highest levels, but life would be a dull sausage without the garlic of hope. And after all, he had well-placed friends and achievements to his credit—not the least being that he had brought the great Boris Semyonovich Nikolayev back from Paris in a propaganda coup, and was still the man responsible for him.

It had been three days, he realized, since he had spoken to Boris. He reached for one of his phones and dialed, his long fingers graceful. After eight rings he frowned and hung up. Often Boris chose not to answer. If the maid was not there, as she apparently was not, a trip to the apartment was necessary. There couldn't be the smallest chance of allowing Boris to change his mind or, even worse, to sink into the state of silent brooding that made everything impossible. Boris's appearance at the festival was to serve two purposes, one prestigious, one political: to remind the world that one of its greatest living composers was Russian, and to provide a painless way of improving the Soviet image. On second thought, Rodion reflected, both purposes were political. And he had given his personal guarantee that Boris would fulfill them.

He took some papers from a drawer and tucked them in an inside pocket. Then he stood, smoothed his hair, and stepped out of the office. "I am going to see Boris Semyonovich," he told his secretary, "and I will not be back. If the minister should want me . . ." His shoulders lifted in a shrug well understood by the secretary and in turn used by her in speaking to others. The shrug meant that the minister was almost certainly drunk by that hour. The minister, who had been an engineer and knew nothing about art, had begun his new position by aggressively promoting amateur art festivals as if they were tractors, but had soon lost his enthusiasm and begun drinking instead. When important decisions had to be made, the minister would call on Rodion Sergeivich, if he was sober. If he was drunk, he made the decisions himself.

Boris lived where he always had, near the conservatory, in an old pre-Revolutionary building that he had refused to leave when a large apartment block was built exclusively for composers. Even when he was most out of favor, even when they took away his dacha, he had been allowed to remain in the apartment. Since it was not far, and the weather was pleasantly warm, Rodion Sergeivich, who believed in mild exercise, decided to walk.

He went up Gorky Street, like a tourist, he thought, except that tourists were still looking for dissidents. As if dissidents were in some way typical of the Soviet people. A ridiculous, insulting notion.

He passed a stand where people were happily eating ice cream. Russian ice cream was the best in the world; touring artists all said so when they returned. One must make certain they did return. Rodion recalled the violinist who had slipped away in London six months before, and then dismissed her; he had not been personally involved. What is a Soviet trio? A quartet that has been to the West. The first time he heard the joke he had laughed heartily. What would life be without its cushion of jokes?

Outside a store was a long queue. A woman scurried up, asking another, *"Chto dayut?"*—What are they handing out? Apparently the answer was oranges. He might have stopped if there hadn't been a queue, but there always was. He never needed to stand in them, thanks to his position, but it was a fact of life that Russian women had to spend much of their day in queues and never left the house without a good supply of rubles and a string bag, to join any queue they saw. However, changes were now being ordered, to achieve more efficiency. Change was necessary, even desirable. As long as it did not go too far.

No, communism had not created the perfect society, as his father had been certain would happen. One learned that early if one had eyes and ears. Rodion could still remember, in his first year in school, singing a song on Lenin's birthday about how Grandfather Lenin had created for children the best country on earth, and wondering, since that was true, why there was always a shortage of oranges. He had been six at the time.

That year he had started violin lessons. His teacher had encouraged him, but he had known his talent was modest, knowledge that had made him so angry he had smashed his violin and told his father some strange boys had stolen it. Talent, or its lack, was something he could always recognize. There was no point in becoming an ordinary violinist; better to be in a position to help artists deal with the cumbersome machinery of the State. Besides, the world was made so that artists could achieve status, but only politicians could achieve power. To some, that was a tragedy; for Rodion Sergeivich, it was a fact of life.

He went into Boris's building, with its dark, high-ceilinged vestibule, and up in the double-doored wooden elevator, which creaked unmusically as if to defy the artistry of the man it so often carried. Rodion had to knock and ring at the apartment door for a long time. He felt as if he were a boy again and his father was holding his hand and saying, "Now, Rodya, you will meet a man who is going to compose very great music for his country, a man who went to school with your own papa," and when the door opened, he looked up at an oak.

Then the door actually did open and he felt relief, for he could see that Boris was fine. He smiled and said, "Good afternoon, Boris Semyonovich." No matter how long he had known him, or how much had passed between them, he had never used a more familiar form of address.

Boris regarded him from under sagging eyelids, nodded, and turned to walk back into the apartment, expecting him to follow.

Boris was still a big man, though his whole body had sagged like his eyelids. When he walked, he swayed lightly, but his feet moved firmly in carpet slippers. He wore, as always, shapeless pants and an ancient white shirt, over which his hair, very white, lay like a ragged silk collar. He padded through the apartment, past the small room where he had obviously been working, its table piled high with scores and the carved bed at one end gaping unmade. In the kitchen he sank into a chair. Before him on the table was a glass of tea and a plate with a half-eaten jam tart and a boiled sausage. In the center of the table was a small vase with a wilting flower. He pushed a swag of hair from his forehead and looked at Rodion with eyes that were bright and watchful beneath their overhang, like animals at the mouths of their caves.

Rodion sat across from him. "I called but there was no answer."

"You mean I chose not to answer."

"Very well. Where is the maid?"

"Spending the afternoon with her mother, who is ill. I told her to go."

"I see." The woman had orders not to leave for such reasons; she would have to be reprimanded. "Were you working?" Rodion asked. No answer. "How are you, then, Boris Semyonovich?"

Boris shrugged and said, "Not in my prime. You didn't need to come over to know that."

"What do you mean? Is something wrong? Tell me and I will have it taken care of immediately."

"Good. Then you can make me twenty years younger." Rodion merely smiled.

"So, there is something Rodion Sergeivich Orlov cannot do?" Boris picked up the half-eaten sausage and contemplated it, or his comment, with satisfaction.

"You are in fine shape for a man who is nearly eighty."

"How would you know?" Boris said dryly.

"I know the doctors say you are in good health."

"Doctors." Boris snorted. "If you tell them to, they will prescribe the mental ward." He bit into the sausage and put what remained back on the plate.

"I assure you," Rodion said, "that I do not give orders to doctors."

Boris chewed, the flesh of his cheeks moving but not his eyes, which gave Rodion one of the cold, disbelieving looks that were part of the intricate fabric of their relationship. When he finished, he said, "I trust my music to the future and my health to God."

"Neither of whom, unfortunately, can be held accountable."

"Neither of whom, fortunately, belongs to the Party."

Rodion sighed. "Dare one hope that you are composing again, Boris Semyonovich?" That would be the best possible news: something stirring inside that leonine head, to be transmuted into sound by some alchemy no one understood.

"One may hope whatever he likes." Boris got up, went to the refrigerator, and took out a bottle of vodka, which he held up in a question.

Rodion shook his head. "I am not staying. I came by only to see if you are well." He hesitated. "And to remind you that we leave for Finland in two weeks."

Boris went to a cupboard, got brandy and a glass, sat down, and poured himself an inch of liquid. "I don't want to go to Finland," he said.

Rodion spoke firmly, over a sudden ringing in his ears that made his voice sound tinny to him. "Boris Semyonovich, the trip was approved at the highest level, and you know that I mean the very highest. News was released months ago to the bourgeois press. The whole world is expecting your presence in Finland."

"And if I don't go, you will call in your doctors to diagnose my mental health?"

"There can be no question of your not going."

"There is always a question, Rodion. About everything. That is the nature of life."

"When you speak like that, I don't understand you. I am not a philosopher, Boris Semyonovich."

"No, you are a man of action, like your father." Boris's eyes fixed on him, guilelessly.

Rodion altered his tone to match those eyes. "Of course you are right. There are always questions. I will put it differently: Where there are questions, someone must provide answers. In this case, me. Now, if you were to say that you are not able, after all, to make the trip to Finland, I would have to answer to many people, not only to those at the highest level but to others. Say, to Alik, who will be distressed to learn that he is unable to make the trip. Perhaps you will be distressed too, since you insisted that no one but Alik could play the premiere of your guitar concerto."

Rodion sat back and studied Boris's face. Boris had made Alik's performing in Finland a condition of his own going; he had simply refused to go otherwise, and there had been no way to force him. No acceptable way, although some in the KGB would have had certain ideas if it had been left to them. Finally Rodion had accepted Boris's condition; Alik's behavior in recent years made it possible to do so.

Boris continued to look at him, still guileless. The gaze that stretched between them was like an invisible pole balanced by their eyes.

Why, exactly, Rodion wondered, was Boris so keen on Alik? He had of course said it was for musical reasons, and undeniably—and surprisingly—Alik had become an excellent classical guitar player. No doubt it was also a factor that the two men—again, surprisingly—had become friendly in recent years. But Rodion did not truly understand the relationship between the two men, who were both linked to him, although not through him, for he was not the source of their contact: one the child of his dead mother's cousin and the other, the friend of his dead father. In Rodion's view, many things in life could not be understood—for instance, why one composer was an original genius, like Nikolayev, while others were imitative and dull, like most members of the Composers Union. But friendships should be understandable, for they were reducible to a question of who needed what from whom. It was clear what Alik Markov gained from an association with Boris Nikolayev. But what gain was there in the other direction?

Still watching Boris, Rodion pulled the little vase on the table toward him, took out the wilting flower, and rolled it between two fingers. "Shall I have the unhappy task of telling Alik that his trip to Finland has been canceled?"

Boris sighed. His eyes dropped their end of the gaze and fixed instead on his glass. "I said I didn't want to go to Finland. I didn't say I wouldn't."

"Ah," Rodion said casually. "Good." He put the flower back in the vase, wondering whether he had averted disaster. Or had Boris simply been baiting him? There was no way to know; there never was. However, he had established the way to handle any recalcitrance on Boris's part: to threaten Alik. That was valuable to know, if puzzling.

"Boris Semyonovich," he said, making his voice a little harder and darker, as if he too were a musician, able to gauge the slightest effect of tones, "we expect that the trip to Finland and back will be smooth and uneventful, and the week we spend there marked only by events that will do honor to you and the Soviet Union. You will be required, incidentally, to talk to the bourgeois press at least once, as part of the new image we are showing to the West."

"The bourgeois press are jackals," Boris said. As if to wash the thought from his mouth, he drank his brandy.

Rodion took some papers from his inside pocket and placed them on the table. "Here is the statement you will be delivering to the jackals. I thought you would want to study it so you'll be able to read it easily."

Boris's eyes glittered with contempt. "I have never read such things beforehand or thought about them afterward."

Rodion shrugged and made his voice lighter again. "I

know it pleases you to talk that way. Fine. I allow it because of our friendship. No one else knows you, and your loyalty to the Party, as well as I do. No one else knows the truth of Paris, isn't that so?"

After a moment Boris said, "Leave me alone." The contempt had not left his eyes, only changed its object.

"Of course, Boris Semyonovich," Rodion said. "I always do as you wish. Do I not? I help you to do what you wanted to do anyway." He smiled. It wasn't the first of their conversations to end that way, nor would it be the last.

Alone, Boris sat for a long time without moving, staring at the hands that rested on the table in front of him like alien objects. Fingers gnarled like the roots around which he had used to dig for mushrooms. Skin muddied with age spots, veins puffed as if they were swollen. The miniature death of decay occurring every day, in every part of him. Except in his mind.

In his head he was listening to Bach, clearing his mind with the clean architecture of one of the fugues. He had begun listening before Rodion left, in order to drown him out, as well as the memories he so slyly invoked: Rodion Sergeivich Orlov, who knew how to do everything, who could step on whatever heads were necessary and lick whatever asses but could not see, or hear, into a man's mind. Who had had no idea he was being drowned out. No one ever did. People—nonmusicians—thought that music needed sound to exist. Of course music was meant to be played, but in the mind it could go directly into one's awareness, like a drug injected into a vein. He had written all his own works in the mind, never going to the piano until late in the process—just as the way to read someone else's score was to do it visually—so as not to be bothered by any difficulties with the fingers. The fingers gnarled and darkened and stiffened, but the mind was always young.

At length he felt peaceful again. He rose slowly, his big body not wanting to fight the gravity to which, he prayed, death would soon return it; all life was a fight against gravity, with music helping it to ascend, and he was tired of fighting. He lumbered down the hall to his workroom, where he sat at the table and pulled toward him the notebook in which he had been making musical notations when the doorbell had rung.

The day was hot, and the heat smelled of pine, as if the air had speared itself on the needles of the trees surrounding the dacha. The sky was so bright that the guests winced when they got out of their cars. The place was close to Moscow, so the drive was interrupted by only two checkpoints. Eight of them, an actress, two novelists, a Swedish businessman, and their current partners, walked across the field full of wildflowers to the dacha settlement.

Sofia Mikhailovna greeted them on the shady porch, her short red hair glinting harshly in the sun, her body slat-thin in tight American jeans below a peasant-style blouse. She had a long but pretty face with very red lips, which formed again and again into kisses planted on both cheeks of each guest and returned as profusely as they were given. At length everyone trooped inside.

The dacha was a large old wooden house with more charm than conveniences. Sofia's father, a high official in the Ministry of Justice, had procured it for her shortly after her marriage by means he had not explained and she had not inquired about. It was unthinkable that she and her husband should not have the prestige of a private dacha. The furnishings were simple and sparse, but the largest room had a fireplace. Sofia had known how to throw a hand-woven rug over the back of an old sofa and to brighten one wall with posters of French and Italian films and another with her own painting of some lilacs. The kitchen, where an old woman was preparing a meal, had proper cupboards, and the original old iron stove had been replaced at last.

The guests moved about, shaking the constrictions of Moscow from their bodies and minds, admiring the beautiful cover of a French magazine, exclaiming over a new videocassette recorder, telling the new joke about a Politburo member, gossiping about the painter whose wife had left him and who had had three canvases removed from his show by a Ministry commission on the grounds that they were religious propaganda, and above all, discussing the new atmosphere of candor and debating what its ultimate limits would be. One of the writers had a novel the censors had refused for years; would it now have a chance? Although he had interrupted his chain-smoking to inhale the country air, he started up again, and people began helping themselves to the vodka on the dining table. Suddenly the actress cried, "Sofochka darling, where is Alik? We must see Alik!"

Everyone stopped talking at the mention of the host. It was not as if they had forgotten him but rather as if they had been pretending not to wonder where he was and had left it to the actress to ask, because she was the only one of them as well known as he.

Sofia raised both hands defensively. "You know Alik," she said. "He's out in the woods. He must not have heard you arrive."

"Let's go get him," the actress said.

Sofia smiled, but at the same time her face hardened. "Irina, darling, I'll go."

"I insist!" the actress cried. "Everyone into the woods to hunt the wild man Alik!"

The others picked up her enthusiasm, which, along with her gaiety, made her the most popular member of the cast of a current TV detective series. Trying to look as if she too thought the idea was great fun, Sofia led them all out the back door of the dacha, from which she directed them to fan out into the trees and bushes. She watched them leave, then struck off determinedly to the right.

She had gone only a hundred yards when she saw something white through a break in the trees: his shirt. Clumps of young birches were scattered among the pines, and he was sitting under one of them, his head leaning back against its graceful trunk, his eyes closed. Wishing that he were as simple a man as he looked when he was lounging under a tree with his face at peace, Sofia stopped a few feet away, to enjoy the sight of him. Even before she met him, when she had seen him only on a stage, she had had such a physical craving for him that she had thought there must be something abnormal about her. Finally she had found someone to take her to a party where Alik sang his political songs. The one about the factory that made sunglasses so dark one could not see the sun through them, based on an actual newspaper story, was dangerously funny ("How much better *Pravda* reads! How much more handsome Brezhnev is!"), and she had been surprised that he would sing it in her presence, knowing whose daughter she was. In point of fact, though, her father had enjoyed some of Alik's *magnitizdat* songs; everybody did, even some KGB.

She moved a step closer to him. Although he must have heard her, he didn't stir, nor did the peace leave his face. She felt sure he was thinking of going to Finland. Alone. "Hello," she said, too loudly.

He didn't answer. She went closer still. "Alik, everyone has arrived."

He sighed and said, "It's so beautiful out here."

"I don't see how you would know. Your eyes are closed."

They stayed that way. "Don't be small-minded, Sofia." But his voice was lazy and gentle.

"They've all come out to look for you."

He frowned. "Why?"

"Because Irina wanted to see you." Sofia bit her lip. "Why are you out here? Why couldn't you be with me to greet people when they arrived?"

He opened his eyes and sat erect. "If I stand on the porch and play the friendly host, what happens to my image?"

"Why do you say things like that?" she asked, not sarcastically but in perplexity. Eight years of marriage had not helped her understand or predict his moods, any more than she had understood the one in which he had asked her to marry him, saying, "I want to become respectable. It's the one thing I haven't tried." Had he been joking or serious? Not that she had cared. In fact he had behaved circumspectly with her father and had stopped singing his more dangerous and provocative songs. When she told him how pleased she was, he had sunk, comically, into an old man's stance and cried in an old man's voice, "Ay, I have no teeth left." Then he had disappeared for two days and come back with stubble on his cheeks, vodka stiffness in his movements, and dirt all over the clothes he was usually so fussy about. Fortunately, a mood like that was rare.

She watched him get to his feet, and moved to brush off some twigs clinging to his expensive new shirt.

"Why do you pull away from me?" she said.

"I don't think I did."

"Yes, yes, I could feel that you wanted to."

He took a deep breath. "If you're going to imagine things, Sofia, why not make them nice ones?"

"I don't imagine things."

"Whatever you say. Why would I want to pull away?"

"I don't know," she said uncertainly.

He lifted his arm. For one crazy moment she thought he might hit her, but he had never done anything like that; the violence in him always stayed inside. He casually dropped the arm around her shoulder. "You see? I am a man who knows what is good for him."

"Why do you always say that to me?"

"Because it's true. I have no reason to pull away." But in a moment he did.

They began walking back toward the dacha. The air, heavy with pine, tried to keep Sofia's words in her throat, but they spilled out anyway. "In two weeks you'll be in Finland. It's not right that I can't go with you. I've always been a good Party member. I don't see why Rodion Sergeivich couldn't arrange it. Did you really ask him?"

"Yes." It was more a growl than a word.

Even so, she went on. "I don't think you really tried. I think you like the idea of going to Finland alone."

Alik snorted. "Since when is the KGB staying home?"

That kind of comment was best to ignore. "It's not right! I haven't been allowed to take a trip outside for ten years, and the reason is you, I know it is. And now you're able to go and I'm not. It's not right."

"If you're looking for justice," he said, "ask your father. It's his ministry."

"You know Papa tried his best to get permission for me to go. Which is more than you did, I'm sure of it."

He stopped and turned to her. The sun coming through the leaves hit one side of his face and cast the other into shadow. Patience holding reins on his voice, he said, "Sofia, if your father couldn't manage it, how the hell could I? I know you'd like to go there and be seen as the wife of Alik Markov—I don't know why, but I know you would, and if I could give you that, I'd certainly do it. But I can't. I did try, believe it or not, whichever makes you feel better. Hostages have to be left at home, you know that. Unfortunately for you, I guess they figure you're the best hostage for me."

"Why do you use words like *hostage*?" she said.

"Because I'm a poet," he said, and moved on.

She hurried after him. "I don't care. It's not right. Just because Boris Nikolayev said he wouldn't go without you. Nikolayev! A man whose wife and daughter defected!"

He stopped again. She saw that some kind of struggle was taking place within him. She could identify the combat but not the combatants. At length he said, "Boris Semyono-vich is not responsible for the actions of his wife and his daughter. You should remember that."

Irina and one of the novelists came into view. "Alik!" Irina cried, running toward him, breasts moving beneath her light sweater as if they couldn't wait to reach him. When they did, he crushed them against him in an enor-mous hug.

He started toward the dacha with his arm around Irina, his laugh a dark rumble below her soprano chatter. Had he slept with her? Sofia wondered. Had he slept with any of them, or all of them? Would he sleep with someone in Finland, and if so, could she get her father to find out? He couldn't have been faithful to her no matter how convinc-ingly he insisted that he was. No matter how unable she was to find evidence that he hadn't been.

"Tell me," said the novelist, falling in beside her, "how will you amuse yourself while Alik is in Finland with Nikolayev?"

"I'll be fine," she said. A bird called so raucously above her head that the words were drowned.

"I didn't hear you," the novelist said.

"I said, he'll only be gone for a week. A week is nothing." Then she heard herself add, "And he is a man who knows what is good for him."

PART
2

ALIK

CHAPTER SEVEN

The jet lifted easily from the runway and then canted up sharply into the sky.

Seated by a window, Hedy watched the city and the huge, glittering sprawl that surrounded it fall back in dizzying angles. She put a hand against the glass to steady the land, and to tie herself to it as long as possible, for in proportion as it receded, she felt a rising need not to leave it.

She had left it before—gone to England for the Brontë book, to Spain to do research on Lorca—and had felt momentary twinges, foolish fears that the captain would somehow announce the flight destination as not London or Madrid but Moscow. What she felt now was different: a powerful desire to get back by any means to the country her heart had chosen long before she saw it, even by smashing through the window.

She looked down, hoping the plane's wide circle might take it over the Statue of Liberty. On the centennial celebration for the statue she and her mother and the *babushki* had gone down to Battery Park almost at dawn to get a good spot. It had been an extraordinary day, uniquely American in its blend of show business, commercialism, and patriotism. Throughout it, she had been buffeted by two emotions: a desire to cry, which rose in waves each time she looked at the statue, rose so strongly that she kept having to turn away; and, equally, to grin because Americans for once were feeling the same thing. So often they frustrated her with their failure to prize their liberty properly, or their shocking willingness to abandon it: That very week the Supreme Court had gone out of its way to express its moral support for a state law outlawing private homosexual conduct. On that day, despite the party atmosphere, she saw her own emotion reflected on hundreds of faces, as if the concept that had fired minds all over the globe was for once grasped fully by those who had never needed to think about it. She had felt tied to everyone in Battery Park, in Manhattan, in the United States. How ironic, she had thought, that the sense of the *kollektiv*, which years of Soviet admonitions had failed to instill in her, should come upon her there, in the country founded on individualism.

That day she had allowed herself to think of Alik, to believe he would share what she was feeling, and to wonder again, without having an answer, what it was that had made him and her and a relative handful of others want desperately to come to America while most of their countrymen had no desire to leave Russia. For once, the memory of him had been cloudless.

She pressed closer to the plane's small window, straining to discover the statue down there somewhere, but the lights were receding into anonymity, and Liberty was nowhere to be seen.

"Excuse me, ma'am, are you feeling all right?"

It was the man next to her: square face, cropped, graying hair, accent she had learned to recognize as midwestern. His gaze was direct and concerned.

"Oh, yes," she said. "I'm fine." The trip was beginning with a lie; appropriate, she thought.

"Good. I thought maybe looking out the window was making you dizzy."

"Not at all. I was just thinking of leaving my . . . my family."

"Ah." He nodded and sat back.

She tried to do the same, but her body turned once more to the window.

Somewhere down there, in the carpet of lights that was pulling away but was still supporting her, her mother was sitting, probably staring at television, looking through the screen to the past. Hedy had wanted to hire someone to stay with her, or at least to look in on her, but Vera had been adamant. "I'll be fine!" she had said in exasperation. "If you're going to face danger in Finland, I think I can surely face the perils of my own apartment." They had compromised finally: The *babushki* would take turns going by to have lunch and dinner with Vera, and one of them would always be on call at night.

When she left, Vera had said, "Good-bye, my darling, darling girl. When you see your father, tell him that I . . . tell him . . ." She had raised her fingers to her mouth, and her dark eyes had glittered above them as if she were looking over bars. Hedy had knelt by her chair and put both arms around her, and the two of them had rocked in a long, wordless good-bye.

Jess was down there somewhere, too, on his way back to Manhattan, his cab nothing more now than a mote of light. When she had finally told him that she was going to change her appearance for the trip, and shown him how, his eyes had darkened, his jaw had tightened like a military salute, and his thought had been as visible as if he'd spoken: It's so goddamned dangerous that you need a disguise? She had seen his determination not to say it, followed by a deceptively mild "It doesn't look like you. I mean the real you, the one inside." It had been odd to hear her own assessment come from his mouth. Did he really see her as she saw herself? "I guess that's good," he had added, "that it doesn't look like you."

Later, when they were lying in her bed, just holding each other, he had suddenly said, "I don't care if I said I wouldn't try to stop you. Dammit, I don't want you to go!"

She hadn't answered, and after a while he had sighed and buried his face in her neck.

At the airport, after he kissed her good-bye, he put his hands around her face and said, "Go and face the past, then. I hope you can get it out of your system. Because if you can't . . ."

"Yes? If?"

"Ah, hell. Good luck. Go."

So she had.

There was a scraping noise, and a voice came over the plane's public address system: the captain, announcing the route to London and the arrival time.

But they were still in America, Hedy thought; she was hearing American voices on an American airline. She had told her travel agent to book her that way despite the layovers, not to use the European lines until the last leg of the trip, from Helsinki, when there was no alternative.

The man beside her cleared his throat and asked, "Been to London before?"

"Yes."

"Going to be there long?" His face was weathered, and his neck a stretch of dry, cracked land.

"Only long enough to take a connecting flight."

He nodded, looked away, then swung back. "Say, I hope you didn't mind my asking if you were all right."

"Not at all. It was kind of you."

"Reason was, you looked kind of peaked."

"No, I'm . . . just tired. I need to sleep."

She leaned back and closed her eyes, but the man was looking at her, she was sure. Studying her face. Wondering if she was wearing a wig? If she was Anna Borisov— No. It was just the kindness of a stranger; no way could the man be KGB. She thrust the thought out of her mind, reached for something else. *Peaked,* he had said. Strange word. Did anything rhyme with it? *Naked, crooked, wicked . . .* nothing. She turned her head to the window to look out once more, but the lights and the land had melted into the blackness of space and night. Her gaze went deep into it and beyond it . . . scanning every corner and street and crowd . . . for gray men in unmarked cars, or women waiting at bus stops with big shopping bags but never getting on buses, or scrubbed-looking young men in neat suits . . . the KGB presence that was always there, in reality and, sometimes worse, in one's mind, with a permanence no American friend could fully grasp . . . a presence numbering in the hundreds of thousands, plus a huge network of informers, all ceaselessly watching for "deviant behavior" . . . sometimes hidden, sometimes open . . . on May Day standing in gray uniform jackets with red GB on the shoulders, lining the paths to Red Square while thousands roared "Long live Soviet power!" . . .

The tiny oblong of the aircraft window came back into focus. If she could set herself shivering, she thought, because of a few words from her seatmate on the plane, what in God's name would happen to her in Finland?

She turned to the man beside her. He was leafing through a magazine, not looking at her. He was completely and obviously American, and she would prove it, even though he did remind her of a farmer from the Ukraine. She hesitated; small talk was a skill she hadn't developed, whether because of growing up in a world of distrust for strangers or because her personality didn't want to bend that way, she could never be sure. She had warned Jess she'd be terrible at political dinners, but he told her you could keep a conversation running for a long time just by saying, "How interesting! What exactly do you mean by that?" She looked at her seatmate and said firmly, "Will you be staying in London?"

He put down the magazine. "No, I'm making a connection too."

"I see."

He grinned. "Matter of fact, I'm going on to Helsinki. Finland."

"Finland? Really?" She hoped it had a casual sound.

"Yup, I'm going back to the old country. Well, not really *my* old country, my family's. My grandparents come over from Finland around 1910 and settled up on the Iron Range. Know where that is?"

"Not exactly."

"The Mesabi Range, up by Duluth. I got a farm implement store near there." He took out a business card, snapped it on his thumb, gave it to her, and said something in what she presumed was Finnish. "Yup, I'm real proud to be a Finn. Say, I bet you didn't know they're the only country who ever beat the Russian Commies in a war."

She opened her mouth to protest, then panicked. What would she know about the Winter War and the Continuation War that followed it if she had never heard about it in school, if she were just an American? Was he trying to trick her? "I don't know much about Finland," she said lamely.

He grinned and began talking about the country as if he were selling it: Did she know it had more saunas than cars?

that the language had only nineteen letters? that the Lapps had over a hundred different words to describe snow?

She began to relax, and to feel almost grateful to him for giving her a first, easy lesson in the caution she would need, the monitoring she would have to do before she spoke or replied to anyone. As he went on, switching to the economic problems of the farm states, she listened with half her mind, then a quarter. "Really?" she said at intervals; it seemed all he needed.

She was thinking of telling Jess she had acquired the skills for any political dinner party he cared to take her to, when the man's words penetrated. "Say," he said, "you're smiling. Are you maybe going there too?"

"I'm sorry," she said, "I didn't quite catch the last thing you said."

"I said, believe it or not, I'm not going to Finland to talk farming. I'm going to a music festival, a new one, up near the Arctic Circle. I catch a morning flight out of Helsinki."

She managed to produce a smile, as artificial as a fan, and said, "How interesting. What exactly do you mean by that?"

The sky in Finland was an omnipresence, a brilliant, icy blue that became part of every perception and might have been distilled from the thousands of lakes lying beneath it like pieces of dark glass. The sharp green of trees was everywhere, and the soothing colors of stone.

At the airport there were Lapps in traditional costumes, and clear air as fresh as snow. Hedy drew in great lungsful of it, which, confusingly, made her whole body yearn for sleep even while her blood fizzed with new energy. The canyons and chaos of New York, even the sprawl of London, seemed impossibly distant; when she tried to recall them, the images that came were like photographs in someone else's album.

A *taksi* deposited her at a hotel centrally located to the events of the festival. She had hoped to stay in the same hotel as her father, to make it easier to try to see him alone, but festival headquarters had been unable or unwilling to tell her travel agent where the Soviet musicians would be quartered. She had chosen the largest of several hotels that were close to one another; if she wasn't in the same one as her father, she might at least be in one nearby.

There was a group at the desk when she checked in, but she was fairly sure they were speaking Swedish. Someone was begging one of the desk clerks in German for a room, and being told they had all been booked many weeks in advance. There was no sound of Russian in the lobby, no faces that announced, by wariness or any other means, that they might be Soviet. She said to the desk clerk, "I heard that some of the festival musicians are staying here. Is that so?"

"Yes, madam."

"The Russians? The Moscow Symphony?" Ironically, one of the festival's two visiting orchestras was the same group with which she and her parents had once made the trip to Paris.

"No. We have here the chorus from West Germany and some others." The clerk looked at her registration. "Miss Lucas, if we can do anything to help make your stay enjoyable, you have only to ask."

His English was excellent, but in the elevator and the hall she heard Finnish, full of "l" and "sh" and "k" sounds, so that it seemed both liquid and harsh—a language made, like the country, of lakes and wilderness. Her room was pleasant. After the long flight and its tensions, the bed called to her like a siren, but she knew she couldn't rest until she'd learned where her father and . . . where the Russians were. She went into the bathroom and jumped as a blond stranger walked toward her in the mirror. She splashed water on her face before thinking that it might make the strange eyebrows run; she saw that the new slant of her mouth had been chewed or eaten off along with the lipstick.

In the toilet things she unpacked were the travel soap and lotion the twins had given her the weekend before. "I mean," Laura had said, "who knows what kind of weird stuff they might have in Finland?" And Lindsey had added, "Think of us when you use it." When they parted, the girls had hugged her tightly, their sturdy bodies making a sandwich of hers, one smooth, fresh face pressed against each of her cheeks, and she had found herself not wanting to let go. Now they seemed to be in some far country she had never known, where there were no concerns other than growing up.

She fixed her face, combed the wig, changed into a skirt and cotton sweater, and left to get a taxi to the festival's main building. Her driver was a stocky man whose English was strained through a thick accent like soup through a mustache. She asked him several innocuous questions before mentioning the Russian musicians. "Oh, yes," he said, "I take some Russians from airplane to hotel. Very quiet for whole trip." He grinned. "Maybe Russians think I am spy."

"Do you remember which hotel?" she said, and when he gave her the name at once, she felt such a lift of the spirit that she expected him to feel it too and turn around in amazement. She had gotten her first piece of information so easily. It had to be a good omen.

She realized the hotel was not one of those near hers. Then she realized it was the same hotel where her flight companion had said he was staying.

The name on his card was Raymond Salmi, "but everybody calls me Ray." All the way to London she had kept changing her mind about him, back and forth. What were the odds that a man with a touch of the Ukraine about him would sit next to her on the same flight to the same destination in Finland purely by coincidence? Why would an American farm implements salesman care about a festival celebrating Nikolayev, Brahms, and contemporary Finnish chamber music? But why should she assume that a farmer couldn't have an interest in serious music? He said he came to Finland every summer to attend one or more of the country's many arts festivals, without his wife and children, who had no interest in music. The story was so poor a cover it could well be real. In fact he spoke of music credibly enough to support it. He had asked about her in a way that could be quite normal. She had told him only that she was a writer hoping to interview some festival musicians.

The taxi delivered her to the new concert hall that also housed the festival offices: a spare structure made of wood, stone, and glass, which captured the sun at every angle yet looked cool. Inside, scraps of music came faintly from a dozen places; the dissonance was a comforting reminder of walking into her mother's apartment building. She located the press office and presented herself to a friendly young woman with a skier's body and white-blond hair that fell to her waist like poured milk. Hedy felt as if she should pull off her wig and confess.

Instead she said, "I'm preparing a book about Boris Nikolayev. I never expected to have the chance to talk to him in person, but now that he's here, I'm anxious to arrange an interview." She smiled. "You might even say I'm desperate."

"Yes, yes," the young woman said. "That is understandable." She consulted a schedule and looked up with a brilliant smile. "Nikolayev is going to meet the press on Tuesday morning at ten o'clock, here, on the second floor."

Hedy's heart gave a single, great beat, like a tympanum.

Intellectually she had known for weeks that she would see her father, but in that moment, for the first time, her blood knew it too. "That's good," she said, "but I'd also like to arrange a private interview with him."

"Yes, other journalists have asked for the same thing. Unfortunately, we are not permitted to arrange interviews for Soviet musicians. And we have been told that Nikolayev will see all the press together, and only the one time."

"Can you tell me whom I could speak to about it, then?"

The young woman shook her head. "I don't think it will be any good."

"I'm sure you're right, but I must try. You can understand that."

"Yes, yes." The woman thought, biting into a full, naturally pink lip. "I will tell you the Soviet official who is in charge. You are lucky today, because he is coming to this office in about a half hour, and maybe you can try to speak to him then. His name is . . ." She checked some papers that were out of Hedy's sight, below the counter. "Yes. Rodion Sergeivich Orlov."

"I beg your pardon?" Hedy said.

"Rodion Sergeivich Orlov. Yes. From the Soviet Ministry of Culture."

It was too perfect, Hedy thought. Even the jailer would be the same. She wanted to laugh, as if someone had planned it for her and she must be courteous and show her appreciation. "I see," she said. "All right, I'll . . . I'll be back."

The woman seemed satisfied, and no one in the halls or out in front of the building glanced at her oddly, so Hedy assumed she looked normal enough. She found a stone bench under a birch tree and sank gratefully onto it.

Mama and Papa were at the table in the kitchen, talking with a man who came to see them once in a while. She

didn't like the man, although she supposed she should because each time he came he brought her something from
Detsky Mir: a doll, a little washboard, a toy drum. This
time he had brought a little tea set, and Papa had said, as
if the man was her uncle, which he wasn't, "Now give your
Uncle Rodion a kiss." The tea set would break, of course,
as the other things had, but that wasn't the man's fault; toys
always broke, no matter how careful you tried to be. No,
the reason she didn't like the man was his hands. They
were too white, with shiny, squared-off nails on long
fingers, and they were too busy, always stroking the tablecloth or tapping on a tea glass as if they'd rather be doing
something else. But no, the reason wasn't really the man's
hands; it was what happened to Papa when the man came.
Papa, who was so tall and strong and always felt rough—
his skin, his jaw, the cloth of his jackets—Papa somehow
got smoother when the man came, as if he had shaved more
than his face.

Hovering in the kitchen entrance while the three adults
talked, she watched the man's hands and her parents' faces,
listening not so much to the words as to the sound of her
parents' voices, which was different in some way—as if the
words were being pulled on a tight string. She didn't try
to understand the conversation, but she recognized some
names: Lenin, of course, whom they sang about in school
all the time, and Stalin. When she first went to school, they
had sung about Stalin, too, but she couldn't remember any
songs about him lately. She was glad, because Stalin had
done something to Papa that made them not have enough
money, although she didn't know what. Usually his name
sent a shadow over Papa's face. She leaned in to see, but the
shadow was not there. Curious, she tried to understand
what they said. The man was saying what a bad person
Stalin had been, and suddenly Mama lifted her chin and

with her eyes flashing asked how did they really know they were any better off now?

Papa's eyebrows shot up like startled birds. The man shook his head at Mama as if he was angry, but it was strange because at the same time one side of his mouth was smiling.

He glanced over toward the doorway. His face changed as quickly as if by magic. "Little Anna!" he said. "Come here and tell me what you are learning in school." She knew even without looking at Mama that she would have to do it.

Standing before him, she visualized the bookshelves in her classroom. "We are reading about collective farm labor, and our glorious Red Army, and transportation, and our motherland. And Grandfather Lenin."

"Splendid," the man said. One of his hands began to move up and down her arm. "Soviet education is a splendid thing."

She hesitated, then spoke firmly. "I don't like those books too much. I like to read *Dr. Aibolit* and fairy tales by Pushkin."

The man turned to Papa. "Boris Semyonovich, you must be sure your daughter learns to fit into the *kollektiv.*" Then he smiled and said to her, "Do you know our good Russian proverb?—'In a field of wheat, only the stalk whose head is empty of grain stands above the rest.'"

"Yes," she said unwillingly, hating both him and the proverb, which had been cited to her many times.

"Good." He just sat there, stroking her arm, shaking his head, smiling with part of his mouth.

A feeling had rolled in her stomach like bad milk: Papa should be telling the man to go away, but Papa couldn't, and she didn't know why. Was it possible Papa didn't want him to go away?

. . .

A car stopped less than fifty feet from the bench she was sitting on, and he got out: Rodion Sergeivich Orlov. Without question, it was he. Shorter than she remembered, well dressed, his red hair barely grayed. Face knotted in a frown, he came toward the building, talking to an aide. He was going to glance over and see her, she knew it, and then he would summon the KGB to deal with her. Her muscles screamed to run, but she forced all motion inward except for the clutching of her hands on the edge of the bench. She felt paralyzed by him. . . . As on that day, when she was sixteen, when she came home and found him at the table with her father, discussing the two writers who had been tried for having their work published abroad; they had dared to demand that the State respect their constitutional rights. She had heard the news of their sentence the day before: five and seven years, respectively. And there was Rodion Sergeivich, smiling and speaking of it as necessary. The State had no choice, he said, because such commerce with bourgeois decadence was anti-Soviet and must be punished. Prison for being published in the West! A rocket of rage had started inside her; she had to cross her hands on her throat to push it down before she could greet the man pleasantly—as prudence, and her father, demanded. She had felt as if her face were paralyzed, severed not only from her body but from her mind and spirit. *This,* she had thought, *is how I will feel for the rest of my life if I stay in this country.* In that moment she had sworn to leave it, somehow, by any means.

She had looked at her father, the brooding, enigmatic artist who deeply questioned the State—and should despise the smiling man in the kitchen who was its representative—and wondered how he could keep silent and bear such a paralysis. Was he so enslaved by his music that he didn't realize he was free to move no part of himself but his mind? However much she loved art, she thought, she would never let its dark power blind her to reality.

Rodion Sergeivich was approaching the building. He would hear her heart if she didn't quiet it. *I am an American citizen*, she thought, and said it over and over, like a mantra, as he came closer: *I am an American, an American.* . . . He looked in her direction, looked right at her.

Then moved on, uninterested, and entered the building with brisk steps.

Slowly she took her hands from the edge of the bench. The grit of the stone had pushed angry red imprints into her palms, which were numb from the pressure of her grip.

She had done it, she thought. She had sat still while he looked right at her. He had seen only an anonymous blond woman. Yes, the glance had been brief and yes, talking to him would be quite different, but even so. . . . Her palms stung back to life, and she felt a spurt of exhilaration. She would have jumped up to run after him and put her questions to him if common sense hadn't remembered that she wasn't supposed to know who he was.

She made herself sit there for ten more minutes, to plan what she would say and rehearse it softly, to make sure no hint of accent would creep in under the pressure of fear. Then she rose and went back into the building.

There were several people in the press office, and he was behind the counter, speaking with the young blond Finnish woman. Hedy stopped in the doorway for a moment, then walked to the counter. The young Finnish woman looked up, smiled, and went on talking to him. She was explaining a rehearsal schedule, saying, "We have arranged for the orchestra to have three hours on the stage in the morning . . ." Saying it in Russian, so Hedy must not react to a word of it because she couldn't understand Russian because she was an American, an aggressive American journalist who was afraid of nothing. . . .

She let them talk for several minutes. Then she leaned closer and said to the young woman, "Excuse me, may I just ask you whether Mr. Orlov from the Russian Ministry of Culture has come in?"

They both turned to her, the woman with a smile and Rodion Sergeivich Orlov with the cold, blank stare she hadn't seen in almost twenty years—the stare that wasn't his in particular but belonged to the face of Soviet official-dom. The woman started to answer, but he interrupted, in English. "Who is asking for Orlov?"

"I am. Are you he?"

Again the Finnish woman started to speak, but thought better of it.

"What is your business with him?" Orlov said.

Hedy looked at his hands, at the fine hairs that lay along their backs like ink lines on soft white paper. "It's about . . . one of the Russian musicians," she said.

The Finnish woman decided to plunge in. "This lady is an American writer. I told her that if she came at this time, she might have the chance to speak to . . . to Mr. Orlov."

His eyes were a smoky blue that Hedy had forgotten. They rested on her face, seemed to scald it. Nonetheless she said, "My name is Hedy Lucas, and I must speak with Mr. Orlov."

"State your business. He will hear of it."

It was ludicrous: Why was he hiding who he was? Was he suspicious of her? Or simply of everyone, like a good Soviet? "I think it would be better," she said, "if I spoke to Mr. Orlov directly."

"Do you wish to state your business or not?"

She couldn't see that there was a choice. She gave the speech she had rehearsed. "I'm a writer of biographies, three of them published so far. I'm planning to do my next book about Boris Nikolayev, mostly about his music." She took out a paper. "Here's a letter from my publisher confirming that fact." He took it and placed it into a folder without looking at it. She went on. "I'd like to include material about Nikolayev's life and a personal statement from him. I came to the festival in the hope of getting an interview with him."

"Nikolayev will meet press people Tuesday morning."

"I know, but I must speak with him alone. After all, for a book . . ."

"It is not possible. No individual interviews with Nikolayev."

"Are you the one who makes that decision? Are you Mr. Orlov?"

He looked at her blandly, then smiled with half his mouth. When he spoke, his tone was suddenly amicable. "Yes. I am Orlov. So I can tell you definitely, it is out of the question. Now, you will please excuse me . . ." He turned to the young Finnish woman, and all Hedy could see was the back of his head, where his thick hair formed into curls, like rows of reddish cocoons.

She was in another taxi, heading back to her hotel, when she thought of another old Russian proverb: The wise man does not climb the mountain but goes around it. She smiled and gave the driver different instructions: the hotel where the Russians were staying.

CHAPTER EIGHT

A Russian newspaper open in front of him, the man sat in the lobby of the hotel, reading in short takes that alternated with casual glances toward the elevator. He was a stocky man with mild blue eyes and a round face given texture by thin wires of broken blood vessels, which clustered on his cheeks.

He had left his current charge taking a shower in the room they shared. There was no reason not to give the man some time alone, provided one knew where he was, and why. The function of a companion was to be diligently aware and to prevent certain kinds of activities, but normally they did not include showering.

When the companion had finished the paper, he began to read it again. Fortunately, patience was a strong element in his character, for boredom was a frequent presence in his work, although it was offset by the comfort of belonging to the official power structure and, in recent years, by a certain amount of foreign travel.

Finally he saw the subject of his concern come out of the elevator. He folded the paper, slid it inside his jacket, and walked over. "Aleksandr Romanovich," he said with soft heartiness, "you are going out?"

His subject nodded, squared his broad shoulders, and shoved his hands into the pockets of his sweater. "Come on, then," he said in the deep, grating voice that had become so well known on records and tapes. The companion hurried along. He himself had enjoyed some of Markov's underground songs, which could make a man bellow with laughter at their slyly accurate depiction of certain facts of Soviet life, or feel his blood slowing with their mournful portrayal of the pain of war and prison.

When Markov was younger, he had gone too far, of course, and his bouts with the security organs were as well known as his songs. Three years in the camps had taught him nothing, for at the end of the sixties he had seemed to want to be arrested again. He had signed protest letters, published poems in an underground literary journal, and written and performed mocking songs that could not be ignored, like "Anti-Soviet Behavior," in which that criminal charge consisted of such things as being happy. Or worse, one in which Stalin came back from the dead and walked about Moscow looking at the buildings and saying how glad he was to see that nothing had changed—and everyone could tell he wasn't really talking about the buildings. With songs like that, how could officialdom look the other way? Markov's concerts, which were unofficial in any case, had to be stopped. He had been called in many times, reprimanded, detained; and it was still a mystery why that tongue, sharp enough to cut beef, hadn't been sent to a hospital with him attached. Instead, he had disappeared from Moscow for a while. Roaming the country, they said, living outside society and the law. But he had come around, learning the line between what could be tolerated and what could not, even gaining acceptance into the appropriate union, and finally here he was: allowed to tour to Finland, walking about in boots and a sweater that could have been bought only at a special shop for those with very good connections, sauntering along like a tourist.

It was an odd kind of saunter, though, for as slowly as he was going, occasionally even stopping to take big breaths and stare up at the sky, something about him wasn't casual at all. A strange thought came into the companion's mind: He was out walking not with Markov but with some jungle animal, which he held on an invisible leash. He was so surprised to be having such a thought that it was several moments before he shook it from his head.

Markov, in fact, was causing him no difficulty—neither ignoring him in the ostentatious way that sometimes happened nor seeming bothered by his presence. However, there was no predicting what would catch Markov's interest. He stopped to read a festival poster, then to look at a display of local ceramics. He walked in and out of a self-service cafeteria and for a long time stood across from a church, apparently to study its architecture. Too interested in the products of Western decadence? Looking for places to buy Western literature or to make contact with foreigners? Too early to say. Markov simply seemed interested in everything, the companion decided, like an explorer, but, of course, the man was on his first trip outside the Soviet Union. It occurred to the companion that although he and his charge were the same age, forty-six, he had seen more of the world than Markov. The thought pleased him.

Markov stopped to study a display of jewelry: birds with bodies made of some kind of minerals or semiprecious stones, hanging on golden chains. When he entered the shop, the companion took his time about following. Once inside, he heard Markov speaking to the saleslady in English, a language the companion understood, but not easily. He made out something about "Finnish design" and "for my wife," and felt a mosquito-sting of irritation. He hadn't been informed that Markov spoke English. Then came an itch of worry—why hadn't he been informed?

Suddenly Markov turned around and dangled one of the birds by its chain. "Handsome, don't you think?"

"Yes, Aleksandr Romanovich," the companion said, although in fact he didn't think it looked much like a bird. There was nothing resembling feathers, just a colored oval body. Not enough realism to suit his taste.

The package bought and wrapped, Markov walked on, and on and on, as if determined to do the whole area in a single afternoon. The companion's durable feet were, like patience, one of his assets, so he did not get tired, but he did think that he had been to parts of the world more important and interesting than this Finnish corner on the edge of a wilderness, where the sun didn't even set properly at night. He had been to East Berlin on an assignment the year before, to Sweden, and even to America, where he had accompanied a chamber ensemble during an earlier period of cultural exchange. Foreign travel was useful, not only because of all the goods it allowed one to take back home but because it showed so clearly the superiority of the Soviet system, which might have economic shortcomings but was deeply committed to peace and provided its citizens with order and security. For a moment the companion recalled the chaotic, disordered life he had seen in America, where people faced constant insecurity about everything from unemployment to street violence—more than once he himself had felt the menacing presence of Negroes in both New York and Washington, whereas he had never known a moment's fear on the street of any Soviet city. The recollection so absorbed him that when he next looked, he couldn't see Aleksandr Romanovich. There was a beat of panic, then of reproach for having failed in his duty, however briefly, then of relief as he saw Markov's tall figure emerging from the door of a shop displaying local handicrafts. Knives and pots made by a bunch of Lapps! Who would want such stupid things?

The companion's feet, if not his patience, were sending signals of wear when he finally saw their hotel back in sight at the end of the street.

Inside, as they waited for the elevator, Markov's gaze roamed over the lobby with the same casual intensity it had directed at everything on the street. Suddenly it locked on something. The companion turned and tried to locate its object: those musicians from the orchestra, who must have just come in and were standing by the window? the blond woman talking to an older man, both of them obviously Americans? the taxi driver bringing in expensive-looking luggage for an elderly couple?

"Is something wrong, Aleksandr Romanovich?" the companion asked.

"Nothing at all."

"Good. May I remind you that a sightseeing tour has been arranged for our group on Thursday, to—"

"Just a minute," Markov said, his imperious brusqueness contrasting with his previous amiability.

He started back to the desk but stopped halfway and stood watching beside a column that partially hid him. In turn, the companion moved to watch him but could see only his profile, which was motionless. So was his whole body, in fact. Turned to stone, thought the companion, except that stone did not make one feel it had eyes, burning on someone or something.

"Actually," Hedy said, "I came because I want to ask you a favor. A big one."

"Well, that's fine. How about if we go someplace where we can talk?"

"I'd rather ask the favor first, Mr. Salmi."

"Shoot." He folded his arms as if he meant the word literally. "But I'm not going to listen unless you call me Ray."

"All right, Ray." Hedy hoped the smile she gave was engaging. "I know I told you I was coming here to the festival to interview some of the musicians, but there's more to it than that."

He nodded sagely. "Figured that was so."

"You did? Why?"

"Oh, you look like a lady who might have something up her sleeve."

She hadn't a clue what that meant, Hedy thought. Maybe he was just one of those people who convert new information into prescience as a way of mental life. Unless he was something quite different and dangerous. But whatever he was, she had decided, she had nothing to lose by approaching him.

"The truth is," she said, "that I'm writing a book about Boris Nikolayev, and I'm desperate for a private interview with him. But none are being allowed." Salmi's wiry, gray eyebrows lifted. She went on. "So I have to try something else. I don't know what, but if anything's going to work, I have to be staying in the same hotel as he is. Namely, this one. I've learned that all the Russians are staying here."

Salmi's face, which all the way across the Atlantic had been as animated as a cartoon, was expressionless. "So what's the favor?" he said.

"Would you help me out by changing hotel rooms with me?"

"What?"

"I can't get in here because everything is booked solid, but if the two of us switched, there'd be no problem. My

room is very nice, by the way. It's a single with a shower
and a phone."

Salmi unfolded his arms as if they were heavy. If he was
what he said he was, she had reasoned, he might agree on
grounds of helping out a fellow American. And even if he
wasn't what he said he was, he would still have to pretend
to be.

There was one other consideration: If he made a fuss
about needing time to think over her request, it could be
because he was working for somebody and had to check out
her request before he could agree.

"Well," he said, "I don't know."

"It would make a big difference to me," Hedy said. "And
you'd be helping the cause of art, you know. Oh, and I'll
send you a copy of my book about Nikolayev when it's
finished."

"Oh, yes?" he said without enthusiasm. "Trouble is, this
is the address I gave my wife and everybody."

"If you want to call your wife about the change, I'll be
glad to pay for it." She smiled at him, glanced away for a
second, and couldn't move.

Alik.

She was flung back in time as if caught in an undertow,
breath knocked out of her, perspective spinning.

Finally she righted herself. He was exactly the same, she
saw, yet he was different. She felt her heart turn over and
didn't know which was the cause: the brilliant eyes and the
power of presence that hadn't changed since she last saw
him in Pushkin Square; or the difference, which seemed to
come not from age but from something internal, as if an
inner pressure had subtly shifted the planes of his face,
perhaps of his being.

She made her eyes leave his face, praying he hadn't
recognized her even though he was staring at her with the
most puzzled expression.

"I wasn't counting on anything like this, you know."

She realized that the words had been Ray Salmi's. She remembered that she was talking to him, asking him something.

She looked at him. "Excuse me?"

"I'd like to help out the press," Salmi said. "Especially a pretty lady like you. But I don't think . . ."

"That's all right," she said, and wondered what on earth she was saying.

"I'm real sorry," Salmi said. "Hope you won't hold it against me."

She felt as she had when she first came to America and people spoke too fast for her to follow. Then the context of the conversation tumbled back into her mind. Shifting position so her back was to Alik, she said, "Never mind, Mr. Salmi. Ray. I thought it was worth a try, that's all."

"Well, sure it was. Say, will you let me make it up to you and buy you lunch or something?"

"I don't know. I'm pretty busy."

She managed to escape his heartiness and walked to the front doors. Before she opened them, she allowed herself to look again in Alik's direction, but he wasn't there. Perhaps he had been a hallucination. No, he must have gone upstairs. The thought of him standing in the elevator, staring at its walls with the polite, abstracted look one always had in elevators, made it suddenly, inescapably real that he was in the building—not frozen in the past, in her mind, but there, alive, with a present and a future.

The elevator opened and disgorged a passenger. Alik's height. She took half a step toward him before stopping herself. Anyway, the man was a stranger.

She left the hotel and stood outside, taking long breaths of the clear, sweet air.

· · ·

Boris Nikolayev turned a page of his text and, still without looking at his listeners, continued to read.

"Composers in the Soviet Union have unlimited creative possibilities and all the conditions necessary for a glorious future of musical culture. I can truthfully say that the Soviet people, with their high standard of musical taste and their expectation of highest-quality work from their composers, have been the inspiration for my work, in which I have attempted to reflect not only the great spirit of the collective but also our Soviet dedication to universal peace and brotherhood. From my earliest work, a piano sonata composed while I was a student at the Moscow Conservatory, to the Sixth Symphony of three years ago and the Concerto for Guitar that will have its premiere at this festival, I have always been conscious of my duty to the Soviet people, who are the true objects of the honor this festival is showing to me."

The voice stopped. There was no closing inflection. The sound, which had gone along emptily, like a barrow over cobblestones, simply ended. The hooded eyes, which hadn't once looked out at the room full of reporters, finally lifted from the paper but gave no impression of their perceptions.

Hedy was in the back of the rows of chairs that had been set up in a large rehearsal room. There were reporters from publications all over the world, it seemed, but television cameras were barred. Behind her, standing against the wall, were several men she assumed to be KGB. Perhaps there were KGB among the reporters, too; she knew they often posed as journalists. After a delay Rodion Sergeivich had ushered her father in and announced that he would deliver a statement, which would be made available in print in several languages but which Nikolayev would read in English. Her father had taken some papers from his pocket and begun to read in that flat, heavy voice in which the only life came from his stumbles with English pronunciation.

She needn't have been worried, she thought, because it wasn't her father up there at the podium. It was a wax-museum figure, impressive in its fidelity to life but convincing only to those who had never seen motion. She shook her head, negating what she saw. Into her mind came the various words she had used over the years to hold her father in memory: abstracted, distant, frozen, locked in his own visions. She saw how wrong they were, how alive and vital and fierce he had been, compared with the figure at the podium.

One day, when she had just begun going to school, she had been sent home early because she felt ill. He had been in the kitchen alone, one hand curled around a bottle of brandy like a baby's around milk. He had looked right through her, as if she wasn't there—the way he was now looking out at the room—so she had gone very close to him and stood between his knees and whispered, "Papa." That had made his eyes clear. He had pulled her into his arms and hugged the breath from her, saying softly, more to himself than to her, "Think of the music, nothing else matters, think of the music," saying it over and over, although the repetition didn't make her understand it. Later, when she was in bed drifting to sleep, she heard him tell Mama that he had had to read a speech at some meeting, that he had been given a speech to read, that he knew what some people were saying about him but he didn't care because his music would live long after he was gone and only the music mattered.

She had lain in her bed and tried to understand what was so bad about having to read a speech somebody else wrote.

She looked up at the podium and sighed.

He was older, she thought, his hair gone quite white and the center of his gravity lowered from his chest to his belly.

A dark blue suit hung on him awkwardly, as if draped on a tree. She waited to feel something about him, but her own animation seemed to be suspended, waiting for his. Of course, she thought, she was tired, not yet adjusted to sleeping in this strange world where the sun never set and the past was always rising.

When her father finished, Rodion Sergeivich came forward, wearing a smart gray suit and a smile, both of which looked tailored. "Ladies and gentlemen," he said, "many of you have expressed a desire to ask questions of Boris Semyonovich Nikolayev. He has agreed to answer some of your questions, which should be brief ones. Please put your questions in English, German, or French. I will translate as required."

Hands and voices shot into the air. Hedy saw a slight tremor pass over her father's face. She raised her own hand. Rodion Sergeivich stood surveying the crowd, shaking his head until the voices subsided. "Please," he said. "Please! We cannot deal with questions unless they come in orderly fashion." He surveyed the room, then pointed to a hand raised on the right.

In French, someone asked if Nikolayev would explain why he had agreed to come to the festival. Hedy watched Rodion turn to her father, who bent down and spoke to him in a low voice. Rodion nodded, then said to the questioner, "Boris Semyonovich Nikolayev comes to this festival because he is happy to have the opportunity to show the world and all music lovers that he is healthy, happy, and still active at his work. Therefore it is nonsense to suggest, as some have done, that he is not permitted to attend such festivals."

If her father had said that, Hedy thought, she would walk back to London.

Like the others, she raised her hand again. Rodion pointed to someone else, who asked in accented English if

Nikolayev was familiar with the music of his contemporaries in the West. The same performance was repeated on the podium, with Rodion responding that certainly Nikolayev knew such work. "There are hundreds of orchestras in the Soviet Union, and many of them play contemporary music, not only Russian but also German, French, American, and so forth. Certain parties in the West charge that we are inhospitable to what is new in the arts, but this of course is a wrong idea."

If her father had said that, Hedy thought, she would swim from London to New York.

Two more questions followed—clearly plants, like the first two—before the crowd of journalists began a restless, whispering rebellion. Finally one man stood without being called on and said, first in English and then in heavily accented Russian, that he would like to hear Boris Nikolayev answer a question in his own words. "And that question is, sir, given that your music has been attacked and denounced by your government at certain times and praised at others, I think the world would like to know how that situation has affected you and your music."

Rodion Sergeivich smiled, as if to say, you think I am afraid of such a question? You think I will not let him answer? He turned to Nikolayev, folded his arms, and waited.

So did the rest of the room. Finally the answer came. "To make connections between a composer's life and his art, that is the work of critics and of the future. It is not of interest to me. Only the music interests me."

That, Hedy thought, was her father.

Rodion Sergeivich smiled. "I may just add that in the Soviet Union we concentrate on making a better future, not on contemplating mistakes of the past."

Another voice came quickly, an American one. "Mr. Nikolayev, there has been a lot of speculation as to why you

finally joined the Communist Party. Do you consider yourself a good Communist, then, particularly in light of what
you just said, that only music interests you?"

Stupid, Hedy thought, and swore silently. If they kept
asking such questions, Rodion Sergeivich would stop the
press conference and she would lose what could be her only
chance to speak to her father. She watched Rodion's face,
on which the smile had left no trace, and her father's, still
impassive. He brushed at the hair hanging close to his eyes
and said, in Russian, "The motherland is the source of my
music. Like all good Russians, I love her."

Clever, Hedy thought. But clever enough?

"Boris Nikolayev," Rodion said in English, "is too modest to speak of the high regard in which he is held by the
Party, for the many services he had performed for his country."

"Does that include," called another voice, "signing at
least three letters condemning artists who fled to the
West?"

The room went very quiet.

"Nikolayev came here to talk of music," said Rodion, in
a hard, dry voice. "If the press is not interested in such
matters—"

Hedy leaped to her feet. "I am! I have a musical question!
Please!"

"Yes?" If Rodion recognized her from their encounter,
he gave no sign.

She couldn't ask the question that was her real goal; she
couldn't worry that if she spoke with even a hint of accent,
her cover was blown; she couldn't do anything but plunge
in with something, anything.

"You have written a lot of vocal music, Mr. Nikolayev,"
she said, "but never an opera. Have you considered various
subjects and rejected them, or does the operatic form not
interest you?"

He lifted his head to look into the back row, and something seemed to flare in his eyes, like fire darting out when
a furnace door is opened for an instant. He had recognized
her, she thought, in spite of the years and the blond hair
and the words in English. A feeling she hadn't expected
and couldn't identify washed through her, like a wave carrying so many objects that none could be discerned. Barely
able to take in what he was saying, she was aware only that
he spoke in Russian, in the living voice she remembered,
not in the flat, heavy thing that had labored through his
other answers like a tired ox. Not until Rodion Sergeivich
translated did she know what he had said: that two sources
for operatic material had intrigued him all his life, Chekhov
and Shakespeare, and that although he had actually given
some thought to *The Sea Gull,* he had never found the musical idiom that satisfied him.

Ah, Chaika, she could hear him saying, as he put down the
beautiful leather-bound volume of Chekhov and sighed.
What a marvelous creation Arkadina is, and Nina. . . .

She smiled up at him on the podium, and was almost
certain he smiled back.

Someone from a British publication asked a detailed
question about the thematic relationship between the Sixth
Symphony and one of the song cycles of the 1950s. He began
to answer, still in Russian, saying that in the fifties a certain
theme had come to his mind, which became central to
Forests of Childhood, but he had always felt there was an
expression of it still to come, particularly the passage beginning with the augmented triad. . . .

His manner, Hedy saw, was the same as it had been
during her own question. What had sparked him to life was
not the realization that he was speaking to his daughter, but
the call of music.

That, she thought, was her father.

Someone asked him another purely musical question, but

she forgot the press conference. She was standing at the
door of the tiny room where her father worked, motionless
over his score paper, eyes fixed on something she could
neither see nor imagine. A cigarette smoldered in a tray
beside him. She watched it teeter, fall off, and land on some
crumpled papers on the floor, into which it began to bite,
leaving black-rimmed holes. She knew she should be calling to Papa, but something made her wait to see if he would
notice the fire, something that made her both desperate and
angry. She prayed for Papa to look up and see the fire. If
he didn't, it would mean something important, although
she didn't know what. She found herself thinking of the
Young Pioneer they always talked about at school as a hero,
the twelve-year-old boy who informed on his own father
and even testified against him at his trial. It confused her
to be thinking of him. She flushed with guilt. Unable to
speak, she watched the black mouths in the papers widen
like laughter and begin to send up curly lines of smoke.
"Papa!" she yelled finally. He turned to her blankly. Then
realization came into his eyes, and he leaped up and
stamped out the fire. Although she must have been only
nine or ten, she had never forgotten that day. It lodged in
a permanent corner of her mind, where she could stare and
stare at it. When she grew older, she put words to it: The
surrender demanded by her father's music prevented him
from dealing properly with reality. That was the danger of
all art . . . of passion of any kind, she came to think, after
what her feeling for Alik had driven her to tell him. . . .

She saw that at the podium her father was still speaking
with some animation, apparently about the guitar concerto. "I liked the idea of using a folk instrument to express
contemporary musical ideas. The past and the future in one
work, you might say, meant to be experienced in the present. Also, we have in Russia a popular performer on the

guitar who is also an excellent classical player, and I wished to write something for him."

Rodion Sergeivich translated the words into English and then added, "An old Russian folk song is in fact the melodic basis for the first movement of the concerto. The Soviet people, you see, inspire their composers frequently."

Many hands went up again. Hedy raised hers, too, but after three more questions Rodion Sergeivich said, "Only one more, please, ladies and gentlemen. Boris Nikolayev is becoming tired."

Hedy waved her hand frantically, but Rodion pointed to someone from an Italian paper who wanted Nikolayev's opinion of the future of music.

His voice strong, his large hands gripping the edges of the podium, he said that too much contemporary music was either "sugar water" or "noise," exhibiting neither originality nor knowledge of craft. Mastery of craft was all, he said, in the blunt way Hedy had heard him express those thoughts at the dinner table; concern with the emotions, be they the composer's or the audience's, was self-indulgence. The future of music, like its past, lay with mastery of craft.

Knowing how he would embroider on that theme, and for how long, she got up and moved as unobtrusively as possible down the aisle, until she half stood, half crouched beside someone in the front row.

"Ladies and gentlemen," Rodion Sergeivich said, "Nikolayev and I thank you for coming, and we—"

"Just a minute!" Hedy cried.

Rodion looked down with his practiced smile. "Sorry, the meeting is over."

"No," she said. Then, as loudly as she could, directing her gaze and all of her being at her father, she said, "I am Hedy Lucas, an American biographer. I am writing a book on you, Mr. Nikolayev, but I've been told I can only talk to you here, at this conference. Is that true? Won't you grant me an interview?"

Her father was looking at her impassively, but there was attention within the hooded eyes, she was sure of that. Rodion Sergeivich moved close to him and whispered to him. Nikolayev's face did not change.

"The press conference is now concluded," Rodion said.

"Mr. Nikolayev," Hedy shouted, "I wish you would refuse me in your own words, in the presence of all these people."

Rodion took Nikolayev's arm, as if to lead him off.

"I've interviewed your wife in America!" Hedy cried, her last resort. "Does the Soviet Union wish me to get all my information about you from one of its defectors?"

She was aware of a slight motion behind her—as if the two KGB men had taken a step forward—but she couldn't think of them, not now. She kept her eyes, and her mind, on the podium. Nikolayev squared his shoulders and pushed away Rodion Sergeivich's arm. He looked down at her, his eyes like probes. But what did they see? The room had gone quiet again, and it seemed to Hedy that she and her father hung suspended in time.

At length he shook his head, scattering the white hair on his collar, and said—to Rodion, but loudly, so that everyone heard it—"I will speak with this lady. You will arrange it, please."

CHAPTER NINE

Anya. Could the woman have been Anya?

Stretched fully dressed on the single bed in the hotel apartment he shared with three others, Alik Markov stared at the ceiling and the question that seemed to be written there. For two days it had appeared wherever his eyes rested, whenever they and his thoughts were quiet.

The woman had been thinner than Anya, with different hair and coloring. Though he hadn't been close enough to hear individual words, he thought she had sounded like an American. But perhaps Anya would now sound that way? Certainly the age was about right, at least as much as one could tell with women who took care of themselves when they entered that smooth country between thirty and fifty; and the face, though Anya's had been much fuller, was still like hers. Something in the carriage was like Anya, too, especially when the woman had lifted her shoulders. That had frightened him—the shoulders and some intangible projection of personality that had struck him at once.

Of course, Alik thought, some people looked remarkably like others. Once, during one of his officially approved concerts, he had looked into the front row and seen a man he recognized as a cellmate from the camps—clearly the comrade, with enough flesh back on him to make him look human again. But it hadn't been the comrade after all, only someone who resembled him strongly. Probably it was the same with the woman, and she was a stranger.

How likely was it, though, that someone who happened to look like Nikolayev's daughter would show up at a festival honoring him?

And if it was she, did Boris Semyonovich know?

Alik studied the ceiling so intently that when he finally turned away, its pattern of squares left a grid on his vision. He put his hands behind his head and stared down the length of his body at his feet, which rested on the footrail, in shoes that gave him pleasure whenever he glanced at them. It had been years since he had first tasted the joys of dressing, eating, and living well, but apparently he was never going to be able to take them for granted. *Sold out for a pair of shoes,* he thought mockingly, and a scrap of melody formed in his mind, ready to become the opening phrase of a song if he wanted to encourage it.

He didn't. He looked to the other end of the room, where the watchdog-companion sat at the small table, writing in a notebook. They were alone in the apartment. The two others had gone with a group, with another "companion," to visit a Lapp museum. The watchdog had been glad to pass up that one.

The man must have felt his gaze, for he raised his eyes, looked at Alik as if he were making some difficult calculation, and said, "You are not tired, then, Aleksandr Romanovich?"

"Very tired," Alik lied. "But I keep going over the re-hearsal in my mind."

The watchdog nodded as if he understood, though as far as Alik could tell, he wasn't interested in music, or in any-thing except his notebook and his two grandchildren, whose pictures he kept in his wallet and looked at every night.

For the watchdog's benefit, Alik had propped a snapshot of Sofia against the lamp on his table. She regarded him with the earnest, intense expression that was often on her face, out of which she would burst into a tight, bright smile, like a swimmer breaking to the surface.

The woman couldn't be Anya, Alik thought. Not in Fin-land, of all places. Not now, of all times.

He closed his eyes. Whoever she was, he thought, *so be it*. He had first used those words in the camps, in the crawling hours when the fountain of songs that was the source of his being would dry into a scream, when he could no longer think or write in his head because his angers and hungers were rattling his starving body as if it, not the cell, were the prison. *So be it*, he would say to them, let it go, nothing can be done now, so accept. Ac-cept and wait. Of all the things in the world he had ever had to do, that was the hardest—forcing himself to learn patience. And the most necessary.

Whenever he had refused to accept things as they came, he had paid for it. The refusing might be as glorious as fireworks, but its glow faded as quickly, whereas the pay-ment took months or even years. Like the time in a win-dowless gray office, when a captain was asking the same questions so many times that he had wanted to stuff them back down the man's throat with his fist—"Who was at the party where you sang these uncivic songs? Where is the typewriter located on which you copied out your anti-Soviet verses?"—until finally he let it spurt out of him, like relieving a bursting bladder, and sang, right in their faces, an "uncivic" one about a bulldog who was too stupid to find his own balls. Oh sweet moment while the faces turned red. But then it was two months in a sour cell while he decided he had been as stupid as the dog.

Alik Markov had given up being stupid.

He heard a sound and turned to look between slitted lids. The watchdog sat on the edge of the opposite bed, unlacing his shoes. He put one down neatly, then the other, sighed, and swung up to stretch out. He lay as straight as Lenin in the mausoleum, hands folded on his stomach. It was nearly five o'clock; he liked a nap before he ate.

Alik lay quietly too, running his mind over that morning's rehearsal of the concerto and the tricky passage at bar thirty-seven, which Boris Semyonovich had wanted to work again and again, his head tilted back as if he were not looking at the orchestra although he saw and heard everything, one hand beating time in the air in the jerky way that was uniquely his. The concerto was brilliant, using the guitar so that it had sometimes to hold swift, ironic dialogue with brasses, at others to provide a syncopated base against which the violins agitated. The concerto juxtaposed classical effects and startling angularities—and was a devil to play. "I don't have twenty fingers, you know," Alik had said to Boris the first time he saw the score. Boris had given one of his contemptuous "humphs" and said, "Show me that you have one musical brain." After an hour of work he had looked at Alik from the sides of his great hooded eyes and said, "You will do it. You must do it."

A strange man, Boris. If his music came straight from the soul—and all true music did—it was the only thing that did. All else came wrapped in bitter humor or self-deprecation or a yawning pretense of indifference, which perhaps was not always a pretense, so that to come to know Boris, one had to translate him: That kind of sigh means disgust, that look in the eye signals true interest, and so on. He was not quite the same man Alik had first met through Anya; but who had stayed the same? At that time Boris had seemed aloof, though warm and protective to his daughter. Of course Alik had been so awed by the genius that he had had little to say to the man. Years later, when he decided to try renewing the acquaintance, the aloofness had grown thick and hard: a wall of glass through which Boris could be seen but not understood unless one allowed for refraction. Approaching Boris hadn't been easy. He would open his apartment door, stare, then slam the door into its frame like the cymbal in his Third Symphony. But Alik kept returning. One day Boris stared, then sighed and walked back into the apartment with the door left open. Their first conversations had been about Boris's music. Then they talked about Alik's, and finally, briefly, about the two women who were gone. Several years later, when Alik said he was going to marry, Boris had blinked and rumbled and patted his shoulder and offered his good wishes. Translation: I understand, but must you do it?

Answer, never spoken: Yes, I must.

Alik opened his eyes again and saw the ceiling. Could the woman be Anya?

After a while he heard a noise and turned his head. The noise came from the watchdog's open mouth, a soft bee-buzzing of sleep that made Alik think, incongruously, of being in the pines near the dacha.

Quietly he sat up. No reaction from the watchdog. He ran both hands through his hair and stood up. No reaction. He patted his pockets and looked around the room as if counting its contents, then moved toward the door slowly, freezing into a statue after each foot of progress, reaching out once to take his guitar case from a chair. When he turned the lock on the door, it gave a little snick, like a laugh cut off before it started. He moved on without stopping, to the elevator. As if expecting him, its doors opened, like arms. The person stepping off was a stranger who paid him no attention.

When he walked out into the lobby, he shifted the guitar and stopped to look around for a moment.

The woman was standing at the desk.

He looked toward the lobby doors and the sun shining on the world beyond them.

He moved toward the desk and the woman.

She was talking to the same American man as before, smiling, her face angled up to his. Slowly Alik moved closer. He heard her say, "I can't thank you enough. But what made you change your mind?"

Anya's voice, so American?

The man laughed and said something about his . . . conscience—was that the word?—and wanting to help the press.

The woman moved her head slightly, and the motion, which let the soft pad of an earlobe show beneath her hair, pierced Alik with certainty, although he didn't know why, for there had been nothing special about Anya's ears. In fact he couldn't remember them at all, so there was no reason for one little oval of flesh to make him know it was she. But it was, and he knew it. Thin and blond and American, but Anya.

She turned and saw him. And turned away again.

"OK," the American man said to her, "I'll go upstairs and start packing."

"Yes," she said. "We may as well do it right away."

The man walked toward the elevator.

She started toward the lobby doors. Without planning it, Alik was beside her. He said her name, softly.

She stopped. "My name is not Anya," she said. She didn't turn to look at him when she spoke.

"Do you think I wouldn't know you?" he said in Russian.

She stood in profile to him, not moving except for the blue sweater that rose and fell with her breathing, which was too rapid.

"I don't mean to upset you," he said, still in Russian. "If you can't speak to me, tell me to stop bothering you and go away."

The muscles around her eyes seemed to shiver. She turned to him and said in English, "You must have mistaken me for someone else. My name is Hedy Lucas. I'm sorry."

"Why are you sorry?"

"Because . . . because I have to go now." But she didn't move.

Behind him he heard a voice, flat yet breathless. "Aleksandr Romanovich! Aleksandr Romanovich!" It was the watchdog, his hair pushed into little spears by the pillow, his face askew with urgency.

In English, to Anya, loud enough for the watchdog to hear, Alik said, "I am afraid I cannot be interviewed, as you request."

The watchdog was beside them now.

"Oh," Anya said. "Well . . . I am sorry. Good-bye, then." She gave Alik the smile of a stranger and walked away toward the door.

He watched her push it open and step out into the sun, and the world.

So be it, he thought, *so be it*. But it was hard to let go.

At least he had learned who she was. If there had been a shadow of doubt, it would have been dispelled by the quick way she had adjusted to the story he was telling the watchdog. She had understood the need for it and known what to do. She was Russian. She was Anya.

"Who was that woman?" the watchdog asked.

"An American reporter, I think. She wanted to interview me."

"Why? Does she know who you are?"

Alik shrugged, to gain a moment; was it safer to say that she knew who he was, or not? "I think she just guessed that I'm one of the musicians," he said, hefting his guitar case.

"I remind you, Aleksandr Romanovich, of the proper behavior of a Soviet citizen, who does not seek contact with citizens of imperialist countries."

"Have I not just told you, Alexei Grigorevich, that I did not initiate the contact? Members of the bourgeois press, as you know, are very aggressive."

The watchdog patted his hair down with one hand. "You did not say that you wished to go out."

"I didn't want to disturb you," Alik said, playing out the stupid fiction that he had the man as a companion by choice.

"And you have your guitar with you?"

"I felt like playing. I wanted to find a room down here that I could use."

"It does not disturb me if you play in the room. For me it is an honor to listen."

Really? Why don't I shove it up your ass and play us a tune? The words were so near the surface that Alik had to cough to keep them in.

"Ah!" The watchdog's eyes had gone to the door. "Here are our friends."

Alik turned and saw a group of orchestra musicians entering the lobby, including the two others quartered with him and the watchdog. "I'm going back upstairs," he said abruptly. At eight o'clock was a concert in which a magnificent Finnish baritone would sing the Brahms *Schöne Magelone.* Until then, Alik thought, he would lie on his bed and wait. Patiently.

. . .

Hedy hung the last of her things in the new closet.

The room was similar to the one at the other hotel: airy and clean, with birch chairs and bright fabrics, these in an orange, red, and yellow design. The main difference was a cool view of a grassy courtyard. Ray Salmi's call had surprised her: "Is that my friend the lady writer? Say, I been thinking it over. Decided to change hotels with you after all. If you still want to."

She had hesitated. If he wasn't just a good Samaritan, the delay could mean he'd had to check with someone for orders. Then, once in the room, fear had stabbed her—the delay had been needed to install bugging devices. For an hour she had gone over the room carefully but frantically, doing everything she could recall from spy stories—thank God for them: checking behind pictures, unscrewing anything hollow, even managing to take off the base of the phone. She had found nothing. For whatever that was worth.

It might have been a mistake to switch hotels, she thought, but she had had to do it. Rodion Sergeivich had not yet given her the interview, even though a room full of journalists had heard her father request it, and not honoring it would be asking for trouble. She had been twice to the press office and the blond Finnish woman with no result except learning the woman's name, Aini: "I am sorry, no message was left for you by the Russian gentleman. Yes, I will ask him when he next comes in." Now that she was in the hotel, Hedy thought, she could sit in the lobby and catch Rodion going in or out. Or even her father.

Or Alik.

Alik knew her.

He had spoken to her, his voice exactly the same. She had clutched her purse so tightly that the leather probably still bore nail marks: to admit or not to admit that she was

Anya? To ask Alik's help in getting to her father, and risk his reporting it all to Cousin Rodion?

To trust him again, or not?

That decision, still to be made, had been postponed when the man rushed up—obviously someone who worked for the security organs. Alik was under constant watch; that was normal. Would she be watched now, too, because Alik had spoken to her? Add that conversation to her behavior at the end of the press conference and her wish to change hotels, if indeed Salmi had reported it. . . . They could very well be suspicious of her.

She shut the closet and turned back into the room, feeling a strong need to talk to Jess, knowing why she felt it. Her watch read seven P.M. Washington was seven hours earlier. America was so far away it was already in the past. Would she ever live in the present again, let alone the future?

She walked to the phone and placed a call to Jess's office.

Waiting for the hotel operator to ring back, she thought of her inconsistency: For someone so impatient with the past, she had chosen a career that meant she was always exploring it. Of course the past in her books was other people's, or had been until now. Would she let the world know that the biography of Boris Nikolayev was written by his daughter—or would she keep her identity secret even in the book? That was a question she couldn't answer, not yet.

An odd thought crawled into her mind, like a strange child poking through a hedge: If only she could write the book as a novel. She blinked in surprise. If she wanted to write fiction, her father's biography wasn't the place to begin. In any case, literature was not her calling. Once Jess had asked her why she didn't try it. He seemed to think her fascination with language and imagery would lead her in that direction. Answering him, she had groped to say that biography and fiction had a lot in common. Both portrayed people and their actions—except in one you used your imagination to create them, and in the other, to decipher them. "If they're so close," he had said, "why not write novels too?" She had had no answer at the time—the question hadn't needed one—but now an answer came, so incongruous that it made her blink in surprise and then almost laugh: She wrote biographies because being a biographer was . . . safe.

Safe? When it had brought her to a country bordering on Russia? When she had to search her room for bugs and wonder if the KGB was on to her?

The phone rang. Her party in Washington was not in his office. Would she speak with someone else at the number?

"No, thank you," she said, and after she had hung up, "Dammit, Jess, where are you? Why are you leaving me here alone with my father and . . . and . . ." She sat on the edge of the bed, staring at the hands folded in her lap as if someone else had dropped them there. *Think of something else. Anything. What are the most beautiful words in the English language? Fresh, luminous, tranquil . . .*

Hedy lifted the phone again and gave the operator her mother's number, even though they had spoken the night before. She had talked as if she were just a biographer in pursuit of her subject; the word "father" wasn't to be used in their calls, so she had simply reported seeing Nikolayev at a press conference.

In truth, it was easier to say "Nikolayev" than "father," for it had been a long time since she had felt much like a daughter.

She blinked, aware that she had never put that thought into words. Her mother's presence wouldn't allow it. Now, thousands of miles away, her mother's perspective was no longer binding. She pushed her bare feet farther into the colorful throw rug and lay back on the bed. It was always "your papa" and "your father and I," but in truth Hedy had had no sense for years of the three of them as a family, a unit—or, for that matter, of her parents as a pair.

Even as a child, she remembered, she had puzzled over how they came together. How had her mother, the bright butterfly, been caught in her father's dark net? Only gradually had she learned, and accepted, that it was the butterfly who had had the net.

The phone rang. She sat upright so fast she saw stars.

It was Aini from the press office. "Is that Hedy Lucas? I have spoken finally to Rodion Orlov, who says you will have an interview with Nikolayev tomorrow, for one hour. No tape recording allowed. At noon you will be at the desk of your hotel. Someone will come to fetch you. This is agreeable, I hope?"

Two final stars sailed across Hedy's vision. "Yes. Absolutely. How did you manage it?"

"It is only my job. However, I spoke to Rodion Orlov about your request at a time when several other Western journalists were standing close by."

Hedy laughed. "Thanks. Will you let me buy you lunch or dinner?"

"If I can find a free time."

"I'll drop by and make sure you do."

As soon as Hedy hung up, the phone rang again. She answered with an upbeat still in her voice.

"Hedy, is that you? All the way over in Finland?"

It took her an instant to place the voice. "Dorothy? What's wrong? Why are you calling me? Is something the matter with Mama?"

"No, she's fine. I mean, she's . . . I'm getting our lunch ready. And I'm not calling you. Aren't you're calling me? Calling your mother, I mean?" The bewilderment carried across the Atlantic.

Hedy began to laugh.

"What's so funny?" Dorothy asked, but she began to laugh too, until Vera apparently said something that made her stop. "Hedy, your mother says you can't afford to laugh. I mean, you can't afford to waste your money laughing all the way from Finland. I mean . . . oh, I'm putting your mother on. Good-bye!"

"Dorothy," Hedy said, "don't ever change."

"But . . . why on earth would I?"

"I don't know. Just don't."

"I promise," Dorothy said. "Here's your mother."

And in a moment, as clear as if she were only across town, so that the little tremor in her voice had a darker cause than distance: the familiar "Hello, my darling girl! Are you all right?"

"Fine, Mama. I have a new phone number to give you. I've switched to a different hotel."

"Why? Something is wrong?"

"It'll be easier to get the interviews I want, that's all." Hedy decided not to mention the call she'd just received—not until the interview was over.

Vera took the new number. "I'm glad you called because I didn't ask yesterday, have you seen Kim Wan Lee?"

"Not yet."

"You will give my regards to him and his family? And tell him to remember his bow arm."

"I will, Mama. I miss you, and I love you."

"You are the best daughter in the world, I have always said it. Now, tell me, who has given you a fortune, that you can make these telephone calls?"

Boris Nikolayev looked up from the chair beside his bed, where he had been sitting for some time, making occasional music notations in his notebook. "Yes?" he said, impatience thickening his voice. "What is it?"

Rodion Orlov stood in the doorway to the combined

kitchen and living area that separated the two bedrooms in their suite. "I remind you that the woman will be here soon."

"What woman?"

"The American author you demanded should have an interview—in spite of your opinion that the bourgeois press are jackals."

"If one never sees the jackal, one forgets his bite." Boris lifted his head, stared intently upward for a moment, then said, "She is coming here?"

"Didn't you ask not to leave these rooms again for any reason except your festival appearances? You see how I accede to your wishes."

"Such as my wish not to appear at that press conference."

"Unfortunately your presence there was required by the Ministry."

Without sarcasm, as if he were simply stating a fact, Boris said, "Surely you are able to influence the Ministry's requirements."

"Only," Rodion said, "because I know which ones not to argue with."

Boris shrugged and turned away.

"When the woman arrives," Rodin said, "I'll call you. Unless you prefer not to see her after all."

"Call me." Their eyes locked briefly in the familiar, unacknowledged combat before Boris bent again to his notebook.

Rodion looked for a moment at the top of Boris's head, where hints of scalp had begun to show through the white hair. Then he left, closing the door behind him. In the kitchenette, he made sure that all food and vodka were stored in the cupboards and the small refrigerator. In the living room area, he adjusted a chair so it was nearly at a right angle to the small sofa. He picked a scrap of paper from the floor and a speck of lint from the cuff of his jacket. As if it had been timed to coincide with the completion of those motions, a knock came at the main door of the suite. Rodion opened it, nodded to dismiss the aide who escorted the woman, and motioned her in.

"Good afternoon, Mr. Orlov." She walked into the center of the room and stood there.

Rodion looked at her steadily but with no expression, an approach he often used, his gaze moving from her face to her brown linen jacket and skirt, to her sandals, back to her eyes. She did not appear to react. "You are a persistent woman, Miss Hedy Lucas," he said.

"Thank you."

"You think I pay you a compliment?"

"Didn't you?"

Rodion let ten seconds pass before he smiled. "I understand you have moved from your hotel to this one."

"Yes. I prefer this location."

"You will please take a seat over there." Rodion gestured to the chair he had arranged and sat across from her. In Russian he said, "We wish to know why you interest yourself in Boris Nikolayev."

She put her purse on the lamp table beside her. "I'm sorry, I don't speak Russian."

"No? Knowledge of Russian would, I think, be important in your case."

"Perhaps I will start to study it when I get back to America."

"Ah. But for now I must act as translator?"

"Boris Nikolayev speaks English."

"Yes, but there will be some difficulties for him." Rodion crossed one leg neatly over the other. "You have written about a British family of authors, a Spanish poet, and the Frenchwoman who chose to call herself George Sand. Yes, do not be surprised; we inform ourselves of such matters.

But those persons are dead. Why do you wish now to write about a living artist?"

The woman took a notebook and pen from her purse. "I thought I was coming to do an interview, Mr. Orlov, not to be the subject of one. But I'll answer your question. I write about artists whose work I admire. The fact that Boris Nikolayev is still alive is irrelevant to my decision, since I never expected to be able to speak to him."

Rodion sat looking at her as before, without expression. "How odd that you, an American, can find no American artists who are worthy subjects."

The woman opened her mouth, closed it, then said, "I don't choose my subjects by national origin. I choose them by—"

The door to Boris's room opened, and he stood in the doorway, nearly filling it. Rodion went to him and led him to the small sofa, on which he sank heavily, the flesh of his face and neck quivering slightly with aftershock.

The woman had risen. Slowly she said, "It is a very great honor to meet you, Maestro."

Boris waved a hand in dismissal. "Sit. Please. I like to know who you are. Why you are wishing to write book about me."

"I write biographies of artists," she said. "You are an artist, a great one. And no biography of you has been done in the West."

Boris frowned. "You like to be first?"

"Yes, but . . . That's not really the reason. I admire your music."

"Why?" he said.

"Because it's . . . I think your influence is . . ." The woman took a breath. "No one else sounds like you or has your kind of musical ideas. You are original. I admire originality above everything."

"You are musician?"

"No, but there has always been music in my life. My fam— I grew up with music."

There was silence. "Boris Nikolayev would like to know," Rodion said, "why you imagine yourself qualified to write of him and his music." Boris narrowed his eyes but said nothing.

"I don't believe that I—" The woman stopped, began again. "I am a professional writer and, though not a professional musician, someone who loves music deeply and has studied it. I am, for example, very familiar with Russian music and its history. In addition, for the specifically musical parts of my book, I will be advised by professional musicians."

Boris leaned forward. "What questions?"

It was not possible to do, yet it had to be done: Looking politely at Papa's face, where age had settled like the weights that hold down a curtain, as if she didn't know that he hated to shave those cheeks and that they smelled, for some reason, faintly of yeast. *I know you trained at the Moscow Conservatory, Maestro; how were you influenced by your professors there?* Listening to the voice halt and stumble in English as if she didn't know how it could splash and roar in Russian. *I'm interested in your awareness of music as a child; do you recall when and how you knew that it would become your life?* Watching his eyes, sunk more deeply now, as if she had never watched their erratic cycle of absorption, irritation, fear, and love. *We all know your* War Choruses, *Maestro; could you tell me where you were during the war?* Turning occasionally to smile at Rodion Sergeivich, as if there were no claws of fear digging at her with every move of his hands, to which they seemed to be paired.

Remember the goal, she told herself: to find a way to let him know who she was, or to get some signal that he knew it.

Concentrate on the list, she told herself: just keep going down the list of questions in the notebook. She had spent much of the night and all the morning writing them out, trying to wipe from her mind everything she knew about him and to consider what a stranger would need to ask. It would be like acting, she had thought—and wondered if it was true that actors chose their profession in order to escape their identities. Or was it to be able to look on themselves like disembodied spirits? Now the scenery and the audience were real, and it was like nothing she had imagined.

Maestro, how, if at all, do you think you have been influenced by The Five? By Tchaikovsky? Stravinsky?

While he gave answers she already knew but found odd to hear in English—"At conservatory I have marvelous composition professor, very old, very musical man"— while he took time to remember, to frown, to collect his thoughts, like anyone else she had interviewed—"Stravinsky influence everyone. All who write music after him have Stravinsky sound in ear. He visit Soviet Union before his death and we speak of music"—while he struggled to say the difficult English word *rhythm,* she felt herself wishing more and more strongly for him to say that he knew who she was, to call her Anna, even as she worked to contain her fear that he would do just that. The wish and the fear grew together, making her a neutral site for their struggle, forcing her to appease first one, then the other.

She recalled her goal and thought, Ask about the West, draw his mind to the West. *I assume you have heard records of Western conductors performing your music. I'd like your reactions to some of their interpretations.* No, that was not good. Rodion Sergeivich's long fingers were busy; he was ready to interrupt unless. . . . *Maestro, you said in your statement at the press conference that the Soviet people are the inspiration for your work. Could you explain what you mean by that?* Surprisingly, that made him shake his head and then, as if shaking off the burden of English, burst into Russian, through which she had to sit impassively until Rodion translated: "Boris Nikolayev explains that he deeply loves the Soviet people. He compares their courage and their . . . their solidity to forests he knew as a boy. To tall, strong trees where he used to walk and to find, ah, refuge. Boris Nikolayev feels that his music comes from the soil of the Soviet Union, and from the soul of the people." It was a reasonably accurate, if condensed, translation.

Her father was looking at Rodion. Silent, as she had so often seen him in Rodion's presence. A wax-museum figure trained either to speak or to let Rodion speak for him, as needed. What tied him to Rodion?

Why didn't he give a sign that he knew who she was? Or, after what she had shouted to him in the press conference, why hadn't he asked about Mama? Was it possible that he didn't recognize her, that he could sit beside his own daughter for nearly an hour and take her for a stranger? She bit her lip because the urge to shout "Papa" was so strong—as strong as her fear of shouting it. Between them she was paralyzed: her face as it had used to be in Russia, unable to reveal her thoughts or express her desires, the face of a wax figure in a State museum. *I am an American citizen,* she thought. *I am an American citizen.*

She released her lip, looked at her father the maestro, and said carefully, "As I told you, I have spoken to your wife."

Rodion leaned forward—only a small motion, but it made her think of the cocking of a gun.

Papa-Maestro did not move, but something in his eyes turned over. "She is alive?"

"Yes. I have had several conversations with her about your music and your life together."

Rodion got to his feet in one smooth motion. "Boris Nikolayev has no wish to speak of a defector. You are insulting him to mention such a person. In any event, the time allowed for this interview has been exceeded."

"No insult." Boris raised a hand so imperiously that Rodion stepped back. The two men looked at each other, their gaze like shields that met and were immobilized by the equal pressures behind them.

At length Rodion shrugged and folded his arms.

"Vera Andreyevna," Boris said softly. He looked again at Hedy. "She knows you come to see me?"

"I told her I was going to try."

"She is . . . playing violin?"

"No. Not anymore."

There was silence. *Ask about your daughter,* Hedy thought, begging him, *your daughter.* Rodion looked at her as if he could hear the words.

Boris pushed the white hair off his forehead. "Please, where is she?"

"Under the circumstances, she asked me not to say where she is living."

Boris nodded and sighed. "She is well?"

"No. She's . . . she has cancer."

He didn't seem to know the word. "She will die?"

"I'm afraid so."

There was a long silence. Rodion's hands moved as if he wished to break it, but he didn't speak.

"I wish also to hear of my daughter," Boris said. "You see my daughter?"

No words would come properly. Hedy lifted her head and nodded slowly, fixing her eyes on Papa-Maestro's, willing him to know who she was.

He nodded too, as slowly as she had, and sank back against the sofa.

"Boris Nikolayev is tired," Rodion said. "The interview was too long."

"Yes. Tired."

"I'm not finished!" Hedy said. "I have more questions— many questions."

"I am sorry," Rodion said, not even bothering to sound as if he meant it.

"Maestro!" she cried to her father. "I must talk to you again, please!" But he seemed as oblivious of her as if he were composing and she were a child in the doorway of his workroom.

"Miss Hedy Lucas," Rodion said, "I must now ask you to leave."

"Not until I have another appointment. I haven't asked about . . . about the film scores or his method of working or . . . There must be another interview. There must!" Hedy heard her voice heading toward hysteria and forced it back. "Don't you want the truth about the maestro to be known in the West? I won't mention his family again. I swear it."

A smile grew slowly on Rodion's cold, official stare, like a worm uncurling on a stone. Was it a taunt to Nikolayev's daughter? Or an attempt at politeness to an American writer? Hedy hung between the possibilities, watching his lips, unable to move.

"Very well," Rodion said. "We will allow another interview. You will be advised."

She was able to nod, but not to decide what the smile had meant.

CHAPTER TEN

Low in the sky, the sun slanted into the parklike courtyard and laced through its trees. Across the intent faces of
the violinist and pianist, shadow-patterns seemed to move
in rhythm with the Brahms sonata. It was nine-thirty at
night; the air was cool and crisp and the sunlight a musky
dark gold—the color of the music, which moved in liquid
swells. The light, the trees, the music, the faces and hands
of the two musicians—all were joined. No clear boundaries
seemed to separate the art, the artists, and the setting.

When the final notes sounded, there was a long intake of
breath from the listeners, the players, and the wind, before
the first pairs of hands ignited the applause.

On the small stage, Kim Wan Lee and his colleague
began to bow, faces emerging from the spell and the effort
of the music and breaking into wide smiles. Loath to return
from the place the music had taken her, Hedy finally had

to accept the end of the journey and release her breath. She joined in the applause, pounding her hands together so long and hard that they felt hot. All around her, she saw other faces holding her own feeling, and marveled at music's capacity to weld the deepest individual response into a common experience, to lift everyone, by its abstract nature, above the divisiveness of particular experience and specific idea. Atheist and priest could both love Brahms. Or, wretched thought, tyrant and victim.

It was the third night of the festival and Kim Wan Lee's first appearance. The crowd, eager to see and hear a man heralded as one of the next world-class violinists, had gathered early and spread beyond the courtyard. Coming in, Hedy had spotted Rodion Orlov in one of the front rows—he had been particularly fond of the violin, she recalled—but her father wasn't there, which made her feel an obscure relief. She glanced over at Orlov and saw that he was applauding as enthusiastically as she.

All right, so Orlov knew and loved music. Presumably that fact was part of what kept her father tied to him. Another part was being the son of her father's school friend. But those two factors still weren't enough. There was something else, but it had always eluded her.

Did Orlov know who she was? That was eluding her too. She had gone back and forth between yes and no so often she was dizzy.

The crowd in the courtyard was rising and moving for intermission, faces releasing the stamp of their common experience, individuating again. One of the Nikolayev sonatas would be on the second half of the program, the first piece of her father's music that Hedy would be hearing at the festival. She had hesitated before coming, not quite sure why, then giving in to the lure of the Brahms and the chance to try to speak to Kim Wan Lee after the concert.

That morning she had vowed to forget her mission and
to focus on the festival. Not only would such behavior look
normal, but absorption in music for a day would make her
function better by clearing her mind and spirit. It hadn't
quite worked out that way, with her father's name appearing on every poster everywhere and her vision snagged by
anyone whose demeanor hinted, even remotely, of surveillance. Still, she had gone to hear three different Brahms
works, trying in the hours between them to behave and
think like a tourist.

She had tried the lavish spread the Finns called
voileipapoyta, "bread and butter table," eaten more of their
wild mushroom relishes than seemed possible or safe, and
sampled cloudberry liqueur. She had wandered the streets,
enjoying the spectacle of a whole town concentrated on
music: instrument cases being carted along the streets, festival programs poking from pockets, restaurants ringing with
discussions of performers and performances in languages
from French to Japanese. Even the bracing life in the air
seemed to come as much from sound reverberations as from
nature. As the newest addition to Finland's summer full of
arts, the festival seemed on its way to being a success. Odd
that Finland, with all its wilderness, should become a summer arts capital. But perhaps not. After all, two of the great
springs that feed the soul are art and nature.

The crowd was taking its seats again. Hedy saw Orlov
come in, chatting with someone she didn't recognize. Resolutely, she turned away from him and saw a man looking
at her, a solid man in a gray suit. KGB, she was sure. His
gaze shifted as soon as hers met it. Tiny buds of fear rose
on her arms. She made herself pick up her program, calmly.
Sonata for Violin and Piano, Opus 63. "Composed in the
summer of 1954, at Nikolayev's country home," read the
notes, "the second of his three violin sonatas is perhaps
the most melodious, incorporating into its dark sonori-

ties the strains of several old Russian folk songs. Nikolayev has used such materials throughout his career, but in ways that . . ."

She put down the program and looked up at the nightless night sky. From somewhere, she heard a snatch of the opening theme; Kim Wan Lee warming up. Except the notes weren't produced by bow and strings, they came from a throat. Papa's. Papa singing them, at the dacha. Papa in a grand mood, carrying her around on his shoulders, singing loud enough "to teach the birds," he would say, gripping her hands, which gripped his neck, bouncing her up and down as he walked so that her braids flapped like wings. Papa breathing deeply as soon as they arrived, as if he would suck in not just the air but the trees and the sky. Papa coming out to the yard where she sat making mud pies, squatting beside her and putting his big hands into the earth, saying, "Good Russian soil. Where my music comes from," and then roaring with laughter when she gathered a handful and held it to her ear. Papa sitting on the porch, holding her in his lap and reading her a tale from Tolstoy: about Sergei, who for his birthday got a cage for trapping birds and caught a little finch, whose heart beat so fast. On the third day Sergei forgot to feed it. When he went to do so and to clean its cage, he left the door open. The finch flew out, to the window and freedom. But the window was closed; the bird struck the glass and was hurt. Though Sergei tended it, it died in the night. When Papa read the last line, it hung shivering in her mind: "After that Sergei never again wanted to trap birds."

She heard applause all around her. Kim Wan Lee and the pianist were coming back onto the small stage. Feeling her whole body tense, she got to her feet.

Minutes later she was on the street, not quite sure how she had got there or why it had been so imperative to leave, to avoid the music.

It was less than half a mile to her hotel. She walked home slowly, in the dark gold light.

Something woke her; she didn't know what.

She sat up in the bed and tried to pull her hands through her hair but was stopped by the wig. Though it was uncomfortable to sleep in, doing so made her feel safer. Her nightgown was pulled to one side. She adjusted it, stared into the artificial gloom created by the drawn curtains, and turned on the bed lamp. Everything was as it should be, including the chain on the door.

She knew no one had come in while she was at the concert. Before leaving for any length of time, she put a wet hair across the door and arranged clothes and papers so she could tell if they had been moved (spy novels to the rescue once more). She turned off the light, swung out of bed, opened the curtains, and was looking out at the sun, shining in the moon's place, when she heard something again.

A small noise at the door, between a knock and a scratch.

She put her hands over her heart, which seemed ready to leap into them. After three breaths, she got her robe and pulled it on. At the door she stood willing the noise not to come again.

It came.

"Who is it?" she said, so faintly she had to repeat it.

The answer was faint too. "Alik."

"No," she said.

A whisper: "Yes."

She took another breath. Trying to sound puzzled, she said, "Who are you?"

"I must speak with you. Please."

Twenty years went by. She undid the chain and opened the door.

He came in, closed the door behind him, and leaned against it with his arms folded. He was wearing jeans and

a dark red sweater that made her realize there were shards
of gray in his hair, which was still thick and wiry. She
knew exactly how it would feel.

"I don't know you," she said. "Why are you bothering
me?"

His smile was pitying. "I first saw you at Lidiya's. You
wore a white sweater. I sang songs from the camps. I
thought, Who is this girl who always watches me? The next
day I thought, Why am I always thinking about her?"

"I told you, you're mistaking me for someone else."

"Why do you tell me in Russian, then?"

She was angry at herself. Then she sighed, and forgot to
be angry, and stood and looked at him, letting her eyes
abandon the pretense that he was a stranger. He didn't
move, but after a time something in him seemed to open
itself, like the wings of a large bird. Soon he was going to
come toward her and put his hands on her bare arms, she
knew it, and knew exactly how it would feel. If she didn't
stop it.

Coolly she said, "All right, I give up. How are you,
Alik?"

His face changed, settling back not into age but into the
subtly different planes that had struck her when she saw
him first, in the lobby. He walked to one of the birch chairs,
sat, and put his hands behind his head. "I am fine," he said
in a plummy, hearty voice. "Thank you, Lenin, for that."

That voice had used to make her laugh. So had the
changes he would ring on the endless sloganeering about
Lenin. "What shall I ask you, then, Alik?" she said. "What
you've been doing?"

"Working to turn Moscow into a model Communist city!
Working to increase wheat production according to the
next five-year plan! Supporting the peace-loving Leninist
foreign policy of the Soviet Union!"

"I gather the slogans haven't changed."

"May the deeds of Great Lenin live forever!"

He looked as if he drank too much, she thought. And as if there weren't enough vodka in the world to soothe him. "Did you always sound so bitter?" she asked, more of herself than of him.

"I don't know." He brought his hands down, and his tone returned to its normal rasp. "Did I?"

"I don't . . . remember you that way."

"So, you do remember?"

To answer would be to say everything. She said nothing.

A breeze came through the window like a lazy scarf and fluttered over her. She realized she was still standing and moved toward a chair, but the bed caught her eye, unmade, the space between the sheets as secret and inviting as a cave. She pulled up the spread and sat on the edge. When she looked down at her feet, they seemed very white and naked.

"Are you here to see your father?" Alik asked.

She lifted her gaze. "Papa doesn't know who I am."

Alik raised both eyebrows.

"I mean, I haven't told him—or anyone—who I am. I'm here just as a writer. Who wants to interview Boris Nikolayev."

"So you did become a writer."

"Yes."

"And an American citizen?"

"Yes."

"Ah." Something—the strange light, or the deep color of his sweater—turned his eyes from blue-green into the color of fire opals. "Is it . . . as you expected?" he said. "America?"

"Not exactly. Some things can't be imagined."

"Better, then?"

"Some things. Not all."

He nodded. "Was it hard to adjust?"

"Yes," she said truthfully. "But wonderful, too."

"Tell me how it seemed at first. What struck you the most."

She made an effort. "How full of color everything was—the clothes, the shops, the streets. How beautiful the city was, New York, but at the same time how dirty." Her words sounded as hollow as stones dropping into a bucket.

"So, you went to New York City."

"I'm still there. I live there. Are you in Moscow?"

"A three-room apartment on Alexei Tolstoy. And a dacha. And a car to go between them." He said it mockingly but angrily, as if daring her to ask how he had acquired the taste for such things. Or what kind of man he had become.

"You are married," she said quietly.

"My wife Sofia is a painter. What else?"

"What do you mean?"

"What else about America? The shops, the food? Of course," he added, using the old ritualistic phrases, "in Russia we have everything. And ours is best."

Was he expecting her to laugh? "Things came in so many kinds," she said, "that sometimes in the supermarket I'd just stop and stand with my shopping cart and feel overwhelmed. Fruits and vegetables and beef . . . and something called peanut butter. Peanuts ground into a sort of paste. You spread it on bread, and it's . . ." Suddenly it came on her like a fever, the full awareness that she was talking to Alik. Two events were defying reality: The sun was shining in the middle of the night and she was talking to Alik. And not saying the things she had wanted to say for so many years. Talking about peanut butter. The craziness of it bubbled up, threatening to become laughter. But the laugh died, for she remembered so well that chronic hunger for material things—a hunger she had heard derided by people who had never known it; who were not able or willing to understand the draining of energy and spirit required by the constant hunt for material things, or the precious gift of time that material comfort provided.

Alik was looking at her quizzically. She knotted her hands and said, "It was the things that *weren't* there, too. The internal passports, the work passes, the permits. The checkpoints when you took a drive of any length. And Lenin. Sometimes I would forget for a moment and find myself expecting to see him, but he was never there. No pictures, no statues, no posters. Nothing."

"Ah," Alik said again, the syllable grating in his throat.

"And I couldn't believe the newspapers, the radio and TV, the books. They told everything. I wanted to get drunk on learning things, learning the truth of them. I must have read without stopping for the first six months."

Alik folded his arms again, shoulders bulking large in the dark red sweater. "We are also well informed, you know." He was using the plummy voice again. "*Pravda* had a story on your party when the Statue of Liberty was one hundred years old. A highly commercial celebration. Freedom in America is the freedom to sell and be sold."

What did he want to hear, she wondered—that freedom was not as wonderful as he had believed? Why was he was so defensive? *Was* he defensive? "When did they tell you about Chernobyl?" she asked.

He didn't answer, only shrugged, as if bored.

"I have one of your records," she said. "I found it in a store in New York. 'Birches' was the only song I knew."

He stared at her.

"Didn't you know that one of your records was being sold in the West?"

"Yes. But I . . . that you would go into a store and find it . . ." He lifted his hands, dropped them to his thighs. "As you said, some things can't be imagined." Suddenly his face was just as she remembered it. There was no difference at all.

"Alik . . ."

"Yes?"

In one moment, she thought, if she didn't stop herself, she would get up and go to him; she would take that face in her hands and taste the mouth. If she didn't stop herself. "Did you betray my father to Rodion Sergeivich?" She made the question ring in her mind so loudly that for a moment she thought she had actually asked it. But he was still looking at her, in the way that made it imperative not to get up. She closed her hands over the edge of the bed. "It was dangerous for you to come to this room."

"Oh, yes," Alik said softly.

"I mean, dangerous to elude your watchdog."

"The man sleeps soundly, especially if you drink a little vodka with him before bedtime. And he knows I can't get out because the lobby doors are locked for the night." With no change in his tone, Alik asked, "Are you married?"

"No. But I'm . . . with someone." She tried to visualize Jess, but when she did, his face was like Alik's. She tried to see the twins, her mother, the *babushki*, her publisher; but her memory was a black hole down which everything had vanished except the man sitting in a birch chair across the room from her.

"Who is the someone?" he asked. "What does he do?"

"He's . . . a member of the government. Of Congress. A representative from the state of New York."

Alik's eyes glittered. "A member of the militaristic, imperialist government. I thought you would be with a poet or a musician."

"With someone like you—is that what you mean?"

For the first time since he had come in, he looked surprised. "I wasn't thinking that."

Suddenly she was angry with him, furious without knowing why, except that she wanted him to be exactly the same and he wasn't. She couldn't know what had happened

to him in twenty years, even if he told her. She wanted to
have back the sense that they could talk *po dusham*, soul to
soul, that she could trust him with anything, but the sense
was gone, unrecapturable. So then why should the other
have remained—the desire to lay the full length of her body
against his and forget everything else?

She pushed her naked feet hard into the bright throw
rug.

"When did you change your hair?" Alik said. "The color
was beautiful. A perfect match for your eyes."

"It's not . . . I changed it a while ago."

"For him?"

"Who?"

"The someone."

"No. I wanted a change, that's all."

"Tell me about your writing, will you?"

She lifted her shoulders. "I've done biographies, three of
them. One on the Spanish poet Garcia Lorca, one on
George Sand." She hesitated. "The first one was on the
Brontës."

She was sitting with him on the bed in his corner, resting
her chin on his shoulder, breathing in the smell of him
while they read one of the books in English she had
brought from home; helping him because his English was
self-taught, studied while he was in the camps, but hers had
come from school; trying to say the strange names, like
"Eyre" and "Thornfield" and "Rochester"; stopping to discuss the dreadful treatment the heroine had to surmount,
or the author's having to hide that she was a woman—did
no society let a writer just *be?*—or to let their mouths
join. . . .

"You don't write about Russian authors?" he asked.

"I haven't. No."

"You want to get away from everything Russian, even
the good things." He didn't put it as a question. He didn't

need to. "In America do they love their poets the way we do?"

"Not very much. That was one of the hard things."

"You write in English, do you?"

"Yes, of course."

He shook his head wonderingly. "You can truly write whatever you want? Without getting permission?"

"Yes."

"What is it like?"

"It's . . . I don't know how to answer, Alik. You just write. You don't think about anything except what you want to say."

The expression on his face was so strange to it that she needed a moment to identify what it was: He looked wistful.

"I want to hear about you," she said. "Life must be . . . different now."

The expression disappeared. "Yes. There has been progress, wonderful progress! We can now say certain things without being sent to the camps. We can admit that there are certain social problems. We can—"

"I meant, your own life. Your career."

He sat back, crossed his long legs at the ankles, laid a hand on each thigh. "I give official concerts at which I am allowed to play Western music. I have been appearing on television for a long time. I have had poems and stories published officially. Thank you, Lenin, for all that!"

How did you become respectable? she thought. *By betraying my father?* She compressed her lips.

"Of course," he said, "people still come to my concerts hoping I will sing or say something that takes a real poke at the Party. You remember how that is—how we Soviets go to concerts or poetry readings or plays and sit through two hours of safety in order to get two minutes of honesty. We are patient people. And not very demanding. Two hours for two minutes. Maybe ten, now." He swung his head in a motion so familiar that she didn't know how she had forgotten it: as if he were shaking something off his neck. "Well?" he said. "Do you remember?"

"Yes."

"Good."

"I also remember the postcard."

"What?"

"The one from your neighbors upstairs, who went to America but came back. We didn't understand. You kept saying, What matters to her? To any of them?"

"That's right. I said that." His gaze was steady.

"Why did you come here tonight?"

"Because I couldn't stay away."

Or because you were sent? She knotted her hands again. "Are you going to tell Rodion Sergeivich who I am?"

"I tell Rodion Sergeivich as little as possible."

"Can't you just say yes? Or no?"

He inhaled deeply. "No, I am not going to tell him who you are."

"It's very important to me, Alik. Will you swear it to me, on . . . on the past?"

"All right. I swear on the past." He rose abruptly and then stood looking at her, his eyes as they had been when she first saw them, over a guitar. Could a man change without having his eyes change too?

As if he read her thought, he turned away. In a moment he said, "How is your mother?"

"She's . . . all right."

"You may have trouble getting to your father. I could deliver a message."

For an instant she considered it, until she made herself think that it could be a trap. Alik was a Soviet citizen—who could be ordered to do anything the State asked, spy or set a trap, anything. "No," she said firmly.

"I suppose it seems odd to you, but he and I have become friends."

"Why should you think I'd find it odd?"

He hesitated. "No reason. I started going—"

The phone rang.

Alik's head jerked toward it, and the skin tightened across his cheekbones as if something had pulled it. "Who is calling you at this hour?" he said.

"I don't know."

"I must leave."

She nodded, lifted the receiver, and answered.

"Hi, sweetheart."

"Jess?"

"None other. I know it's the middle of the night over there, but every time I've been free to try you, I couldn't get you. And now Vera tells me you've changed hotels."

"I . . . Yes. Yes, I have."

"Did I wake you? You sound strange."

"No, I'm awake."

"It better be because you're thinking of me."

"Yes. I mean . . ." Jess's voice was in her hand, Alik's eyes on her face.

"Hedy, is something wrong?"

"Just a minute," she said. She looked at Alik, covering the receiver as if she could hide the look from Jess.

Alik came to her. She watched his hand lift slowly, half expected to find it laid against her cheek, instead felt it press on her shoulder. Her robe offered no resistance to the warmth of his fingers. Then he turned and walked to the door. She stared until it clicked behind him.

Finally she took her hand from the receiver and said, "Sorry, Jess."

"Don't tell me you've got someone in your room? At this hour?" Please God he was making a joke.

"No, no," she said. "I just had to . . . close a window."
A breeze sailed in and reprimanded her.

"I miss you," he said.

"Me too. I tried to call you yesterday, about noon your
time. I knew you wouldn't be there, but I tried anyway. I
needed to talk to you."

"Sweetheart. About what?"

"Nothing special. I just wanted to hear your voice."

"At noon? I'm afraid I was raising it in a committee
meeting, against my nemesis from Texas."

"What?" she said, aware of his words, but separately, like
beads from a broken chain.

"You know, Emmett from Texas. The immigration bill?
My losing battle for open immigration?"

"Yes, of course."

"Is everything all right? Have you made the contact you
wanted? Hedy?"

For a terrible instant she thought he was referring to
Alik. "I . . . yes," she said. "I got an interview with Nikolayev."

"You did?"

"You sound surprised."

"Worried is more like it."

"There's nothing to worry about," she said sharply.
Maybe she hadn't found a bug in the phone, but the hotel
operator could be listening. "I'm fine."

"Good. Did you get what you wanted from Nikolayev?"

"I . . . Some of it. I'm going to see him again."

"When?"

"I'm not sure. They'll let me know."

"Does he seem in good health?"

"Yes."

"And he's answering your questions? Not being difficult?"

"Not really." She made her voice brighter. "So tell me

about you. About your meeting with Nemesis from Texas."

There was a pause, but no chuckle. "Emmett. He thinks it's great that Immigration uses that old McCarthy-era law to keep out people advocating Communist ideas. He thinks it's fine if America bans *ideas*, for God's sake. And *I* think there are better things than Emmett to spend my transatlantic nickel on. Like how you're feeling. Who else you've talked to besides Nikolayev."

This time he had to mean Alik. "What do you mean?" she said, knowing it sounded defensive.

"Gee, I didn't think it was complicated. Who've you been spending your time with?"

"Nobody. Casual chats with some of the other journalists, that's all. And I go to concerts. Nothing worth talking about."

"I see." Another pause. She knew how his face was starting to look: patient and tight. "So what is worth talking about?" he said. "The weather in Finland? The food?"

"Jess, it's not easy for me to sit and chat in a situation like this."

"Then what the hell did you try to call me for?"

She said nothing.

More gently, he said, "I'm concerned about you, Hedy. I want to know what you're going through, what you're feeling."

"How I feel doesn't matter right now. I'm just concentrating on doing the job I came for."

"Sure. Of course. My fault for asking. As usual."

"Do we need sarcasm?"

Silence. Then his voice uncoiled. "Why is it so goddamned hard for you to open up to me?"

"Why do you always grill me? Jess and his Inquisition."

"Dammit! You always make me feel like the bad guy for caring about you!"

How on earth had they gotten to this? she wondered. She wanted them to stop, but suddenly her voice wasn't working right; it seemed to have torn into pieces whose edges hurt her throat.

He was silent too.

Finally she managed, "I'm sorry, Jess."

"Yeah. So am I."

But they both sounded dutiful. Because they had both meant what they said.

"How are the twins?" she asked.

"The twins are fine." Another pause, long and awkward. "Well," he said, "I'd better let you get back to sleep."

"Yes. I'm glad you called, Jess."

"OK. I'll let you go, then."

"Jess?"

"What?"

"I miss you. And I . . . need you."

"Right," he said. And hung up.

She sat staring at the phone, contemplating the things she had said. Then, as if she could create the truth ex post facto, she rose, went to the window, and shut it, even though the breeze, which had grown more vigorous, was wonderfully refreshing.

Eyes closed against the strange night sunshine, his breathing maintained at a regular pace, the companion listened to the sounds, barely audible, of clothes being removed, of a bed cautiously giving, and finally of a body sliding carefully between the sheets.

The companion smiled to himself, without of course moving his lips. Markov had returned after only thirty minutes, but that was quite long enough, he thought, considering the door on which he had seen Markov knock.

CHAPTER ELEVEN

"**O**h, Dad, *really*!" said Laura Newman. Her twin Lindsey rolled her eyes.

"What?" Jess said. "What did I do?"

Patiently Laura leaned over the table at the restaurant where the day and a half they had spent together was ending with lunch. Jess bit back a desire to say that Laura's long blond hair was hanging too close to her dish of ice cream, and waited to hear the latest evidence of his lack of understanding and generally prehistoric perspective. "Dad," Laura said, "do you think we're truly dumb? Of *course* we know about drugs. Everybody knows about drugs. The teachers talk about it, and it's on TV all the time, and Mom carries on, and *really*."

"Drugs are scary," said Lindsey. Matter-of-factly she added, "Doing them is stupid. Don't you think we know that?"

"Sure. I know you know it." Jess hoped he sounded convincing, though actually he had no such knowledge, and little about whatever else his daughters might or might not comprehend at their age. He couldn't recapture the sense of being an adolescent; he knew he had gone through the agony and the foolishness, for he had specific memories of some events, but he couldn't remember how it felt. It seemed to him that he had been a child for a while, and then gone directly to feeling adult. No doubt it was because the family had had no money and he had had to find out young whether or not he could count on himself. But if he said that, the girls would say *really* again. "It's only that I worry about you," he said, hoping to sound casual. "There must be people in the school who use drugs, or know how to get them. Aren't there?"

Laura shrugged. "We know guys that do it. But not us." Lindsey scraped up the last of her ice cream, then held the spoon vertical and licked it.

Darts of panic hit Jess's chest. Were they lying? Or only sublimely ignorant? How could he be sure they wouldn't feel different in six months or a year? How could they be left to cope with ugliness and craziness, those two splendid beings with hair the color of rock candy and eyes as blue as morning? They couldn't even get their eye makeup on properly yet; there was a purple smudge on Laura's right lid, as if a tiny hand had pinched it. How could he let them go into the world alone? He couldn't. He would have to make sure they were guided, supervised, directed. . . . He heard his inner words and stopped them. The politician's vice, he thought: planning what other people should do. How the hell, he thought wryly, could he be out speaking and working for political freedom around the globe but unwilling at home to accept that his daughters should be free to make their own mistakes?

His right hand was resting on the cloth; Laura began drawing circles on his knuckles with one finger. "Dad, we know you worry about us. But can't you trust us? If we say we're not doing drugs, then we're not."

"OK, guys," he said, hoping his voice did not betray the mush to which she had just reduced him. "OK. I trust you."

Lindsey frowned. "Dad? Some people say that drugs wouldn't be such a problem if they weren't illegal. What do you think?"

It was the last thing he had expected, a serious question on an issue. He wondered if they would ever cease amazing him, hoped not, and told them what he thought: that making drugs illegal greatly aggravated the problem, and was arguably unconstitutional, but the problem itself was to make people understand that drugs altered their minds, therefore their lives, and that mixing two or more drugs was like sending death an engraved invitation. The twins listened, talked, questioned, sounding adult enough to make him feel disoriented. And disarmed. Then, when they left the restaurant and he was hailing a cab to take them back to Alice's, they pointed at a record album in a window, collapsed into shrieks and giggles, and sounded about five years old. Child-women, that's what they were, and Jess never knew which half would predominate at any given time. Perhaps they didn't know either.

In the cab, Laura leaned across her sister. "You know something, Dad? We asked you about Hedy today and you hardly said anything. How come?"

"How come?" He realized he was using a politician's trick, restating a question rather than answering it, but sometimes tricks were necessary. He resorted to another one: "Now, what makes you ask that?"

"It's just a question. I mean, she's away, so don't you miss her? Aren't you crazy about her?"

"Am I?"

"Dad!"

"OK, OK. I didn't say much because there isn't any real news about her."

"But you talked to her last night?"

"That's what I said, didn't I?"

Lindsey cleared her throat and asked, "You guys didn't have a fight or something, did you?"

"I mean, we wondered," Laura added.

Child-women, Jess thought. He and Alice had never fought in front of them, but they had always known anyway. In fact it was the sight of their woeful but knowing little faces that had made Alice and him decide divorce was best for all concerned. Now their antennae had detected something in his voice or manner: a hint of that sour mix of anger and self-reproach he had been tasting since he hung up the phone on Hedy. Should he frame an answer for children or women?

"Hedy and I are having a difference of opinion," he said lightly. "But it's nothing serious." But why did she always hold back from him? What the hell was happening in Finland? Had she seen that old lover he wouldn't be jealous of if he could ever get her on the phone and if she didn't sound so evasive when he finally did get her? Why the hell couldn't she ever say she loved him?

The cab swayed to avoid a bicyclist, and Lindsey slid against him. He put out his arm to hold her even closer, and Laura, too, on her other side. "Guys," he said, "people can fight without having it mean anything. That is, anything fundamental."

The cab rolled on, and the twins righted themselves. They sat silently, as close together as if they were Siamese. Sometimes they surprised Jess by their closeness, sometimes by their distance. They were struggling, he thought, to find separate identities without losing the comfort of a mirror image. Often he had tried, and failed, to imagine being born with a double. Surely that made it harder to acquire the sense of one's uniqueness that he had always felt—and took for granted in others? The compensation, according to the typical twin experience, and to what he could observe in his own girls, was that the bodymate became a built-in soulmate.

Did it all prove that the deepest intimacy came from similarity, not from difference; that the attraction of opposites was less than that of mirrors?

Weeks earlier, Hedy had asked that question casually. They hadn't pursued it, but it had stayed in his mind. Was the heart of his feeling for her a matter of commonality or of difference? And why the hell was there so much difference lately?

Laura said, "Are you going to marry Hedy?"

They had never asked the question, although he had wondered a hundred times if it was in their minds. Suddenly it was as real as a fourth person in the cab, one who demanded a truthful answer. "We've got some things to work out," he said, finally. "I don't know whether we'll want to always be together, but as soon as I do know, you will, too." Neither of the twins responded. "Would you be for it or against it?" he asked.

A silence, during which his heart gave several loud bumps. Like the Speaker's gavel, he thought, and prayed for the right ruling.

"For, I guess," Laura said. He felt Lindsey nodding agreement.

They rode another block in silence. Then Lindsey said, "Hedy has secrets, doesn't she?"

"What do you mean?"

"I don't know. She just seems like she has secrets."

"Don't we all?" he said, lightly again, but suddenly he knew that after he dropped the girls off, he wasn't going to catch an early plane back to Washington.

"Roses! Again? You will spoil me."

Vera Lucas put her face deep into the flowers. All that could be seen of her was the short cap of her dark, graying hair and her thin fingers, one with a plain gold band, holding the green florist's paper. When she looked up, she said, "The smell of roses makes me think always of concerts. Going to them, playing in them. Yet I can't remember any special incident about roses at a concert. Isn't that strange?" She held them out. "Zoya, you will put them in the big white vase, from the top shelf of the kitchen cupboard?"

"Of course," Zoya said. "Then I will do some shopping for you." She gave Jess another moment of the intent scrutiny with which she had greeted him when Vera introduced them, then took the flowers and sailed into the kitchen.

"My friends look after me well," Vera said.

"So I hear. I don't think Hedy would have gone to Finland otherwise."

Vera cocked her head to one side and regarded him. Jess thought she looked about the same as the last time he had seen her, a month earlier. She could go along this way for months, the doctors had told Hedy, before another, probably final, decline. Apparently Vera had expressed little interest in the doctors' prophecies.

"You didn't want Hedy to go to Finland, did you?" she said.

"Hedy told you that?"

"Not in words. But I know my darling child. From the way she doesn't tell me, I know you don't want her to go."

Jess hesitated. He wanted to ask how Vera could permit, let alone encourage, her darling child to take the risk she was taking. He had wanted to come and ask her that for weeks before Hedy left, but Hedy would never have forgiven him. And now that he looked at Vera, thin and serene, he knew he wouldn't have done it anyway. If she was physically much the same as the last time he'd seen her, something in her psyche had altered. She was in the room with him, in the conversation with him, yet he felt that she was at a distance—gone to spend the rest of her time in some place deep within her, where her dark eyes could look out intently, as they were at the moment, but where her absorption in herself, in the deeply private process of facing death, was laying an uncrossable moat between her and everything else.

"I thought Finland would be a painful experience for Hedy," he said. "Naturally that worried me."

Vera nodded. Silence hung between them like a picture at a crooked angle, which neither knew how to straighten.

Zoya burst in with the vase of roses and put it on the small table beside Vera. "Now," she announced, "I am going shopping, so the two of you can be alone to talk."

"No, please . . ." Jess started to protest, but Zoya thrust out one arm in a queenly gesture of refusal and announced, "Vera, I will look for raspberries."

"No, no, too expensive," Vera said.

"I will decide what is too expensive and what is not. And I am very fond of raspberries."

Vera smiled. When her friend had gone, she turned to Jess. "Zoya is right. You want to talk to me alone, don't you? About Hedy."

"Yes. I guess I do."

She looked at him expectantly, but when he couldn't decide how to begin—when he was thinking that maybe his

visit on impulse had been a bad idea—she said, "You are
good for her, I think."

"Do you?" He felt absurdly pleased.

"You are smart and strong, but also kind. I think it is
hard for someone to be all of those things. Maybe especially
hard for a man. The strong ones are so often cruel, and the
kind ones weak."

Jess didn't know what to say. He had never considered
whether he was kind or cruel; the issue didn't arise in those
terms, if at all. Politicians, he thought wryly, wanted to be
regarded as kind; "compassionate" was the magic word. He
had seen too many crocodile tears shed in Washington,
where the deepest motive for concern with the poor was
often the desire for power. Where all motives, he sometimes thought, including his own, were the desire for
power. He wanted to achieve things he thought were right,
but to achieve anything, one first had to have the power. At
least he didn't want power for its own sake. Within six
months of arriving in Washington, he had seen what the
dividing line was: those who wanted power for a purpose,
and those who just wanted it. He had sworn that if he ever
thought he was becoming one of the latter, he'd resign his
House seat.

"You don't agree with me?" Vera asked.

"I was thinking about it. You may be right." With surprise he heard himself add, "I like to be in control." He
laughed. "Which I'm not at the moment, because I had no
intention of saying that."

"In control of Hedy, do you mean?"

"No. Not in any obvious or traditional sense. I don't
want to run her life or set her goals. God forbid. But
she . . ." He pushed his hands through his hair. "One of my
daughters said something about her today. She said Hedy
seems as if she has secrets. Lindsey likes Hedy a lot, they
both do, but what she said is true. There's always some part

of Hedy that I can't reach, that she won't let me reach, and I . . . I was going to say I can't stand it, but that's too strong. I'm puzzled by it, challenged by it, frustrated by it. Ah, hell, I can't stand it. But that's my problem, not hers." He wondered what the hell he expected her mother to say to such stuff, and why he was blurting it out.

"Hedy is private, that is true," Vera said. She reached toward the roses, touched a petal gently, then curled her hand around the vase. "In Russia we are all private. We cannot be ourselves in public, you know. Everything is supervised, everyone is observed. You go about with a kind of official mask. You don't dare open up to people for a long time; you have to be sure you can trust them politically. Once you do find friends, however, they become terribly important, the closest people in the world. But it takes a long time. That is what I am trying to tell you."

"Were you like that?" Jess asked. "I thought, Hedy told me the story, that the very first time you met your husband, you went up to him and kissed him."

Vera smiled. "I was different. Sometimes impulsive . . . impetuous? One of those words. But Anna, Hedy, she is more cautious. Although once she too—" Vera stopped. Her hand slid from the vase and began to do delicate violin fingering on the table. "You must take Anna as she is."

"Of course. As she must take me."

"Of course."

The two of them were silent, the awkwardness gone. Through the walls Jess could hear faint sounds of singing. Patches of late sun lay on the carpet and the blue velvet sofa, sucking their color.

"One cannot push Anna," Vera said. "No one ever could. Even when she was a tiny child, she had her own opinions. I used to watch her go off to school each day and worry that she would say something to call attention to herself, but she learned to do what was necessary. To keep her thoughts private. That was the trick, you see: not to let them stop your thoughts, but never to let them know what those thoughts were."

Jess leaned forward, to say, Tell me about her, tell me what she was like then. He said, "Tell me about Alik Markov."

Vera looked as surprised as he felt. "Alik? But what does he . . . You know about Alik?"

In for a penny, in for a pound, Jess thought. "I don't know enough. Just that he's in Finland at the festival."

Vera blinked slowly. Her hand went protestingly to her throat.

"I'm sorry," Jess said, cursing himself. "I assumed you knew."

"No. She never said . . ." Vera sighed. "It is true, your daughter's idea. Hedy has secrets. But what would Alik be doing . . . She has told you about him?"

"Enough to make me feel she's still tied to him in some way. Or could be."

Vera was silent for so long that Jess wondered if she had retreated entirely to her inner space. The distant singing stopped, and as he looked around the room, he began to feel sealed off from the rest of the building, and the world, his own life and concerns, like the colors of the sofa and carpet, paling in the glare of the sun. He sat back in his chair to watch the only reality, Vera Lucas: the dark eyes, the tilted head, the pale, fine skin beneath which her blood beat in its closed circle and life tried to sustain itself. She had always been "Hedy's mother," her features and gestures most vivid to him in the ways that reflected Hedy's. Now, even when she began speaking of her daughter, Hedy's presence receded from hers, like a double image resolving into one.

"Alik Markov," she said at length, "was a young man with a fire inside him. He had a talent for music and words, which he wasn't free to use as he wanted, so he was angry.

I think he may have tried to accept, the way so many people did, but he couldn't. I thought him very attractive, but also dangerous, politically dangerous, because he took great risks. Anna was terribly in love, with no reservations, no holding back. I don't like telling you that, but it is true. She kept it to herself for a time—being private, you see. And then, she lived her own life more than many young Russian girls because her father and I were busy with our music, each of us in our different way. But I knew she was in love. I made her bring him to meet us. The first time he came, he made me think of coal in a grate, which can look so gray and cool, and then suddenly it shifts a fraction of an inch and glows red and sends out fire. I never saw the shift, he was always quiet and cool with Boris and me, but I knew it was there."

"And that's why she loved him," Jess said. "Because it was there."

Vera sighed. "Do people know why they love each other? You can say a hundred things about a person—he is smart, he is good-looking, we like the same kinds of music, he has nice eyes—but when you have finished making such a list, does it tell you why you love him? The country of the heart, it is strange terrain. Yes, surely Anna was attracted by that fire inside Alik Markov, though I assure you he was not the only young man in Moscow with such a fire. But he was the only one she had to leave."

"What do you mean?"

"She was in love with him, yet she had to leave him. She had to choose between him and leading a new life, in freedom. Can you imagine how that is?"

"No," Jess said quietly.

Vera tented her hands and pushed each fingertip against its opposite. "The only thing harder than choosing between two things you love is making that choice because you are forced to it. And when that happens, the thing, or the person, you had to leave is always there in your heart, perhaps even more powerful than if you had been able to stay with him. You think always, What could have happened? What might have been?" Vera was silent again. The shadow presence in her face, no longer Hedy's, was the young, intense woman she must have been. "You understand what I am saying?" she asked. "It's not that you say to yourself, Did I make the right choice? Because you know you did, the choice that was best for you and . . . No, you think, How could I have chosen against something—someone—that I love? Even though you know you had to choose, were made to choose, you can't accept it." She stared at her hands, braced against each other, and let them fall to her lap. "The only choices they give you are the ones that break your heart."

Jess said, "I've upset you. Hedy would be angry with me if she knew, and I don't like it much myself."

"No, no." Vera shook her head. "You love my daughter, and you want to understand her. That is not something to upset me. But I don't know if what I say can help you to understand."

"It does." But even more than what she said, Jess thought, was the story that had relived itself on her face, the inner life she had exposed without self-consciousness.

"Perhaps," she said, "it is good that Alik is in Finland."

"Perhaps it is."

She turned to the roses, pulled the vase toward her, and inhaled strongly. Her cheeks seemed to flush, as if she had taken in not only scent but color. "I will tell you this," she said. "When Hedy says that she loves you, she means it deeply and totally. And she assumes the same from you."

Jess was silent.

"I will be glad," Vera said, "if you are with her when I . . . am not. No, no, do not try to think what you can say to me, there is no need. Perhaps you will go into the kitchen and make us a cup of tea."

"Of course." He got up, went to her, and kissed her cheek, which felt like very fine, thin linen.

Rodion Sergeivich crossed one leg over the other, took a drink of tea from the glass at his elbow, and said, "You were seen. So please do not attempt to lie. It would not only be pointless, it would disgrace your mother's memory."

"Very well." Alik stood in the kitchenette of the apartment he shared with the watchdog and the two other musicians, all of whom Rodion had sent out. "I won't lie. I did go to the woman's room last night."

Rodion's eyes and lips narrowed; his round face seemed to flatten like a cat's when it readies for attack. "Why?" he said.

Alik reached to take one of the chairs at the table. "I have not asked you to sit down," Rodion said, his voice as light and sharp as a dart.

Alik shrugged, folded his arms, and said nothing.

"I am responsible for your presence at this festival," Rodion said. "What am I to do when Alexei Grigorevich reports that you seek unauthorized contact with Westerners?"

"Commend him for being a good watchdog."

"I am sorry to hear you still think insolence is effective."

"I think it's all I have left."

Rodion sighed. "You are never content. No sooner is one song approved than you are demanding another. No matter what you are allowed, you push at the edges of the allowable."

"And you shove back." Alik added mockingly, "All art is compromise, isn't that so?"

"Do not push any further. I have allowed you the maximum privileges consistent with your behavior." Rodion took more tea, exaggerating his enjoyment just enough to stress that he alone was drinking. "When you were six years old," he said, "I took you ice-skating one day. At my mother's suggestion, so I could get to know my young relative. A special treat, just the two of us. Do you remember?"

"No, I don't."

"You refused to skate with the others. You wanted to play by yourself in the snow outside the rink." Rodion put down his tea and laid a finger on the sharp crease of his trouser, above his knee. "I thought that since your marriage, you had finally learned when and where to skate."

"I have," Alik said. "But once in a while I must skate with insolence."

The two men regarded each other. Between them lay fourteen years, a chasm of political difference, and no family resemblance at all except a certain angle of the nose and a stubbornness that they expressed in ways as different as a cat was from a bulldog. Their mothers, close from childhood, were cousins, but the two men inherited their physical beings almost exclusively from their fathers: Rodion's a thin, ascetic man, loyal to the system, who had taught piano to beginning students and died young of emphysema, Alik's a burly sailor who cared much more for vodka than for politics and who one day went to ship out from Murmansk and never returned. The mothers had retained a childhood closeness. When Alik's died, her cousin had implored her son Rodion not to abandon Alik and to try to keep him out of trouble.

Many families had to face the fact of political differences within their ranks. Some responded by a painful severing of relations between parents faithful to the regime and children acting against it; others, by keeping dissident activity completely outside the family circle, even outside its knowledge. In Alik and Rodion's family, silence had been preferred to rupture. On Rodion's side was a cousin who had worked to smuggle out documents about the arrests and trials of dissidents but had used a pseudonym and avoided signing protests to spare his father, a Party official. Rodion had expected the same consideration from Alik. When he began to hear of Alik's underground songs and his helping to arrange public readings of protest poetry, he had gone to him and demanded that, out of love and respect for the family, he be discreet. "If I am discreet," Alik had said, "how will you become known as the second cousin of the famous Alik Markov?" There was enough truth in the remark to feed Rodion's anger, which in turn had made him hide his relationship to Alik from the circles in which he was rising, until Alik's fame grew sufficient to be useful.

"Now, Alik," he said. "You will tell me the truth about why you went to the room of the American writer."

"Very well." Alik's voice was indifferent. "The woman accosted me in the lobby the other day, as Alexei Grigorevich surely reported to you. Apparently she has heard a record of mine. She said she admired it and wanted to interview me. She invited me to her room for a drink."

"You should have reported the contact to me at once. This is not a matter in which you can play by yourself in the snow outside the rink."

"I believed it was my duty to the State to find out what the woman wanted."

"I believe you are not a man who thinks in terms of his duty to the State."

"I must be. How else could you have allowed me to attend this festival?"

For the first time since he had come into the apartment, Rodion smiled—not thinly, but genuinely. As he recognized musical talent, so he appreciated verbal agility. Whatever difficulties the relationship presented, he enjoyed the parrying, and the fact that his opponent had a degree of

power derived from his fame. But only a degree; Rodion
had the rapier with the unshielded tip. "I allow you to
attend," he said, "because Boris Semyonovich insisted on
it, and because you are Aunt Lena's son. Now. What did
the American woman tell you about herself?"

"Her name is Hedy Lucas. She is a writer. She is here at
the festival to interview musicians."

"Did she mention Boris Semyonovich?"

There was a beat of silence. "Yes. She wants to interview
him in particular. That was what made me think I should
try to find out what she wanted."

"I am to accept that concern for Boris Semyonovich was
your motive?"

Alik shrugged. "It's the truth. Why not accept it?"

"Did the woman ask you to help her make contact with
Boris Semyonovich?"

Another beat. "Not directly."

"Indirectly?"

"I think she may have been hinting at it."

"What did she actually tell you she wanted?"

Alik shrugged again. "An interview with me. But in fact
I think she wants to go to bed with what she would call a
'Soviet star.' I believe American women are quite casual
about these things."

"Did she get her wish?"

"Rodion, I was barely there half an hour."

"Answer my question."

"She did not."

"What did you do, then, for half an hour?"

Alik unfolded his arms and ran his hands through his
hair. "May I sit down now?"

"Very well."

Alik pulled out a chair, took it, and put his hands on his
thighs. "She asked questions about my life and career. I was
careful to explain the excellence of our system. I think her

questions were a pretext for her physical interest in me, which her behavior made obvious."

"Why didn't you stay, then?"

"The woman got a telephone call. I took advantage of her preoccupation and left."

"Why? Didn't you find her attractive?"

"I didn't come to this festival to sleep with other women."

"You leave that to do at home? I'm afraid you may have to change your plans."

"What do you mean?"

"I mean that you are going to see the woman again. To learn exactly who she is and why she is interested in Boris Semyonovich."

Alik was motionless, but his eyes grew paler and more brilliant. "I don't understand," he said slowly. "Do you have reason to think the woman isn't who she says she is?"

"You are not required to understand, only to see her again. To do whatever is necessary to learn about her, including to sleep with her if need be. A prospect I can't believe you will find unpleasant. Or will refuse, for that would make me question your desire to do your duty to the State."

Alik looked into the distance, then at his relative. "Very well. I will sleep with the woman."

"You will do what is necessary. The goal is information, not sex."

Alik smiled faintly.

"And to make sure that we don't lose any piece of that information, you will be wired."

Alik sat erect, as if something he didn't dare look at were crawling up his spine. Rodion smiled, as if he could see what it was, and said, "Now, why don't you have some tea?"

CHAPTER TWELVE

"This has been real nice," Ray Salmi said. "But you can't rush off without dessert. The desserts are good here. How about whipped berry pudding?"

"No, really, I must get back to my hotel. I have notes to catch up on." Hedy pushed aside her cup of the typically dark, intense coffee, which, after five days, her stomach was still picketing in protest. "I must thank you again for changing rooms with me. And of course for this lunch."

"My pleasure," Salmi said. "And, Hedy, don't forget now, I get a copy of your book when it's done."

"I won't forget." He looked expectant, so she added, "Ray." He beamed.

He had called her twice, insisting with hearty gallantry that she let him give her lunch. To refuse might seem odd, so she had spent an hour and seventeen minutes with him over food that lost its taste by the time it was siphoned through her caveats. He had tried to ask about her book. When she said she didn't discuss work in progress, he had asked about where she lived, whether she was married. The questions could have been normal, or suspicious. When she answered as briefly as possible, he had talked about Finland again. She had carefully considered each reply. Would it seem natural to comment on how the Chernobyl fallout had hurt the Lapp reindeer herds? How much should she seem to know about the golden caviar he insisted she try, which she had had so often in Russia? Why would he be so damn interested in her unless he was either making a pass, which he showed no sign of doing, or reporting to Rodion Sergeivich?

She leaned over to pick up her bag. As she straightened, her gaze caught on someone across the room. "What's the matter?" Salmi said.

"Nothing." She shook her head. "Nothing." But it was the man from the Brahms concert, solid in his gray suit, the KGB man, she was sure of it, sitting half hidden so she hadn't noticed him before.

"Listen," Salmi said, "if there's anything else I can do to help out, just let me know."

She looked at his pale brown eyes, set in weathered skin, and felt an almost overpowering desire to trust him. Surely he was what he seemed: American, friendly, someone she could ask to help her if . . . She wouldn't think of the things that could come after "if." She wouldn't say anything but "Thank you, Ray. I appreciate that" and make her way out of the restaurant, not looking to see if KGB eyes were on her but feeling them on her back like fishhooks.

She walked the few blocks back to her hotel, forcing herself not to run. Most people were heading in the other direction, toward the afternoon concerts. Only five days of the festival left, she thought, and three days since Rodion had promised her another interview. Surely this time there would be a message for her, to schedule it. She walked faster, telling herself it was only because she was growing more and more certain of finding a message waiting for her.

There was one. Smiling, she took the folded paper and read, in English:

> Hedy Lucas,
> I want very much to see you again. It will be difficult. If you will be tonight in your room, I will try.
> Alik Markov

She stared at the paper, then buried it inside a fist and walked away from the desk until she could go no farther because a window stopped her. The sun, the eternal sun, was shining on the inner court, sifting through the leaves of a tree. She didn't know what kind it was, but a laurel came into her mind. Daphne . . . pursued by Apollo, begging for escape, finally rescued by her father the god of the river, who rooted her feet to his bank and turned her into a laurel. . . . A sense came over her of escaping into stillness; of skin hardening into bark and a great downward pulling into roots. She wanted to write of how it felt to be freed and trapped at the same time, but her fingers were reconfiguring into leaves, words were losing shape and blurring into sighs. . . .

Stop it, she thought, bewildered by the desire to solace herself with imagery. To escape into language—as her father had escaped into music, and out of reality. It was the fault of the strange sun, and the music.

Standing at the window, she thought that she had been running to words as if they could replace, or even cure, the immobility Alik's note had caused. Immobility that was the only possible compromise between her wish to have him come to her again and her fear that he could betray her. Or could make her betray Jess. Jess, who had made her angry, whom she missed and needed. . . .

She opened her fist and smoothed out the note, trying to think clearly.

After Alik's visit she had been sure of nothing—not even whether the visit confirmed that the room wasn't bugged. Surely Alik wouldn't speak as he had if he knew he was being recorded. On the other hand, though his tone had been mocking, his words hadn't been anti-Soviet. He could have been ordered to trap her into revealing her identity, an order he couldn't dare refuse. And now he had written to her. Why in English? To warn her? But of what? Why not simply come to the room again? Why write, unless he had been ordered to bait a trap?

If he was really a friend of her father's now, as he had said, then surely he couldn't have betrayed him twenty years ago. But yes, he could simply have lied to her father about it. Or he could be lying now by telling her that he and Boris were friends, lying so she would reveal something. . . .

One of the desk clerks came over and asked if she was all right.

"Yes, of course," she told him. "Thank you."

As he moved away, she made up her mind to act, not to stand immobilized by messages she hadn't expected, or to wait passively for those she hadn't yet received. She put Alik's note in her bag, headed to the elevator, and pushed the button for the floor two above hers.

The long hall was empty, though faintly redolent of cooking—as the hall had been at the hotel in Paris where they had stayed, the three of them, the family that had been a unit. She went down to the corner apartment and rapped on its center door. No one answered. She knocked again, sharply.

There was a noise of chains and keys. She straightened, ready. The door opened. She looked into her father's face.

No words came. Those she had prepared were for Rodion. Her mind spun, trying to decide what language to use and whether she dared to say "Papa."

"What is it?" he said, in Russian, squinting so that she could see little of his eyes except the flesh that hooded them.

"Maestro," she said; Italian was safe.

"What is it?" he repeated.

"Don't you . . . know me?"

His eyes began to open wider.

She waited, unable to breathe, willing him to whisper "Anna."

His mouth opened slightly and the tip of his tongue, like a cautious hand, hooked over his lower lip. But he said nothing. Something else—preventing him from speaking?—entered the narrowed field of Hedy's vision. It was Rodion's face.

"Hedy Lucas," he said sharply. "What are you doing here?" He was smoothing his clothing. Perhaps he had been asleep or in the bathroom.

The prepared words came to her. "I haven't heard from you. You promised me another interview with the maestro." It was absurd, speaking about her father as if he weren't there, talking over and around him. But he made no attempt to speak.

Rodion said, "I told you that you would be advised."

"But I haven't been advised. And there are only five days of the festival left. Why can't you give me the interview right now?"

"That is not possible," Rodion said. Her father was still silent.

Why didn't he push Rodion Sergeivich aside and tell her to come in? Why didn't he push Rodion out of his life?

In Russian, but without turning his head, so that he was

staring at her as he spoke, her father told Rodion that the next day would be suitable.

Rodion said nothing, only looked at her, his gaze as still as a trap. She couldn't fall in. She gave no sign that she understood what had been said. Finally Rodion said, "Three o'clock tomorrow. For one hour. Be at the desk. Do not come again alone to this door, please, or there will be no interview."

Her father seemed to fade back into the apartment, and the door shut.

If only she had been quicker, she thought. If only she had told her father at once who she was, before Rodion got to the door. She would find a way, she swore it, to tear her father out of Rodion's grip, to get him to whisper "Anna" and tell her why he hadn't come with them in Paris.

"No, please, it's quite all right." Smiling at her from a chair in his hotel room, Kim Wan Lee held up a hand in reassurance. "We can speak for ten minutes or so. That is no problem at all."

"I'm very grateful," Hedy said. She had prevailed on Aini at the press office to help her locate the man, who turned out to be resting at his hotel before his performance that night of the Brahms and Nikolayev violin concertos. She had introduced herself on the phone as Vera Lucas's daughter. If something was important but couldn't be talked about on the phone, he had said, that made him curious and she should come by at once. No one had followed her.

Everyone knew him as Kim, he said; she must call him that. He was a small, intense man who looked about twelve when he smiled. "I studied only one year with Vera. My parents had to move to San Francisco when I was nine. But my brother, he studied with her. I remember he would tell

me how hard she made him work. And do you know what?
I was jealous!"

"Mother said to tell you to remember your bow arm."

Kim laughed. His age sank to around nine. "Vera is
well?"

"She's . . . fine."

"Good. Good. Now, tell me this important thing you
need to ask me."

"It's about Boris Nikolayev," Hedy said. "Have you met
him?"

"He came yesterday to our rehearsal of the concerto. A
difficult piece, to make it all come together as one is not
easy. We discussed it, Nikolayev and I. An old man, but he
still has much creative power, I think."

"I'm writing a biography of him. I have my second interview with him tomorrow afternoon, but the man from the
Ministry of Culture will be there, Rodion Orlov." Kim
nodded. "I need to speak to Nikolayev alone," Hedy said.
"I know I'm asking a lot, but Mama thought that if I needed
help, you might give it. If you're not rehearsing at the time,
could you come with me and distract Orlov? I hear he
especially likes the violin, so he must be an admirer of
yours."

Kim was silent, his smile gone. Hedy didn't want to look
at him like a beggar, even though she was one, so she
glanced around his room, at the familiar paraphernalia of
the violinist: rosin, strings, extra shoulder pads. He played
a Guarnerius del Gèsu, which lay in its open case on the
gold velour lining, its wood gleaming like dark skin. *You
love your violin,* she could hear her mother saying, *but then
you realize it's not perfect. It has limits. So then you ask, Is it up
to me to adjust to the weather and the seasons and so forth, or do
I keep adjusting the instrument? Are the limits in me or in the
fiddle? The greatest players, I think, believe the limits are in themselves.*

"Why do you need to speak to Nikolayev alone?" Kim Wan Lee asked.

She had expected the question and thought carefully about the answer. "I have two reasons. For one, some of my questions involve his dealings with the Soviet government, and with Rodion listening, I can't know if the answers are genuine."

Kim looked dubious. Perhaps he thought she wanted him to help her make some kind of protest.

"But even more important," she said, "I have a private message for Nikolayev from someone in America, which I want to deliver privately. Someone he would like to hear from."

"Ah," Kim said. His face gave a little explosion of comprehension, after which his smile returned. "What time tomorrow afternoon?"

The concert hall was handsomely proportioned, with walls and ceiling made of different woods fitted together in a tapestry of textures, and chandeliers that seemed made of cones and squares of ice.

Hedy joined the crowd pouring in and found her seat in the sixth row. Kim had pressed the ticket on her when he heard she didn't have one. In the circumstances, she couldn't have refused.

She had ordered tickets for most of the performances of her father's music. It would have looked odd if his biographer didn't. But so far his daughter had used only one—and then she had escaped from the concert before the Nikolayev began. This time there could be no avoiding. She took off her sweater, folded it in her lap, and looked around the hall, telling herself she was calm.

A door opened at the side of the stage, and Rodion Sergeivich led her father out, down three small steps, and to a seat on the third row aisle. The audience applauded; her father lifted his hand in acknowledgment but kept his gaze fixed in space. He had always been ambivalent about audiences, admitting their necessity but disliking to face their actuality. The same dark blue suit he had worn at his press conference hung on him with the same indifference. He sank heavily into his seat. The applause faded to a patter. Orlov looked out over the crowd, then sat beside him. In the rows around them, KGB were planted.

Tension began to flicker in Hedy's body, like distant heat lightning. It was because of Orlov, she told herself. Orlov the Keeper. The Music-lover. Once he had actually sat with her and her mother, in the Great Hall of the Moscow Conservatory, at the premiere of her father's Third Piano Concerto. From the opening measures, with their long chain of parallel chords, the music had seized her, not by its beauty but by the angry, stamping power of its rhythms and the uncanny, unexpected leaps in its melodic lines. She had felt as if she were riding bareback on a huge wild horse, with no way off unless it chose to stop and let her slide down. When it did, she had looked at Rodion Sergeivich; his face showed that he had been on the same ride, with the same excitement. The knowledge had frightened her. No matter how hard she applauded, she could not make her hands warm.

The applause surged again as the concertmaster appeared on the stage, followed by the conductor, and finally by Kim Wan Lee. The lights dimmed, and the audience rustled into stillness.

The trickle of sound began with an oboe, like tendrils of fog over a lake, then grew and spread to the other reeds, to the cellos, to the muted brasses, until a great wall of chords had been built for the violin to pierce with its long, arching melody. The concerto that began so quietly and melodically and would turn so angry and harsh before it finished, as if her father were putting himself into the sounds—there was no defense against it.

"Annushka!" Papa said. "Come in, give me a kiss."

He was in his tiny workroom, in the old black sweater, with his pencils and score paper and smoke rising from the eternal cigarette. She had looked in as she always did when she came home from school, expecting to find him in his usual state of impenetrable concentration and wanting to make sure the cigarette was safely in the ashtray; but it was one of the rare days when he looked up and saw her— actually saw her—and motioned her in.

She left her book bag in the hall and went to him. He smiled and tugged on her braid. She was years too old for his lap, but she bent down to kiss him, feeling the little pins of stubble on his cheeks and smelling the smoke and yeast and mustiness that she had associated with him as long as she could remember. "Shall I make you some tea?" she asked.

"No, no. Sit and talk to me." He put out his cigarette and with his foot pulled over the low stool with a red velvet cover.

She sat on it, tucked her skirt around her legs, and asked, "What are you working on?"

He waved a hand dismissively at some papers covered with notation. "A film score. It's nothing."

"Why do you call it nothing? I liked the last music you did for a movie. Better than I liked the movie."

For a moment she was frightened, unable to connect the look on his face with what she had said. "Papa, please . . ."

His eyes met hers, and the look changed into something softer, if sadder. "Why did you like it?" he asked. "Can you put it into words?"

She wanted to try; everything was better in words. She thought of the movie, which had taken place in the country, on a collective farm. "It didn't matter what the people in it were like," she said finally. "They were there, really, to talk about communism. I think the movie was about communism, not about people. But your music was about people."

Her father put a large hand on her head. It felt almost like a cap. "That is a nice thing to hear from my daughter." He sighed. "All right, so a film score is something, not nothing. But it's not a very big something."

"I understand, you know, Papa. Why you compose for films, I mean."

"Do you?" He took his hand away and leaned back in his chair.

"Yes. You have to have work. And sometimes a film score is the only work they will give you to do."

"That's true," he said. "I've done many of them. You haven't seen all the films I've composed music for. When you were very small, I did scores for some films that were about Stalin. Stalin the great, the wise, the handsome." His voice began to sound like a knife. "And now, when Stalin is no longer great and wise and handsome, and the few years are over when we were able to breathe without him, now I do scores for films about the collective farms and the glorious Red Army and anything they offer, because we have to keep on eating. And because I don't want to hear a knock in the middle of the night. The knock that drives out music! So I do enough of what is safe, so they will let me . . . Safe! And my own daughter likes it!"

She was growing alarmed. The knife had plunged into him and released a stream of infection, and somehow her words were responsible. "I didn't mean to say it, please," she said. "I didn't mean to."

He didn't answer. She began to pray that her mother would come home, even her grandmother. At last his eyes cleared. He reached down and pulled her up to sit across his thighs. "Listen, Anna," he said, "I want you to understand. There is nothing wrong with the film scores. The music is all right, some of it is even quite nice, but it is all safe. Do you know what I mean?"

"Not exactly," she said.

"Safe means that anybody could write it. Anybody in the Composers Union, even that idiot who licked and crawled his way to the head of it."

"I don't believe that," she said, indignant. "His music doesn't sound a bit like yours. Only yours sounds like you."

He swung his head, impatient yet pleased. "All right, all right. You are getting too damn smart, aren't you? Safe means that you try not to do anything very different from what has been done before. No new harmonies or rhythms, just new combinations of the old ones, keeping in mind all the while that the Central Committee likes beauty and refinement. If you are good, you can do that very well. But what if you have sounds in your head, in your ear, that are not beautiful and refined? Safe means that you keep them to yourself, the best of them, you put them down on paper and know they may never be played, not while you are still alive."

"I understand," she said slowly. "It's what I do in school. You keep your best ideas and feelings to yourself."

"I . . . Yes, that's right." He picked up the paper on which he'd been working and looked at it as if he had never seen it before. She looked, too, at the notations drawn in fine lines. One of her earliest memories was sitting on his lap while he explained the symbols for the clefs, the rests, and all the notes, from whole to sixty-fourth. She had loved it,

not only because it was what her mysterious father did all
day and sometimes half the night but because it was a kind
of writing, in sounds instead of words.

He raised his hand and with its palm stroked her cheek.
"You are my smart and wonderful girl, the best girl in all
of Russia." Then he did what he had used to do when she
was a child. He said her name and a list of diminutives—
Anya, Anechka, Anyuta, Nyusha, Annushka, Anyusya,
Anyulenka—going down the scale with each, ending the
octave on a deep bass "AN-NA." She laughed and kissed
him and leaned into his neck, where the smoke-smell was
trapped in his beard like a fox in a hedge. They sat for a
while, motionless except for their breathing, which settled
into exactly the same rhythm.

She was lulled into happiness, but then he sat erect so
abruptly that she slid off his thighs and had to scramble to
stand beside him. He patted her hip and began searching
in his papers, pushing them aside until finally he came on
what he wanted. "Yes," he said, "yes," to himself more than
to her. She looked at it over his shoulder: something for
violin. That would please her mother.

He lit a cigarette, put it in the ashtray, and picked up his
pencil, which he tapped absently while he looked into that
distant place where he found his music. She turned and left
the room.

A week or so later, when she came home, he and her
mother were together at the piano in a corner of the big
room, and her mother was playing something new, a melody that was lovely but painful. "And then," her father
said, his hands busy on the keys, "then it does this . . ." The
melody began to turn on itself and grow angry. "And
this . . ." With her mother following, he played on, pound-
ingly, a fierce look on his face. "This is Nikolayev," he
shouted over the music, "Nikolayev who cannot permit
beauty to be made into a prison, who must leave its safe-

ty sometimes and go where the sounds in his head take
him . . ."

She wondered if he had had too much vodka, if both of
them had, for her mother was laughing even while struggling with the difficult notes.

On the stage Kim Wan Lee's torso was swaying, his
shoulders twisting, black hair falling to his eyes and snap-
ping back. The whole string section was bowing furiously.
There were high, sharp chords in the brasses and a wild
rhythm from the tympani. The tension in her body was
racing. The music was harsh and wild and bitter, and she
didn't like it. What was in her father that made him want
to create sounds like that? She twisted in her seat, trying
to get away from such thoughts.

The music stopped abruptly. After a full measure of
silence, the solo violin returned, its theme nearly the same
as in the opening, but not quite: still long and arching, but
heavier, sadder, more yearning.

She looked at her father, slumped in his third-row aisle
seat, broad shoulders bent like an overloaded yoke, body
unmoved by the music. She heard his voice—*After that,
Sergei never again wanted to trap birds*—not knowing why she
heard it, knowing only that she was weeping.

The music dissolved as it had begun. Applause began to
crackle around her.

Yes, she thought, all right, accepting what the music had
done to her. Perhaps that was why she had been avoiding
it. The music had made her know that she could not see
Papa and talk to him, and then simply leave while he went
back. She would have to try to finish what had begun
twenty years before: to help him leave the chains, and the
suffering. To bring Mama the gift of smiling at him one
more time.

Perhaps that decision had been implicit in the decision

to come to Finland. If so, she hadn't known it. Perhaps Jess had; perhaps that was why he worried so about her. She had known only that she must come. And that, once here, it was dangerous to listen to Papa's music.

In its grasp, in the shadow of his presence, she was helpless not to feel the love and anger and pity, and the guilt they spawned by pulling her among them. She was not capable of being so close to Papa without trying to help him defect. The music had known.

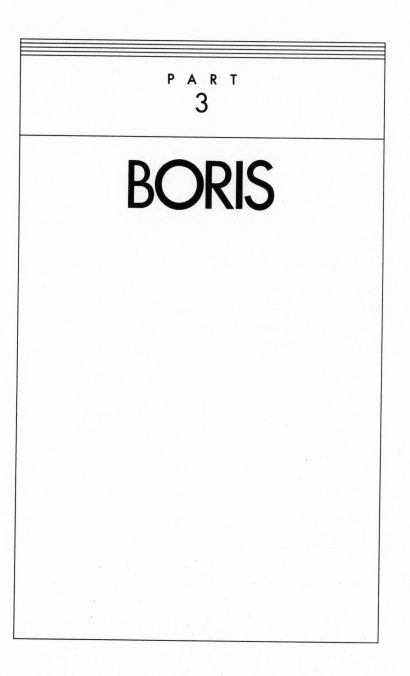

PART
3

BORIS

CHAPTER THIRTEEN

Rodion Orlov lifted the bottle of vodka and made a face at its Finnish label. "Ours is better," he said half mockingly, and poured himself another glass. "Boris Semyonovich? May I give you some?"

Boris pushed his glass closer, across the table in the kitchenette of their apartment. There were plates of sausage, caviar, stuffed eggs, and pickles, and a loaf of dark bread—an after-concert supper that Rodion had laid out when they got home. They could have stayed in the concert hall, held by Boris's admirers; they could have joined some of the musicians or even gone to a small, exclusive party being given in the town, but Boris would have none of it and had demanded to return to the hotel. Rodion had smiled, said, "Whatever you want," and brought him back.

Boris's gaze, fixed on his glass, lifted slowly with the vodka that was running into it. When it was full, he pulled the glass back to him with a gnarled hand and tossed down a drink. The motion made his baby-fine white hair bell out over the collar of the suit jacket he still wore.

"You haven't told me," Rodion said, "how you liked the performance tonight."

Boris set down his glass. "Suppose I didn't like it at all?"

Rodion blinked. "You didn't?"

"Yes, yes. I only said 'suppose.' It was fine. A little slow in the opening, brasses too loud in the last of the third movement, but fine."

"And Kim Wan Lee?"

"Excellent. Though not of the Russian school." With sudden savagery Boris added, "And of course ours is best."

Rodion ignored the outburst. "I have never heard the Brahms better played than tonight. Your own concerto . . . excellent, yes, though perhaps not quite equal to the Brahms, which I suspect Kim feels somewhat closer to. Don't you agree?" When there was no answer, he said, "No matter. Kim has a great talent. I find him exciting." Delicately Rodion took a stuffed egg from one of the plates and put it in his mouth. Boris watched the egg disappear.

Rodion went on. "Alik wasn't there tonight. I would have thought he would come to hear the violin concerto. Since he is such a good friend of yours."

"Alik has heard the concerto many times."

"Tell me," Rodion said, "how is he enjoying his first trip outside the motherland? Has he given you his impressions of Finland?"

"Since we arrived, I have talked to Alik only at the rehearsal of the concerto he will play. As you no doubt know."

"He must have given you his reactions to Finland. Since you are responsible for his presence here."

"We discussed the music. As usual."

"Come now, Boris Semyonovich, surely you speak of things other than music."

"Not often."

"You have no personal matters to discuss?"

"I am not interested in Alik's personal life, nor he in mine."

"Is that so? In spite of the interest he used to have in your . . . Perhaps that's wise. Events that took place so long ago—why would either of you want to discuss them?" Rodion let the sentence dangle, like bait, but Boris did not take it. Rodion pulled off a chunk of bread, tore it precisely in half, and ate one of the pieces. A crumb lodged in the corner of his mouth, which he removed with a fingertip.

"I told you before," Boris said. "I don't need you to sit here with me. Go, be social. It's part of your duty."

"My duty, which I do happily, is to be with you."

"An eighty-year-old man does not need a keeper."

"He doesn't have a keeper. He has a friend."

"Your father was my friend."

"Boris Semyonovich! Do you not know that I am your friend too? That you are of the greatest importance to me?"

"Yes," Boris said heavily.

"For me you are not only the living genius of Russian music but a living connection to my father."

Boris lifted his drink. "To Sergei Viktorovich."

"To my father." The two men's eyes met above the tops of their vodka glasses, then disengaged. They drank.

Rodion said, "At the end, when his breathing was so bad he could barely talk, he spoke of you. He told me to do whatever I could for you because you did not understand politics or anything else in the world except music. As usual, he was right."

"Not at all. I understand fear, disgust, loneliness, and anxiety."

Rodion leaned forward. With no calculation in his curiosity, he asked, "Weren't you happy when you were young? When you and my father were boys?"

Boris drank again. "I suppose I was. Yes. We used to throw spitballs behind the teacher's back. Sergei had a good aim. We went into Young Pioneers together. I didn't understand what all the fuss was about, but Sergei was excited. I liked his face when he was excited. I liked to watch him when he was at the piano. We discovered the piano together, you know—Clementi and Czerny, over and over, until you thought you would go mad, the Moszkowski etudes. . . . We were like two explorers. Look at this Bach fugue! I would say. Listen to these variations by Glazunov! he would say. The first thing I thought when I woke in the morning was, What can I dazzle Sergei with today?" A smile crept like a stranger across Boris's face. "He didn't think I practiced enough. True. I was more casual than he because I knew the piano would not be my life, so Sergei would scold and jabber at me. 'You must practice for the glory of the school,' he would say. He always said it the same way, in the key of E flat. Sometimes we fought about music, too. I could never cure him of a fondness for Anton Rubinstein. Rubinstein! Third-rate German romanticism, not a Russian sound in it! But your father liked it. And he could be stubborn. Those were bad times, you know, when we expected the Bolsheviks any minute to come and take his parents' piano, but somehow Sergei got hold of a two-piano transcription of *The Afternoon of a Faun*. I was wild to see it, but he wouldn't show it to me until I read through some political tract he was excited about. The whole thing! Oh, yes, we had our differences. But still . . ."

Boris sat with a memory frozen on his face. After a while Rodion said, "My father was a good Communist."

"Yes." Boris sighed. "It all mattered to him. A great deal."

"But not to you?"

"I didn't say that. There was revolution in the country, and there was revolution in art—Stravinsky, Meyerhold, Eisenstein. For a time the two revolutions were together, and Sergei and I were both excited, he for one, I for the other. Then his revolution turned on mine. Politics turned on art. So we stopped discussing our excitement."

"You never stopped caring for each other."

"Friendship has its own laws. Like art. Ideology interferes with them only at its peril." Boris looked away. "Art has no laws except truth, originality, technique. I told your father that. To graft politics onto art is ridiculous. To place ideology above mastery of craft is contemptible." His hooded gaze swung back to Rodion like a challenge.

"I am not going to discuss art and ideology with you, Boris Semyonovich."

"Your father was not afraid to."

"Fear has nothing to do with it. I simply don't see that it's practical."

"Ah," Boris said, the sound blending comprehension and contempt.

Rodion asked in a light, cheerful voice, "May I give you some sausage?"

"I am not hungry."

"Caviar? Pickles? Eggs? Bread? More vodka?" Rodion chuckled. "As the Party secretary said, I don't understand how people can afford all this eating and drinking without being Communists." He laughed, head tilted back, sound rolling easily from his throat. Boris looked at him blankly. "That is an old joke," Rodion said. "You haven't heard it? The Party secretary goes to a restaurant, eats hugely, drinks much vodka, and has to spend the Party dues he has collected in order to pay for everything? And then says he doesn't understand how people can afford such eating and drinking without being Communists?"

"Why do you think it amusing to joke about corruption?"

"Corruption is part of life. Jokes make life easier and more pleasant."

"Your father did not think corruption would be part of our life."

Rodion smiled boyishly. "I admit it, I am a cynic, Boris Semyonovich, and you are one of the few people to whom I can reveal that fact. My father, and for this we should both be thankful, died before life could make him cynical."

"Do you believe in the same things your father did?"

Rodion picked up the sausage, cut a wedge, and began to eat it in small bites off the knife. "I believe in facts, Boris Semyonovich. We live in a certain kind of world, which requires saying and doing certain kinds of things. Therefore, I interest myself in saying and doing them in such a way that I can live easily in that world and get from it the things I want. But I also believe in art. When I sit at a concert, as I did tonight, hearing Brahms and Nikolayev, then I am content, at peace with the world and its facts. Art is what makes facts bearable."

Watching Rodion's face, Boris nodded.

"And what did you think of tonight, Boris Semyonovich, when you sat there and heard your concerto?"

Boris looked out the small window, where the dark sun hung in a sky of old brass. He sighed and said, "Stalin."

"Excuse me?"

"I thought of Stalin."

"But . . . why?"

"Because I was thinking of him when I wrote it, of the things he made me feel. All of us—a country full of composers, bowels turning to water because of Stalin. A man who knew nothing of music, yet his face and his words had to be in your mind when you composed, because if he didn't like it . . ."

"Stalin had been dead for six or seven years when you wrote the violin concerto. He had been exposed. He was finished."

"The things he made one feel—they never finish. To hear yourself called an enemy of the people, because of your music . . . to see people turn away from you on the street, in the halls of your own building. . . . Do you remember Stassov? Taught composition at the conservatory. A colleague, and a splendid one, I thought. He understood what I was trying to do in my music. When your father died, I thought, well, thank God, a bit of Sergei's spirit lives on in Stassov. Then comes the denunciation, and two months after that comes Stassov's article attacking me and my music as decadent, to save his own hide. Such things do not go away just because the ugly little man who made them happen falls into his grave. They become part of your dreams, and then part of your music, until one day you wake up and realize you are composing music that is proper and safe. So you grab your pen and write something that bursts out, something you know Stalin would denounce if he were still alive—that is why you write it. And then you realize, dear God, in trying to escape him, you are still thinking of him."

Rodion had raised both eyebrows. "I am distressed to hear such things, Boris Semyonovich. Stalin has no effect on your music anymore. He is gone."

Boris brushed hair from his eyes. "Ink in the well water. Always traces of it, no matter how many times you pull up the bucket. And didn't you tell me the truck drivers still keep his picture on their windshields?"

"My friend, who cares what the masses do? Stalin did build a powerful nation, however. That can't be denied—in fact we must be grateful for it, even though he was overzealous and caused harm."

" 'But he got things done!' " Boris said, savage again.

"He led the Party off its track and suffered the necessary consequences. He has no effect on your music any longer. So why think of him and the problems he caused? There is no reason for such thoughts. They will cloud the pleasures of the festival for you. I want you to enjoy the festival, to bask in the glory of being Russia's most revered composer. I recommend that—"

"A man has whatever thoughts he has! I do not particularly like to hear the violin concerto because certain thoughts come with it. Nor do I wish to be questioned about those thoughts." Boris locked both hands around his glass, and his eyes retreated to some far country.

"Very well," Rodion said amiably. "We'll talk of something else." He cut and ate another slice of sausage. "The American author was at the concert tonight." Boris was silent. "Why do you wish to see her again? Her questions and musical insights are not unusual. And surely you don't wish to hear more from her about the wife and child you decided to be finished with years ago in Paris?"

Rodion studied Boris's face, which did not change. "No, certainly you don't. Therefore your desire to see the American author again is puzzling."

"Therefore you are not going to let her come tomorrow?"

"Would that disturb you?" The knife was empty, but Rodion kept it lifted to his mouth, parallel to his gaze.

Boris shrugged.

Rodion did too, as if imitating him. "She may come," he said. "I find her interest in you . . . interesting." Boris's eyes flicked to his, then away. "However, when she comes tomorrow afternoon the conversation should be restricted to musical matters."

"Then restrict it," Boris said. "You are the expert at such matters."

"Why do you say such things?" Rodion's voice rose hurt and angry, like flesh after a slap. "I am a man devoted to the arts and the artists in my care."

"I say things like that for the same reason you dislike hearing them."

Laying his thumb against the point of the knife, Rodion said, "Sometimes, Boris Semyonovich, you speak as if you are too old to remember certain things. Who was chiefly responsible for the restoration of your teaching post at the conservatory, for your acceptance into the Party? For the regular programming of your works, not only in Moscow but throughout the republics? Who makes it possible for you to compose in peace and not have to concern yourself with Party politics? These are things you cannot afford to forget. These are facts."

Boris's heavy lids lifted in surprise. Seldom did Rodion speak of the services he had rendered. Usually the nature of their relationship was observed in words connected only obliquely to the reality they seemed to express. Gradually the obliqueness had become the reality.

"I do not forget, Rodion Sergeivich," he said. "Anything. Remember that I conduct my music always without a score."

Rodion put down the knife, aligned it with a plate, and said nothing.

Softly, using a diminutive, as he almost never did, Boris asked, "Tell me, Rodya, what are you afraid of?"

"Why should I be afraid of something?"

"Everyone is."

"Perhaps I am not like everyone."

"I think you are. I think you fear losing your power."

"Not as long as you and I are friends," Rodion said in a serious tone that had just a small edge of mockery, like an escape clause. Then he shrugged and added, as if it were not a change of subject, "Did I tell you that Tartikoff has been complaining again? Nikolayev is heard everywhere these days, whereas Tartikoff's compositions receive insufficient performances."

"He is a lackey with no talent and a plagiarist."

"True. He is also head of the Composers Union. Shall I make sure that he causes no trouble for you?"

"Yes, yes. Take care of him, Rodya. You know that I can't be bothered to deal with such people."

"Of course not, Boris Semyonovich. You are an artist."

Their glances locked, then slid away from each other.

Boris gave a sigh so heavy that it strained the shoulders of his jacket. "I am tired now. I will go to my room."

"You have barely eaten a thing."

"I am not hungry. I wish to be alone." Boris hoisted himself to his feet and padded out of the kitchenette. Rodion watched him go, with a smile that was superior but affectionate.

In his room, Boris took off his suit jacket, removed his notebook from the inside pocket, and lowered himself into the bedside chair. There was not enough sunlight to read by, so he snapped on the bed lamp and, with a small pen that nearly disappeared inside his hand, began to make musical notations, his lips working silently.

Still in the green dress she had worn to the concert, only her shoes removed, Hedy lay stretched on top of the bed. Her eyelids trembled against the pressure of trying to stay closed and finally flew open. Her gaze went to the clock. The concert had been over for two hours, she back in the room for one and a half. Without being followed.

The golden night seemed thick with silence, but as the minutes passed and she forced her eyes to stay closed, she went deeper into that silence, which began to reveal its life: far away, the hum of a motorbike; closer, the sputter of a cough. A muted step, a scrap of laughter, a muffled rush of water—the soft night-chorus of sounds that maintained the human presence. Beneath them, emerging gradually, once one learned to hear through them, was another world, non-human. The motion of the curtain was not soundless, but a sigh prolonged beyond easy recognition. The clock whirred with energy, the bed gave little sighs and clicks of adjustment, even the floor seemed to strain against the confines of its shape. It was a child's world, she thought, where everything could come to life; where the nutcracker quite naturally became a prince and you were dressed up and taken to the Bolshoi to watch it happen, sitting in velvet between Mama and Papa. . . . She became aware of another sound, deeper than the others: the surf, heard at a distance. She frowned, then realized it was her own blood beating in her ears. Waiting for Alik.

She sat erect, yanking her mind up through layers of concentration, and stared at herself. Was it better to be fully dressed when he came, or should she be in her robe? Or more casual, in jeans and a sweater? Which would make her look the least eager to see him? She had gone around in that circle of indecision when she got back to her room, and finally decided to stay with the dress. But should she be lying on the bed? Perhaps it would be better to be sitting in the chair, working at the small desk—although that might look as if she were waiting for him. If she truly didn't care whether or not he came, she'd be in bed, asleep, in her nightgown. She swung off the bed, fingers working on the buttons of the dress, and headed into the bathroom.

She took a drink of water and stared in the mirror at the blonde with higher eyebrows and thinner mouth, who was becoming less of a stranger if no less an alien. Why preserve that face for this meeting, since Alik knew who she was? Why not give herself the luxury of wiping it off and letting her skin, and her true self, breathe? She got a tissue and made several good swipes with the cleansing cream, until

it occurred to her that Alik might interpret her looking
more natural as some kind of welcome for . . . for something. She crumpled the tissue and tossed it, then grimaced
at the figure in the mirror with her dress half open and her
makeup half off. It wasn't her clothes and face she couldn't
decide about; it was how to deal with Alik.

Staring at herself, she finished wiping off the makeup,
watching the familiar face emerge around the dark eyes.
Then she rebuttoned her dress. Naked face and covered
body, she thought, as good a way as any to greet him. If in
fact he was going to come, surely he'd have done so by now?
I want very much to see you again. It will be difficult. . . .

Back in the bedroom, she sat at the small desk. Her notebook lay as she'd left it before going to the concert—on top
of the desk, where anyone could easily find it and verify
that it contained lists of a biographer's questions. She
opened it to a clean page and wrote "3 P.M." across the
top.

In fourteen hours, by three the next afternoon, she
would be with her father, revealing her identity—learning
whether he had already guessed it—and telling him she
wanted to take him to Mama, and to freedom.

Would he agree to come? And if so, how in God's name
was she going to get him out?

She had to have a plan. Sitting through the rest of the
concert, barely hearing the Brahms concerto, she had tried
to devise something that would be possible for Papa to do,
nothing too taxing or elaborate or frightening. What she
had come up with was hardly brilliant. The scheme was
ordinary, but she knew that something like it had once
worked for someone else. Someone strong and agile, not
eighty years old.

On the notebook page she wrote "Kim. Cab. Embassy."
and frowned at the words.

Alik would know what to do, she thought. Alik had schemed against the organs half his life. He would have good ideas.

Her sudden inhalation was sharp enough to hurt. How could the desire to trust Alik again come from nowhere? Whatever else she said to him, she must not let slip any clue that she was planning to get her father to the West. She could not give history a chance to repeat itself. She pulled the page from her notebook and tore it into increasingly smaller pieces, took them into the bathroom, and flushed them down the toilet.

But desire didn't have to be translated into action, she thought. You could control what you did, if not what you felt. If she held to a strong, clear idea of what she wanted to say to Alik, there would be no danger of saying something else inadvertently.

With renewed purpose, she went back to the desk and the notebook. On a clean sheet she wrote, in Russian, the only thing she needed to say to Alik: "Did you tell Rodion Sergeivich that my parents and I were going to defect in Paris?" She would find a way to ask him—not in those blunt words, to which she couldn't trust his reply, but in a subtler form that would elicit the truth. If the truth were Yes, she would find out how. And why. And never forgive him.

She tore off the page, folded it, and put it into the pocket of her dress. She lay on the bed, keeping a hand in her pocket, touching the note as if it were an amulet.

CHAPTER FOURTEEN

The companion sat at one end of the hotel room, hands folded across his stomach. On the small table beside him were a Russian newspaper and a German magazine, both of which he had read from first page to last. Patiently he regarded the wall across from him, its plaster surface an expressionless match for his face. After a few minutes he looked at his watch. "It is getting later and later," he said to the figure lying motionless on the bed that faced his own. "Hadn't you better go soon, Aleksandr Romanovich?"

"I'll go when I'm damn good and ready."

"But you are ready. The device is in place, and you are dressed."

"I'm the judge of when to go."

"That is true," said the companion pleasantly. "But have you considered that the woman may be asleep by now?"

"Then I'll wake her up."

The companion shrugged. Earlier, at Rodion Sergeivich's direction, he had placed a tiny recorder inside a
pack of cigarettes, which was now in the pocket of the blue
shirt Markov wore. After commenting on the companion's
good work in tracking Markov to the woman's door, Rodion Sergeivich had explained that Markov would now pay
her another visit, for official reasons. "Let him go in his
own time, but make sure that he does go," Rodion had
ordered, and so the companion had to wait for Markov to
move, although he would have preferred to be in bed,
asleep by now. He checked his watch again, permitted a
small yawn to escape, and resumed his bland study of the
wall.

Without warning, Markov sat up, swung his legs off the
bed, and put on his shoes.

"Are you ready then, Aleksandr Romanovich?"

"What the hell does it look like?"

"It looks like you are ready," the companion said without
offense. He stood up.

Markov grunted and took from a chair his gray cardigan,
heavy-knit like a fisherman's sweater. He swung it on,
pulled his hands through his hair, lifted his shoulders as if
hoisting something.

"Excuse me, Aleksandr Romanovich, please wait. I am
instructed to make certain you take nothing with you but
the device. Please empty your pockets."

Markov opened his mouth, bit it shut, and took out keys,
Finnish money, a handkerchief, a pencil. "Raise your
arms," the companion said, and searched him expertly;
there was nothing but the recorder in his shirt pocket.
"Thank you, Aleksandr Romanovich. You understand that
I only follow orders."

Markov headed to the door, then swung back to the table
in their kitchen area and picked up the bottle of vodka it
held. "I am taking this," he said, his voice a rasp. He opened

the door and walked out without a backward look. The companion closed the door and moved down the hall behind him.

The hall was an empty tunnel. At intervals there were dimly glowing lights in the shape of icicle clusters, which made Markov's shoulders loom even larger when he passed one of them. The previous time he had gone to see the woman, when the companion had followed him surreptitiously, Markov had moved slowly, even unwillingly. This time he strode to the exit door that led to the stairs, flung it open without looking back, and went down two flights to the woman's floor, the metal steps reverberating under his tread. When he reached the woman's door, he stopped and stood silently, as if his energy had run out and he hadn't enough left even to knock. The companion stopped several doors away, watching and wondering why Markov was hesitating, what he could be thinking.

Bitter, it was bitter. To be doing what he wanted—but under orders. If They wanted to remind him that he was their creature, They couldn't have devised a better way. Once, with Anya, he had planned to be free, but here he was, still following orders: sending her a note, then going to her as a spy, capable only of the tiny rebellion of not going quite as quickly as his masters wanted.

The path to the West that he had once told her about—it hadn't worked. Or he hadn't known how to make it work. He had cut his feet for years, dancing on the razor's edge between rebellion and obedience, terrified the former would put him back in the camps, or the latter creep into his soul. He had sung and mocked and become one of the stars of underground song, and if his fame had kept him from going back to prison, it had become his jailer in another sense, for his very popularity seemed to be the reason They would not exile him to the West. Either that, or They knew how badly he wanted it. Whatever a man's soul thirsted for—that was the one thing not to be allowed, in the glorious Soviet Union, no matter what reforms They made.

Or perhaps there was no reason at all. Perhaps They were simply like cats who batted a beetle between their paws until They grew tired and the creature was able to crawl away on whatever legs They had left it. He wasn't one of the brave ones, with spirits of blue flame, who could suffer prison for a decade and more. He was just a poor beetle who wanted to be a singer of songs and a teller of tales.

Only one path was left, he finally had decided: the path of no resistance at all, of seeming to become tamed. Of singing "proper" songs; of marrying the Party official's daughter who was mooning after him, and who wasn't bad in her own way, so that he had always tried to be decent to her; of saying and doing what had to be said and done, and yes, damn his soul, enjoying the rewards, the shoes and the dacha and the car; of praying that one day they might let him go to the West for some reason, on some pretext— perhaps a trip with Sofia, if he did not grow too old to travel before it happened. And when the miracle finally occurred and he got to Finland. . . .

If there were gods to believe in, one might think it was their doing, something to amuse themselves while drinking vodka: See that poor fool down there? Prays all his life to get to the West? Let's let him go—let's even let him get away from his watchdog and get down to the lobby of his hotel with nothing but the clothes on his back and the guitar in his hand, ready to walk out the doors and find a taxi or a bus or something that would take him to freedom. And then—yes, then! when he could walk out the door!— let's have him see the woman in the lobby. He'll have to stop, poor fool; he'll have to take precious moments and find out if she is Anya. And while he takes those moments, let's send the watchdog panting after him, chain in hand. *Here sheep, good sheep, get back in the fold, bleat as you're told.* . . . Ha, ha! Godlike laughter and clinking of god-size glasses.

To have found her again was like finding one's youth when it had passed, one's dream after one had ceased to dream. But could a man of forty-six bear his youth and his dreams? Or trust them?

Two nights earlier he had been afraid of revealing himself to her. Almost twenty years had gone by, and who could know how she might have changed? Now he must keep both of them from revealing anything. Smiling, Rodion had said, "Of course there will be no such behavior as turning on a radio loudly or running water in the shower. Nothing to change my belief that you are a man who wants to do his duty to the State."

Alik glanced back down the hall, where the companion watched and waited. He reached into his shirt pocket and activated the recording device. He lifted his shoulders, and then his hand to knock.

It was barely audible: just three quick moments when silence intensified into sound. Hedy stood up. Her shoes were on the floor by the bed, but she pushed them aside and went to the door with her feet bare. "Yes?" she said.

There was no reply, only another knock. She opened the door.

Alik came in quickly, as if he were being followed, and closed it behind him. He wore jeans again, and beneath a heavy cardigan, a blue shirt that made his eyes look pale. In one hand was a bottle of vodka. He put the other in the pocket of his sweater and stood looking at her. *King of pain,* she thought, *king of pain,* the phrase coming into her mind without reason, for he was smiling.

"Hello, Miss Hedy Lucas," he said, in English.

"Hello," she said, trying to match his tone but not quite able to identify it nor to read anything in his face.

He moved into the room and seemed to be looking for something. "Alik—" she began, but he interrupted. "Yes, I am here. Aleksandr Romanovich Markov, Soviet artist you are wishing to interview. Too bad you speak no Russian. You will have to understand my English." His voice was close to the hearty, plummy one he had used two nights before.

She said nothing. He went to her desk, put down the vodka, and picked up her notebook, which still lay open, and her pencil. He began to write, talking at the same time, but slowly, frowning with the dual effort. "So, you like to learn more things about me? About my life in Soviet Union and my music? We can talk as you wish, and then perhaps we amuse ourselves. We can have good time. Russian good time. I have brought vodka, you see. In Russia, talk is better with vodka. Everything is better with vodka. Yes?"

She said nothing, until he gave her a look that made clear he wanted her to speak. "Yes," she said. "All right. That's exactly what I want—to talk."

"So," he said, "you want to interview me for some magazine or newspaper? Why are you choosing me?" He finished writing and came toward her, holding out the notebook.

She took it and said, "Why don't you fix us a drink first? There are glasses on the dresser."

"Yes. Good."

She read what he had written, in Russian:

> They know I came before. I said you asked me. Tonight I have to record our meeting, to find out why you are interested in Boris. They don't know who you are. I said you are an American writer who

heard a Markov record and just wants to sleep with
him. We must make them believe it.

She lifted her head to stare at him. He shrugged and held
out a glass of vodka, his eyes glittering with irony and
helplessness. Something had to be said, she knew, but her
mind did not seem capable of words, only of a scuttling
indecision between laughter and desperation.

"I show you how we drink in Soviet Union," he said.
"Here." He put the glass in her free hand. "You take much
in one swallow, fast. First you push air out—I forget English word . . ."

"Exhale," she said automatically.

"Yes! Exhale. Then head back, vodka down, do it fast."
She watched him drink, saw the quick, familiar convulsion
in his throat. "For you, best to take food right away," he
said. "Piece of bread, maybe."

"I don't have any bread, just some crackers." Her voice
sounded tinny, as if it came from a distance.

"Good." His didn't. His was too close.

She went to the desk, put down the notebook, and got a
half-eaten pack of crackers from the drawer.

"Now you drink," he said. "Please."

She tossed back some of the vodka, which burned her
throat as if she'd never had it before.

"Quick, eat now!" he said.

She took a bite of a cracker and swallowed it slowly. "I
don't really like to drink," she said.

"What do you like, then, Hedy Lucas?" His voice was
soft and mocking.

She plunged her hands into the pockets of her dress and
felt the note that was still there. The reality of the situation
crawled along her skin. She had been prepared to find out
the truth about the past, and instead she must pretend to
want to sleep with him. To pretend to want what part of

her actually had wanted, so perhaps this was retribution. *I can't do this,* she thought.

She would tell him to leave. She would say she was ill. But tomorrow Rodion would see that she was perfectly well, and be suspicious.

She would say she was too tired. But wouldn't Rodion just make Alik come back?

She would say she had changed her mind. But what would become of the story Alik must have told, in order to protect both of them?

"What is wrong?" he said.

She swung her head. "Nothing. Except it's too strong for me. Your vodka. No wonder we hear that alcoholism is a major problem in the Soviet Union."

"America has alcoholism too. And homeless people. In Soviet Union we do not have unemployment problem as you do. Or racial problem."

She almost smiled; he sounded like the perfect Soviet citizen. "I hope you didn't come for a political discussion," she said.

He took a pack of cigarettes from his shirt pocket and wandered toward the dresser. "I may smoke?"

"I'd rather you didn't."

Holding the pack in front of him, he mouthed words as if it were a microphone, laid it carefully on the dresser, and nodded Yes to the question in her eyes.

She sank into the desk chair, staring at the cigarette pack, unable to summon any thoughts except the wry one that if Alik had come wearing a recorder, that was proof the room hadn't been bugged before.

"I came," he said, "to ask why you are wishing to interview me."

He was looking at her intently. She had to say something. For the tape. This was supposed to be a seduction scene. She must have read and seen a thousand of them, she thought, begging her subconscious for a cliché. One floated up. "Let's just that say I find you interesting," she said.

Alik lifted his glass as if to drink again, then lowered it and cradled it in both hands. "I do not think it is Alik Markov you find interesting. I think it is Boris Nikolayev."

He was speaking for the tape too, she realized—he had to seem to be trying to learn why she was interested in Nikolayev. Unless he was trying to learn for real—for Rodion. But no, if he were really spying, he wouldn't have told her they had sent him. Unless telling her was a particularly clever way to convince her she could trust him. . . . The possibilities nested inside one another like Chinese boxes. *I can't do this,* she thought. But she had no choice.

"I find both of you interesting," she said. "You and Nikolayev. Are you friends?" *Did you betray him and then dare to try to become his friend?*

"We are musicians together," Alik said.

"No more than that? When he writes a concerto for you?"

"Not for me, for guitar."

"Have you always been a classical musician?"

"No." The look he gave her underlined his next words. "Boris Semyonovich influences me."

"You admire him, then? You would never do anything to harm him?"

Alik's surprise seemed genuine. "Certainly not. Nikolayev is hero in Soviet Union."

She couldn't help saying, for Rodion Sergeivich, "That wasn't always the case."

He frowned but said nothing.

"How long have you known Nikolayev?"

"Since . . . about nine years."

"Tell me what he's like."

"Tell me first why you are wishing to know."

"I thought I had. I'm writing a book about him."

"Why?"

"There's no biography of him in English. I think there should be."

"And you will make much money?"

She was going to protest, but his look warned her. "I hope so," she said firmly. "I'm a good capitalist."

He nodded. Apparently she had said what he wanted.

"I gave you my reasons," she said. "Now tell me what Nikolayev is like. Tell me about the man himself. The things you can learn only by knowing someone well." For a moment she forgot the tape; she simply wanted to know what Alik would say, and whether she could trust it.

He looked away, toward the window, where the open curtains let in the sun's dark light. Suddenly, in profile, he was the man of twenty years before; if she walked across the room to him, he would turn to her without guile. "Nikolayev is a man . . . to himself," he said. "If that is correct English."

"A man who is unusual, no one like him? Or do you mean a man who keeps to himself, who is hard to know?"

"Both of those ideas. Some days I am with him, he talks of music in ways to make me hear things I never hear before. Some days, he talks not at all."

"What kind of life does he lead?"

"I know what he does when I see him. Other times, I know nothing." Alik knocked back the rest of his drink, went to the dresser to refill it, and came toward her with the bottle.

"No," she said. "No more for me."

"Yes," he said harshly. "With vodka, it is easier." He filled her glass, set the bottle down beside the notebook, and picked up the pencil. Very quickly, in Russian, he wrote, "We will act everything with our voices. But you must pretend you want me to sleep with you."

He stood looking down at her, defiantly. Defying her or himself? She could see that on the fullness of his lower lip there were small, fine vertical lines. Had they always been there?

I can't do this, she thought. But she had no choice; that was why she could do it. She picked up the glass and drank in the Russian way, to clear her throat.

"Good. You are learning."

"I'm trying." She added a small laugh—in seduction scenes a woman would surely give small laughs. Yes, she could see it on the page of some paperback: *Looking at him from beneath lowered lids, the woman gave a small, throaty laugh.*

Alik put his hand on her shoulder, as if to give her courage. Her paper imaginings disappeared, and her awareness shrank to the shape of five fingers and a palm—and panic, because she couldn't want him to touch her. She moved away from his hand and steadied her own by locking it around the vodka glass.

"Why," he said, "are you not wishing to write about American composer? Why Boris Nikolayev?"

"Because. . . . I don't want to talk about Nikolayev anymore."

"Why?"

"I don't want to talk at all. I want to . . . to listen. Yes. To hear you sing. You must know hundreds of songs that weren't on the record I found in New York. Sing one for me."

"I don't have guitar."

"Can't you sing without it?"

Alik frowned. "Yes."

"Well, then?"

His eyebrows rose in a helpless protest, and he walked away, to the window, where he stood outlined by the light. At length his shoulders squared and he turned around.

"OK, Hedy Lucas, I sing for you." He walked to the bed and sat on its edge. "Song is called 'Nichevo.' You know this word? In Russian it means 'nothing,' but we say it to mean 'never mind' or 'that's all right.'"

"Really?" she said. She had heard the word all her young life, used everywhere, often as a fatalistic comment on the fact that something wasn't ready or possible or had been arbitrarily changed. A word that could breathe of futility and indifference: "Don't let it bother you."

"We use this word every day in Soviet Union," Alik said, "but the way I use it in song is different." He lifted his hands, seemed surprised to find they held no guitar, and let them fall back to his thighs, where his fingers moved in mute chords. His eyes fixed on her, and he sang softly, the rasping voice sheathed in velvet.

> They met on the bridge,
> A man filled with sadness, a woman, with hope.
> Shall we love each other forever? she said.
> I may not know how, he said.
> Nichevo.
>
> They loved by the river,
> A man full of darkness, a woman, of light.
> Will you stay with me always? he said.
> I may have to leave you, she said.
> Nichevo.
>
> They parted by the statue,
> A man full of emptiness, a woman, of—

He stopped abruptly. "Enough."

She knew she had been staring at him too intently. But what else could she do when he sang lyrics like those? "It's . . . a lovely song," she said. "You wrote it yourself?"

"Yes."

"I like the—" She stopped because he was shaking his head violently. What was wrong? "I'd like to hear the rest of it," she said cautiously.

His eyes flashed warnings. "This song is no good without guitar."

Then why had he sung it, except to try to make her feel— Suddenly she grasped what he was signaling. He had sung in Russian, which Hedy Lucas wasn't supposed to understand. She clutched the vodka glass angrily. Then why the hell had he done it: to trap her? As he almost had? No, not if he was warning her at the same time. And he hadn't volunteered to sing; she had asked him. But why a song like that one, except to make her feel . . . "What was the song about?" she said.

He nodded, relieved. "About two people. They meet, they love each other, they have to say good-bye."

"What does *nichevo* have to do with it?"

"The man and woman try to say, Oh, never mind, this is just how things are, nothing can be done about these things." He gave her a look of such intensity that she blinked. "You understand what I am saying?"

"The man and woman try to pretend that the way they feel doesn't matter, but it does. Is that what you mean?"

"Yes. Yes." He stood up and said, his voice reverting to mockery, "You are smart, Hedy Lucas. Smart cookie, that is right American expression?"

"It's an expression. I'm not sure it's the right one."

"OK," he said. "No more songs."

And no more talking about Nikolayev; she had said she didn't want to. So there was only one thing left to do.

She glanced again at the cigarette pack on the dresser. Trying to make her voice huskier, wondering who was listening, or would be—Rodion Orlov?—she said, "I've never known any Soviet musicians. I mean, any who still live in the Soviet Union."

"No?"

"I don't know very much about Russian men. Are they supposed to be good lovers?"

He laughed—he was a much better actor than she—and said, "You would have to ask Russian woman."

"You . . . you're a very attractive man," she said.

"Thank you, Hedy Lucas." For a moment the pain in his face deepened, like a photographic image developing to full strength. He shoved his hands into the pockets of his cardigan and stood looking at her. In the musky light his skin was dark and his eyes not the blue-green she remembered but a color she couldn't name.

She stood too. From the corner of her eye she glimpsed herself rising in the dresser mirror: green dress, blond woman. She had forgotten that she was blond, but the sight was a comfort. She was not doing any of this; it was a blond stranger, who had no choice.

Another inane line came to her. "Let's see whether the two of us could improve relations between our countries."

"Excuse me?"

"Never mind. What I mean is . . ."

"Yes?"

"What I'd like is . . ."

"Maybe I know what you like," he said.

She looked at him helplessly, trying with her eyes to force comprehension into his: They could not do it—there was no way. Were they to utter stagey sighs and groans? Was one of them to manufacture sound effects by making the bedsprings creak? Maybe he could do it—he was a performer, but she was not. She no longer lived where deceit was part of life.

He nodded, as if he understood, and moved a little closer, holding out his hands across the distance that lay between them.

Yes, that would help. Maybe, if they supported each

other with their hands. . . . She held hers out too. They
were so cold that when he took them, his seemed to be
burning.

"I would like . . . no more talking," she said.

"Yes. Yes." His voice was nearly a whisper.

A certain kind of sky, before a storm—that was the color
of his eyes. And when the sky was that color, the birds
called in noisy agitation but everything else grew quiet.

Her hands lay unmoving in his, which didn't move either yet seemed to be full of small tremors. He took a deep
breath and let it out in an aspirate sigh. She watched the
cloth of his shirt move. She felt suspended in time as well
as space; only the presence of his hands connected her to
the reality of the room and the tape recorder. They were
not in a hotel room; they were behind a curtain. She could
almost smell the faint odors of his brother's apartment, of
potatoes and linoleum, which she would block out with the
taste of his skin, a taste like cloves and lemon. They would
have to move slowly and quietly because someone was listening—his brother or his nephew or someone else, it
didn't matter, always there was the fear of someone listening, there wasn't even a word in the language for "pri-
vacy," the nearest thing meant a pitiful condition, like
loneliness.

She pulled back—how had they come so close to each
other that his face no longer held expression, only color?
And how did she come to be leaning against his shoulder,
when she had moved to pull back? Her face was in his
sweater, her nose filling with the scents of wool, and of
cloves and lemon. She raised her head, and his mouth was
so close that she tasted it without touching. *I have no choice,*
she thought hazily, *I'm doing this because I have no choice.* He
moved his lips to her ear and whispered in Russian, "Forgive me, Anya, please forgive me." His mouth moved to the
side of hers, then to her throat, then to the hollow of her

collarbone, where his thumb pushed aside the fabric of her dress.

She lifted her hands to push him away, but they went inside his shirt; she felt her dress slide away and her skin meet his. She thought she would have remembered his body exactly, but she was wrong. She did not know what it would do next, or her own, yet each thing that happened made the blind warmth of memory roll inside her. The two of them seemed never to have made love before, yet never to have stopped. She heard herself say his name, and was dimly afraid that he would call out "Anya." She smiled at her foolishness, because his mouth was busy with things other than words. She forgot the smile and the fear and everything else.

Reality returned after a long while: the light, the room, Alik sitting naked on the edge of the bed, not facing her. She put a hand on his back. He reached around to touch it with one of his own but didn't turn to look at her.

She took her hand away.

After a while, glancing at the dresser and the pack of cigarettes, she forced herself to laugh and to say, "Well, I certainly like the way you do things in the Soviet Union."

Alik neither moved nor spoke.

She gave as credible a yawn as she could manage. "I seem to be awfully tired. I hate to be rude, but I think I'm going to have to ask you to leave so I can get to sleep. I have a lot to do tomorrow."

"Yes, I must leave now," he said, his voice flat. "The man who is watching me, perhaps he is waking up." He rose, took his clothes, and went into the bathroom.

She lay without moving or thinking until he came back, dressed. The light of the dusky sun fell across his face, turning it into a metal mask of pain. She lifted herself on one elbow and forced herself to say, "Maybe we can get together again before the festival is over."

"Yes." He started to cross to her, but his shoe struck a piece of paper, which he bent to pick up.

She realized what it was: the note she had been keeping in her pocket. *Did you tell Rodion Sergeivich that my parents and I were going to defect in Paris?* It must have fallen out when her dress came off.

She sat up quickly and held out her hand for it, but she was too late. She saw his perfunctory glance at it, his perception that it was in Russian, his comprehension.

When he looked up, his face wore the expression that is the refusal to permit expression. He laid the note on the bedside table. Then he got the cigarette pack from the dresser and put it in his shirt pocket. "Good-bye, Hedy Lucas." His voice was as grating as she had ever heard it. "We had good time, did we not? Good Soviet-American time."

"Yes. We did." But he had already reached the door. He was gone.

She lay without moving and thought of Jess: the look of his hand when it held a coffee mug, the nick in his right eyebrow. His robe hanging in her apartment in New York. The twins.

She sat up, stood up, took her clothes, and dragged herself into the bathroom. Half afraid to look at herself, she lifted her eyes to the mirror above the lavatory.

She blinked. Something was written across her face. On the mirror, in Russian, with one of her lipsticks: "Anya, can you help me to get out? Please. If you can find some way . . ."

She stood there naked, shivering, wanting to cry.

After a long while she took a tissue and wiped the writing off.

CHAPTER FIFTEEN

The sun was in its right place and time once more, high and white and normal, as if its dark side had never been. Hedy's eyes opened on its light. The windows were wide, curtains skittering in a good breeze. She lifted her hand and saw that her watch read nine.

She leaped out of bed as if late for something and then stood, staring around the room and the memory it now held. Then, without conscious decision, she began to tidy and clean as thoroughly as if she were one of the maids, even scouring the bathroom. When she found she was scrubbing the lavatory mirror over and over, she finally stopped. In that mirror, her eyes burned with tiredness. All night they had kept fluttering open and staring into the sun-gloom, seeking certainties that were not there. The way to deal with what had happened with Alik, perhaps the only way, she thought, was to call it a rising of ghosts, condemned to walk the earth, like old Marley, because their accounts were not settled yet.

The hours until the appointment with her father stretched ahead with no end, so she decided to go out and eat. When she put on the wig and makeup, they seemed even more alien to her than the first time she had tried them.

After breakfast she went for a walk so long and brisk that it felt as if she were shaking out her body in the fresh air, which was exactly what she wanted. Resolutely she pushed aside the thought of Alik and began to review her plan for getting her father out.

The plan rested on two key assumptions: that the door to the right of the center one in her father's and Rodion's suite led to her father's bedroom and could be unlocked, and that Kim Wan Lee would agree to distract Rodion Sergeivich a second time. She would broach it to him when they met in the lobby before being escorted to the suite at three that afternoon. If he didn't agree, or wasn't able to, then what? She must have an alternative to Kim Wan Lee. Could Aini at the press office call Rodion out on some pretext?

Equally problematic was finding a cabdriver who could be trusted. Could she just go up to one and say, How about helping with a defection? As she walked along, she studied every *taksi* she saw and even started to approach one before changing her mind. To let a stranger know of the plan in advance would be crazy. But then, how and when to find a driver? Ray Salmi had said he would help her if she needed anything else; could she ask him? Why not accept that he was only who he said he was, an American, by acting like one herself and trusting him? She considered it, debating how much he would have to be told. Or would it be better—safer—to confide in Aini?

She was still five or six blocks from the hotel when something nudged its way into her conscious awareness: A man had been behind her for some time. The same man, at the same distance. A solid man, wearing a gray suit in spirit though not in fact, a camera hanging lifelessly around his neck. She walked a bit faster. A block later, he was still keeping pace. Fear bloomed in her stomach. He was the man from the concert and the restaurant. He had to be. The KGB was following her. That was definite now. Her legs and lungs stopped functioning automatically and had to be ordered, one step and breath at a time. She gave another order: not to look back. When she disobeyed, he was still there.

Her strange puppet's legs got her to the hotel, into the lobby and the elevator, and down the hall. The wet hair she had placed across her door was still there. Inside, she rushed to the dresser. Her sweaters were aligned exactly as they had been. On the desk, her notebook was as she had left it, open to the same page, angled precisely with the pencil. The room was still safe. How could it not be, since they had sent Alik with a tape?

She sank into the desk chair, to make herself calm and rational again. Instead, the fear spread upward and swelled in her throat. Irrelevantly, she thought of how venom is said to paralyze its victims in minutes; the thought made her unable to move. The KGB knew who she was; they were going to come for her and take her back to Russia. Unless she could find someone to help her. Ray Salmi. There was no one else. She would call Ray Salmi as soon as she was able to move. Staring at the window and the mockingly normal sun, she fought to take deep, even breaths, but the venom had reached her lungs. It would head for her mind if she didn't stop it. *Think, think. Think straight.*

They had begun following her because they were suspicious of who she was. After listening to the tape, Rodion was even more suspicious, so he . . . Or had Alik told them whose daughter she was? She would be foolish to think that because he could still hold her tenderly, he couldn't have betrayed her. Why had he whispered, with such intensity, *Forgive me, Anya*? Forgive him for what he had done twenty years before—and for what he was about to do? It didn't follow that because he had looked agonized, the plea he had scrawled on her mirror was his true reason for coming to her room. After all, he was an actor. And a Soviet citizen. He could have been ordered to leave the message. Someone could be coming to knock on the door and barge in and "discover" the message—as evidence that she wasn't who she claimed to be. No, that didn't make sense. . . .

It was Ray Salmi after all. He had found out who she was and told Them, she had been going to call him for help, but he was one of Them, to trust was insane, everybody was one of Them, and They were going to come for her, the knock in the night that Papa had always dreaded was finally going to come—

There was a knock at the door.

Her hand jerked like a fish on a line. She made it lie still on the desk. The maid was knocking; it had to be the maid. "Come in," she called, but heard no key scraping. There was another knock. She rose and went to the door. If Alik had come back, she would . . . She didn't know what she would do.

"Who is it?" she called, and refused to believe the answer.

But when she opened the door, it was true. Jess stood there, smiling half in apology, half in pleasure, carrying a raincoat and the travel case he used for going between Washington and New York.

"I hope I'm not the shock of your life," he said.

She couldn't speak.

"Going to let me in?"

Relief started to flood through her; she wanted to run

into his arms and feel safe, but guilt pinned her back. She cleared her throat and said, "Jess, I . . . What are you doing here?"

He grinned. "I don't know. Guess I always wanted to see Finland." He moved past her. She closed the door behind him and tried to fit the reality of his tall presence into the sunny, breezy room—thank God she had straightened it. Against her will, her gaze went to the bed. The red, yellow, and orange spread looked back with a manic, innocent cheeriness.

Jess put his coat and case on it, turned, and held out his arms. Surely he was a figment of her imagination—like old Scrooge's Spirits. But what those Spirits did had turned out to be real, and so was Jess. She could feel his kiss. Surely he would taste guilt in the kiss, or sense it or guess it, and would move away, suspicion narrowing his eyes like a pursestring.

He pulled away, smiling. His eyes were browner than she recalled; had she ever really looked at them? At him? "I can't get used to you as a blonde," he said, "but you still taste the same. Awful damn good." He kissed her again, lightly, then pulled her down to sit beside him on the bed.

It was going to be worse than suspicion, she thought. He wasn't going to suspect a thing, and the entire burden of what to tell him about Alik—if anything—was going to roll on her like a boulder. Why did it have to matter? The world was full of casual sex. Why couldn't she call it that and shrug it off?

Because that would demean both her and Alik, and Jess. Jess most of all—to think she had done that to him casually.

"Is it all right to talk in here?" he said. "Is the room safe?"

"Yes."

"Sure?"

"Yes," she said, thinking of why she was sure.

"OK. First things first, then. I came to apologize."

"For what?"

"That phone call. I was out of line."

She had to work to remember; the call seemed to have happened to someone else. "I don't know if you were out of line, but I know I was mad at you."

He smiled again, the cleft deepening in his chin. His hair seemed even curlier than she remembered, and darker. "I went to see your mother Sunday evening. We didn't talk about any of this directly, but after I left her, I found that . . . Maybe I understood better what kind of pressure you're feeling over here, where your past is so . . . close."

It was a perfect opening. She said nothing.

"I can never understand that past," he said, almost ruefully, "no matter how much you tell me about it, or how little. Sometimes I try to fight that fact. Which is stupid. Gets me into trouble on phone calls. Then I have to fly to Finland and say I'm sorry."

She looked at the square face, the dark eyes, the confident grin, and wanted suddenly to tell him everything about Alik, including last night, to let him comfort her and say he understood, it was only a sealing of the past, not a betrayal of the present, please God, there were enough betrayals in the world. . . .

"What's wrong?" Jess said.

"Nothing. I just . . ." The words trembled in her throat, but she couldn't say them. Why should Jess have to carry the burden of knowing? When she was young, she had thought there could be no secrets between a man and woman who cared for each other. But she was almost forty, and secrets were necessary. "Don't apologize," she said. "The call was my fault as much as yours. A Hedy-Jess coproduction. I'm difficult and impossible and I can't bear for you to apologize. Please."

"OK, then, I came because I missed you like hell." He sighed. "And to make sure you're all right. I suppose you don't like to hear it, but if you want the truth, the whole truth, and nothing but—"

"I want to hear it," she said fiercely, and leaned in to kiss him. Afterward he held her very close. She felt loved, and lucky, and rotten with guilt.

He pulled away and said, "Now, tell me how everything is going. Are you all right? When you opened the door, I thought you looked scared."

Without thinking, she said, "I was."

"Why? What's happened?"

She rose and walked to the desk, to give herself time to think. She wanted badly to tell him about being followed, but that would mean explaining that she had seen Alik, that he had been sent with a tape recorder, that they had—"Sometimes," she said, "I see KGB on the streets, or at a concert, or in this hotel. I saw one of them this morning when I was out. When that happens, I feel scared. I can't help it."

"Jesus," he said softly. "How could you help it? But I'm here now, and I'll stay till the end. I don't want to crowd you, sweetheart, but I'm here to be with you and to help you if I can."

Slowly she said, "That's true. You could help me, couldn't you?"

"Name it."

She walked to the window. A breeze blew across her face like a premonition. "In a couple of hours I have an interview with my father. I'm going to tell him that I want to help him defect." She turned back. "Will you help me do it? Will you use your connections to help me?"

There was a pause. "You're quite sure it's safe to discuss that in here?"

"Yes. Trust me." She winced inwardly. If only she'd used any words but those two, which hung in the air, ringing like bells on a jester's cap.

"OK," he said. "Have you got a plan?"

"Yes. But it has weak points."

"Let's hear it."

Hands pushed deep into her skirt pockets, she told him the situation as it stood, including Kim Wan Lee's willingness to go with her that afternoon. "I'm hoping he'll agree to go and distract Orlov a second time. When that time comes, my father will have to say he doesn't feel well and stay in his own room, and he'll have to leave his door unlocked. I'll be at that door to help him to the elevator and out of the hotel, where I'll have a cab waiting to drive us to the nearest American embassy—either in Helsinki or across the border in Sweden. I don't know which is better. Either way, it'll be the longest cab ride in the world, but I think it'll be safer than going to the airport. Airplanes arrive at known times and places. People can be waiting to meet them."

Until she said the words aloud, she hadn't known how tentative they seemed—as if she had been committed to the plan, but in a dream. Saying them to another consciousness brought the relief of entering reality, and the fear.

Jess was silent. He had taken off his tie and was pulling it taut across his thighs. The tension was in the fabric, not in his face. His face seemed almost naked, like that of someone who rarely took off his glasses. But Jess didn't wear glasses. What he had put aside was the ease of manner—the confident, relaxed connection with his environment that she thought of as American. He seemed hard and intense, as she realized she had always felt he was, at the heart of his personality, even though he kept it smoothed over, under control.

He folded the tie and laid it on the bed beside him. "The plan sounds workable. Provided the violinist can win you time to talk to your father alone this afternoon. And provided you can get your father out his door. Those are the

weakest points, as you say. I can find out whether Helsinki
or Sweden is the best place to head for, and arrange for the
cab. And be waiting in it for you."

"Jess . . . Thank you. Bless you."

"I think I can even arrange for a driver."

"Someone we can trust absolutely?"

"Yes." Jess hesitated. "I think you've met him. His name
is Ray Salmi."

She stared at him. "The man from Minnesota?"

"Yes. He works for, well, let's just say for an organiza-
tion that wanted someone keeping an eye on this festival.
I managed to find out he'd be here."

"Wait a minute. Wait. Did you tell him to keep an eye
on me?"

"Guilty."

Hedy took a deep, careful breath. When she was very
young, there had been a childless neighbor who doted on
her: sewed things for her doll, brought her little cakes, gave
her fresh fruit when no one else had it. The woman had
bright blue eyes and smelled of roses. The discovery that
she was a KGB informer had been one of the first, bewildering shocks of Hedy's life. Once again she felt that same
sense. "Do you know that I thought he might be one of the
Soviets? That I spent a lot of time worrying about him, that
I was only now beginning to think he might be safe? I was
afraid he was watching me for the KGB, and all the time
he was watching me for you!"

"Sweetheart, I'm sorry. But I was so worried about your
being here alone. What kind of person would I be if I didn't
try to do something about it?"

"The kind I— You should have told me about him. Why
didn't you?"

He raised both hands apologetically. "I was afraid you'd
be furious. I guess I was right."

"You didn't even consult me! You didn't trust me!"

The last words registered—those damn words again. Suddenly she was glad he hadn't told her about Salmi. It meant he too had violated the trust that lay between them. She would tell him they were equal traitors; she would punish him with confession and say: I saw Alik Markov. I slept with him. She clenched her hands.

"I didn't mean to upset you," Jess said. "But I had to do what I thought was right."

He looked firm and calm, not at all apologetic. The desire to hurt him drained away. She wanted to hold him and feel his strength and tell him how much he meant to her, how she had missed him—and at the same time to be left alone with the tangle of her thoughts until she had straightened them.

"I'm an ungrateful wretch," she told him. "I know you did it for me. You were probably right."

Precisely at three, the same "escort" who had taken Hedy to her father's suite the first time approached the desk in the lobby. He frowned when he saw Kim Wan Lee with her. "You come, please," he said to Hedy. "You alone."

Pleasantly, she refused. "My friend goes with me. I guarantee you, Mr. Orlov will want to see him."

The escort's frown deepened, but he bowed stiffly and motioned them to the elevator.

Once inside, Kim gave Hedy a broad, conspiratorial smile. Before the escort arrived, Kim had agreed to help her one more time. He had cocked his head to one side and said, "You will have another message to deliver from someone in America?" She had trotted out her prepared, rather feeble explanation—that the message she was about to deliver would require an answer, which in turn would need an answer, which she would then need to take back to Nikolayev—but before she got out more than two sentences,

Kim had put his hand on her arm and said, "Never mind your reason. You are wanting to do something to help Nikolayev, so I will help you." His face had been grave; she had wondered whether he suspected what she was up to— especially when he had added, as if it were irrelevant, "In South Korea, where my family comes from, a famous comedian is in jail for writing satires, but he smuggles them out right under the eyes of his guards." He had patted her hand and smiled again—it was odd, the way his face and smile were a child's but his manner that of an uncle—and said, "Today is Tuesday. I can go with you again to Nikolayev on Thursday morning at ten. Will that do?" They had agreed on it just as the escort came walking toward them at the desk.

The elevator doors slid open. The escort preceded them down the hall and knocked on the center door of the corner suite. Hedy studied the door to its right: about ten feet away, with no outward evidence of special locks.

After a noise of chains and keys, Rodion Sergevich appeared. The escort began to babble in Russian that another man had been waiting with the woman, there had been no way to prevent the man from coming, it was—

Rodion slashed him off with a gesture and told him to leave. Then he smiled. "Kim Wan Lee, I am honored, and somewhat puzzled as well."

"He has come to help me," Hedy said firmly. "You seemed dubious about my musical qualifications to interview Maestro Nikolayev, so I asked my friend Mr. Kim to come with me."

Kim, smiling, as ingenuous as she could have wanted, said, "Miss Lucas does a great service to the world of music by planning a book on Boris Nikolayev. I wish to be of use in any way I can."

Rodion's gaze slid to one side as if he wanted to look back into the apartment without moving his head. His fingers rattled once against the door; then he held out his hand to shake Kim's. "Come in. Excuse me if I remain puzzled to find a great violinist helping with an interview, but I am pleased." He motioned Kim in as if Hedy weren't there, and called out, "Boris Semyonovich, see who has come."

Hedy saw that her father was waiting on the small sofa, one hand resting on its arm. She had hoped to see him come from his room, as before, so she could confirm its location; her recollection would have to suffice. He wore an old black sweater over a white shirt. Sunlight blurred the edges of his profile. He sat immobile, like a larger-than-life puppet propped in place by Rodion, but when she and Kim walked toward him, he stirred to life.

"Good afternoon, Maestro," she said.

He smiled at her. She felt the small sting of triumph she had always felt when that happened, when Papa smiled—as if she had the power to make the unexpected happen, though she never knew exactly by what means she had done it. She did not know now, either. Quickly she sat beside him on the sofa, leaving the chairs to Rodion and Kim.

Boris blinked, looked at Kim, and asked, "Who is it?"

"I had the honor to play your violin concerto last night," Kim said.

"Ah. Excuse me—the eyes are not good—I do not know you at once. Yes. The first movement we spoke of, bars forty-three to eighty, it was good."

Kim smiled as if he had received the most extravagant compliment in the world.

"Maestro," Hedy said, "I want my book to be as musically accurate as possible, but I'm not a musician myself, as you know. So I asked Kim Wan Lee to come along, to make sure my questions about your music are appropriate. Is that agreeable?" She had spent ten minutes working out the best way to put the excuse, but it was still pretty feeble. Kim was trying to help by nodding as if her words were the embodiment of reason.

"Yes," her father said. His gaze, fixed on her, communicated nothing.

Tenting his fingers, Rodion Sergeivich asked, "You are good friends?"

"Kim is a friend of my mother's. Maestro, I'd like to start by asking about your method of working." Hedy took out her notebook, opened it, glanced down, and saw her father's hand, puffed and spotted with age, only inches away, resting on a leg encased in black slacks; below it, in the dark slipper planted on the floor, each bulge imprinted by his toes was visible. She hadn't been so close to him since they had all embraced one another that morning in the Paris hotel room, before separating to execute their plan. A sudden confidence seized her, banishing the trepidation that had been growing since she met Kim in the lobby—as if the physical closeness to her father put her at an emotional distance from him, and from everything else except her purpose.

She began with her questions, aware of her father's halting answers but apart from them, her perceptions honed by liberation from feeling, so that she seemed to know everything at once: the sun streaming in behind her; Kim's boyish, smiling face; Rodion's fingers moving through various positions, tenting, clenching, tapping.

Time went by. She had no idea how long. Kim leaned forward occasionally, to interject a comment or to sharpen the point of her question. She thought it surely must be time for him to start, but a look at her watch showed that they had been in the room only sixteen minutes. "Maestro," she asked, "for yourself, do you rate or rank the composers of history? Is Beethoven, for example, more important than Chopin? A greater genius?"

Vigorously but slowly, her father said, "One cannot

make list for genius. 'Number one, number two, number three.' No. No. That would be dangerous. Foolish. But if you ask what genius I want to be with, to . . . to pass time with, yes, some more than others. Each day of my life I think of Bach, because it is Bach who . . ."

He went on, but Hedy's perception split because Kim was leaning to Rodion and speaking in a low voice. The reply, barely audible, was something about tea. Rodion got up and walked into the kitchen area. Kim followed him.

So it had begun. It would not be easy. They were only at the other end of the room, so theoretically Rodion could catch some of Hedy's and her father's words, and there was no way of knowing how long Kim could hold him. She must start immediately.

She leaned closer to her father and whispered in Russian, "Papa. It's Anna."

His eyes, beneath their fleshy lids, were as still as smoked glass. She waited, wondering with her strange, distant clarity whether he might call out for Rodion. She repeated, "It's Anna."

She had been wrong. There was something in his eyes—a glaze of tears.

She allowed herself to reach across the inches and rest her hand on his for a moment. When she took it away, his fingers gave one convulsive leap, then fell back.

Bending her head and pretending to be writing in her notebook, she said, "Mama sends all her love to you. She loves you as she always has, and believes you wanted to come with us to America. I want to take you to her now. To New York. To finish what we started in Paris. Will you let me do it?"

She raised her head. Her father looked like someone pulled from sleep by a bright light: disoriented and frozen. Perhaps it had been too much, all at once, but there was no alternative. "Papa," she whispered, but from the kitchen area she heard Kim's voice, as bright and loud as he could reasonably make it, saying something about the violin. She stole a quick glance. Rodion, though listening to Kim, was looking in her direction.

"Maestro," she said briskly, hardly knowing what words would follow, "may we return to Bach for a moment? If you say he's the most personally meaningful of your musical ancestors, has he been a literal influence on you?" Tiny pause. "Maybe that question isn't clear. I'll ask it another way. What do you think Bach's lesson has been? Did you learn specific things from him? Do you think people can listen to your works and hear in them your admiration for Bach?"

Her father's eyes were clearing.

In Russian, Rodion called, "Boris Semyonovich, may I bring you a glass of tea?"

She mouthed *nyet* to her father.

Time hung like molasses on a spoon. Finally he answered, "No tea."

"I'll be back with you in a few moments," Rodion said.

Urgently Hedy whispered, "Papa, I have everything planned. On Thursday morning say you don't feel well and stay in your room. Make sure your door is unlocked. At ten o'clock Kim Wan Lee will come by unexpectedly to speak to Rodion, and I will come to your bedroom door, to help you out. A car will be waiting for us in front of the hotel. This time it will work, you will be with Mama and me. This time you will be free."

Her father's hand moved to rest on hers for a moment, warm and heavy.

"Ten o'clock Thursday morning," she whispered. "Have your door unlocked. Do you understand, Papa? Will you do it?"

The flesh around his eyes quivered, seemed to struggle. Behind her she heard Rodion and Kim coming back toward

them. In English, using full voice, she said, "Do you understand my question, Maestro?"

He cleared his throat. "Yes. I understand."

"What is the problem?" Rodion took his chair again.
"Shall I translate?"

"I understand question," her father said slowly but
firmly. "Does one hear Bach in my music? No. Not in style,
not in passages. But what I learn from him as young man—
as boy, perhaps—is technique, how technique is important
and wonderful. You know Bach fugue that one can play
entirely . . . ah, what is English word . . . same both ways?
Same top and bottom?"

"Backward," Rodion said. "And upside down."

"Yes, yes. You play fugue as written, and it is splendid.
Then you play backward and upside down and everything
is again splendid. Imagine mind that can compose this
thing! So what I learn from Bach is . . ."

He went on, his words clear but distant, like bells on a
mountain. Yet he was close, so close. Hedy watched his lips
move, saw his tongue work behind them, noted a fine down
of stubble on his cheek. She was a camera, storing everything for a consciousness to deal with later. When his voice
stopped, she checked her list and found another question,
then another, none of which seemed to have any content.
Yet they must have had, for her father's voice went on, and
Kim interjected occasional comments as before, until
finally, at some length of time she couldn't possibly deter-
mine, Rodion stood and said the session was over.

"Miss Hedy Lucas, you have been with Boris Nikolayev
for one hour and five minutes. This opportunity you had
is a rare one. We trust you will use it wisely."

"I will certainly try," she said. She stood, turned to her
father, and held out her hand to shake his. "Maestro, thank
you for talking to me. I wish I could spend many more
hours with you."

"Yes," he said. With emphasis, surely? But his hand seemed lifeless and held hers without secret pressure.

Kim Wan Lee came up beside her to say good-bye. They were ushered to the door by a Rodion so affable to Kim that he even said a pleasant good-bye to Hedy.

Moments later they were out in the hall.

They walked to the elevator in silence. Once inside, Kim's smile reappeared. "You delivered your message?"

"I think so. I mean, yes. Thank you, more than I can say."

"Do you know that you were right? Orlov himself played the violin once. How did you know it?"

"I . . . don't remember," she said.

"All I did was to ask if he was a musician too. He looked embarrassed, then he told me. Now, on Thursday morning—let us discuss exactly what we shall do."

She hung on long enough to do it, to explain that while he got in at the center door of the suite, she would be going to the door of Nikolayev's room. But as soon as Kim left her, the detachment that had carried her through the interview whipped away like a scarf in a storm, and she started to shake.

CHAPTER SIXTEEN

Alik was stretched on his bed again, hands behind his head, eyes on the ceiling.

He heard the watchdog, at the other end of the room, clear his throat and say, "You have hardly been out for two days, Aleksandr Romanovich, except to one concert and to the American woman's room. The festival will be over soon."

Alik dug his thumbs into his neck but said nothing. The watchdog went on. "You wouldn't like to try one of the sightseeing tours?"

"I'm not interested in tours. But why deprive yourself? Go without me."

After a moment the man said, "Do you not wish to go out this afternoon?"

"Yes. Alone." The watchdog said nothing. Alik kept staring at the ceiling. "Alexei Grigorevich, don't you ever want

to be alone? No eyes but your own? No ears but your own
two handles? No mind but your own to say, Hey, I'm by
myself in here, let's stretch and look around and see what's
good to think today, let's draw a picture, write a poem?
Sing a song? Beat a drum? Eh?"

"No," said the watchdog.

Alik sat up. "Too bad!" he cried. His guitar was propped
by the bed; he grabbed it, struck off three dissonant chords,
and improvised: "Dark in my head, empty, no thoughts but
my own . . . Hey, I'm rattling around in here, 'I'm lonely
. . . Stuff me with good Soviet ideas, stick an apple in my
mouth . . ."

He stopped as abruptly as he had begun. Baiting the
watchdog was no cure, and staring at the ceiling no ano-
dyne, for the things that had been seething inside him ever
since he had left Anya's room.

The moment he closed her door behind him, his hands
had trembled with the desire to beat on it, or on himself.
On a note she must have intended to give him, she had
written, "Did you tell Rodion Sergeivich that my parents
and I were going to defect in Paris?"—and he had left a
stupid plea for help scrawled on her bathroom mirror. He
was the greatest fool in Finland, or any other country.

Then the watchdog had come up and said, "I am instructed to take the tape from you, to deliver in the morning." Alik had looked at the man—at the round, stolid face,
with its cheeks full of broken blood vessels and the ears like
grips on a sugar bowl, ears that might listen to the tape,
might channel its contents into the small mind that sat
between them. Rage had spurted through his body, and
when he got back upstairs, there was no vodka to choke it
off because he had taken it to Anya's and left it. Along with
his dream.

What had happened for Rodion's microphone—the
travesty that somehow had become genuine, the pretense

he could not keep from turning into reality, so that even as he was despising himself, the loathing had formed a strange hybrid with a fierce feeling of love for the young man he once had been with Anya—that hour of his life was not for anyone to soil with the act of listening.

And the one man he couldn't keep from doing so had not deigned to make his reaction known, not in a day and half.

Alik laid the guitar on the bed and got up. "I'm going upstairs," he said.

"But Rodion Sergeivich has not asked for you."

"I don't give a damn."

He went out, not even closing the door. The watchdog followed at a distance, like a toy soldier pulled on a string, the one toy that never broke.

Rodion answered Alik's knock. "Yes? What do you want?"

"To see Boris. About the concerto."

"He's resting in his room."

"Fine. I'll come in and wait."

Rodion shrugged and told the watchdog to leave.

"May I have a vodka?" Alik said.

"It's on the table."

Alik poured himself a glass and took one of the kitchen chairs. Rodion stood looking at him with the expression of faint amusement that had puzzled Alik when he first identified it as a child. What did cousin Rodion find to make him smile so much? Answer, long in coming: the feeling of outwitting people. But which had come first, the feeling or the outwitting?

"You haven't told me how you liked the tape I made for you," Alik said.

"True." Rodion's amusement grew less faint. "Not very much, in fact."

Alik's glass held no ice, but it was suddenly cold. "What do you mean?"

"I heard you say and do many things, but I heard little effort to learn why the woman is interested in Boris Semyonovich."

Alik swore as if insulted and said, "I asked her many times, and I—"

"Three times."

"And each time she gave the same answer—she is writing a book. Why do you think there is more to learn? What else can there be?"

"Who knows? Since you didn't learn it."

"The woman thinks of nothing but sex and money. That must have been clear to you. She is a typical American, materialistic and shallow. She was not interested in talking of Boris Semyonovich, only in getting into bed with me. I admit it was not entirely unpleasant, as you no doubt could hear, although our Russian women are better. If you had had the same opportunity for comparison, you would agree. One loyal Communist always agrees with another, isn't that so?" Alik knew his voice was wrong: the contempt, for Rodion and for himself, was too audible, riding like a shark's fin above the water, but he could not keep it any farther down. "Now that I have done my duty to the State, I hope I'll be relieved of further contact with the woman, who is not of any special interest, in my opinion." He made himself stop, and wait.

Rodion looked at him blandly. "Enough about the tape. Since you're here, let's discuss what plans the Ministry may have for you for next winter. In the present climate, we may permit more appearances in Moscow . . ."

Mechanically the vodka went down Alik's throat. Mechanically the responses came up. He tried twice more to return to the tape, but Rodion deflected the conversation with a skill honed over many years in the Ministry.

He was not going to learn, Alik thought, whether Anya was under suspicion. He would never see her again, for he

would not be able to evade the watchdog again. He would
return to Moscow and spend the rest of his days wondering
which of his songs could be sung and which poems and
stories published, grateful for every relaxation They permitted, never knowing how long it would last, always fear-
ful They would decide to tighten the screws again, as They
had done before. He heard Rodion asking whether he
would continue playing classical works. "Will my masters
allow it?" he said harshly, and gave the answer a vodka
chaser.

Finally Boris came shuffling from his room. "Boris!"
Alik cried, and went to throw his arms around the old man.
"My friend, we must talk. About the concerto, about to-
morrow night's performance."

"Yes, yes," Boris said, as if he were a child.

Sitting across from each other at the table, they began to
talk, ostensibly about the concerto, because Rodion was
there, but all talk of tempos and fingering and expressive
nuances was beside the point. Such matters had already
been settled. The point was to rest against the bulk of
Boris's presence, and his understanding. The point was to
find a way to tell him, and to ask for comfort. . . . "My
friend," Alik said, "I am afraid you will be disappointed.
The goal we have always had, I don't think I will be able
to do justice to it."

"What are you speaking of?" Rodion said.

Alik turned on him savagely. "The concerto! I am telling
Boris that there is very little chance I will perform as he
would have liked! That tomorrow night it will all be over!"

Rodion looked puzzled, but not Boris. Boris understood.
With terrible sadness in his eyes, he poured them both
more vodka.

Although Hedy and Jess moved constantly, time did not.
They had ample Finnish meals, went to hear Brahms bal-

lades and even a contemporary Finnish chamber music offering, wandered among shops, took walks—without, as far as Hedy could tell, being followed. But no matter what they did, or for how long, the time was always "not yet Thursday morning at ten."

A dozen times—looking at Jess's profile at a concert, lifting her glass to his in a restaurant, watching him emerge in blue pajamas from the bathroom—she considered telling him that she had seen and talked with Alik. Each time she said nothing. That decision would have to stay in suspension, like time.

Tuesday, while they were walking, Jess stopped before a huge poster:

NIKOLAYEV!
World Premiere, Concerto for Guitar,
Conducted by composer / Thursday, 20:00
Soloist, Aleksandr Markov

"I'd like to have heard this," Jess said, "but we'll be gone. Is Markov good?"

All she said was "I don't know. I haven't heard him since I left."

They talked of the twins, of Vera, of Jess's future; they went over and over the details of the plan, including exactly what to do once they were all in the taxi in which Jess and Salmi would be waiting for her and her father; they went to bed and lay close but didn't make love because she said she couldn't and he said he understood that she was too tense.

Wednesday night, at dinner, he pulled a New York paper from his pocket and handed it to her. "Something on page four that might please you."

It was a small story: Representative Jesse Newman had

issued a statement condemning not only the banning of books at a Long Island library but any attempt by religious fundamentalists to impose censorship in American society.

She got up and went around the table to kiss him, bumping into a waiter.

Over their coffee, Jess said, "The fundamentalists have millions of votes, you know. The party bigwigs, the ones who could make or break my political future, don't want any of us to antagonize them. I thought I could live with that at least for a while. But the hell with it. I always said that if I catch myself starting to want power for its own sake, to value it more than principles, I'd leave public life. Let the fundamentalists drive me out, if they can."

He stared into his cup, stirring. "Though maybe I should leave politics."

"What? Why on earth would you?"

"Didn't I just tell you I flirted with expediency and compromise? It's so damn easy to do. I believe in individual rights, but I'm elected to serve all the people, and they have a thousand, a million, different values. That's what individualism *is*—differences. Pluralism. So people's values clash. Half the time the law exacerbates the conflict instead of helping resolve it, because more and more the law sides with the majority, not the individual. So politically, how do you protect people's rights to their pluralistic beliefs? How do you serve both the law *and* the individual? Without compromise and expediency?"

"The way you're doing it. If you stop, you'll leave politics to those who *do* want power for its own sake. You know," she added slowly, "all my life in Russia I heard, Glory to the *kollektiv*, individualism is wrong—for the very reason you named. It's pluralistic, so it's chaotic, anarchic. How can anyone live that way? It's so much easier, so much more comfortable, to have one centralized way of doing and thinking. I never thought of it till now, but in the name of the masses, collectivism leads to oneness, while in the name of the individual, capitalism leads to diversity. A paradox, isn't it?"

"It's also an elegant putdown," Jess said. "I should stop complaining about the difficulty of being a politician in a free country?"

"No. I only mean that freedom isn't always . . . easy." She sighed. "I hope I can help Papa adjust to it."

Was she really doing the right thing? she wondered. What would she do with Papa in America, especially after Mama was gone? But those decisions were in suspension, like time. "Let's go over the plan once more," she said.

Then it was Thursday morning, and ten o'clock, which had never been going to come, was bearing down on her like an express train.

Going up in the elevator, she did word games to keep from thinking.

a	o	a
at	ho	ca*
fat	hop	cap
father	hope	cape
		escape

*(not cheating, it was the Scottish form of *call*)

Kim Wan Lee had met her in the lobby and gone up five minutes ahead. He would knock and get Rodion to let him in by saying he wanted, off the record, to explore the possibility of a Russian tour. Papa would have left his door unlocked. *Unlock, knock, Bach, ten o'clock. . . .*

When she got off the elevator, the hall was empty. There was no sign of Kim, so he must be inside the suite. She began to walk toward it. She was wearing slacks and a sweater and carrying only her purse. Everything else would be left behind, except the few items Jess had squeezed into his case. It must look to any watching KGB as if she was only going to the airport to see Jess off. Muffled sounds came from behind the doors she passed, but she couldn't identify them. It was as if the corridor led through a place where aliens lived.

She stopped at the center door of the suite, listened, heard nothing. Cautiously she moved ten feet to the right, to her father's bedroom door, put her hand on the knob, and turned it.

It moved only a fraction of an inch. When she tried it the other way, there was no give at all. The door was locked.

She stared at the knob disbelievingly, as if it had grown to her hand. When she tried again, the result was the same. It was locked. Somewhere behind her, down the hall, there was muffled laughter.

She knocked the only way she dared: softly. Four times. No response.

She stepped backward to think— Call Aini? try to call the suite? get Jess? find Alik and ask him? ask him what?— and collided with someone.

She didn't believe it until she tried to pull away and found her arm held by a strong hand, which guided her to turn around. Her heart thudded and made her vision jump, so she couldn't tell whether it was the man who had followed her, or perhaps the man who had previously escorted her to the apartment. It didn't matter; they all had the same face. And the same power. "What you do here?" the face said.

She forced her voice to work. "I have seen Boris Nikolayev before. I must see him again. I am an American journalist."

The face didn't respond. The hand, still clutching her arm, led her to the center door of the suite. The other hand knocked. Down the hall, someone laughed again.

The door pulled open a bit and revealed Rodion Sergeivich, expressionless.

In Russian, the face said, "I found her knocking on the
other door."

"Very good," Rodion said, also in Russian. "You may go.
I'll take care of her now."

The hand released her arm, and the man moved away.
She reached inside herself for strength she hoped was there
and said to Rodion, as defiantly as she could, "When I
studied my notes, I found I needed to ask the maestro
something else. I thought I'd try to talk to him alone. We
American journalists don't like being supervised."

"I know very well what your bourgeois press is like."
Rodion crossed his arms and looked at her. His gaze had a
thrusting, impersonal intimacy that felt like gunpoint.
"This is a morning of unexpected visits. Your friend Kim
Wan Lee has also come to see us. But perhaps you know
that."

"No. Is he here?" She hoped she sounded surprised.
"Then you won't mind if I come in for a few minutes?"

Rodion smiled. "I insist upon it." He let her into the
apartment.

Kim Wan Lee was in one of the armchairs, her father on
the sofa, his eyes lowered. She willed them to lift, to somehow signal her what had happened. But the fleshy lids
hung like shrouds.

Kim looked uncertain. He must be wondering what the
hell was going on—why she was there, why Nikolayev
hadn't been in his room as she'd said he would be. Trying
to be sprightly, he said, "Hello, Hedy. What are you doing
here? I came by to have a little unofficial chat with Rodion."

"Boris Semyonovich," Rodion said, "Miss Hedy Lucas
was knocking on the door of your room. She must want
rather badly to speak with you."

Her father's gaze lifted, crossed hers like a plea, then

moved to the window. Kim blinked rapidly. Rodion's hand moved back and forth across the top of a chair like a pendulum.

"I only wanted to ask the maestro one more thing," she said.

"And what would that be?" Rodion asked.

What, indeed? Nothing was in her mind, no question except the one she couldn't ask: Papa, what happened? Then she heard herself say, "I wondered if Boris Nikolayev had any message for me to take back to America."

No one spoke for a moment. Then Rodion said lightly, "Kim Wan Lee, I regret that our conversation must be put off to another time. Miss Hedy Lucas raises something we must be alone with her to discuss."

Panic flew up from her stomach and clotted in her throat.

Kim frowned. "Hedy, this is agreeable to you?"

She nodded. *Don't leave me,* she thought, *please.*

"Shall I leave you, then?" Kim asked. She nodded again. "Shall I wait for you in the lobby?" he said.

"No thanks. I'll . . . I'll speak to you later." He could be a witness, she thought wildly; he could tell people that she had been in the room when Rodion tried to deny it. *I am an American citizen,* she thought. *An American citizen.*

Kim left, a frown still sitting uncomfortably on his face. She moved to stand beside her father. Looking down, she saw his scalp, pink as a baby's, through the fine, white hair. The sight was startling, as if she had seen something private, and unimagined to that moment. She had felt that way once when he was ill in bed with something. She had tiptoed into the bedroom and seen him asleep in the middle of the day, skin pale and mouth hanging flaccidly: the giant of her childhood laid flat, looking weak and almost stupid.

"Now, Miss Hedy Lucas," Rodion said, "let us all be frank together."

"All right."

"I will start, shall I? By telling you that you are not Miss Hedy Lucas."

"I am an American citizen."

"True. But I speak of your life in the Soviet Union. As Anna Borisovna."

"Rodion, be quiet." Her father's voice was strong. "You don't know what you are saying."

"I do, Boris Semyonovich. I admit that I did not suspect at once, but for the past several days I have thought that beneath the American accent and the American clothes and the bourgeois attitudes, we might find your daughter Anna. Recently my suspicions were confirmed."

"How?" she said harshly.

"It would serve no purpose to tell you."

She forced herself not to say, By Alik?

Rodion smiled as if she had, and spoke in Russian. "Do you deny that you are the defector Anna Borisovna Nikolayeva?"

She sat beside her father and took his hand. Also in Russian, she said, "I do not deny it." Unexpectedly the panic in her throat dissolved. A strange relief began to take its place.

She heard her father whisper, "Anna."

"Good." Rodion sat across from them. "I have been asking myself why the daughter of Boris Semyonovich would try to see him while concealing her identity." He made his fingers into a steeple and rested his chin on it. "Several answers occurred to me—perhaps the daughter is ashamed, perhaps she is afraid—but there is also another possibility. Perhaps she hopes to take her father back to the West with her. Perhaps that is what she had in mind to do this morning when she came knocking on his door."

Hedy was silent.

Rodion nodded as if she had said yes. "I can assure you that your father will not go. He did not go twenty years ago in Paris, and he will not go now."

It seemed to Hedy that her father's hand, inside hers, went flaccid. She clutched it harder, forcing life back into it, but said nothing.

Rodion leaned forward. "Boris Semyonovich, if you like, you may leave with your daughter. Now."

"That's an old trick," Hedy scoffed. "As soon as we leave this apartment, you will order KGB to stop us in the hall or the lobby or the street, so you can claim he was caught trying to defect. Is that what you did to him in Paris?"

"No one will stop you. I give my word."

"Which I have no reason to trust."

"Boris Semyonovich does. He knows I mean it. You may leave this hotel, this town, this country, if he wishes. But you will see that he does not wish."

"You ask me to believe that a deputy minister of culture will simply allow him to go to the West—a man as important to the Soviet Union, and to your career, as my father is?"

Rodion smiled. "Perhaps I am simply illustrating the strength of my conviction that he does not wish to go."

She turned to her father and put her other hand over his. "Papa, shall we go, then?"

His gaze met hers, but told her nothing. His lips parted and the tip of his tongue crept between them.

"Please come with me, Papa. To Mama. To freedom." He tried to take his hand away, but she wouldn't let him. "What do I tell Mama, then? That you don't want to go to her?"

"That I love her," he said in a harsh croak.

"Then come to her!"

He shook his head but said nothing.

"All right, Papa, if you don't want to stay with us, then come just for a few months. Until she dies." She turned to Rodion. "You're so eager to make propaganda points for the Soviet Union—let the great composer go visit his dying wife, then tell the world how humanitarian you are."

Rodion pursed his lips. "I couldn't make such a decision on my own, as you well know. But even if I could, I doubt Boris Semyonovich would want to go."

"Why not? Papa, is Rodion right? I know they'd have you under surveillance the whole time, but even so, we could be together, the three of us. . . . Won't you come?"

"Too old," he said. "Too long . . ." He closed his eyes, as if to spare both of them the sight of what he felt, and wrenched his hand away from hers.

"What did you do to him?" she cried to Rodion. "What the hell have you done to him?"

"You should ask yourself the question." Rodion's right hand slapped his knee in rhythm with his words. "You come back into your father's life, agitating him with talk of an old life he has forgotten, prattling about freedom as if he does not have it, thinking of nothing but your own concerns. You are not his child any longer; you are the child of materialism and individualism. I have done nothing to your father. I hold him in the highest esteem and affection. So I make it possible for him to do what he wants."

"This is a man who can never get a note of music published or performed without permission of the State, whom the State can denounce and punish at its whim, and you dare to talk about freedom and doing what he wants?"

"Anna Borisovna, I advise you to curb your cold war rhetoric before it does you harm, and to accept what I have already told you: Your father will not go with you, as he did not go in Paris."

"Why not? I demand to know why! Tell me why he

won't go, one of you, dammit! Tell me why he didn't go in Paris."

"You will not like the explanation."

"How I'll feel about it is my business. Tell me."

Rodion stood. "Boris Semyonovich, perhaps it would be good for your daughter to know what happened in Paris. Will you tell her, or shall I?"

Her father turned to him, confusion muddying his face. Rodion nodded, almost imperceptibly, and her father relaxed a bit. Why do you let Rodion do everything? Hedy wanted to shout, and in the next moment wondered if she had glimpsed, in microcosm, the bond between the two men: the burden of action, of coping, offered to Rodion, who accepted it with a look both imperious and obsequious. Accepted it in return for what?

Rodion walked to the window and gazed down. From the back he looked even smaller and slighter, an improbable vessel for power, but when he turned to face them, he was again the deputy minister of culture, plump not with flesh but with forty years of sitting on the right side of the desk while people queued before him, hats in hand.

He folded his arms. "Very well. I will tell you. You know that a considerable exception was made in the case of your family. Not only was Vera Andreyevna allowed to join her husband on the tour to Paris, but, as a result of Boris Semyonovich's appeals to me, and because of my desire to be helpful to him, I was finally able to obtain permission for you to go with your parents. Naturally, because I am not a fool, I was suspicious of this fervent need to have you with them, although I did not truly believe Boris Semyonovich would do anything stupid or disloyal. Still, one must take precautions. Then I became certain a defection was being planned. Accordingly, I made sure that—"

"How?" Hedy asked, voice pinched as if a hand held her throat. "How did you become certain?"

Rodion's smile screwed into place like a monocle. "I see no reason for you to know. Let us simply say that I found out."

So it was true: Alik had told him. She had trusted Alik and he had betrayed them. Why the hell else would Rodion be smiling like that? She needed to be alone with the knowledge. She could feel the guilt crouching, ready to leap, but it would have to wait because Rodion was going on and she must listen. She locked her hands and forced her mind to his words.

"I had given my personal guarantee to the minister that there would be no trouble in Paris with Boris Semyonovich, so of course no trouble could be permitted. Arrangements were made for your father to be watched even more closely than usual. The three of you stayed together constantly, except for performances. Then your father suggested—no, insisted—that he and I go to a bistro for lunch, a bistro that I knew the three of you had already visited—shall we say inspected? Then, shortly before it was time for that lunch, you and your mother left the hotel to do some shopping. So I wondered. Yes, I wondered." Rodion paused, and this time his smile seemed to be for himself, for his acumen. "We sat at a table near the front of the bistro. I recall that your father ordered veal ragout but barely touched it. I ate little myself because I was busy talking. There were many things to talk about, you know—like your father's previous trip outside the motherland. No doubt you don't recall it. You must have been only seven or eight. Boris Semyonovich went to London and New York to conduct several concerts and represent Soviet artists at an international conference. He was—"

"I know all about it. He went because he was ordered to go."

"He was a loyal citizen. He went, and he did not like what happened." Rodion got up and began to walk about the living area, touching the tops of chairs for emphasis as he spoke. "The bourgeois artists who claimed to be friends of the Soviet Union tried to make a spectacle of him. The bourgeois press hounded him. They asked him dozens of ignorant questions, talked as if they knew best what he should have done, showed him no reverence. The West was not a happy experience for him. So I talked about that at our lunch. There were other things to mention. The difficulty that so many Soviets had had—that they still have—in adjusting to life outside the motherland. Even the dissidents cannot stop loving her, I am told. Then there was the false nature of the concepts on which Western societies are built. The individualism and so-called freedom of America, for example, which is in fact chaos and disorder. Russians are not prepared—why should they be?—for a life that encourages dangerous and antisocial activity and barbaric attitudes and practices, like racism and the worship of weapons. A society of individualism is a society without discipline, for there is no central idea to believe in."

In spite of herself, knowing it was not wise, Hedy had to smile.

Rodion went on as if he hadn't seen. "I reminded your father that in the so-called democracies of the West, the artist is thrown to the mercy of the marketplace. Is his special training paid for? No. Is his teaching position at a conservatory guaranteed? No. Is there a composers union to provide him with the necessary materials and support? No. Is there an apparatus in position to guarantee publication and nationwide performance of every work that serves the needs of the Soviet people? No. Is there housing provided for him and his family, and medical care if there is illness? No. None of these things. Instead he must go with his cap in his hand and try to find some orchestra willing to play his works, to try just one of his works, and if the work is unusual in some way and the orchestra thinks it will not make money for them, then what happens to your artist? He is in the street, with only his cap to eat for dinner and no doctor if it gives him indigestion."

Hedy turned to her father. He had leaned back and was watching Rodion through half-closed eyes, as if the conversation were about someone else. "Papa, what did you reply to all this?"

"There was no need for your father to reply," Rodion said. "I was merely discoursing on topics of interest—idly, as one will sometimes do over a good lunch. I did not insult him by asking why he had wanted to have lunch in that particular bistro or whether he was contemplating doing anything inimical to the interests of the Soviet people. No, no. I merely drank my wine and let my mind wander among various subjects I thought would be of interest to him. The lunch was a long one. Even though I did most of the talking, I knew that I had reached his heart. When I was finished, I sat back and sipped my wine. Neither of us spoke for some time. Then your father excused himself and went to the men's washroom. He was away for a very long time. But I wasn't worried. No, no. I ordered another *demi-bouteille*. And I was right not to worry, for eventually your father returned to the table."

Hedy looked at her father. His eyes had closed completely. She swung back to Rodion Sergeivich. "Don't you mean that he was forced to return? That you had KGB waiting for him in the alley so he couldn't get out the back door?"

"No, no," Rodion said as if to a child.

"You ask me to believe you didn't have KGB watching the bistro?"

"Why don't you ask your father?"

"Papa?"

Silence.

"He doesn't know," Rodion said. "I will tell you why." He was standing behind his chair. He tapped the rhythm of his next words on its back with one finger. "Your father doesn't know because he never got into the alley. He returned to the table because that was his wish. The truth is exactly as the Soviet Union has always stated it. Boris Semyonovich resisted the traitorous appeals of his wife and daughter. He did not want to leave his country."

CHAPTER SEVENTEEN

"**I**s that true, Papa?" Hedy said, her voice childish with disbelief.

She turned to him. The sun's position had shifted; coming through the window at a higher angle, it made a white corona of his hair and hid whatever was in his eyes. "What Rodion says, is it true? Did you *choose* to stay behind?"

He was still silent.

She heard Rodion say, "I warned you that you wouldn't like it."

She ignored him and kept looking at her father, hidden in the sun. "I understand that you can't tell the truth in front of Rodion."

"No doubt it pleases you to think that," Rodion said.

Hedy swung to face him. "Papa doesn't dare say anything except what you want him to say. Let him come to

New York and tell me the story you just told. Then I might believe it."

Rodion smiled, lifted his hands in a graceful shrug, and took his chair again, across from them.

"Papa," Hedy said, gripping his hand, "Mama and I have to understand why you didn't—" She stopped. For his sake, she was loath to use the word *defect* in Rodion's presence, even though Rodion had done so. "Mama and I need to know what happened to you that day," she said. "Isn't there something you can tell me?"

Rodion said, "He has no desire to relive these matters. You are only upsetting him with your questions. With your presence."

"Is that true, Papa? Would you like me to go?"

"No." His hand moved in hers. "Anna."

"I won't leave. But you must talk to me. Tell me something I can take home to Mama."

He shifted his head; his gaze emerged from shadow. "Tell your mother nothing."

It was so surprising that for a moment Hedy thought she had imagined it. But his eyes were on her, as darkly bright as they had used to be when he would finally look away from the distance where his Demon Music lived and would focus on her and Mama as keenly as if he had just discovered them. She had used to imagine their images suspended at the back of his mind, like dolls, until he blinked and set them in motion again. "Why, Papa?" she said. "Don't you want Mama to know what happened?"

"Let her die in peace, Anna."

"Papa, you can't do that! All your life you've held yourself away from us, and escaped into your music, but you can't do it again. I won't let you! Mama and I have lived almost twenty years without knowing what happened in Paris, and why. You've got to tell me now. What Rodion

Sergeivich said, is it true? You didn't even try to come with us?"

Her father wanted to turn away. She could feel the desire trembling in his hand. But the cords in his neck stiffened like brakes; he didn't turn. He looked at her and said, "Yes. It is true."

She released his hand. For all those years she had thought nothing could be worse than learning that, through Alik's betrayal, she had been responsible for her father's staying behind. She had been wrong. This was worse.

"I warned you," Rodion said again.

She stared at her father, at the thin, dark lips through which his words had come, as if she could force them back by sheer will. He hadn't tried to come with them in Paris. No doubt he hadn't tried to leave his door unlocked for her at ten o'clock either.

"Don't tell your mother," he said. "It is easier for her not to know. Easier to think . . . what she thinks."

"She thinks you were caught! That you want to get out but they won't let you!"

He looked away.

Hedy sucked in her breath sharply. "That's why you won't go with me, even for a visit. Isn't it? You can't face her and lie to her, but you can't face her and tell the truth either."

"I sent a letter. Rodion saw that it was sent as I wrote it."

"You mean, 'This way is best, for all three of us'? She got it. She's not going to die in peace, Papa. She hasn't been at peace for twenty years."

"Please," he said. "Don't tell her."

Almost like a physical object, she could feel the burden of that request hovering, ready to settle on her. She stood up, as if she could throw it off, and felt an anger rising in her that had been banked for half her life, perhaps most of her life, so hot it was indistinguishable from cold. She disowned the emotion that had possessed her at the performance of the violin concerto and made her try to liberate her father. She wanted to turn on him, grab his shoulders, shake him, scream at him—to transform him, by the force of her feeling, into someone different: who would love her with a steady flame, as her mother did, no flickering in and out of strange, obsessed states; who would be able to show that he loved her; above all, someone she could understand. She tried to block her emotion by turning to the window and thinking of the world out there—of Jess, waiting in the car and wondering what was happening—but nothing would stop the anger, nothing except the chance to have her life over, to be given it by a different kind of father, to make herself the daughter not of a genius but of a predictable, comprehensible man who would never abandon his daughter and his wife.

Slowly she forced her hands apart, knowing that her anger was futile, that if parents had half a chance to shape their children, the children had none at all in reciprocation. A child was born to the people who conceived it, period—who had to be accepted, and that was that. She had left Russia because she wanted a life of choices, yet in the fundamental fact of her life, those from whom she had received it, there was no choice at all.

Except one, the only choice anyone ever had with another human being: to take him as he was, or not. But first, to try to understand *why* he was.

She glanced at Rodion. He was regarding her complacently. Was there no danger from him any longer? Or was it only that her mind was too crowded for fear? She went back to the sofa. "Papa, please help me understand. Why didn't you want to leave?"

"Because I did not . . ." He stopped and sighed.

"Why," Rodion said, "is it so hard to accept that your

father loves the motherland and the glory of her rich culture? That the thought of never seeing her forests and rivers and skies again, of no longer hearing her beautiful language, would be too much for him to bear?"

Her father gave a strange shiver.

"The world is full of natural beauty and rich culture," Hedy said, "and there are people everywhere to speak Russian with, because they have all left the motherland." She knotted her hands. "Papa, you said . . . You told Mama and me . . . Didn't you want to be free to write? To live where your music could be separated from ideology, and from fear? No more worry that you would be denounced again, under some new Stalin, or lose your teaching post or—"

"He has nothing to fear," Rodion said sharply. "The things you speak of happened long ago. Nikolayev is revered in Russia. He composes as he likes."

"As long as he says and does what *you* like. Yes, I hear you talk about reform and liberalization—but it's not the first time you've talked about them, is it? Yes, it's good if you allow some criticism, if you let some of the dead poets finally be published in their own country—but why must they wait till they're dead? Yes, reform is good, but one thing never changes. It's still the Party using art for political purposes—for better trade with the West, for getting the intellectuals to support you, for safety valves at home. Release this book or that movie so people will forget all the other things they still can't have and do! Whatever is happening happens only because the Party *permits* it. None of it happens by *right*. You can't let it. Today you *permit* Nikolayev to compose as he likes. Tomorrow you could decide that his music—"

"I will tell you what I do not *permit* in this room," Rodion said. "Bourgeois rhetoric from a defector."

"Let her speak. She says the truth." The authoritative voice was her father's. Hedy turned to him gratefully. "I

am going back to the Soviet Union with you," he told
Rodion. "In return my daughter speaks as she wishes."

The two men gazed at each other, a motionless jousting,
until some silent exchange was completed and Rodion
shrugged his acceptance. Acceptance in return for what?
Hedy wondered.

"Papa, if you know that what I say is the truth, then why
don't you—why didn't you—want to live where you could
compose in freedom?"

He shook his head, and there was silence, broken only by
the clatter of a cleaning cart in the hall. The sun had shifted
position and now struck his arm and hand, which, in the
glare, looked passive and pale, like wax.

"Perhaps," Rodion said, "the nature of that so-called
Western freedom was clear to your father. We honor your
father and provide him with security. Why should he want
to go to your free marketplace and sell his work like a
peddler?"

"Let him tell me that, then! Stop putting words in his
mouth."

Rodion shrugged. "Am I telling her lies, Boris Semyonovich?"

Both of them looked at her father. "It is not so easy for
me as you think, Anna," he said.

"Papa, I'll be there to help you now. I don't say it's easy
to be an artist in a free country. Yes, you have to deal with
other people's choices. But they make those choices freely,
just as you do. Their freedom to decide whether to buy
your work is the same as yours to create what you want.
One freedom safeguards the other."

Rodion made a disbelieving sound.

Hedy swung on him. "How can you say you love art and
not understand that artists must be free to think and say
and create whatever they like?"

"It is not Rodion you are angry with," her father said. "It is me."

"I'm not angry, Papa. I just don't understand what happened in Paris. Is Rodion right? You decided you didn't need freedom after all?"

"No," he said with a terrible wistfulness.

"Then what?"

He gave a sigh so heavy that it shook his cheeks. "Do you remember that Stravinsky visited the Soviet Union in the early sixties?"

"Vaguely. What does that have to do with you and Paris?"

"The minister of culture gave a reception for Stravinsky, which some of us composers were chosen to attend. After the toasts, Stravinsky made some remarks about Russia, his love for her, his inability to forget her, his regret for not having created his works there. A man can have only one country, he said, one birthplace, and that is the most important factor in his life."

"Then why didn't Stravinsky stay there? Why did he choose to settle in Paris? To spend virtually all his life outside Russia?"

"Once the ties are cut," Rodion said smoothly, "they can't be made whole again. They can only be regretted. That is the tragedy, which Boris Semyonovich understands well."

"So, Papa," she said, "is that it? You stayed because you . . . didn't want to leave the culture and the natural beauty?"

Her father gripped the arm of the sofa with one hand; she felt that he was bracing to pull something from an inner depth. "I stayed because I was afraid."

"Of what, Papa?" She had always known that there was fear in him, like liquid at the heart of a mountain, but she had assumed it was fear of the knock in the night—of prison, even death, as he had seen happen to so many friends and colleagues. But that fear should have driven him to defection, not away from it.

"I was afraid for my music." It was as if what he said would choke him whether he said it or held it back. "I must be in Russia to write music. If I can't write music, how can I live?"

"I see," she said, trying to keep the words as flat as an alphabet. "You stayed for your music. In the choice between Mama and me and your music, you chose the music."

His eyes met hers, naked for the first time, revealing what that choice had cost him. She struggled not to look away. If he could feel that much pain, she could at least witness it. "Oh, Papa," she said, and put her arms around him, embracing him in the moment of learning that he had chosen against her.

His body was soft and heavy. His arms went around her and he patted her, murmuring, "Annushka, Anechka, *dochka*," holding her more and more tightly, as if he could weld their flesh together and no more words would have to be said because she would be part of him and would know them already.

She couldn't get enough air into her lungs; his grip had grown too tight. Slowly she pulled away from him, but took his hands. "Papa," she said gently, "your music is in *you*, not in Russia. You could compose wherever you lived, in London or Paris or New York—anywhere."

Rodion said, "No composer is more deeply attached to the motherland than Boris Semyonovich. No one's music is more deeply rooted in her soil."

"You say that, you make him say it at a press conference," Hedy cried, "but what does it mean? Music comes from the mind and heart, not the soil. It's not some kind of vegetable! Papa, you wouldn't have been cut off from the language of your art or have to learn a new one, the way a poet does. The language of music is the same everywhere."

He shook his head. "I can't make you understand."

She had to stand, to walk away. When she touched her face, her hands were ice. Locking them on her elbows, she said, "Papa, if you ever loved me, if you love Mama, you *must* make me understand. All my life, in reality and in memory, I've tried to understand you and failed. I loved you, Papa, but I never knew you. Once in my life, make me know you! If you don't, if you won't at least try, then I can't forgive you, for any of the things that have happened. And Mama won't forgive you either, because I'll tell her the reason you didn't come is that you didn't *want* to come. Answer me, Papa! Dammit! Please!"

At first she thought he wouldn't; he angled his head and stared into some private space. Then he righted himself, his hair settling back over his collar like a sigh. "Do you remember the village?" he said. "The old village?"

"Yes, of course." It was a small country settlement, the place where he had been born and spent the first years of his life, before his prodigious talent had been discovered by a visiting priest and he was sent off to music school. The place was not far from Moscow, but like most of the country villages, it was locked in another century: tin-roofed wooden houses with logs piled at their sides and painted fences separating them from one another. Water from a pump, washing in a stream, a church abandoned to decay, streets oozing mud half the year, and only one sign of cheer in the isolation: the heavy frames on the windows, which were painted aqua and carved with magical flowers and beasts, so that one could stare into them as into a book of tales.

"There was a stream not far away," her father said. "Once I took you there—do you remember?" He didn't wait for her answer. "It was a splendid stream. Magic. No matter how hot the weather, the water always ran clear and cold. When you put your hand into it in summer, you would gasp with shock and pleasure. When you used both hands and drank, you would get a taste of snow. And somehow of berries, too." He was silent, smiling, one hand cupped in memory. Then he went on in a voice she had never heard: soft, almost shy. "There was music in the stream. At first I didn't know what it was. I was too young, you see, and I'd never heard music before—oh, yes, Uncle Dmitri had a guitar, and sometimes Mother would sing, to me or to herself, but nothing was like the sounds I heard in the stream. Voices, high, sad voices, but no words, only vowels. A wonderful instrument that doesn't exist on this earth—part French horn, part harp. And if you bent close, there were skipping rhythms near the stones." He gave the strange shiver again. "Sometimes the sounds were there, sometimes not. I never knew whether they would come, but when they did . . . I was only a boy, but I knew I would spend my life with them, trying to capture them. I had no idea how to go about it, except to sing to myself, in my mind, and try to pluck out things on Uncle Mitya's guitar when he wasn't there. That's how the priest heard me. Soon he insisted that I be sent to have lessons. . . . Ah, well, you know that part of it. But I never told anyone, not even your mother, about the music in the stream."

He was staring into the distance with an odd, blank intensity—as if he were composing; as if the demon had his spirit. But he went on speaking. "After the stream, I thought I would never again hear the music. But I did. Once, skating on the river, when I was in school. Another time walking along Arbat Street just as the first snow began to fall. And in the woods, going after mushrooms, or at the dacha, in the wind. You could never tell when it was going to happen, but when it did . . . you were lifted beyond anything you had known. Then you would run home and try to put what happened into music the world can hear. But you never quite succeeded." He sighed. "People say, 'You are wonderful, ah, Nikolayev, you have written something splendid,' but in reality it is pale. People are ignorant. Party chairmen most of all. All the talk that Stalin understood music . . . He was ignorant. As all of them have been."

Hedy glanced at Rodion Sergeivich, but his face registered concentration, nothing more.

"No," her father said, eyes still on the distance, "you never quite succeed. So you work. Work, work at your craft. Master your craft and keep working. And hope. And sometimes . . . perhaps in the slow movement of the Second Symphony, and the first of the string quartets . . . and there are passages in the songs for tenor and French horn and the *War Choruses* . . . But always something stays beyond your grasp, hovering at the rim of your mind. Still, whatever is best in you, whatever is not ordinary and even stupid, comes from hearing the sounds."

"And if you could never hear them?"

"You could write nothing worth writing. But you do hear them. Often enough to keep you from . . . Each time, you are afraid it could be the last. Each time, you wonder if you will do it again, if you . . ." This time his shiver was a convulsion of his whole body. His eyes were fixed on the space where Hedy stood, but not on her, his features clenched around the sight.

He was looking at nothing, she thought: not at her, nor at anything in reality. "Papa," she whispered, "what are you afraid of? There's nothing there."

He didn't answer. Perhaps he couldn't. It didn't matter; she had said it for herself, to put into words that nothing was there, no demon, nothing but his own fear. Not just the fear of being arrested in the night and sent to prison—though God knew he had had reason for that—but something deeper: the fear of losing not his life but his creative power.

Could he have such a fear? Surely someone who talked of technique and craft, who was contemptuous of emotionalism, couldn't hold the belief that, at root, his music was outside his control.

But that was what he had told her: that it came from somewhere outside him.

"And you believed," she said, "that if you left Russia, the sounds would stop and you wouldn't write again."

"Not what my heart needs to write." His eyes left the distance and came back to her. He shook his head in sad bewilderment. "I can't explain," he said. She saw that, for him, what he had told her paled beside what he felt. Words had never been the voice of his soul.

She sat beside him and took his hand again. Something seemed to pass from his flesh to hers, so that she felt her perception of him altering slowly, like a turning mirror, in which she would appear too. All her young life, she thought, she had witnessed music's power over him and called it dark and demonic. But that could not be so. After all, the power of art was only the power of one's own values, of one's very capacity to value. The darkness she had seen was not in the music but in her father, because he was a man torn in two—by his deep, almost mystical belief that he was free to create only in the place that would not allow him to create freely. That had forced a terrible choice upon him.

"What I wrote you was true," he said. "This way is best. At first it was difficult. I thought I would . . ." He gave a shivering breath. "I missed you."

The silence in the room was total, as if the three of them

had been cut away from all outside existence, from everything but her father's suffering.

"Boris Semyonovich . . ." Rodion whispered. "My friend . . ."

"How did you manage to survive, Papa?" She was whispering too.

He shook his head.

"In your father's distress," Rodion said, almost gently, "he attempted to say and do some things that could have been interpreted as anti-Soviet. Fortunately I was able to prevent significant damage. All difficulties were resolved when he finally joined the Party."

Hedy closed her eyes.

She heard her father say, "I need to be where I was born, where I am . . . nurtured. You and your mother needed . . . something else. This way is best."

She looked at him. His eyes were beggar's bowls. "Perhaps you're right, Papa," she said. "Perhaps it's best."

He clutched her hand till it hurt.

How strange, she thought, to be granting absolution to one's own father. She tried to smile at him, but her mouth would not lift.

"So," Rodion said, his voice once more official, "you have learned what you wanted to know, and in the process you have distressed your father. He must go in now to rest. Tonight he must conduct the premiere of his Concerto for Guitar. That is more important than anything else."

"Rodya is right," her father said. He moved as if to rise.

"Papa, don't!" She was eight again—*Papa should be telling the man to go away, but Papa couldn't, and she didn't know why*—and ten, and twelve, and all the years of watching the two men and hating what she saw. . . . "Don't order him around," she heard herself cry to Rodion. "You're not his master!"

"Of course not," Rodion said. "A preposterous notion. I

am the servant of your father's genius. No one admires him more than I, or cares more deeply about him."

It was so simple, Hedy thought. She had looked at it for half her life and not named it properly. "We must see if Rodion Sergeivich can take care of it"—how often had she heard those words? Her father, disarmed by his view of a talent he did not understand, helpless before a political system that could dole out either prizes or prison at its whim—how much easier for him to retreat further and further into the caverns of his music and let someone else deal with the world. The artist who couldn't handle reality and needed those who could; and the practical man who felt himself inferior to artists—and so needed to control them. Who had worked tirelessly to keep the great Niko-layev imprisoned in his fears, even while professing to love and admire him. Who must have been only too glad to let Nikolayev's wife and daughter go, so his influence would have no competition. Who *did* admire the genius, to be fair, and perhaps even loved the man, in some way; wouldn't the ropes of fear and need and awe that bound the two of them together have a power as strong as that of love?

"It is my duty to look after your father," Rodion said. "I have permitted you to spend this time with him because he wished it, for no other reason. But now that you have heard the truth—"

"Not quite," she said. "Not all."

Color rose in a rash along Rodion's cheekbones. "I have indulged you far beyond any necessity. You are a traitor to—"

"I want to know something else about Paris. You said you learned that a defection was being planned. How?"

"You will hear nothing more."

"Tell me how you knew! Did someone tell you?"

He glared at her, then seemed to change his mind; he stuffed the anger back behind a smile. "I knew *when* it would happen when Boris Semyonovich asked to have lunch in a bistro—after you had so carefully packed your luggage with food, to avoid having to spend your money in Paris on restaurants. And I knew *that* it would happen because . . ." He stopped, dangling the words before her.

"Because someone told you?" He nodded. "Who was it?"

"Why are you so eager to know?"

"Damn you," she whispered.

Pleased, Rodion folded his arms.

"He is lying," her father said. "No one told him about a defection."

"But then . . . how did he know?"

Another sigh rattled deep in her father's throat. "Because of me."

"*You* told him? I don't believe it."

"I didn't have to tell him. He found what I was carrying."

"What you . . . I don't understand, Papa."

Rodion said, "When our customs officials went through your luggage as you were leaving Moscow, they found something in a small wooden box your father was carrying. They reported it to me, but I ordered them not to remove it."

"I would not go into exile without a handful of soil," her father said.

"Oh, no," she said, understanding at last. No good Russian would leave without taking soil from the motherland, to be sprinkled on his foreign grave.

Rodion said, "I knew that if your father was carrying such a thing, it meant he did not plan to return." He smiled. "Fortunately, I was able to help him come to his senses."

Hedy turned to her father, who nodded, then turned away.

In a moment it penetrated: She hadn't betrayed him. Alik

hadn't betrayed her. She closed her eyes; something in her was lifting, rising, turning into a Roman candle of relief. She put her hands to her mouth and stood for a long time, knowing Rodion was watching her, not caring what he saw or thought.

She heard him say, "Excuse me, Boris Semyonovich, what are you doing?"

She opened her eyes; her father had risen. "I wish to give my daughter something," he said.

"Yes? What?"

"I will get it." Her father headed toward his room.

When he was out of earshot, Hedy said to Rodion, "How did you know I was Anna Borisovna? I don't think my own father recognized me—how did you?"

"Someone told me." Something must have showed on her face, for he smiled and said, "Yes, Alik. Not in words, shall we say, but in actions? I know my cousin better than he thinks. I know he is not a man to sleep with a strange woman just because she asks him to. Or to be so concerned over what I think of his behavior with her. These things confirmed to me that, as I had begun to suspect, she was not a strange woman." He smiled. "You are embarrassed?"

She wanted to erase his smile, his whole mouth; no, to sew it eternally shut with neat little stitches, like a zipper. The thought gave her an almost sensual pleasure.

"However," Rodion said, "what happened can be our secret, Alik's and mine. Unless it should become necessary for his wife to know, or his father-in-law in the Ministry of Justice, or someone else in the government. Of course it might be necessary for them to know only part of it—that he was guilty of unauthorized contact with a Westerner. Only in extreme circumstances would they need to know that the Westerner was an enemy of the Soviet Union."

The heat left Hedy's cheeks—embarrassment was childish, irrelevant—taking with it the warmth in her hands and everywhere else, leaving only the knowledge of the weapon her presence at the festival had created for Alik. Had Rodion known who she was *before* Alik's visit, and the tape been only a way, a sadistic way, of getting evidence to hold over Alik's head?

"Why did you do it?" she said to Rodion. "Don't you have enough power over him already?"

He regarded her blandly. No, she thought, his kind could never have enough power over those they could not equal.

She realized then why her fear of him had gone—not because she had suddenly acquired such courage, but because he had ceased to regard her as an active danger. He had shown her his power over both the men she had loved. He controlled both Papa and Alik.

Her father came back into the room, his tread heavy, a small, thick notebook in his hand. He started toward her, but Rodion was at his side instantly. "What is that, Boris Semyonovich?"

"Some of my musical jottings. I want my wife and daughter to have it as a memento. Perhaps Anna may wish to use some of them as illustrations in her book." Her father held out the notebook.

Rodion took it peremptorily and began looking through it. "All work produced by Soviet citizens is the property of the State. You cannot give this to her, or to anyone, without permission."

In one second, as if the paw of a bear had lashed out and retrieved it, the notebook was back in her father's hand. Rodion looked as startled as Hedy felt.

"This is a book of musical scribbling," her father said. "It has personal value only. Musical value? None. I will show you." He took out a cigarette lighter and held it to the edges of the pages, which began to catch before Rodion cried, "No!"

Her father dropped the book and choked the flame with

one slippered foot. "I can burn it," he said, "or I can give it to my daughter. Which shall it be?"

Hedy wanted to cry. The giant of her childhood was back, for a moment.

His gaze did combat with Rodion's until Rodion said, "Very well. If it is so important to you."

"It is. Thank you, Rodya."

"Now," Rodion said, his voice subtly different, as if expert hands were adjusting reins, "I think you must return to your room and rest."

Her father put the book in Hedy's hands and cupped his own over them. "When you write of me, Nyusha, remember that music is the key."

"It has been all your life. I understand that, Papa."

His eyes, very bright, probed hers, and he repeated, "Music is the key. Remember." Then he folded her into his arms like a doll. He kissed her forehead and cheeks, over and over, and whispered against her ear, "Tell your mother that I love her. Only that. And forgive me."

She turned once, at the door, to look back at him: the sad eyes partially hidden from the world, or hiding from it, the bearlike body sagging into itself.

She wanted to love him for being a giant, and to hate him for having chosen against her. She couldn't quite do either.

Then Rodion was saying, "Do not come to see us again. The reception will not be cordial"; and she was in the hall, with her father's image still in her eyes and the rest of life crowding back to block it out. Mama, waiting patiently for her to come back home and say . . . what? Jess in the car, growing more and more uneasy about her. And the hotel to get through first. Would there be KGB waiting somewhere, to kidnap her soundlessly and announce, what a propaganda coup, that Boris Semyonovich's daughter had decided to rejoin him?

The elevator came. On the way down, she thought to check her watch: five after eleven. Barely over an hour up in the room; time had stretched like a watch painted by Dali. The elevator doors opened, and she stepped out. Across the lobby, she thought she caught sight of Jess and some man, heading for the main doors.

No. It was Alik and his "companion."

She lifted a hand, to call him back: to tell him it was all right now, she knew he hadn't betrayed her, he could be at peace in her memory, they could be at peace together. Her hand fell slowly as he pushed through the doors, tall and broad-shouldered, reminding her a little of Jess.

It was the first time she had put it that way, she realized; always the thought, if allowed at all, had come the other way around—that there was something of Alik in Jess.

A man bumped into her from behind. She spun around in a panic, but he was only a tourist, who apologized and moved on. She saw that she was standing in the traffic path, and had been for some moments. She swung her head, took a long breath, and went out the lobby doors to the car.

The rear door opened for her at once.

"My God," Jess said, "what the hell has been going on? I didn't know what to— Where's your father?"

"He's not coming."

Jess swore. "You were caught?"

"In a way. But it's all right." She got in beside him and leaned over the seat. "Hello, Ray. I'm glad you're on my side."

Salmi grinned—a quintessentially midwestern, American grin—and said, "Always glad to help the press. I take it we won't have a passenger?"

"Would you mind giving Mr. Newman and me a minute alone?"

"Here?" Salmi said. "Sure. Why not?" He got out of the car and closed the door behind him.

Hedy took Jess's hand. "There's no time, so I have to do it this way. I wish to God I didn't, but I do."

"Let's have it," he said quietly.

"My father hadn't left his door unlocked. He didn't even try to come with me. He isn't capable of it, psychologically. But there's someone who is, who's wanted it for most of his life. I know he wants it because I've seen him and talked to him. Jess, if we can manage it, will you help Alik Markov come to the West? Instead of my father? Because Alik has the strength I wish my father could have had." She searched Jess's face, but it was carefully expressionless. "I know what I'm asking you, and on damn short notice, because Alik just walked out of the hotel with his keeper and our only chance to help him is to start driving down the street until we spot him, and then see if we can get him into this car—before he goes back to the hotel and his keeper learns that I'm not just an American journalist Alik is allowed to speak to. I'd give a lot if I could give you more time, tell you more, but the choice has to be made now. Can you do it, Jess? Can you think of Alik Markov as just a brave, desperately unhappy man who's wanted all his life to be free?"

Slowly Jess shook his head. "Jesus, Hedy," he said.

CHAPTER EIGHTEEN

The flight left London exactly on time, heading up into dusk, reducing the earth to a matter of geometry and light, until clouds finally closed below it and shut everything else out of sight.

Hedy turned from the window. A breath she hadn't known she was holding escaped in relief. "All right?" Jess said.

"Yes, fine. Now."

"Home in about seven hours."

"Don't forget customs," she said.

"Ah. True."

"And the cab ride."

"OK, nine hours. A stickler for detail, as usual."

"Strange word. What does a stickler do—stickle?"

Jess smiled. Flight noise droned around them for several

minutes, and then he said, "Thinking about your father, aren't you?"

She nodded. "I was wondering whether maybe his explanation wasn't meant to be literal. Maybe it was a parable, the only way he could try to put what he feels into words. I guess I mean an allegory—a parable is supposed to make a moral point. Which I don't see any sign of."

"Suppose it was allegorical. What then?"

"Then . . . I don't know what then. Jess, you were lucky. You could understand your father."

"I think you understand yours well enough. What you can't do is accept what you know. You want your father to have had reasons that *you* might have had, to want what you wanted. But he didn't. That's what you can't forgive."

"Is that it? I can't forgive him?" She returned to the tiny window and the monotony of clouds. "In Russia I felt so different from most of the people around me. I know it's practically a definition of adolescence to feel alienated when you look out at the world, but I'm talking about something quite specific: the way most people accepted their lives. Oh, they complained about shortages and joked about the bureaucracy, but fundamentally they just . . . *accepted.* I couldn't do that. Nor could Mama. Or Papa—I thought."

"Or Alik Markov."

She turned to Jess, but nothing seemed to be hidden in his face. "That's right." She wanted to add "That's why I loved him" but knew it wouldn't come out naturally. "When I got to America, I saw that most people there accept their lives in the same fundamental way, even though those lives are so very different. Do you remember when we first met and I told you that most people in the Soviet Union had no real desire to leave it? You didn't want to believe it. You'd rather believe that everybody in the world, at heart, wants to live in freedom. So would I. But

I can't. I think what most people want is to be happy, or at least comfortable, in the world they're used to. If that world is free, they're incredibly, extraordinarily lucky. If it's not . . ."

"They need courage to leave it. As you should know."

She shook her head. "It isn't courage that makes you leave. Staying and fighting could take just as much courage. Even more."

"True. Well, what then?"

"I've tried for years to put it into words. I think you have to be able to imagine your life differently—to imagine choices for yourself, and not feel threatened by having to make them. To like having them, in fact."

"Ah. And maybe to feel you deserve to make them for yourself?"

"Yes! Deserving—I did feel that. I felt it was somehow . . . part of me to be able to make my own decisions. Part of my identity."

"I thought your identity was supposed to come from the Party."

Jess was smiling; he had been joking, but she knew he'd said something important. Wasn't it true that for her and Alik—and Mama—identity had not come from belonging to some system or group? It had come from belonging to oneself. Perhaps that was the root of wanting to live in a world of choices. The idea felt right, slotting into her mind as if the space had been waiting for it.

"You want a drink when they come around?" Jess said. She shook her head. "You want to read the papers from New York and Washington?"

"No. But go ahead. I think I'll look at my father's notebook again. I can't figure out why he was so keen for Mama and me to have it."

She took it from her purse and opened to a page of the crabbed music notation. As far as she could tell, the music was like nothing he had ever composed before, and hardly something he could have expected to get officially published and performed in the Soviet Union. Some "new sound" he wanted her to smuggle to the West? She studied the page for a while, then leaned back and angled her head just enough so she could see Jess's face.

It was lived-in, she thought; there were lines in the corners of his eyes and mouth. But they hadn't been left there by bitterness and pain—more by good humor. His nose was a perfect line, a straight arrow of a nose, and in the corner of his lip was a tiny, sensuous pad of flesh that she had known was there but seemed to be seeing for the first time. He was the most photogenic member of Congress. More important, he was what politics needed: a man who could recognize the siren call of power and decline to answer.

A man not to be bribed, with money or other coin. When she had run out to the taxi and asked him to try to help Alik, she could have told him what she had understood when she saw Alik in the lobby: that learning he hadn't betrayed her had freed the past to mean in memory what it had meant while she lived it. That it wasn't Alik she wanted, not anymore, but peace for his memory.

To have told that to Jess then would have seemed like a bribe and an insult. So she had waited and watched the struggle on his face, and then, as she had known she would, she had heard the quiet "I think we can do it. Let's try it." He was not the kind of man who could have made any other decision.

Reading, he frowned and rubbed his jaw. A sudden tenderness wrung her—not, she knew, even as she felt it, the same thing she had felt for Alik, but something as powerful. And different in a wonderful way because, now that she had accepted it, she wasn't afraid of its power. Alik had been discovery, and oneness; loving him had been an unfor-

gettable, unrepeatable rebellion against all that was choking her and an act of claiming her identity. She would
always love him in a corner of herself, but she had changed
too much in the years since then—become too American,
perhaps.

If only the new life could change Alik, too. But it might
be too late to ease the pain and bitterness in his face.

If only she could tell him that the strange night they had
spent together had, by some alchemy, freed her to know
that she loved Jess. But wasn't it a legacy of the trip to
accept that some kinds of secrets were necessary?

Jess put down his paper with a snap. "Hedy, I just had
a thought. Could it be that your father had always planned
not to go with you and Vera? That his decision was made
long before the chat in that bistro with Orlov?"

"Dear God," she said, remembering what Alik had told
her. "You mean Papa pretended he was going to go with
us so that *we* would go?"

"You said he seemed to know that you and Vera needed
to be free."

"But . . . why would he take the handful of soil, then?"

"Maybe he thought your mother would be suspicious if
he didn't."

"Oh," she said, three times, slowly, the possibility growing more real each time. "To have done that for us . . . to
have wanted us to be free. . . . If only I could know for
certain!"

"You can think of it as likely, can't you?"

She touched his cheek. Jess the optimist. "Thank you.
Have I told you how altogether splendid you are?"

"About ten times since we left Finland. But eleven is
OK, too." He took her hand and kissed the palm.

"Would you like something to drink?" the flight attend-
ant said.

"You have vodka?"

"Certainly, sir."

After paying for it with the strange money they had given him, Alik had no desire to drink it. He was drunk without it, seeing everything from some clear height but not able to function very well. Yet. The journalists outside the American embassy in Stockholm had been a shock: hundreds of them, it seemed, shouting and pushing like a cloud of bees, stingers out in the form of questions that came so fast he could understand no words and heard only a buzzing. He had missed his guitar sorely; if it were there, he would have sung about how odd he felt, knowing he was free to say anything and not knowing what it should be. *Forgive my tongue, but forty-six years on a leash has made it fat and stupid, gav-gav* . . . No, he couldn't say "gav-gav." In America the dogs went "boo-boo" or some other weird sound he couldn't remember. How the hell would he live in a country when he didn't even know what the animals said?

Ah, but he would. Aleksandr Romanovich Markov would be able to learn, no matter how difficult. He couldn't remember a time when he hadn't known two things about himself: that he wanted to sing and that he could survive anything, except chains. He should have been able to survive them, too; but he didn't have true courage, not anymore. He had courage-to-a-point. The point of getting old and tired and marrying the Party official's daughter.

He wondered what story Sofia would be told about him—what his public would be told, if it came to that. Probably nothing at all. He might simply cease to exist, as other defectors had, his name never mentioned again unless it suited their purposes. Death while still alive. People would have to learn the truth about his escape by listening to Western broadcasts. The few lines they might hear couldn't communicate what it had actually been like.

When the taxi had pulled up beside him and the watch-dog, he hadn't noticed it at first. Then Anya had stepped out and called, in English, in a parody of seductiveness that would have made him laugh if he hadn't been so startled: "Alik Markov! I've been looking for you everywhere. May I see you for a minute?"

The watchdog had looked uncertain, but after all, as far as he knew, Alik was authorized to contact the American journalist. So Alik had walked to the car, and she had put a hand on his arm and leaned up as if she wanted to kiss him but instead had whispered that she would take him to America if he would get in the taxi and drive away with them, no chance to say anything but yes or no. He didn't know what she had seen in his eyes, but then she had added, "Don't come to be with me, Alik. I can be your friend, I hope I always will be, but that's all."

He had seen that she meant it. They had stared at each other, on a Finnish street in summer that had felt like Pushkin Square with snow falling, and he had said yes.

Then, at the periphery of his vision, encroaching on her face, he had become aware of two men. He had felt as if his whole life to that moment was moving to suck him back, and he had lunged for the taxi.

It had seemed to happen in an endless slow spin of time: the two men and the watchdog coming toward the taxi; a man from the back seat leaping out to help shove them off; and somehow the taxi roaring off, the watchdog's stupefied, terrified face receding in the back window. There were quick introductions to the driver and to the man who had helped him, called Newman, then the change after a kilo-meter or so to another car and driver. The ride to Sweden, over two hours, had been silent and tense, although the roads they traveled were quiet. Finally there had been the border, in a wooded area near a river, with no guards, not even a customs man.

When the driver announced, "Now we are in Sweden," Anya had leaned forward and gripped Alik's shoulder, her fingers so strong through his sweater and shirt that he could almost feel them on his flesh.

Yes, he was still drunk on it, and dazed.

He leaned back in his seat. He had insisted on sitting alone, telling Anya and Newman that he wanted to smoke, but really it was so they would not feel he was clinging to them like snow to a roof in January. Anya must see that he had accepted what she told him. And then, of course, he must accept it.

For twenty years, he thought, he had put her out of his mind, so in a way nothing had changed. In any case, to ask for more would be tempting the gods, after what she had done for him.

You get only part of what you want, my friend, he thought. *Which makes you luckier than almost everybody you know.*

He closed his eyes, but his fingers played restlessly on his thighs. In his mind, he heard the opening sonorities of the Concerto for Guitar. Anya had said to him, once they were in Sweden, "It didn't take you any time at all to choose to come, did it?" He had told her the truth: The only regret that had come into his mind was not being able to play the concerto with Boris.

"You won't miss my father himself?" she had said. He had realized that she didn't know—no, how could she?—so he had had the pleasure of telling her.

"Yes, I will miss Boris, but I am exactly where he wants me to be. The trip for me to Finland, it was all his idea— that I should come and try to find a chance to get out. We began talking of it years ago. He wrote the concerto in hopes he might arrange for me to be invited to play it somewhere in the West, and he stood over me and forced me to become a decent classical player. When the festival announced it would be honoring him, we knew it was probably my best chance. He fought hard to make Rodion and the Ministry allow me to go. So I am here, you see, because of Boris Nikolayev and his daughter."

Anya's eyes had filled with tears. Anya's dark, beautiful eyes.

If Newman didn't keep her happy, by God. . . . But Newman looked as if he damn well meant to.

So be it, Alik thought, using the words for the first time in freedom.

"Oh, my darling girl, come here to me!" Vera cried.

She rose from her seat at the big table, head cocked a bit to the left, eyes glittering and arms outstretched. Her fingers worked the air impatiently until Hedy came close enough to be touched. The two of them held each other, rocking and kissing, pulling back to look, then embracing again and again.

Finally they sat down, close to each other, still holding hands.

"Mama, you look good," Hedy said. It wasn't exactly true, but it wasn't a lie, either, for Vera looked as she had before Hedy left. Nothing had changed during the ten days in which everything had changed.

"Never mind how I look," Vera said, dismissively waving a thin hand. "I don't matter. You are what matters, everything that has happened to you. You told me so little on the phone from Stockholm that I didn't know what to say to my friends. 'She says Boris is all right,' I told them, 'and he sends his love to me.' Lucille said, 'For that she goes all the way to Finland?' And then the papers say Alik has defected. Alik? Who you didn't even tell me was going to be at the festival? And it is Jess who got him out?"

"Mama, if you'll stop asking questions, maybe I can answer some of them."

"You are right, my darling. And first . . . you know what I want to hear first."

"Yes." Hedy looked into her mother's eyes, but nothing was there to guide her except longing and caution, together, as equals. She breathed deeply and said, "Papa didn't come with us, Mama, because he couldn't."

"Ah. Ah. They caught him in Paris and made him go back?"

"They . . . Rodion Sergeivich was suspicious and had KGB in the alley of the bistro. Papa couldn't get past them, of course, so he had to go back in. And from then on, it was impossible for him to leave."

Once, Hedy thought, she would have hated lying to Mama. But then, once she had had the irrational certainty that bringing back the truth from Finland would make her mother well again.

"And all these years," Vera said, "they have kept him from coming?"

"Well, yes. They have."

"I knew it must be so."

"He has had to accept the life he has without you, or at least accept the fact that you are not with him."

"I knew he would be with us if he could."

"Yes. He would. But Papa is . . . in prison. Not a literal one, not at all—in fact I think he lives well enough, and he looks in good health for his age—but the chains are still there, invisible ones. And he wasn't . . . he isn't . . . able to break them." That much, at least, was the truth.

She had expected a barrage of questions, but her mother was silent, looking inward, her expression almost serene. It was several minutes before Vera's head gave a little shake, as if she were coming up into the light, and she said, "I knew, you see. I was right all along. Wasn't I?"

Hedy nodded; it was all she could do.

"Ah," her mother said. Satisfaction seemed to fill her being.

Hedy waited, but to her surprise, her mother seemed to have heard all she wanted.

Perhaps she was like Papa, her inner certainties needing only minimal support from reality. And Hedy had just given them all they needed.

Each of her parents, she thought sadly, had an illusion that could not be surrendered: Papa, to justify his fear of leaving Russia; Mama, to justify the pain of having left without him.

Gently she released her hand from her mother's grip. "I have two more things to tell you, Mama. First, about Alik. It wasn't only Jess and I who got him out. No, it was Papa, too. Nothing could have happened without Papa. Papa could not come himself, so he helped Alik to come in his place."

Her mother listened as she told the story, nodding, taking it into herself like oxygen. When it was finished, she said, "You see how wonderful your papa is? How clever, to think of such a way to help?"

"Yes."

"Where is Alik? I would like to see him. To hear about Boris."

"He's gone on to Washington, to see the State Department. With Jess." The words still had an air of unreality, as had the sight of the two men together. On the flight, shortly before they got to New York, Jess had gone back to talk to Alik, and she had been unable not to turn and watch them: rather wary and formal, yet both smiling, as if something about each other was intriguing. When the flight landed, they had stood together and each made a statement, Alik's very short; looking a bit dazed and tired, he had lifted both arms as if he wanted to embrace everything in his vision, and said, "For many years I am thinking this day would not come. It is here. I give deep thanks." Jess's hadn't been much longer. He had simply said that Alik was like the many other artists who had spent their careers struggling under censorship and had been willing to leave their artistic cultures and risk their lives for freedom. "We must be as passionate as they are," he had said. "We must make sure that no kind of censorship is imposed in America, by any agency or group, or else the Alik Markovs of the world will have been betrayed."

She had looked at the two men standing there, of a height, and cried.

"Alik will come to see you soon, Mama," she said. "I promise."

"Good." Vera smiled.

"Here's the other thing," Hedy said. She reached into her purse. "Papa said he wanted you to have this. When he gave it to me, he said, 'Music is the key.' I thought he meant the key to him, to his whole life, but perhaps he meant to this notebook. I don't understand, though, because—"

"Give it to me." Vera's eyes were large, and her fingers trembled until they held the notebook. "He always kept a journal, in books like this one. Not a diary, just the thoughts he had. This must be one of his journals."

"There's nothing in it but music, Mama."

"Yes, yes, he wrote in music, you see. So they could never take him to prison because of what he had written. I found out by accident one day, and he was furious. No one must know, he said, no one. I had to swear it on my father's memory and promise never to tell a soul. Even you."

"What do you mean he wrote in music?"

"The notes equal letters. Ten notes—an octave plus two, C through E in English notation—plus the sharp and flat for each one. That makes thirty letters, the whole Cyrillic alphabet if you leave out the pronunciation marks. So he can write anything he likes. Sometimes in the treble clef, sometimes in the bass, so it won't always look the same." She opened the book, pulled it close to peer at it, and said triumphantly, "Yes! It is a journal! But why are the pages charred? Oh, darling girl, give me my glasses!"

When she had them, she scanned a page, her eyes suddenly the trained musician's. "Look—here he writes about Bach, he calls him 'the sublime architect of sound.'" She turned more pages. "Ah, here he is talking about Stalin . . . I think, yes . . . how Stalin had a painting done of himself, and had the painter shot when he didn't like it." Her lips moved, working something out. "Your father says pictures of Stalin are now being peddled illegally, and in them he should be painted as a butcher with a bloody apron. . . . Ah! Here he writes that music tries to bring out the best in human nature, but the system can only honor mediocrity, and worse. . . ."

She looked up and said, "Hedy, this journal will show people what he is like, how he despises the regime, all the regimes."

"Then," Hedy heard herself say, "it should be published." The idea was wonderful in its simplicity.

"Yes! Yes, it must be."

"Mama, this is the book to do—not a biography of Papa but a translation of his journal."

"But not while he is still alive. That would be dangerous for him."

"No, not while he's alive. And you can help me with it. Nikolayev's journal, by his wife and daughter."

Vera clasped her hands under her chin. "Yes. Oh, yes. And when we are both gone, Papa and me, you can show the world what he was really like."

For Mama's sake, she wouldn't cry, Hedy thought. She simply wouldn't allow it.

"Thank you, my darling," her mother said. "You are the

best daughter in the world. You have given me something so wonderful. . . ." She lifted the journal again, her thin face sharpening in excitement as she read, wordless little cries emerging with each page. Something in her was alive again, ready to act, to do whatever she could for what she loved—the mother Hedy held in her heart.

Had Papa known? she wondered. Had he realized he was sending back a strange gift of life, which would give Mama's last months more purpose and pleasure than would have seemed possible?

She would think that he had, Hedy decided. Let him rest in peace in her memory.

ABOUT THE AUTHOR

KAY NOLTE SMITH was born and raised in Minnesota and Wisconsin but left for New York in the late 1950s to become an actress and writer. She worked in the theater, doing summer stock and Off Broadway plays, and wrote short stories, mostly mysteries. She wrote *The Watcher* (1980), winner of the Edgar Allan Poe Award for Best First Novel. Her acting experience prompted her to write *Catching Fire* (1982), which was followed by *Mindspell* (1983), while a lifelong passion for opera prompted *Elegy for a Soprano* (1985). Mrs. Smith has published a new translation of Edmond Rostand's lyric drama *Chantecler* and written articles for many publications, including *Opera News* and *Vogue*. She lives in New Jersey with her husband, Phillip J. Smith.